"HE DIED THREE THOUSAND YEARS AGO. BUT HE IS STILL THE LITERARY STAR OF THE YEAR. THE RAMSES II SAGA . . . IS A MUST-READ BESTSELLER"
—*Paris Match*

"Officially, Christian Jacq was born in Paris in 1947. In fact, his real birth took place in the time of the pharaohs, along the banks of the Nile, where the river carries eternal messages. . . . Who could ever tell that Christian Jacq, Ramses' official scribe, was not writing from memory?"
—*Magazine Littéraire*

"With hundreds of thousands of readers, and millions of copies in print, Christian Jacq's success has become unheard of in the world of books. This man is the pharaoh of publishing!"
—*Figaro Magazine*

"In 1235 B.C., Ramses II might have said: 'My life is as amazing as fiction!' It seems Christian Jacq heard him. . . . Christian Jacq draws a pleasure from writing that is contagious. His penmanship turns history into a great show, high-quality entertainment."
—*VSD*

"It's *Dallas* or *Dynasty* in Egypt, with a hero (Ramses), beautiful women, plenty of villains, new developments every two pages, brothers fighting for power, magic, enchantments, and historical glamour."
—*Liberation*

"He's a pyramid-surfer. The pharaoh of publishing. His saga about Ramses II is a bookselling phenomenon."
—*Le Parisien*

RAMSES

VOLUME II

THE ETERNAL TEMPLE

CHRISTIAN JACQ

Translated by Mary Feeney

WARNER BOOKS

A Time Warner Company

If you purchase this book without a cover you should be aware that this book may have been stolen property and reported as "unsold and destroyed" to the publisher. In such case neither the author nor the publisher has received any payment for this "stripped book."

Originally published in French by Editions Robert Laffont, S.A. Paris, France.

Warner Books Edition
Copyright © 1996 by Editions Robert Laffont (Volume 2)
All rights reserved.

Warner Books, Inc., 1271 Avenue of the Americas, New York, NY 10020

Visit our Web site at
http://warnerbooks.com

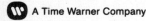 A Time Warner Company

Printed in the United States of America

First U.S. Printing: March 1998
10 9 8 7 6 5 4 3

Library of Congress Cataloging-in-Publication Data

Jacq, Christian.
    [Temple des millions d'années. English]
    The eternal temple / Christian Jacq.
        p. cm. — (Ramses ; v. 2)
    ISBN 0-446-67357-9
    I. Ramses II, King of Egypt—Fiction. I. Title II. Series:
Jacq, Christian. Ramsès. English ; v. 2.
PQ2670.A2438T4613   1998
843'.914—dc21   97-44334
                                         CIP

Book design and composition by L&G McRee
Cover design and illustration by Marc Burkhardt

ATTENTION: SCHOOLS AND CORPORATIONS
WARNER BOOKS are available at quantity discounts with bulk purchase for educational, business, or sales promotional use. For information, please write to: SPECIAL SALES DEPARTMENT, WARNER BOOKS, 1271 AVENUE OF THE AMERICAS, NEW YORK, NY 10020

MAP OF EGYPT

N

Mediterranean Sea

Rosetta
Alexandria
Damietta
Port Saïd

Tanta
Zagazig

Cairo
Ismailia

Giza
Memphis

Saqqara
Suez

*Siwa
Oasis*

SINAI

LIBYAN

Lake Karun

El Faiyum

*Bahariya
Oasis*

El Minya

Beni Hasan

Hermopolis

Tell el-Amarna

Farafra Oasis

Asyut

Nile

ARABIAN
DESERT

Red

DESERT

Akhmim

Abydos

Dendera

Nag Hammadi

Qena

*Dakhla
Oasis*

Necropolis of Thebes

Luxor

Sea

Esna

Kharga Oasis

Edfu

Kom Ombo

TROPIC OF CANCER

Elephantine

Aswan

Philae

Abu Simbel

125 miles

N   U   B   I   A

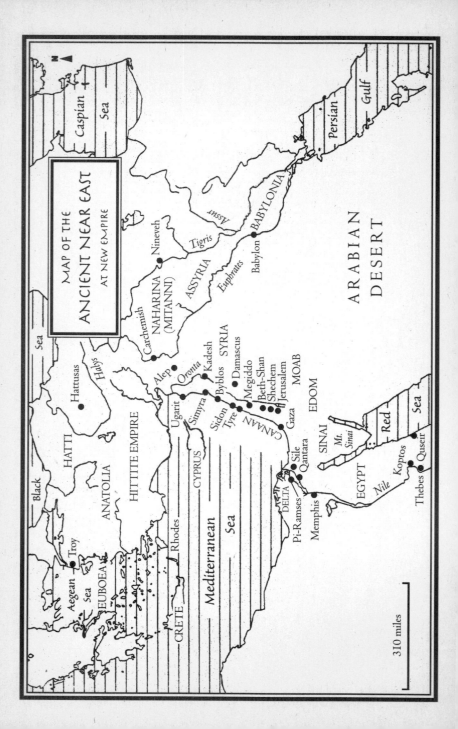

ONE

Ramses was alone, awaiting a sign from the Invisible. Alone, facing the vast scorched stretches of desert. Alone, facing the destiny still just beyond his grasp.

At twenty-three, Prince Ramses was tall and athletic, with well-defined, powerful muscles and a magnificent head of red-gold hair. A broad, high forehead, thick brows arching over small, bright eyes, a long, slightly hooked nose, rounded, delicate rimmed ears, full lips, and a strong chin added up to a commanding, attractive countenance.

He had already been through so much—younger son of Pharaoh Seti, royal scribe, army officer, finally named coregent by his father and initiated into the mysteries of Abydos.

Seti had been a great ruler, an irreplaceable sovereign whose reign had brought peace and prosperity. But now Seti was dead after fifteen remarkable years on the throne, fifteen all-too-brief years that had flown like an ibis in the summer twilight.

At first, Ramses had not even been aware that his distant, demanding, awe-inspiring father was gradually grooming him for kingship. Seti had put him through various tests, beginning with a face-to-face encounter with a wild bull, the symbol of pharaonic power. At fourteen, Ramses had the courage to confront the beast, but not the strength to overcome it. He would have been gored to death if Seti hadn't roped the charging bull, leaving Ramses indelibly impressed with the understanding of a pharaoh's first duty: protecting the weak.

The king alone held the key to true power. Through the magic of experience, he communicated it to Ramses, stage by stage, without revealing his master plan. Over the years, father and son had grown closer, united in faith and purpose. Reserved, unbending, Seti was a man of few words, yet with Ramses he indulged in long conversations, attempting to spell out what was required of the Lord of the Two Lands, upper and lower Egypt.

Those golden hours, those blessed moments had now vanished into the silence of death.

Pharaoh's words had poured like consecrated water into Ramses' heart, where they would be stored as precious treasure, infusing his thoughts and actions. But Seti had departed, gone to commune with his fellow gods, and Ramses was alone, bereft of his father's guiding presence.

He felt defenseless, unable to bear the weight thrust upon his young shoulders. To govern Egypt . . . at thirteen, it had been his dream, a childish longing for a prize that could never be his. Convinced that his older brother, Shaanar, was his father's chosen successor, he had finally surrendered the foolish notion.

But Pharaoh Seti and Tuya, the Great Royal Wife, had decided otherwise. After observing their two sons in action, their choice had fallen on Ramses. Why hadn't they found someone stronger and abler, someone as great as Seti! Ramses felt prepared to meet any challenger face-to-face, but not to steer the ship of state through the uncertain waters of the future. He had proven himself in combat, campaigning with Seti in Nubia; his boundless energy would see him through a war in defense of his country, if the need arose; but he had no idea how to command an army of bureaucrats, dignitaries, and priests, all of whom could outmaneuver him.

The founder of their dynasty, the first Ramses, had been an elderly vizier, unwillingly appointed Pharaoh. When Seti inherited the throne, he was mature and experienced. He, Ramses, was only twenty-three and had been content to live in his father's shadow, following his directives and responding to the least of his demands. It had been so wonderful to have a trusted guide! To work under Seti's orders, to serve Egypt by obeying the Pharaoh, to have him available with the answer to every question . . . that paradise was lost.

Now fate had unfairly dictated that Ramses, a spirited, even rash young man, should take Seti's place. It might be better if he fled, laughing, so far into the desert that no one would ever find him.

Of course, he could count on his supporters: his mother, Tuya, an exacting and faithful ally; Nefertari, his beautiful, calm young wife; and his four boyhood friends. Moses, the Hebrew, now supervised royal construction projects, Ahsha was in the diplomatic corps, Setau was a snake charmer, and Ahmeni had devoted his life to Ramses as his private secretary and sandal-bearer.

However, he could count far more enemies. His brother, Shaanar, had still not given up on claiming the throne for himself. It was anyone's guess what plots he was currently hatching. If Shaanar appeared before him this very instant, Ramses would offer no resistance. His brother might as well wear the double crown if he coveted it so desperately.

But did Ramses have the right to betray his father and abdicate the responsibility with which he had been entrusted? It would be so simple to conclude that Seti had been mistaken, that in the end he might have changed his mind. But Ramses would not lie to himself. His fate depended on the answer he received from the Invisible.

It was here, in the desert, the heart of this "red land" charged with a dangerous energy, that the answer would come to him.

Sitting cross-legged in the classic scribe's pose, Ramses waited. The vast and solitary desert was the place for a pharaoh. The rocks and sand harbored a fire that would either strengthen his soul or break him. Let the fire pass judgment!

The sun approached its zenith, the wind died down. A gazelle leaped from dune to dune. Danger was near.

It came out of nowhere: an enormous lion, twice as big as normal. The blazing mane made it look like a triumphant warrior, the sleek dark brown body rippled with muscles.

At the sight of Ramses, it loosed a fearful roar that echoed far into the distance. Teeth flashing, claws bared, the big cat studied its prey.

Seti's son had no way to escape him.

The lion came closer, then stopped a few yards from Ramses, who noticed his golden eyes. For a few seconds, they stared each other down.

Flicking his tail at a fly, the lion loped forward, suddenly tense.

Ramses rose to his feet, still staring hard.

"It's you, Fighter, whom I saved from certain death. What do you have in mind for me?"

Forgetting the danger, Ramses remembered plucking the baby lion from the brush as his army left Nubia. Fighter's remarkable constitution had allowed him to survive a cobra bite. Cured by Setau's remedies, the cub grew to colossal proportions as Ramses' pet.

For the first time, Fighter had escaped from the pen where he was kept in his master's absence. Reverting to the wild, he was ready to pounce on the man who had raised him.

"It's up to you, boy. Kill me now, or fight at my side for life."

The lion reared on his hind legs and set his paws on Ramses' shoulders, nearly knocking him over. The prince held steady. Fighter's claws retracted. He sniffed Ramses' face. There was friendship, trust, and respect between them.

"You've sealed my fate, boy."

There was no longer any choice for the young man Seti had named Son of Light.

He would have to fight like a lion.

TWO

In Memphis, the palace was deep in mourning. Men stopped shaving, women wore their hair down. The mummification process took seventy days, and during that time the country was in limbo. The throne remained vacant until Seti's successor was officially proclaimed, which could happen only after the Pharaoh was entombed and his mummy united with the heavenly light.

The frontier posts were on alert, troops ready to check any attempted invasion, at the order of the prince regent and the Great Royal Wife. The principal threat was from the Hittites, to the north in Asia Minor. While there appeared to be no imminent danger, a surprise attack was always possible. For centuries, the rich agricultural provinces of Egypt's Delta had been tempting prey for Bedouin raiders roaming the Sinai desert, as well as for Asian princes who occasionally managed to form coalitions and storm the northeastern border.

Seti's departure for the Land of the West was cause for alarm. Whenever a pharaoh passed away, the forces of chaos might prey on Egypt, destroying a civilization that had lasted through eighteen dynasties. Would young Ramses be able to keep the Two Lands safe from danger? Some of the notables were less than sure he could and wished he would step aside in favor of Shaanar, his more prudent and craftier brother.

The Great Royal Wife, Tuya, had not changed her habits since Seti's death. Forty-two years old, slender and regal, with a fine, straight nose, piercing almond eyes, and a nearly square jaw, her moral authority was unquestionable. She had always been Seti's full partner; when he was forced to leave the country on state business, it was she who ruled Egypt, and ruled it firmly.

At daybreak, Tuya liked to stroll briefly in her garden, among the tamarisk and sycamore trees, organizing her workday as she walked. Her time was divided between secular and religious duties.

With Seti gone, all her activity seemed devoid of meaning. Tuya's sole desire was to join her husband in a world without conflict, far from the vanity of men; yet she was resigned to serving out her time on earth. Great happiness had been hers. She must repay her country by serving until she drew her last breath.

Nefertari's elegant silhouette emerged from the morning mist. "More beautiful than the palace beauties," as the common folk said, Ramses' wife had shining black hair and sublime blue-green eyes. An accomplished musician who played at the goddess Hathor's temple in Memphis, a gifted weaver, educated in classical literature (including her husband's favorite, the sage Ptah-hotep), Nefertari was not of noble birth; but Ramses had found her beauty, intelligence, and unusual maturity for her age an irresistible combination. Nefertari never called attention to herself, yet attracted everyone. Within moments of meeting her, Tuya had recruited the girl to oversee her household, a position Nefertari continued to fill even after her marriage to the prince regent. The two women were very close, almost reading each other's thoughts.

"The dew is thick this morning, Majesty. A blessing on our fair land."

"You're up early, Nefertari."

"Not as early as you, and you're the one who needs rest."

"I can't sleep anymore."

"What can we do to ease your pain, Majesty?"

A sad smile fluttered on Tuya's lips. "Seti is irreplaceable. The rest of my life will be bearable only if Ramses prospers in his reign. The thought of it is all that keeps me going."

"I'm worried, Majesty."

"Tell me what you fear."

"That Seti's wishes will not be respected."

"Who would dare go against them?"

Nefertari remained silent.

"You're thinking of Shaanar, I know. He's vain and ambitious, but he would never be so foolish as to defy his father's will." The soft gold of dawn began to light the queen's garden. "Do you think I'm naive, Nefertari? You don't seem to share my opinion."

"Majesty . . ."

"Has something happened to . . . ?"

"No, it's only a feeling."

"Daughter, you're intuitive and quick as lightning. I know you never speak ill of others. But at this point nothing can stop Ramses from being crowned, short of his death."

"That's exactly what I fear, Majesty."

Tuya stroked the branch of a tamarisk. "Would Shaanar resort to murder as his stepping-stone to power?"

"I hate the idea as much as you do, but I can't get it out of my mind. You may think I'm a fool and tell me it's all in my imagination. Even so, I had to say something."

"What security measures has Ramses taken?"

"His lion and watchdog guard are always on duty, along with Serramanna, the head of his royal bodyguard. Since he came back safe from the desert, I've finally convinced him of the need for constant protection."

"We're only ten days into the mourning period. In two months, Seti's body will be placed in his tomb, preserved for eternity. Then Ramses will be crowned and you will become Queen of Egypt."

Ramses bowed to his mother, then pressed her tenderly to him. Seemingly so fragile, she was a lesson in dignity and nobility.

"Why has God put us to such a cruel test?" he asked.

"Seti's spirit lives on in you, my son. His time is over, yours is beginning. He will never die if you continue his work."

"His shadow dwarfs me."

"You, the Son of Light? You must part the darkness, overcome the chaos that looms around us."

The young man pulled away from his mother.

"My lion was loose in the desert. He approached me as a friend."

"The sign you were hoping for, wasn't it?"

"Definitely, but may I ask you a favor? Whenever my father went abroad, you filled in for him."

"Yes, according to tradition."

"You have experience. You have everyone's respect and admiration. What keeps you from replacing him now?"

"You know that was not Seti's wish. He represented the law we must all try to follow. *You* are the one he chose, my son, and you must succeed him. I'll help all I can and advise when you ask."

Ramses did not press her. His mother was the only person who could alter his destiny and lift this burden from him, but she would never swerve from the course her late husband had set. Despite his misgivings, Ramses would have to make his own way.

Serramanna, Ramses' Sardinian bodyguard, stuck close to the king-to-be, never leaving his wing of the royal palace. Naming the former pirate to this prestigious position had been a controversial move. Some were convinced that sooner or later the mustachioed giant would turn on Seti's son.

For the time being, he checked all visitors to the palace himself. The Great Royal Wife had urged him to screen them carefully and to feel free to use his sword if threatened.

Hearing distant shouts, Serramanna hurried toward the entryway.

"What's going on here?"

"This one was trying to force his way in," replied a guard, gesturing toward a tall, broad-shouldered man with flowing hair.

"Who are you?" challenged Serramanna.

"Moses the Hebrew, royal construction supervisor and friend of the prince."

"What do you want?"

"Ramses will see me."

"Not unless I say so."

"Is he in seclusion?"

"Security measures. State the reason for your visit."

"None of your business."

"Then you'd better leave and steer clear of here, or I'll have you thrown in jail."

It took no fewer than four guards to restrain Moses.

"Tell Ramses I'm here, or he'll have your hide!"

"You don't scare me, mister."

"Listen, you big lug! My friend is expecting me. Go ask Ramses."

Years as a pirate captain and scores of fierce battles had

honed Serramanna's ability to read situations. Despite this Hebrew's muscle and swagger, he seemed to be on the level.

Ramses greeted his boyhood friend with a hug.

"Is this a palace or a fortress?" Moses asked.

"My mother and my wife, Ahmeni and Serramanna all fear the worst."

"What is that supposed to mean?"

"An attempt on my life."

The regent's audience chamber looked out on the gardens. In the doorway, his huge pet lion dozed, with Watcher, the yellow dog, curled between his front paws.

"With them to guard you, you ought to feel safe enough."

"Nefertari is convinced that Shaanar still thinks he should be king."

"A coup before your father's laid to rest? Hardly his style. He likes to set things in motion and watch from the background."

"He's running out of time."

"You're right. But he won't risk a confrontation."

"God willing. It could only bring harm to Egypt. What do you hear at Karnak?"

"Opinion is running against you."

Moses had been running Seti's vast construction site at Karnak, where the royal architects had been instructed to add a huge hall of columns to the temple. The Pharaoh's death had brought the work to a halt.

"Whose opinion?"

"The priesthood of Amon, some nobles, the vizier of the south . . . Your sister, Dolora, and her husband, Sary, have stirred them up. They didn't take kindly to being exiled from Memphis."

"Sary tried to have me killed and nearly did have Ahmeni eliminated. Fine behavior from our old teacher! He and my sister could have faced much stiffer consequences than being sent to Thebes."

"The southern sun did nothing to dry up their poison. You should have banished them from Egypt once and for all."

"Dolora is my sister. Sary practically raised me."

"Should a king have different standards for his relatives?"

Ramses was hurt to the quick. "I'm not king yet, Moses."

"I still think you should have taken them to court."

"If the two of them pull any more tricks, I'll show no mercy."

"I wish I believed you. You don't realize how ruthless your enemies can be."

"Right now I'm grieving for my father."

"And forgetting your duty to your country. If Seti is looking down from heaven, do you think he approves of your passivity?"

If Moses weren't his best friend, Ramses would have hit him.

"You want me to be hard and impersonal?"

"You've suffered a great loss, but keep your eyes open. Shaanar approached me, even knowing how close to you I am. He tried to turn me against you. Does that give you some sense of the danger you're in?"

Ramses was speechless.

"You're facing a tough opponent," Moses continued. "Wake up, friend."

THREE

Memphis, where the Nile Valley began branching out into the Delta, was the country's economic capital. Now it slumbered. In the harbor, called "Safe Journey," merchant ships stayed in their moorings. For the seventy-day mourning period, trade was suspended, and the nobles refrained from entertaining.

Seti's death had sent the town into a state of shock. His reign had brought increased prosperity, but the most prominent businessmen feared a weaker pharaoh would reverse the trend. A pharaoh less firm in defending Egypt's interests—and who could be as strong as Seti? Shaanar, his elder son, would run the country capably, but in his waning days Seti had designated the young and fiery Ramses, who seemed more like a dashing playboy than a head of state. The most clear-sighted of leaders can make mistakes, and Memphis quietly agreed with Thebes that Seti might have chosen the wrong son to succeed him.

Shaanar restlessly paced Meba's parlor. A fit-looking

man of sixty with broad, appealing features, Meba was Seti's longtime secretary of state. He had secretly worked against Ramses, supporting Shaanar, whose political and economic views more closely resembled his own. Opening the Mediterranean and Asian markets, strengthening commercial ties, was the wave of the future, even if it meant forgetting a few traditional principles. After all, he felt, the arms trade was preferable to armed conflict.

"Is he going to show up?" asked Shaanar.

"He's in our camp, rest assured."

"That could change any moment. You can't trust a bully."

Seti's older son was short and heavyset, with a round face and plump cheeks. His thick, sensual lips betrayed his love of good food, and his dark, beady eyes were perpetually agitated. He avoided the sun and all forms of exertion. A cultivated voice failed to mask his uneven temper.

Shaanar was a pacifist for financial reasons. Egypt's economic isolationism was folly, in his opinion. *Treason* was a term for moralizers without a nose for profit. Ramses was too old-fashioned to understand business. No matter how you looked at it, he didn't deserve to be king. It was easy for Shaanar to rationalize the coup he would soon be orchestrating: Egypt would thank him for it.

First, though, he still needed his most important ally.

"A drink," Shaanar demanded.

Meba served his illustrious guest a cup of cool beer.

"We never should have included him," said the prince.

"I'm sure he's still with us. Don't forget how eager he is to get home."

Finally, the secretary of state's doorman announced the long-awaited caller.

Blond, sharp-eyed Menelaus, son of Atreus and King of Sparta, was lucky in war. He wore the breastplate, back armor, and wide belt with golden buckles that had served him well in Greece's victory over Troy. With his fleet in tatters, he had sought refuge in Egypt. Now his wife, Helen, refused to leave the land of the pharaohs, fearing bitter treatment from her husband once they reached home. Since Queen Tuya had taken Helen under her wing, Menelaus was unable to strong-arm his wife. Fortunately for him, Shaanar had stepped in to enlist his cooperation in overthrowing Ramses, promising to hand over Helen in return.

The moment Shaanar became Pharaoh, Menelaus would take Helen back to Greece.

For several months, his troops had settled in, the officers joining the Egyptian army, the soldiers and sailors finding ways to make a living, all seemingly content with their good fortune. In reality, they anxiously awaited their commander's order to spring into action, like a new and improved Trojan Horse.

The Greek eyed Meba suspiciously. "Tell him to leave," he ordered Shaanar. "You and I talk, no one else."

"The secretary of state is one of us."

"Don't make me repeat myself."

Shaanar waved the older man out of the room.

"Where do we stand?" asked Menelaus.

"It's time."

"Are you sure? This infernal mummification takes so long I'm beginning to wonder about you people."

"We need to act before my father's mummy is laid in his tomb."

"My men are ready."

"I don't want any unnecessary violence or . . ."

"Out with it, man! You Egyptians are afraid of a good fight. We Greeks kept after the Trojans for years until we destroyed them. If you want Ramses dead, say so. My sword will do the rest."

"Ramses is my brother, and sometimes deceit is more effective than brute force."

"They go hand in hand. And who are you to be lecturing me on strategy?"

"You need to win Helen back."

"Helen!" he spat. "The woman makes me sick, but I can't go home without her."

"Then let's try my plan."

"Fill me in."

Shaanar smiled. Luck was with him this time. With the Greek's help, it would work. "Only two things stand in our way: the lion and Serramanna. Two solutions: poison and a sneak attack from inside. Your men kidnap Ramses and we hide him until you're ready to take him off to Greece."

"Why not just kill him?"

"I don't want blood on my hands when I take the throne. The official story will be that Ramses renounced his claim and decided to see the world. Unfortunately, a tragic accident will occur during his travels."

"What about Helen?"

"Once I'm crowned, my mother will have to obey my orders and release her. If Tuya resists, she'll be placed under house arrest in a temple."

Menelaus nodded. "Not bad, for an Egyptian. Do you have the poison on hand?"

"Of course."

"Our man in Ramses' guard troops is one of my best officers. He'll have no trouble slitting Serramanna's throat while he sleeps. Name the day, Prince."

"It won't be long. I have business in Thebes. As soon as I'm back, we'll strike."

To Helen, freedom was an unexpected bonus, and she enjoyed every moment of it. In a light, nectar-scented dress, with a veil on her head to protect her from the sun, her life in Tuya's household was a waking dream. She had somehow slipped out from under her bullying lowlife of a husband. "Evil bitch," he told his men to call her.

Tuya and her daughter-in-law, Nefertari, had given Helen friendship and employment. It was a pleasure to live in a country where women were not forced to live as prisoners in their homes, even if that home was a palace.

Was Helen truly to blame for thousands of Greek and Trojan casualties? She had never wanted the long years of frenzied killing, yet somehow she had been tried and convicted without ever having the chance to defend herself. Here in Memphis no one condemned her. She wove, she listened to music and played it, she swam in the palace pools and strolled in the endlessly delightful gardens. The clash of weapons grew distant, yielding to birdsong.

Several times a day, fair-skinned Helen prayed for her dream to continue. Her only wish was to leave her past, her country, and her husband behind.

On a sandy path lined by persea trees, she spotted a dead crane. Walking closer, she saw that the bird's handsome body had been torn open. Helen knelt and examined the entrails; her gift for prophecy had been acknowledged by both the Greeks and the Trojans.

It was a long while before she struggled to her feet.

What she read in the crane's shattered body appalled her.

FOUR

Thebes, the southern capital, was home to the cult of Amon, the god credited with helping to drive out the Hyksos, a cruel, barbarian Asiatic people who had occupied the country several centuries earlier. Since Egypt's liberation, every pharaoh for generations had paid tribute to Amon and further embellished his temple at Karnak until it had become the largest and richest of cult centers, a sort of state within the state. The high priest of Amon acted more the powerful government leader than clergyman.

Upon his arrival in Thebes, Shaanar immediately requested an audience with the high priest. The two men talked in the shade of an arbor dripping with wisteria and honeysuckle. A cooling breeze blew from the sacred lake nearby.

"You came without an entourage?" the high priest asked in wonder.

"Very few people are aware I'm here."

"I see . . . we need to keep it quiet."

"Are you still opposed to Ramses?"

"More firmly than ever. He's too young and hotheaded

to be Pharaoh. He'll go overboard. Seti made a mistake designating him."

"Will you go along with me?"

"Where would you rank the temple of Amon, if you wore the crown?"

"At the top of the list, naturally."

"Your father had other ideas. He favored Heliopolis and Memphis. Karnak must no longer be second best; that's all I ask."

"Then don't ask Ramses."

"What do you have in mind, Shaanar?"

"We need to act, and act quickly."

"In other words, before Seti's funeral rites."

"Yes. It's our last chance."

What Shaanar did not know was that the high priest of Amon was seriously ill. His doctor told him he had only months, perhaps weeks, to live. A speedy resolution would be a final blessing from the gods. Before he died, he would see Ramses deposed and Karnak saved.

"I cannot condone violence," the high priest decreed. "Amon gave us peace; which must be preserved."

"I agree completely. Unfit as he may be to rule, Ramses is my brother, and I hold him dear. I have never for one second intended him any harm."

"What are your plans for him?"

"He's an energetic young person, in love with adventure and the open road. An extended trip abroad will be a welcome prospect once he's freed from his crushing responsibilities. When he returns, his firsthand observations will be extremely valuable."

"I would also like to see your mother remain as your close adviser."

"That goes without saying."

"Be faithful to Amon, my son, and your future will be assured."

Shaanar bowed deferentially. This gullible old prelate was a godsend.

Dolora, Ramses' older sister, rubbed soothing unguents into her oily skin. Plain, gangly, bored since birth, she hated Thebes, hated the south. A princess belonged in Memphis, in the thick of court gossip.

Thebes was tiresome. High society had welcomed her with open arms, of course, and showered her with invitations; she was, after all, a member of the royal family. But Memphis set the fashion, and besides, her husband was sinking into a deep depression. Affable, paunchy Sary had been Ramses' tutor, then head of the *Kap*, the royal academy where Egypt's top students were sent. His talents were wasted here, and it was all her brother's fault.

Yes, Sary had come up with a less than successful scheme to have Ramses killed. And yes, she, Dolora, had thrown her lot in with Shaanar. Yes, they had both made mistakes. Even so, shouldn't Ramses grant them his pardon, now that Seti had died?

Revenge was the only possible response to his cruelty. Ramses' luck would turn eventually, and when it did, she and Sary would be ready. Meanwhile, she kept up her skincare regime while her husband read or dozed.

Shaanar's unannounced arrival was like a blast of cold water.

"My dear brother!" exclaimed Dolora, kissing him. "Bearing glad tidings, I hope!"

"Possibly."

"Don't keep us in suspense!" Sary demanded.

"I'm going to be king."

"Our day is coming soon, then?"

"Come back to Memphis with me. I'll find a place for you until we dispose of Ramses."

Dolora blanched. "Dispose of him, you say?"

"Don't worry, little sister. I'm only sending him on a grand tour."

"Will you have a job for me?" asked Sary. "Something important?"

"You've made it just a bit awkward," replied Shaanar, "but I can use a man of your intelligence. Be loyal to me and the sky's the limit."

"You have my word, Shaanar."

Iset the Fair was biding her time. Before she gave birth to their son, Ramses had sent her to Thebes; now she was raising her beloved Kha in the royal palace. A striking young woman with green eyes, a small, straight nose, and finely drawn lips, she was energetic, vivacious, Ramses' first lover and now his lesser wife.

Lesser wife . . . hard to accept the title, harder still the status. Yet Iset found it impossible to be jealous of Nefertari, so lovely, gentle, and serious, who, even with the title of queen, still seemed devoid of worldly ambition.

It would have been easier if she were consumed with hate, if she could lash out at the two of them, but she still loved the man who had given her so much happiness and pleasure, the man to whom she had given his firstborn son.

Iset cared nothing for power and prestige. She loved Ramses for himself, his intensity and verve. The pain of living apart from him was sometimes unbearable. Why didn't he realize how much it hurt her?

Soon Ramses would be king and come to see her only rarely, briefly. Each time, she knew, she would give in to her love for him. If only she could meet someone else—but other men paled in comparison to Ramses.

When her majordomo announced Shaanar, Iset was amazed. What was Seti's older son doing in Thebes before the funeral?

He was shown into a room with narrow slits of windows high in the walls, letting in fresh air but little direct sunlight.

"You look magnificent, Iset."

"What do you want?"

"I know you don't care for me, but I also know you're intelligent enough to look out for your own best interests. I think you have the makings of a Great Royal Wife."

"Too bad Ramses doesn't share your opinion."

"What if it weren't up to him?"

"What do you mean?"

"My brother isn't a complete fool. He finally sees that he's not fit to govern Egypt."

"Meaning . . ."

"Meaning that I'll take over and you can be Lady of the Two Lands."

"Ramses would never step down. You're lying."

"It's the truth, dear lady. He's planning to leave the country with Menelaus. When he's done traveling, he'll be treated with all the respect due a member of the royal family."

"Has he said anything about me?"

"I'm afraid he's forgotten you and his little son. All he can think of is seeing the world."

"Is he taking Nefertari?"

"No, no . . . too many fish in the sea." Shaanar laughed. "You know his appetites."

Iset seemed distraught. Shaanar would have liked to take her hand, but it was too soon. He mustn't frighten her away. First he needed to offer comfort, then slowly begin to woo her.

"Kha will have the finest education," he promised. "You won't have to worry. After Seti is laid to rest, we'll go back to Memphis together."

"Will Ramses be gone by then?"

"Of course."

"He's not attending the funeral rites?"

"It's a shame, but there's no help for it. Menelaus refuses to wait any longer. Forget Ramses, Iset. Concentrate on becoming queen."

FIVE

Iset spent a sleepless night.

Shaanar was lying. It wasn't like Ramses to leave Egypt at a time like this. Not for the world would he miss Seti's funeral.

Ramses had treated her badly, true, but she would never

betray him to his brother. Iset had no desire to be queen, no matter what Shaanar thought. The moon-faced, smooth-talking, ambitious, conceited fool! She hated him.

She knew what she had to do: warn Ramses that his brother was plotting a coup.

On fresh papyrus, she composed a long letter relating her conversation with Shaanar. Then she summoned the local head of the royal courier service.

"This needs to reach Memphis as soon as possible."

"I'll see to it personally," he assured her.

River traffic at Thebes had slowed considerably, as in Memphis, while the country was in mourning. Guards dozed at the river landing where boats for the north customarily docked. Iset's messenger hailed a sailor.

"Raise anchor, we're leaving for Memphis."

"Sorry, can't leave port."

"Why?"

"The high priest of Amon at Karnak has the boat reserved."

"Without going through my office?"

"Just got the order."

"Well, I'm telling you to ignore it."

A man appeared on the bridge of the boat in question.

"Orders are orders, my good man. Don't contradict him."

"Keep your nose out of this, whoever you are."

"I'm Shaanar, Seti's older son."

The official bowed. "Forgive my insolence, Your Highness."

"All right, if you give me the message Iset the Fair wants delivered."

"But . . ."

"It goes to the royal palace in Memphis, correct?"

"Yes, to your brother, Ramses."

"That's where I'm heading tonight. Or don't I meet your standards as a courier?"

The official handed the letter to Shaanar.

As soon as the boat pulled away from Thebes, Shaanar tore Iset's letter to shreds and scattered them in the wind.

The night was warm and fragrant, belying the fact that Egypt had lost a king as great as the Old Kingdom pharaohs. As the country mourned, the usual lively nightlife was nowhere to be found. In village squares and city streets, no dancing, singing, or storytelling; no tales of animals turning human and teaching humans a lesson or two, no games and laughter.

Watcher, Ramses' yellow dog, slept with his head against Fighter, the huge lion that patrolled the regent's private garden. After the gardeners finished the evening watering, the two pets liked to stretch out on the cool grass.

Among the gardeners was a Greek, one of Menelaus's men. Before leaving for the night, he tucked poisoned chunks of meat into one of the lily beds, where the greedy beasts would surely find them. Even if the lion took hours to die, no treatment could save him.

Watcher picked up the scent first. Yawning, he stretched, sniffed the air, and trotted over to the lilies. His snout quickly led him to the meat; he nosed and pawed it thoroughly, then backtracked. This was too good a find not to share with his friend.

The three soldiers perching on the garden wall smiled as the lion sleepily trailed the yellow dog back to the flower bed. Just a little longer and the coast would be clear. They could slip into Ramses' bedchamber and hustle him away to Menelaus's waiting ship.

The lion and dog lay with their heads in the foliage. Before long they seemed to go limp. Ten minutes later one of the Greeks jumped down from the wall. Given how deadly the poison was and how much had been put in the meat, the big cat must already be paralyzed.

The scout motioned to his companions, who followed him down the path toward the regent's suite. They were about to go inside when a growling sound made them wheel around.

Fighter and Watcher stood staring at them. Among the trampled lilies lay the tainted meat, which the lion had shredded after confirming his friend's suspicions.

The three Greek soldiers huddled together, daggers raised.

Fighter sprang at them, teeth and claws bared.

The Greek officer who had infiltrated Ramses' royal bodyguard crept through the prince regent's wing of the silent palace. Since he was assigned to patrol the hallways, none of the other soldiers on duty would think a thing of it.

He headed toward the granite threshold where Serramanna slept. The Sard always boasted that anyone coming after Ramses would have to deal with him first.

Once the regent lost his mainstay, Shaanar could easily take command of the guard troops.

The Greek stopped and listened. Not a sound, except for the steady breathing of deep sleep. Even a giant had to rest sometime. But he might have a cat's reflexes on suddenly waking to danger. The Greek must move swiftly and surely, allowing the Sard no time to react.

Cautiously, he listened a while longer, until there could be no doubt. Then he unsheathed his dagger and held his breath, striking furiously at the sleeping figure's throat.

"Nice try, for a sneaking coward," a deep voice snarled from behind him. He whirled around.

"You just killed a dummy," said Serramanna. "My breathing was real, though. I had a hunch that something was up tonight."

Menelaus's man gripped the handle of his dagger.

"Drop it."

"I'm still going to slit your throat."

"Want to bet?" The Sard loomed over him. The Greek's dagger connected with air. For his size, Serramanna was surprisingly quick on his feet.

"You don't even know how to fight," he taunted.

The Greek tried a feint, stepping aside, then rushing forward, blade pointing at his opponent's stomach.

The Sard's right hand chopped at his wrist, breaking it, as his left hand slammed into the Greek's temple. Tongue dangling, eyes glazed, he collapsed and was dead before he even hit the floor.

"One fewer coward to deal with," muttered Serramanna.

Wide awake, Ramses considered the two-pronged attack. Fighter had taken care of the soldiers in the garden. On his doorstep lay another dead Greek, a member of his personal bodyguard.

"They were after you," Serramanna said flatly.

"Did the one you killed say anything?"

"I didn't have time to ask questions. No great loss; he wasn't much of a soldier."

"Menelaus has to be behind this."

"Just let me at that bully! I'll send him off to meet all the heroes he's always lamenting."

"For the moment, just double the watch."

"Defense is fine, but we'll never be secure unless we strike back."

"First we need to know who the enemy is."

"You just told me it's Menelaus! Never trust a Greek. Send them all packing before they try again!"

Ramses laid a hand on Serramanna's right shoulder.

"With you on my side, I don't have to worry."

Ramses spent the rest of the night in the garden with his pets. Fighter was fast asleep; Watcher dozed fitfully. The prince contemplated human folly. The struggle for power had begun even before Seti's mummy could be laid in his tomb.

Moses was right. Lenience toward his enemies had only made them more likely to keep up their attacks, convinced he would not retaliate.

With the dawn, the prince's spirits rose. No one could take Seti's place, but it was time for Ramses to start acting like a pharaoh.

ƧIX

In Seti's Egypt, temples were responsible for redistributing excess donations, as well as the food produced on their extensive domains. As long as there had been pharaohs, the law of Ma'at, the fragile goddess of truth and justice, maintained that this land of plenty should be free from want. What god could bless a feast day if even the humblest soul went hungry?

As head of state, a pharaoh was both the rudder that steered a steady course and the captain who held his crew together. He must inspire the cooperation essential to any lasting society.

A key government department maintained strict control over the redistribution of goods. However, the temples were allowed to commission a few independent merchants to travel the length of the country, trading freely.

One such trader was Raia, a Syrian living in Egypt for over ten years. With his cargo ship and herd of donkeys, he was constantly on the move, selling wine, preserved meat, and vases imported from Asia. He was of average height and build, sporting a trim goatee and a striped tunic. Polite, discreet, and honest, he attracted a faithful clientele with quality merchandise at reasonable prices. His work permit was renewed year after year in recognition of his service to his adopted country. Like many other immigrants, the Syrian had become practically indistinguishable from the natives.

No one knew that Raia moonlighted as a secret agent for the Hittites.

The information he fed the warlike Anatolians would help them decide when to attack Pharaoh's foreign domin-ions, seize those lands, then invade Egypt itself. Raia had cultivated contacts in the military, the customs department, and the police. Tidbits from their dinner conversation ended up in Hattusa, the Hittite capital, by way of coded messages inserted into the alabaster vases Raia exported to southern Syria, Egypt's official ally. Customs had searched his shipments more than once, finding only what appeared to be routine business letters and invoices. The importer made a profit selling the vases and a bonus for delivering the messages to an agent in Hittite-controlled northern Syria, who relayed them directly to Hattusa.

It was a simple way for the Near East's greatest military power to receive monthly briefings on Egyptian politics from a primary source.

Seti's death and the subsequent mourning period would be the perfect time to attack Egypt, but Raia had argued forcefully against it, telling the Hittite generals it would be madness. If they thought the Egyptian army had been demobilized, they were sadly mistaken. Fearing a possible invasion before the ascension of Seti's successor, the border patrols had been reinforced.

Furthermore, Seti's loose-lipped daughter had made it plain that Shaanar, her elder brother, was not resigned to his fate. Seti had passed him over, but Shaanar planned to correct this obvious error before Ramses' coronation.

Raia had made a thorough study of the disgruntled prince. Ambitious, clever, devious—and ruthless when his personal interest was at stake—he was altogether different from his father and brother. Seeing him become Pharaoh was devoutly to be wished, for he seemed more inclined to believe the current Hittite propaganda that closer diplomatic and trade relations would bring an end to the old hostilities. Even Seti had failed to take the key fortress of Kadesh when he had the chance, suing for peace instead. The King of the Hittites had proclaimed his intention to check his expansionist tendencies. He hoped the new pharaoh would believe him and let down the country's defenses.

Raia next began to ferret out Shaanar's co-conspirators and determine how he planned to proceed. His unerring instincts led him to the Greeks who had recently settled in Memphis. Menelaus was no more than a cruel mercenary who boasted of razing Troy. Rumor had it that the blood-thirsty Greek was restless, eager to sail home as a conquering hero with his wife, Helen, in tow. Shaanar, he surmised, would pay the Greek contingent handsomely to eliminate Ramses and help him reclaim his rightful place as Seti's successor.

Raia was convinced that Ramses would mean trouble for the Hittites. Unafraid to fight, he had inherited his father's determination. He was young, hot-blooded, unpredictable. Shaanar, on the other hand, was a known quantity, reasonable, open-minded: clearly the better choice.

Unfortunately, a palace servant in Raia's employ had just brought the information that several Greek mercenaries had been killed while attempting to enter Ramses' bedchamber. The attempted coup had apparently failed.

The next few hours would be telling. If Shaanar managed to avoid being implicated, he still had a future. If not, he'd have to be crossed off the list.

Menelaus stomped on the shield that had warded off so many blows on the battlefield. He broke one of the spears that had dispatched many a Trojan. Then he grabbed a vase and threw it against the wall of his antechamber.

Still fuming, he turned to face Shaanar.

"A complete failure! How can it be? We always win. It took us ten years to beat the Trojans, but we did it."

"I sympathize, but the fact is that Ramses' lion got your three soldiers and Serramanna killed the guardsman."

"Someone gave away our plans."

"No, your men were simply outmaneuvered. Ramses suspects you now. He'll probably order you out of the country."

"Without Helen."

"Yes. You let me down, Menelaus."

"Your plan was stupid."

"You seemed to think it would work."

"Get out!"

"You'd better be prepared to leave soon."

"I know what I have to do."

Ahmeni was Ramses' sandal-bearer and private secretary, but first and foremost his lifelong friend. His allegiance was complete and unconditional. Short and slight, with thinning hair, his frail physique did not prevent him from being a tireless worker and peerless scribe, forever studying official documents and briefing Ramses on their contents. Devoid of personal ambition, Ahmeni was nevertheless a strict taskmaster, holding his administrative staff of twenty to the highest standards, prizing accuracy and discipline above all else.

Although he had little use for a brute like Serramanna, Ahmeni admitted that the bodyguard had dealt effectively with the Greek assassin. Ramses' reaction to the attack was surprising. The future pharaoh simply asked his secretary for a thorough description of the main branches of government, how they worked, how they related to one another.

When Serramanna came in to announce Shaanar, Ahmeni was irritated. He did not want to be interrupted as he pored over documents concerning the reform of outdated laws regulating public ferries.

"Don't let him in," Ahmeni urged Ramses.

"Shaanar is my brother."

"He's a self-centered schemer."

"I think I should hear what he has to say for himself."

Ramses had his brother shown into the garden, where Fighter lazed in the shade of a sycamore tree and Watcher gnawed on a bone.

"Your security is much tighter than Seti's!" exclaimed Shaanar. "You certainly screen your visitors."

"Haven't you heard that some Greeks broke in here last night? They were after me."

"I heard. I've come to tell you who's responsible."

"How would you know that?"

"Menelaus approached me."

"What was his proposition?"

"To put me on the throne."

"And you're going to tell me you turned him down?"

"I do love power, Ramses, but I know my limitations. No one but you can be the next pharaoh. Our father's wishes were clear; they must be respected."

"Why would Menelaus risk his neck?"

"He's dying to sail home as a conquering hero, but to do that he needs to bring Helen. He's convinced that you're holding her against her will. In exchange for making me king, he wanted me to banish you to the desert, hand over Helen, and clear him for departure."

"Helen is free to leave whenever she chooses. I have no say in her decision."

"No Greek would believe you. Menelaus assumes a man is telling her what to do."

"He's a dolt."

"Perhaps, but he's used to bullying his way through life. You'd better be careful."

"What would you advise?"

"He's violated our hospitality. It's time that he left for good."

SEVEN

The poet Homer lived in a fine new residence not far from the palace. Ramses had provided a cook, maid, and gardener to look after him. The cellar was stocked with Delta wine that Homer spiced with anise and coriander, and there was a liberal supply of the fragrant olive oil he liked to rub on his skin. The old poet was so comfortable that he rarely left his garden, seeking inspiration in the shade of his beloved lemon tree.

He would smoke crushed sage leaves in a pipe fashioned from a giant snail shell and a hollow reed. Hector, his black and white cat, purred in his lap as he dictated verse after verse of his *Iliad* to Ahmeni or one of the scribe's assistants.

Ramses' visit was an added pleasure. The cook brought a Cretan wine jug with a very thin spout, pouring just a trickle of cool spiced wine. The garden pavilion—four acacia columns with a palm-frond roof—gave some relief from the summer heat.

"This nice hot weather helps my aching bones," said Homer, stroking the flowing white beard that was such a contrast to his lined and craggy face. "Do you have storms like we do in Greece?"

"Tremendous ones," answered Ramses. "When our god Set unleashes his fury, dark clouds fill the sky, lightning flashes, thunder rumbles, and bolts crash to the ground. The rain floods dry riverbeds, sweeping rocks through the canyons. You'll understand why Set is called 'The Destroyer.' "

"Wasn't your father named for him?"

"For a long time I couldn't imagine why a pharaoh would place himself under the protection of the god who murdered Osiris, his own brother. Then I realized that Seti wanted to harness the powers of darkness and use them to do good."

"Strange, strange country! And it seems you've been having your own stormy weather, son."

"I didn't know you could see from your garden to mine."

"My eyesight is failing, but my hearing is excellent."

"So you heard that your countrymen tried to eliminate me."

"The other day I wrote these lines: '*I greatly fear that you will be caught tight in the enemy's net, that you will all become their prey and spoils of war. They will sack your cities. Think on it night and day, fight on, if you wish to hold your heads high.*' "

"Are you a seer?"

"I can guess why a future pharaoh would take time from his official duties to seek the opinion of an obscure old poet—not that I don't appreciate your visits."

Ramses smiled. He liked the way Homer spoke his mind.

"All right. Do you think the soldiers who came after me were acting alone or on orders from Menelaus?"

"Beware of Greeks, my friend! Hatching plots is their

favorite pastime. If Menelaus wants Helen, and you're standing in his way, it's goodbye Ramses."

"But I'm still here."

"Menelaus is as single-minded as he is unprincipled. He'll keep trying, attack you in your own backyard, without a thought for the consequences."

"What do you recommend?"

"Pack him off to Greece with Helen."

"She won't go."

"Through no fault of her own, that woman sows death and destruction in her wake. If you think you can alter the course of her destiny, you're sadly mistaken."

"She's free to choose where she lives."

"Don't say I didn't warn you. By the way, I could use some new papyrus and more of that wonderful olive oil."

Some might have said the white-bearded poet should be less brusque with his royal patron. Ramses, however, valued the old man's frankness. There were yes-men to spare in the royal court.

The moment Ramses walked through the gate to his wing of the palace, Ahmeni came running, in a most uncharacteristic state of agitation.

"What's happening?"

"Menelaus," Ahmeni panted.

"What now?"

"He's taken hostages down at the harbor—dockworkers, women and children. Says he'll kill them unless you deliver Helen to him today."

"Where is he?"

"On his ship, with the hostages. His whole fleet is ready to sail. Not one of his mercenaries is left in town."

"And where were our naval police when all this happened?"

"Don't be too hard on them. Menelaus took the guards on duty by surprise."

"Has anyone told my mother?"

"She's waiting for you, with Nefertari and Helen."

Seti's widow, Ramses' wife, and Menelaus's reluctant spouse were all looking anxious. Tuya sat on a low gilded chair, Nefertari on a folding stool. Helen stood, her back against a light green column with a lotus capital.

The Queen Mother's audience chamber was cool and restful, with subtle, pleasing scents in the air. On Pharaoh's throne, a bouquet of flowers marked the temporary absence of a monarch.

Ramses bowed to his mother, kissed his wife gently, greeted Helen.

"How much do you know?" asked Tuya.

"Only that it's serious. How many hostages?"

"Around fifty."

"Even one life is more than I'm willing to sacrifice."

Ramses turned to Helen. "If we attack, will Menelaus really kill the hostages?"

"He'll slit their throats with his own dagger."

"How could he live with innocent blood on his hands?"

"He wants me back. If he can't have me, he'll kill before he gets killed."

"It's barbaric."

"Menelaus is a warrior. To him, everyone is either friend or foe."

"And his own men . . . doesn't he realize none of them will survive if the hostages are executed?"

"They'll die as heroes, with their honor intact."

"Heroes or murderers of defenseless bystanders?"

"Menelaus knows only one law: kill or be killed."

"There must be a special hell reserved for Greek heroes."

"Frightening as it may be, their need to fight is more intense than the simple desire to survive."

Nefertari drew closer to Ramses. "What will you do?"

"I'll board Menelaus's ship alone and unarmed and try to reason with him."

"You must be joking," Helen said with a bitter laugh.

"The least I can do is try."

"He'll take you hostage, too!" Nefertari interjected.

"You have no right to put yourself in such danger," Tuya told him. "Won't you just be falling into his trap?"

"He'll take you away to Greece," Nefertari prophesied, "and someone else will be Pharaoh—someone who'll use Helen as a pawn in trade negotiations."

Ramses shot a questioning look at his mother. She seemed to agree with Nefertari.

"If persuasion won't work with Menelaus, we'll have to resort to violence."

Helen approached the prince regent.

"No," he said, "we won't let you go to him. Protecting a guest is a sacred duty."

"Ramses is right," the Queen Mother seconded. "Giving in to your husband's blackmail would be in violation of the law of Ma'at. It could only bring unhappiness to Egypt."

"But I'm the one who caused all this to happen and it's—"

"Don't, Helen. Since you've chosen to live among us, we're bound to help you stay free."

"I'll think of something," Seti's son concluded.

Trembling and sweating, Meba, the late pharaoh's secretary of state, stood on the pier shouting back and forth with Menelaus and fearing that a Greek archer's arrow would pierce him at any moment. However, he did win one concession from the King of Sparta: Ramses would be allowed one night to host a farewell banquet in Helen's honor.

Menelaus stipulated that the hostages would be given no food whatsoever until Helen boarded the ship. He would release them once he sailed clear and was sure no Egyptian warships were trailing his fleet.

Unharmed, Meba walked briskly away from the flagship, not minding the Greek soldiers' taunts. Ramses' praise for his able negotiations was some consolation.

The prince now had a few precious hours to formulate a plan to free the hostages.

EIGHT

Average in height, strong as an ox, with dark hair and skin, the snake charmer Setau was making love to his lissome Nubian wife, Lotus, whose slender curves were a constant call to pleasure. Their large home on the edge of the desert, far from the center of Memphis, also served as their laboratory and workshop. Several rooms were filled with flasks and vials of various sizes and the strange contraptions they used to produce pharmaceuticals from snake venom.

Lotus was a marvelously limber and willing participant in her husband's seemingly endless variations on a theme. Besides her talents in bed, her thorough and insightful knowledge of reptile behavior never ceased to impress him. Their mutual passion for snakes led to important discoveries and, after a great deal of experimentation, the creation of new remedies.

As Setau caressed his wife's breasts, tender as flower buds, their pet cobra suddenly rose to attention in the doorway.

"Someone's approaching," said Setau.

Lotus glanced at the splendid reptile. Its swaying told her whether their visitor was a friend or a stranger. Tonight it did not seem alarmed.

Setau slid off the cozy bed and grabbed a club. While he trusted the cobra's judgment, at this time of night it was best to be careful.

A galloping horse pulled up in front of the house. The rider jumped off.

"Ramses! What are you doing here in the middle of the night?"

"Hope I'm not disturbing you . . ."

"As a matter of fact, Lotus and I were just—"

"Sorry, but I need your help."

The two had attended the royal academy together, but Setau had shunned the traditional administrative career path to devote himself to the study of snakes, unlocking their secrets of life and death. When they were still in their teens, he had dared Ramses to face the master of the desert, a lethal species of cobra. Setau was immune to the cobra's bite, but the prince was not. Their friendship survived the challenge, and Setau belonged to the limited circle of Ramses' closest confidants.

"Is the kingdom in danger?"

"Menelaus has taken hostages and threatens to kill them unless we hand over Helen."

"A fine mess. But why not let her go? The woman did cause the destruction of an entire city."

"Violating the laws of hospitality would make us no better than the Greeks."

"Let the barbarians work it out for themselves."

"Helen is a queen. She wants to stay in Egypt. It's my duty to keep her out of Menelaus's clutches.

"You really sound like a pharaoh. It must be your destiny. But then it's not a job any sane man would ask for."

"I need to storm Menelaus's ship without harming the hostages."

"You've always liked beating impossible odds."

"The commanding officers of the regiments stationed in Memphis haven't come up with one worthwhile idea. Every plan they suggest would end in massacre."

"Does that surprise you?"

"No. That's why I thought of you."

"You think I'm going to storm Greek warships?"

"Not you—your snakes."

"Let's hear it."

"Before dawn, we'll send swimmers to climb up the sides of the ship, carrying bags with snakes in them. Then they dump the snakes near the soldiers guarding the hostages. A few of the guards will be bitten, and in the confusion, our men can free the hostages."

"Original, but awfully risky. What makes you think the cobras will go for the Greeks?"

"I'm fully aware of the enormous risk we'll be taking."

"We?"

"You and I will be leading the raid, of course."

"You expect me to risk my life for some Greek woman I've never met?"

"No, for Egyptian hostages you've never met."

"What will happen to my wife and my snakes if I die in the process?"

"They'll be taken care of."

"No, it's too risky. And how many snakes would you expect me to commit to fighting these bloodthirsty foreigners?"

"You'll be paid triple the going bounty, plus I'll designate your laboratory as an official research center."

Setau looked back toward Lotus, so appealing in the warm summer darkness.

"Enough talk. We'd better start bagging the snakes."

Menelaus paced the bridge of his flagship. The lookouts had noted no unusual activity on the riverbanks. Just as he supposed, the Egyptians were too afraid of bloodshed to make a move, the cowards. Taking hostages wasn't pretty, but it had worked. There was no other way to pry Helen loose from Tuya and Nefertari.

The hostages had stopped their crying and moaning. Hands tied behind their backs, they huddled on the poop deck, guarded by ten soldiers who were relieved every two hours.

Menelaus's aide-de-camp came up to the bridge.

"Do you think they'll attack?" he asked.

"It would be counterproductive. We'd have to slaughter the hostages."

"In that case, we'd have no buffer."

"We'd kill a lot of Egyptians before we were back at sea . . . but don't worry, they won't endanger the lives of innocent victims. I'll get Helen back at dawn and we'll sail home."

"I'll miss this place."

"Have you lost your mind?"

"Didn't you think life was good in Memphis? Peace at last."

"We were born to fight, not laze around palaces."

"How safe will you be when you do get home? By now there must be plenty of pretenders to your throne."

"I can still handle a sword. When they see Helen under my thumb, they'll realize who's in charge."

Ramses had selected thirty of his best soldiers, all strong swimmers. Setau showed them how to avoid being bitten when they released their snakes. The volunteers' faces were tense. The regent made a rousing speech. His strength of conviction, along with Setau's obvious competence, convinced the commandos they would win the day.

Ramses hated keeping secrets from his wife and mother, but neither of them would have wanted him to take part in the raid, thinking it put him in too much danger. He assumed full responsibility for the surprise attack. If he was truly meant to be Pharaoh, fate would see him through.

Setau talked to the snakes inside their sacks and chanted spells to calm them. Lotus had taught him the sounds that had a magical effect on reptiles.

Once the secret weapons were ready, the raiders marched quietly down to the far end of the harbor, out of the Greek lookouts' sight.

Setau touched Ramses' wrist.

"Wait . . . Am I seeing things, or is Menelaus casting off?"

Ramses confirmed his suspicions. "Stay here," he said, dropping the sack that contained a sand viper and running toward the Greek flagship. In the silvery moonlight, he saw the warrior king standing on the prow, holding Helen in front of him.

"Menelaus!" Ramses shouted.

The Greek, wearing a double breastplate and a harness with golden clasps, recognized the prince's voice immediately.

"Ramses! You came to see me off. It will be a second honeymoon for me and Helen. She'll be glad she decided to come. Believe me, she'll get the royal treatment back home!" Menelaus snorted with laughter.

"Free the hostages!"

"Never fear, you'll get them back alive."

Ramses trailed behind the Greek fleet in a small boat with two sails. When the sun rose, Menelaus's soldiers raised a racket, beating on their shields with swords and spears.

Under orders from the regent and the Great Royal Wife, the Egyptian navy made no move, giving the Greeks free passage to the Mediterranean. Menelaus could start his northward crossing.

For a second, Ramses thought he had been fooled, that the King of Sparta was about to slit his prisoners' throats. But then a boat was lowered and the hostages climbed down a rope ladder to board it. The able-bodied men among them took the oars and rowed away from their floating prison as fast as they could.

On the prow of her husband's ship, white-armed Helen, wearing a purple cloak, a white veil, and a collar of gold, gazed at the coast of Egypt, the country where she had known a few months of happiness, where she had hoped in vain to be free of Menelaus.

Once the hostages were beyond the Greek archers' range, Helen twisted the amethyst on her right hand and drank the contents of the minuscule vial it concealed: poison stolen from a Memphis laboratory. She had sworn never again to become her husband's slave; she refused to end her days beaten and humiliated in the palace gynaeceum. Returning with nothing but her corpse, the black-hearted conqueror of Troy would be a laughingstock.

She gloried in the touch of the summer sun, wishing her fair skin could turn a warm Egyptian copper, that she could be like her newfound friends, free to love whomever she chose, satisfied body and soul.

Helen quietly slumped, head rolling onto her shoulder, eyes wide open and fixed on the bright blue sky.

NINE

By the time Ahsha returned from a brief State Department information-gathering mission in southern Syria, Memphis had already been in mourning for forty days. The next day, Tuya, Ramses, Nefertari, and key government figures were set to depart for Thebes, where Seti's mummy would be laid to rest and the new king and queen would be crowned.

The only son of a wealthy family, well bred, elegant, with a long, fine-featured face, a pencil-thin mustache, lively, intelligent eyes, and a compelling, sometimes haughty manner of speaking, Ahsha had also been a classmate of Ramses'. Though Ahsha was distant and dispassionate, Ramses considered him both friend and critic. Ahsha knew several languages and from an early age had loved to travel and study other cultures. A diplomatic career had been a natural choice for him, and he was considered a boy wonder because of his accuracy in reading several crisis situations. At twenty-three, he was one of the top Asia experts in the Foreign Service. He was brilliant in the field and a gifted analyst as well, qualities rarely combined in one man. Some of his colleagues even called him a visionary. Be that as it may, Egypt's security hinged on correctly assessing the Hittite empire's intentions.

When he reported to Meba, Ahsha found the cabinet officer on the defensive, offering little comment and recommending only that he try to see Ramses as soon as possible, since the Pharaoh-to-Be was asking to meet with all high-level diplomats.

Ahsha was admitted by Ahmeni, the regent's private secretary. The two old school friends greeted each other warmly.

"Still thin as a reed," Ahsha noted.

"And you're wearing the latest fashion, as usual."

"We're all grown up now, so I have my choice of vices! It's good to see that your talents are appreciated, Ahmeni."

"I pledged my loyalty to Ramses and I've given my all."

"Wise choice. It won't be long before Ramses is crowned, if the gods are willing."

"They are. Did you hear he's already survived one assassination attempt? Our Greek visitor, Menelaus, sent his henchmen after Ramses."

"Menelaus is a minor king and a scoundrel."

"To put it mildly. He took hostages and threatened to kill them unless we handed over Helen."

"What did Ramses do?"

"He refused to violate the laws of hospitality and planned a counterattack."

"Risky."

"What alternative did he have?"

"Negotiate, then negotiate some more. Though I admit it would be almost impossible to get through to a ruffian like Menelaus. His plan worked, then?"

"No, Helen gave herself up without his knowledge. She felt responsible for the hostages. As soon as they were free and Menelaus's ship headed out to sea, she took her life."

"A grand gesture, but rather final."

"Ironic as ever, I see."

"I find that making fun of everything, including yourself, helps keep things in perspective."

"Helen's death doesn't seem to affect you."

"I say good riddance to Menelaus and his crew. If Egypt is looking for allies in Greece, we can do better."

"Homer stayed behind, though."

"Ramses' old poet," Ahsha said with a smile. "Still writing his account of the Trojan War?"

"I've had the honor of taking it down for him. His verse is tragic, but not lacking in nobility."

"Literature will be your downfall, Ahmeni! Do you know what plans Ramses has for you once he's Pharaoh?"

"No. I like what I'm doing now."

"You deserve better."

"What about you? Do you have your eye on something?"

"My first concern is to meet with Ramses."

"Urgent business?"

"Do you mind if I save it for him?"

Ahmeni blushed. "Sorry. You'll find him in the stables. No matter what he's doing, he'll want to see you."

Ramses seemed strikingly different. The prince was regal and sure of himself, driving his chariot with consummate skill, leading his horses through incredibly complex maneuvers that left the old stable hands gaping.

The tall adolescent had become a powerfully built athlete with the incontestable authority of a monarch. Still, Ahsha noted a rashness and drive that could lead to errors in judgment. But what use would it be recommending moderation to someone burning with so much energy?

As soon as he caught sight of Ahsha, the prince steered his way. The horses pulled up short only a length or two from the young diplomat, splattering his spotless tunic.

"Sorry, Ahsha! These young war horses can be a bit hard to handle."

Ramses jumped down, called two grooms to look after the horses, and took Ahsha by the shoulders.

"More trouble brewing in Asia?"

"I'm afraid so, Majesty."

"Majesty—I'm not Pharaoh yet!"

"A good diplomat always looks toward the future. As it happens, your future is fairly easy to predict."

"You're the only one who thinks so."

"Does that bother you?"

"Asia, my friend—I asked you about Asia."

"Outwardly, all is calm. Our protectorates are ready to welcome you as Pharaoh, and the Hittites are making no move to expand their territory."

"Outwardly, you say."

"That's what the official reports will tell you."

"But you don't see it that way."

"There's always a calm before the storm—but how long before?"

"Come have a drink with me."

Ramses checked on his horses, then sat down with Ahsha under a sloping roof with a view of the desert. A servant instantly appeared with cool beer and scented towels.

"Do you believe that the Hittites really want peace?"

Ahsha considered this, enjoying the delicious brew. "The Hittites are fighters and conquerors. To them, the word *peace* is a sort of poetic image with no concrete meaning attached."

"So they're lying."

"They hope that a young, peace-loving leader may place less emphasis on defense, gradually weakening the country."

"Like Akhenaton."

"A prime example."

"Are they still manufacturing arms?"

"In fact, they've stepped up production."

"Do you think war is inevitable?"

"A diplomat's job is to make sure it isn't."

"How would you go about stopping them?"

"I'm unable to answer that question. My current duties don't afford me a broad enough view to suggest effective countermeasures."

"You'd like a more responsible position?"

"It's not up to me."

Ramses looked out at the desert.

"When I was a boy, Ahsha, I dreamed of becoming Pharaoh like my father, because I thought power was the best game of all. Then Seti had me face the wild bull. The traditional test of will, you know. He opened my eyes to the perils of ultimate power, and I found another dreamworld: living in my father's shadow, relying on his strength. Now his death has brought reality crashing in on me. I prayed to be relieved of the burden of power I no longer sought, and I looked for a sign from the gods. Menelaus sent his men to get me; my lion, my dog, and my bodyguard saved me as I communed with my father's soul. From that moment on, I decided to stop swimming against the tide. What Seti has ordained will come to pass."

"Do you remember that night just before graduation, when we discussed true power with Setau, Moses, and Ahmeni?"

"Of course. Ahmeni found it serving his country, Moses building monuments, Setau studying snakes, and you in the diplomatic corps."

"You're still the only one who will have true power."

"No, Ahsha, it will pass through me, come to life in my heart, my sword arm, but it will leave me if I misuse it."

"Living only for Egypt . . . it's a terrible price to pay."

"I'm no longer free to choose my destiny."

"It's almost frightening."

"Do you think I'm never afraid? No matter what stands in my way, I plan to rule and to continue my father's work. I need to leave Egypt stronger and more beautiful than ever. Will you help me, Ahsha?"

"Yes, Majesty."

TEN

Shaanar was dejected.

The Greeks had failed him miserably; Menelaus, obsessed with stalking Helen, had lost sight of their ultimate goal of eliminating Ramses. The only consolation, which was not inconsiderable, was being able to convince his brother he had not been involved in the coup. Now that Menelaus and his men were gone, no one would dare point a finger at Shaanar.

But Ramses would ascend to the throne and rule Egypt single-handedly . . . and he, Seti's older son, would be forced to bow and scrape to his brother. No, he refused to accept this reversal of fortune.

That was why he had arranged a meeting with his one remaining ally, a friend of Ramses', a man above suspicion, who might help him fight his brother from within and undermine his authority.

At dusk, business was still brisk at the pottery stands. Strollers and serious shoppers passed the displays, eyeing vases of all different sizes and prices. At the end of an alleyway, a water bearer hawked his thirst-quenching product.

That was where Ahsha waited, almost unrecognizable in an ordinary kilt and common wig. Shaanar, too, was carefully disguised. The two men bought a water skin and shared a bunch of grapes like simple peasants, sitting side by side against a wall.

"Have you been to see Ramses again?" asked Shaanar.

"I no longer work for the State Department. I report directly to our future Pharaoh."

"What does that mean?"

"A promotion."

"To what?"

"I'm not sure yet. Ramses is forming his government. Since he's a loyal friend, Moses, Ahmeni, and I should be given high-level appointments."

"Who else, besides you three?"

"His only other close friend is Setau, but he's so devoted to his dear old snakes that he'll never come to the city."

"Did Ramses seem determined to rule?"

"He realizes that it's a crushing responsibility and admits he's not fully prepared, but he won't give up now. Don't expect him to change his mind."

"Did he mention the high priest of Amon?"

"No."

"Good. Then he underestimates the man's influence and potential to do him harm."

"I heard the old fellow was rather intimidated by royalty."

"He was afraid of Seti . . . but Ramses is young, with little experience of power struggles. Now, as far as getting help from Ahmeni, it's hopeless. He worships the ground Ramses walks on. On the other hand, I think I may be able to work with Moses."

"Have you tried to recruit him yet?"

"He wouldn't have anything to do with me, but it was only my first try. He's a tortured soul, seeking some personal truth that may end up clashing with Ramses' views. If we offer him what he needs, he'll switch sides."

"That makes sense."

"Do you have any influence with Moses, Ahsha?"

"I don't think so, but give me long enough and I'll find his weak spot."

"And Ahmeni?"

"He does appear absolutely loyal," Ahsha commented, "but who knows what strange tastes he may develop in time? If he does, we'll be there to exploit them."

"I don't intend to wait until Ramses has his network firmly in place."

"Nor do I, Shaanar, nor do I, but we must be patient. Your experience with Menelaus should teach you that a successful strategy leaves no room for guesswork."

"How long do I have to wait?"

"Let's let Ramses get settled on the throne. Being the center of attention will turn his head. What's more, I'll be one of his advisers on Asia, the one he'll listen to most closely."

"What's your plan, Ahsha?"

"You want the throne, correct?"

"It's my birthright. I know how to lead."

"Therefore, Ramses must be overthrown or eliminated."

"I see no other way."

"Two avenues are open to us: a coup or an attack. As for the first possibility, we would need to enlist a number of influential figures. The onus would fall largely on you. The second scenario would require determining the Hittites' true intentions and preparing a conflict that would ruin Ramses, but not Egypt. If the country is devastated, a Hittite king will take over the Two Lands."

Shaanar's displeasure was obvious. "It sounds too risky."

"Ramses is no easy target."

"I don't see how the Hittites could win and not overrun the country."

"It can be done, I assure you."

"Do you have a miracle up your sleeve?"

"Not a miracle, but a trap that we'd set for Ramses, without our country being involved. If he survives, he'll be blamed for the defeat. In either case, he'll no longer be a credible ruler. Then you can step in to save the day."

"It sounds too easy."

"I've built my reputation on accurate predictions. When I know exactly what my role in the government will be, I'll set things in motion. Unless you'd rather stop before we begin."

"Never! Dead or alive, I want Ramses out of my way."

"If our plan works, I hope you won't prove ungrateful."

"Don't worry. My right-hand man will be richly rewarded."

"Can I really be sure?"

Shaanar was taken aback. "Don't you trust me?"

"Not in the least."

"But why . . ."

"Don't pretend you're surprised. If I were that naive, you'd have gotten rid of me long ago. When a man is ambitious like you, no one ought to believe his promises. The sole basis for his behavior is personal interest."

"Are you a cynic, Ahsha?"

"I'm a realist. When you become Pharaoh, you'll form a government based on your needs at the time. There may be no room for those who, like me, have paved your way to the throne."

Shaanar smiled. "Your intelligence is exceptional, Ahsha."

"In my travels, I've encountered a great many cultures and all different sorts of people, but wherever I've been, it's survival of the fittest."

"Not in Egypt as we know it."

"Seti is dead now, and Ramses can't wait to flex his military muscle. We need to help him find the right war."

"In exchange for your research, I suppose you want immediate compensation."

"It's my turn to compliment you on your intelligence."

"Tell me exactly what you expect."

"My family is well-off, of course, but who's ever rich enough? Since I'm constantly on the move, having several residences would be both a help and a pleasure. I'd like villas in upper and lower Egypt to use whenever I feel the need. Three houses in the Delta, two in Memphis, two in Middle Egypt, two near Thebes, one in Aswan ought to meet my present needs when I'm here at home."

"That would cost me a small fortune."

"A trifle, Shaanar, a mere trifle when you consider what I'll be doing for you."

"I suppose you want precious metals and gemstones as well."

"It goes without saying."

"I wouldn't have thought you so venal, Ahsha."

"I need the best of everything. A collector of fine vases like you must understand what I mean."

"Yes, but so many houses . . ."

"Beautifully decorated houses, serving as a background for fine furniture! They'll be my earthly paradise, pleasure palaces where I'll be the absolute master while you climb the steps to the throne of Egypt."

"When do we get under way?"

"Immediately."

"You haven't actually been appointed."

"I'm certain to have considerable responsibilities. Encourage me to serve you well, Shaanar."

"Where do we start?"

"With a villa in the northeastern Delta, near the border. A sizable estate, a small lake, a vineyard. Fully staffed, of course. Even if I spend only a few days a year there, I want to be treated like a prince."

"I can handle that. Anything else?"

"Well, women. When I'm on a mission, the pickings can be rather slim. I have to make up for that here in Egypt. Yes, a good supply of women. As long as they're attractive and willing, I'm not particular about where they come from."

"I agree to your conditions."

"I won't disappoint you, Shaanar. Just one more thing: we'll continue to meet in the strictest secrecy and you will mention it to no one. If Ramses were to learn of our dealings, my career would be finished."

"Your best interest is my best interest, Ahsha."

"There's no better guarantee of friendship. Farewell, Shaanar."

As he watched the young diplomat merge into the crowd, Ramses' older brother mused that luck was still with him. Ahsha made a first-rate partner. The day he had to be done away with would be a sad one.

ELEVEN

Tuya, the late Pharaoh's Great Royal Wife, sailed at the head of the fleet leaving Memphis for Thebes. On its outskirts lay the Valley of the Kings, where Seti's mummy would be entombed. Nefertari never left the Queen Mother's side, sensing the pain beneath her usual serenity. Simply spending time with the great king's widow taught Nefertari how a queen should behave when faced with the cruelest of losses. The young woman's quiet presence was a tremendous comfort. Neither of them felt a need to express her sorrow, but each felt her heart go out to the other.

As they sailed down the Nile, Ramses worked.

Ahmeni had prepared an impressive stack of dossiers on foreign policy, national security, public health and welfare, public works (including dikes and canals), and a host of other more or less complex subjects.

Ramses was fully aware of the scope of his responsibilities. An army of civil servants would be helping him, but he should have detailed knowledge of how each department worked and keep the government under his control. Otherwise Egypt was liable to pitch and sink like a rudderless boat. Time was working against the Pharaoh-to-Be; the moment he assumed power, he would be expected to make informed decisions and function as the Lord of the Two Lands. The prospect of serious mistakes plagued him.

His mood lifted at the thought of his mother, a precious ally who would help him steer clear of many obstacles and teach him how to deal with turf wars. So many officials had already called on him to plead for their departments!

After long hours of work with the incomparably thorough and insightful Ahmeni, Ramses liked to stand in the prow of the boat, contemplating the source of Egypt's prosperity and enjoying the brisk wind—the breath of the divine. In these stolen moments Ramses had the feeling that all of Egypt belonged to him, from the mouth of the Nile to the desert reaches of Nubia. Would he be able to satisfy her needs?

His dinner guests at the head table were Moses, Setau, Ahsha, and Ahmeni. It was like the old days when they studied together at the *Kap*. Even then they'd thirsted for power as well as knowledge. The pleasant reunion did not disperse the gloom caused by Seti's death. Each of them sensed the difficult days that might lie in store for Egypt.

"This time," Moses told Ramses, "your dream is about to come true."

"It's not a dream anymore, but a frightening obligation."

"What?" objected Ahsha. "You're not afraid of anything!"

"It's the last job you'd ever get me to take," muttered Setau.

"But I was my father's choice. If I stepped down now, how would it look?"

"As if you'd come to your senses. Your father's funeral may not be the only one we end up attending on this trip."

"Have you gotten wind of another plot?" fretted Ahmeni.

"There won't be just one. That's why I'm here, with a few of my trusted assistants."

"Guard snakes," teased Ahsha, "the latest in security."

"At least I have something concrete to contribute."

"Criticizing diplomacy, are we?"

"It complicates everything, when life is basically simple. Good on one side, evil on the other, and nothing in between."

"Your simplistic outlook is the problem," retorted Ahsha.

"It suits me," Ahmeni chimed in. "You're either for Ramses or against him."

"And what if the balance tips in the wrong direction?" asked Moses.

"My position will never change."

"Soon Ramses will no longer be our friend, but Pharaoh of Egypt. He'll view us differently."

Moses' words were disturbing. Everyone waited to hear how Ramses would answer.

"Moses is right. Since this burden has fallen to me, I accept it. And since you're my friends, I'll call on you for help."

"What will you have us do?"

"The four of you have already gone far. I'll ask you to join me on a new journey, seeking the greater good of Egypt."

"You know where I stand," declared Setau. "The minute you're safe on the throne, I go back to my snakes."

"I still plan to try and convince you to work with me."

"Waste of time. When this security mission is over, I leave. Moses can be your master builder, Ahsha can head the Foreign Service, and more power to them!"

"Are you leaving any appointments for me to make?"

Setau shrugged.

"Why don't we get started on the wine?" suggested Ahsha. "A rare vintage, the cellar master tells me."

"I propose a toast," said Ahmeni. "To Ramses' health, and a long, full life in which to enjoy it, by the grace of the gods."

Shaanar had sailed not with the regent, but on his own ship, a splendid vessel with a crew of forty. As chief of protocol, he had invited a party of notables, most of whom were no friends of Ramses. Seti's older son carefully refrained from joining in their criticism, merely compiling a mental list of future supporters. The courtiers thought Ramses too young, too inexperienced to make a go of it.

He smugly noted that his own excellent reputation remained intact, while his brother would continue to suffer in comparison to Seti. There were already cracks in the foundation; the trick would be to expand them, further weakening the new Pharaoh's base of power.

Shaanar's guests sampled jujube fruit and cool beer. His mild manners and moderate opinions made him a favorite with the courtiers, who enjoyed basking in the limelight with an increasingly prominent member of the royal family.

For more than an hour, a man of average stature, with a trim goatee and a brightly striped tunic, had been waiting for an audience. He looked humble, almost submissive, yet calm and collected.

When he found a free moment, Shaanar motioned the man forward. He approached, bowing deferentially.

"Who are you?"

"My name is Raia. I come from Syria, but I've been a traveling merchant in Egypt for a number of years now."

"Dealing in what?"

"Preserved meats and the finest Asian vases."

Shaanar lifted an eyebrow. "Vases?"

"Yes, Sir Prince, I'm the exclusive distributor for some very fine manufacturers."

"Do you know that I'm a collector?"

"So I was told just recently. I came here in hope of arranging a private showing for you."

"Are your prices high?"

"That depends."

Shaanar bit. "On what?"

From a sturdy cloth sack, Raia extracted a small, thin-lipped vase, solid silver, with a palmetto design. "What do you think of this, Sir Prince?"

Shaanar's eyes widened. Beads of sweat broke out on his forehead, his hands grew damp. "A masterpiece . . . an unbelievable masterpiece. How much?"

"A gift, to the future pharaoh of Egypt."

Could he be hearing things? "I think you have your princes mixed up, my good man. My brother, Ramses, is the future pharaoh, not me. So name your price."

"You're the prince I want, all right. In my profession, there's no room for mistakes."

Shaanar tore his eyes away from the stunning vase. "What is your point?"

"That many people are displeased with Ramses."

"He'll be crowned in a matter of days."

"So he may, but will that end the dissatisfaction?"

"Who are you, merchant?" challenged Shaanar.

"Raia, a man who believes in your future and wants to see you on the throne of Egypt."

"What would you know of my intentions?"

"That you clearly wish to expand foreign trade, make Egypt less arrogantly insular, and improve relations with the most powerful kingdom in Asia."

"You mean . . . the Hittites?"

"We understand each other."

"Ah. You're a secret agent. And your employers like what they see in me?"

Raia nodded affirmatively.

"What are you proposing?" asked Shaanar, as excited as if he were being offered another rare vase.

"Ramses is rash and war-loving. Like his father, he wants to flex Egypt's muscle. You, Sir Prince, are a reasonable man, better able to come to terms with foreign powers."

"If I betray Egypt, Raia, I'm risking my life."

Shaanar recalled how Tutankhamon's widow had been condemned to death for her dealings with the Hittites, even though she was attempting to protect the throne.

"A certain amount of risk is to be expected on the way to the top."

Shaanar closed his eyes. The Hittites . . . Naturally, he'd considered them as a weapon to use against Ramses, but that was no more than idle speculation. Now, suddenly, the idea sprang to life in the form of this ordinary, harmless-looking merchant.

"I love my country . . ."

"No one would doubt it. But you love power more. And only an alliance with the Hittites will put it in your hands."

"I need to think this over."

"I'm afraid I can't indulge you."

"You want my answer now?"

"My own safety is at stake, now that you know who I am."

"And if I refuse?"

Raia did not respond, but his expression became fixed and unreadable.

Shaanar had little trouble convincing himself that it was meant to be. He would handle his powerful new partner with the utmost care, exploiting the Hittites without endangering Egypt. Ahsha, of course, would have to be kept in the dark, though he could still be of use.

"It's a deal, Raia."

The merchant smiled faintly.

"You live up to your reputation, Sir Prince. I'll be in touch with you every now and again. Now that I'm supplying vases for your collection, there's no reason for me not to visit. Take this one, please, to seal our bargain."

Shaanar closed his hands around the silver curves. The future was looking brighter already.

TWELVE

Ramses had memorized every parched and rocky inch of the Valley of the Kings, the "Great Place" he had first visited with his father. Seti had shown him the tomb of his own father, the first Ramses, their dynasty's founder, an elderly vizier selected to succeed the childless Horemheb. After only two years he passed on, entrusting his son with the mission of reasserting Egypt's power, a power now invested in Ramses II.

The stifling summer heat felled some of the servants carrying furnishings for Seti's tomb, but it seemed to have no effect on Ramses. Heartsick, he marched at the head of the procession transporting his father's mummy to its final resting place.

Ramses felt a rush of hatred for the place that was claiming his father, leaving him so alone. Then the familiar magic took over: the Valley radiated life, not death.

The stony silence rang with the voices of the old ones. They spoke of light, transfiguration, resurrection. They demanded worship and respect for the celestial world that gave rise to all forms of life.

Ramses was the first to set foot inside Seti's vast tomb, the longest and deepest carved into the Valley. Once he was Pharaoh, he planned to decree that no other tomb surpass its dimensions. In the eyes of posterity, Seti would remain without equal.

Twelve priests carried in the mummy. Clad in a panther skin, Ramses was to conduct the rites of judgment and rebirth. Ritual texts on the walls of the tomb would guide his father on the journey and serve his soul through all eternity.

Seti's mummy was a masterpiece of the embalmers' art. He looked perfectly at peace with himself and his life on earth, as if at any minute the eyes might open, the lips might speak . . . The priests placed the lid on the sarcophagus, to be enclosed in a gilded shrine where Isis would work her alchemy, making the Pharaoh's mortal remains immortal.

"Seti was a just ruler," murmured Ramses. "He upheld the law of Ma'at and was beloved of the light. He walks living into the West."

All over Egypt barbers toiled, shaving off beards now that the official mourning was over. Women again pinned up their hair, and society ladies summoned their hairdressers.

On the eve of the coronation, Ramses and Nefertari gathered their thoughts in the temple of Gurnah, where mortuary prayers for Seti would henceforth be said on a continuous basis, maintaining his *ka*—his spiritual essence—and affirming his presence among the living. Then the couple proceeded to the temple of Karnak to see the high priest, who welcomed them with cold formality. After a frugal dinner, the regent and his wife withdrew to the royal quarters within the god Amon's earthly residence. Each of them meditated before a separate throne, symbolizing the primordial mound that emerged from the ocean of energy at the beginning of time. It figured in the hieroglyph for Ma'at, the timeless law, "She Who Is Righteous and Gives Good Direction," the law that they must embody and impart to their subjects.

Ramses had the feeling his father was close at hand, seeing him through these last tense hours before his life changed forever. As king, his life would no longer be his own. His only care would be for his people's welfare and his nation's prosperity.

Once again, the prospect overwhelmed him.

He wished he could flee this palace within a temple, take refuge in his lost youth, Iset the Fair, the carefree pleasure they once knew. But now he was Seti's designated successor and Nefertari's husband. He would have to master his fear and ride out this one last night before his coronation.

The shadows parted and dawn came forth, announcing the sun's rebirth. Once more it had won the nightly struggle with the monster from the depths. Two masked priests, one in the guise of a falcon, the other an ibis, stood on either side of Ramses. They symbolized the gods Horus, protector of royalty, and Thoth, master of hieroglyphs and sacred learning. Pouring the contents of two tall vases over the prince's naked body, they cleansed him of his humanity. Then they remade him in the image of the gods, applying nine different unguents in the order, head to toe, that would open his energy centers and give him a perception of reality different from other men's.

The ritual garments also helped construct his new and unique identity. The two priests dressed the prince in a kilt of white and gold, the same as the first pharaohs wore. On the sash, they hung a bull's tail, the emblem of royal potency, that recalled to Ramses the terrifying encounter with a wild bull his father had arranged as a test of his youthful courage. Now he would embody the bull's power, which he must learn to exercise with care.

Then the ritualists fastened a large jeweled collar, with seven rows of colored beads, around his neck, placed copper bracelets on his wrists and upper arms, and shod him in white sandals. They presented him with the white club he would use to strike down his enemies and make the darkness into light. Around his forehead they tied the golden band called *sia*, meaning "intuitive seeing."

"Do you accept the ordeal of power?" asked the Horus priest.

"I do."

Horus and Thoth took Ramses by the hands and led him into another room. On a throne were the crowns of the Two Lands. Protecting them was a priest wearing the mask of the god Set.

Thoth stepped aside as the brothers Horus and Set embraced. Despite their eternal rivalry, they were bound together in the person of the Pharaoh.

Horus lifted the red crown of lower Egypt, basket-shaped with a spiral flaring in front. On top of it, Set placed the white bulb-shaped war helmet of upper Egypt.

"The two powers are united in you," declared Thoth. "You govern and unify the black land and the red land, you are the rushes of the south and the beehive of the north, you make both lands green.

"You alone will be able to lay a hand on these two crowns," revealed Set. "Within them is thunder to strike down any usurper."

Horus gave the Pharaoh two scepters. The first was called "Mastery of Power" and was used to bless offerings. The other, known as "Magic," was a shepherd's crook serving to keep his people together.

"The time has come to appear in glory," Thoth decreed.

Preceded by the three god-priests, Pharaoh left the temple's hidden rooms, heading for the huge inner courtyard where the privileged few allowed within the temple gates had gathered.

On a platform, beneath a dais, was a gilded wooden throne, rather modest and squarely built. Seti's throne, the one he had used on official occasions.

Sensing her son's hesitation, Tuya took three steps in his direction and bowed low.

"May Your Majesty rise like a new sun and take his place on the throne of the living."

Ramses was deeply moved by this welcome from the Pharaoh's widow, the Queen Mother he would worship until the end of his days.

"This is the testament of the gods that Seti left you. As it legitimized his reign, so will it yours, so will it your successor's." Tuya handed Ramses a leather case containing a papyrus written in Thoth's own hand, at the dawn of civilization, declaring Pharaoh the heir to Egypt.

"Here are your five royal names," continued Tuya in her clear, steady voice.

"Strong Bull, Beloved of Ma'at,
Protector of Egypt, He Who Binds Up Foreign Lands,
Rich in Armies, Powerful in Victories,
Chosen of the God of Light, Powerful in His Rule,
Ra-Begot-Him: Son of Light."

Total silence fell as she chanted the titles. Even Shaanar felt the poison of ambition drain from him as he surrendered to the magic of the moment.

"A royal couple rules the Two Lands," Tuya said now. "Step forward, Nefertari. Take your place beside the king as his Great Royal Wife and Queen of Egypt."

Despite the solemnity of the occasion, Ramses was so entranced by his bride's fresh beauty that he wished he could take her in his arms. In a long linen gown, with a golden collar, amethyst earrings, and jasper bracelets, she gazed at the king and repeated the time-honored formula:

"I recognize Horus and Set united in one being. I sing your name, Pharaoh, you are yesterday, today, and tomorrow. I live through your word and will keep you from evil and danger."

"I recognize you as Queen of the North and South and of all lands, lady of utmost sweetness who pleases the gods, who is mother and wife of the god, who has my love."

Ramses set a crown on Nefertari's head. Its two tall plumes declared her Great Royal Wife and associate ruler.

Like a blot on the sun, a falcon spread its wings, circling above the new king and queen, then dove for them so suddenly no royal archer had time to react.

A cry of horror and disbelief rose from the onlookers as the raptor landed on the new king's back, digging its claws into his shoulders. Ramses stood absolutely motionless; Nefertari stared.

Time stood still as the awestricken courtiers registered the miracle. The falcon was Horus, protector of the monarchy. This man was truly chosen to govern Egypt!

The falcon flew back toward the sun, strong and serene.

A single cheer proclaimed Year One of the reign of Ramses, beginning this twenty-seventh day of the third month of summer.*

THIRTEEN

As soon as the ceremony was over, Ramses was swept up in a whirlwind of activities.

The chief steward of the Pharaoh's household had him inspect his palace at Thebes, both public rooms and private quarters. As head of state, he toured the grand reception room bedecked with columns, mosaics, and wall paintings in lotus, papyrus, fish, and bird motifs; the smaller private

---

*Early June 1279 B.C., according to one of the most commonly used estimates.

audience chambers; the scribes' offices; the balcony for official appearances, a winged solar disk above its window; the
dining room with a table in the middle laden night and day
with baskets of fruit and flower arrangements; the bedchamber with colored pillows piled high on the bed; the
tiled bathroom.

Ramses was introduced to the members of his household: the priests in charge of secret rituals, the scribes of the
House of Life, the physicians, the chamberlain who super-
intended the private quarters, the head of the royal messenger service, the royal treasury, granary, livestock, and so
on, all eager to meet their brand-new pharaoh and assure
him of their continuing devotion.

"And this is . . ."

Ramses got to his feet. "That's the end."

"Majesty, please!" the chief steward spluttered. "So
many important people . . ."

"More important than I am?"

"Pardon me, I didn't mean . . ."

"Take me to the kitchens."

"That's not your place!"

"Who would know better than I where I belong?"

"Pardon, I . . ."

"Do you pass all your time finding excuses? I'd rather
hear why the vizier and the high priest of Amon weren't
here to pay their respects to me."

"I have no idea, Your Majesty. That's completely beyond
the scope of my authority."

"To the kitchens, then."

Butchers, bakers, pastry chefs, brewers, vegetable peelers, makers of preserved foods—Romay, the palace chef, commanded a small army of specialized workers, jealously guarding their turf and highly particular about their schedules. Jolly, round-cheeked, slow-moving Romay never worried about his multiple chins and bulging belly. He'd do something about his weight when he retired. For now, he concentrated on ruling his domain with an iron fist, preparing delicious and flawless meals, keeping the peace among his staff of prima donnas. A stickler for cleanliness and fresh ingredients, Romay personally tasted each dish that left his kitchens. Whether or not Pharaoh and the members of his court were in Thebes, the chef never settled for less than perfection.

When the chief steward appeared with a young man in tow, impressively built and dressed in an immaculate white kilt, Romay groaned inwardly. Mr. Big must be planning to saddle him with yet another useless worker in exchange for some favor from the boy's family.

"Hello there, Romay! I want to introduce you—"

"I can guess who he is."

"Then shouldn't you be bowing?"

"That's rich!" guffawed Romay, hands on ample hips. "Why would I bow to this young buck? First let's find out if he can even wash dishes."

Flustered, the steward faced the king. "I *beg* your pardon . . ."

"I can wash dishes," Ramses said. "Do you know how to cook?"

"Cook? I'm the palace chef! And who do you think you are?"

"Ramses, Pharaoh of Egypt."

Romay froze, convinced his career was over. Then he crisply removed his leather apron, folded it, and laid it on a low table. Insulting the king was a punishable offense, if it ended up in court.

"What's on the menu for lunch?" asked Ramses.

"Quail," Romay managed. "Roast quail. Nile perch with herb sauce. Fig puree. Honey cakes."

"Tempting, but will it taste as good as it sounds?"

"I stake my reputation on it!" Romay protested.

"Your reputation means nothing to me. Let me try some food."

"I'll have the staff prepare the dining room," the steward said unctuously.

"Don't bother. I'll eat right here."

Ramses lunched heartily as the steward looked on in dismay.

"Excellent," he pronounced. "Do you have a name, chef?"

"Romay, Your Majesty."

"Romay. 'Man.' It fits. All right, Romay, you're my new chief steward, cup bearer, and director of royal kitchens throughout the land. Follow me, I have a few questions for you."

Stunned, the former chief steward stammered, "Your Majesty? Pardon me, but where will I . . ."

"I have no use for inefficiency and pettiness. There's always a shortage of dishwashers, though."

The king and Romay ambled beneath a portico.

"You'll report to my private secretary, Ahmeni. He looks frail and doesn't much care what he eats, but he's a tireless worker. More than that, he's the most faithful friend I could ever hope to have."

"I was trained as a cook," Romay said bluntly. "Are you sure I'm ready for this much responsibility?"

"My father taught me to judge men according to my

instincts. If I'm wrong, I have only myself to blame. I'm looking for loyalty. Do you think I'll find it at court?"

"To tell the truth . . ."

"Do, Romay. That's all I ask."

"Then I can say that Your Majesty's court is the biggest collection of hypocrites and back-stabbers in the entire kingdom. In fact, they seem to think they own the place. Your father kept them in line, but as soon as he was gone they started showing their true colors, like desert flowers after a downpour."

"They hate me, don't they?"

"That's the least of it."

"What do they hope will happen?"

"That you'll trip yourself up before long."

"If you're with me, Romay, I demand your loyalty."

"What do your instincts tell you?"

"A good cook isn't thin. A talented chef has everyone trying to steal his recipes. Rumors fly through his kitchen and he has to sort through them with the same care he takes in selecting ingredients. What are the main factions I have to deal with?"

"Almost the whole court is against you. The general opinion is that anyone would suffer in comparison to a pharaoh of Seti's stature. They see you as a transitional figure until a serious contender appears."

"Will you risk leaving your own little kingdom here to run my households?"

Romay smiled broadly. "There's more to life than feeling comfortable. As long as I still get to cook, I'd be willing to try. But I do have one reservation."

"Tell me."

"With all due respect, Your Majesty, you don't stand a chance."

"What makes you say that?"

"You're young and inexperienced. You'll have the high priest of Amon and a host of government insiders trying to make you their puppet. The odds are bad."

"A pharaoh doesn't wield much power, according to you."

"Of course he does. That's why everyone wants to take a shot at him. What chance does one man have against an army?"

"Pharaoh is supposed to be endowed with the might of the bull."

"Not even a wild bull can move mountains, Your Majesty."

"Am I to understand that you're advising me to abdicate, on the day of my coronation?"

"If you let the powers that be take charge, who will even notice, and who could blame you?"

"You, Romay?"

"I'm only the best cook in the country. What I think isn't important."

"You're chief steward now, aren't you?"

"Would you listen, Majesty, if I offered some advice?"

"It all depends on what it is."

"Never let yourself be served food or drink that's less than the best. It's the beginning of the end. Now, if you don't mind, I think I should get to work. Starting here in Thebes there's a great deal to be done."

Ramses had made no mistake. Romay was the man for the job.

Relieved, he headed for the palace garden.

FOURTEEN

Nefertari tried her hardest not to cry.

What she most feared had finally come to pass. As a girl, she had dreamed of a quiet, cloistered life; now she had become public property. Immediately after the coronation, she had been separated from Ramses to make her first round of appearances as his consort, visiting the temples, schools, and weavers' guilds she officially sponsored.

Tuya introduced Nefertari to the managers of the queen's various estates, directors of the harems where young women were educated, scribes in charge of administering her affairs, tax collectors, priests and priestesses who would perform daily rites in her name as "the spouse of God," protectress of the creative principle.

For several days, Nefertari kept up a grueling pace, meeting hundreds of people, finding the right thing to say to each of them, smiling constantly, never showing the slightest sign of fatigue.

Each morning a hairdresser, makeup artist, manicurist, and pedicurist worked to make her even lovelier than the day before. The good of Egypt depended as much on her

charm as her husband's power. No queen could be more
beautiful than Nefertari in her elegant, red-belted linen
gown.

She lay exhausted on a narrow bed, unable to face the
evening's banquet or the thought of being presented with
more jars of perfumed unguents.

Tuya's slight figure moved toward her through the gathering dusk.

"Are you ill, Nefertari?"

"I haven't the strength to go on."

Seti's widow sat on the edge of the bed and took the
young queen's right hand between her own two hands.

"I know what you're going through. It was the same for
me. Two things will help: a special tonic and the magne-
tizing force Ramses inherited from his father."

"I wasn't meant to be queen."

"Do you love Ramses?"

"More than myself."

"Then you'll stand by him. He wed a queen, and a queen
will fight at his side."

"What if he chose the wrong woman?"

"He didn't. Don't you think there were times when I felt
as tired and discouraged as you are now? The demands
placed on a Great Royal Wife are beyond any woman. So it
has always been, and so it should be."

"Didn't you want to give up?"

"A dozen times, a hundred times a day, at first. I begged
Seti to take someone else as his chief consort and let me
become his lesser wife. His answer was always the same: he
took me in his arms and comforted me, yet did nothing to
ease my workload."

"If I can't perform my duties, how can I be worthy of
Ramses' faith in me?"

"Good, Nefertari. You take nothing for granted. Now listen. I'm not going to say this twice."

The young queen's eyes filled with uncertainty. Tuya's clear gaze locked on hers.

"You're Queen of Egypt, Nefertari. It's a life sentence. Don't fight your destiny. Swim with the current, become one with the river."

In less than three days, Ahmeni and Romay had streamlined the government of Thebes, following Ramses' directives. He had met with a wide range of officials, from the mayor to the head ferryman. Due to its distance from Memphis and the fact that Seti had taken up near-permanent residence in the north, the southern capital had grown increasingly independent. The high priest of Amon, with the force of his temple's immense wealth behind him, was beginning to consider himself a king in his own right. Ramses' meetings with local officials made him aware of how dangerous the situation was. Unless he acted quickly, upper and lower Egypt could split into two different, even opposing, countries, and the division would lead to disaster.

From the beginning, Ahmeni and Romay worked well together. Physical and mental opposites, their differences complemented each other. They shared a deep respect for Ramses as well as the conviction he was heading in the right direction. Turning a deaf ear to hidebound courtiers, they forged ahead with their sweeping reforms, making any number of unexpected personnel changes with the king's approval.

Two weeks after the coronation, Thebes was in an

uproar. Some officials had predicted the new pharaoh would prove incompetent. Others saw him as a playboy prince, simply uninterested in matters of state. Yet Ramses had spent his days in the palace, holding meetings and issuing decrees with all the vigor and authority of his father.

Ramses waited for the inevitable reaction, but it never came. Thebes seemed stunned into silence.

Summoned by the king, the vizier of the south was deferential, noting His Majesty's directives with assurances that they would be carried out at once.

Ramses did not share in Ahmeni's boyish excitement or Romay's amused satisfaction. His enemies may have been taken by surprise, but they were far from defeated. They would regroup and come back at him stronger than ever. Open confrontation would have been more to his taste than their insidious plotting, but he would have to learn to deal with intrigue.

Just before sunset he always walked the paths of the palace garden, as twenty-odd workers began watering the trees and flower beds in the cool of the evening. On his left trotted Watcher, the yellow dog, with blue flowers ringing his red collar; on his right loped Fighter, the gigantic lion. And at the entrance to the garden was Serramanna, the Sardinian captain of the royal guardsmen, sitting beneath an arbor, alert and prepared.

Ramses felt an intense affection for the sycamores, pomegranates, perseas, figs, and other trees that made the garden a paradise and a comfort to his soul. He wished all of Egypt could be like this haven where a wealth of essences lived in harmony.

One evening, Ramses was planting a sycamore seedling, mounding soil around the sapling and carefully adding water.

"Your Majesty should wait half an hour, then give it another jug of water, almost drop by drop."

He looked up to see a gardener of indeterminate age. The back of his neck showed a healing ulcer where the weight of his yoke rested. Two heavy earthenware water jugs hung from either end of it.

"Wise advice," Ramses told him. "What's your name, gardener?"

"Nedjem."

"'*The mild one.*' Tell me, Nedjem, are you married?"

"Married to this garden, you might say. The trees, plants, and flowers are my family, my ancestors and descendants. The sycamore you just planted will outlive you, even if you spend a hundred and ten years on earth, the ideal life span of a wise man."

"I must not be so special, then," said Ramses with a smile.

"It can't be easy to be a king and be wise. The human race is too perverse and devious."

"You're a member of it. Don't you share those faults?"

"I dare not say, Majesty."

"Have you trained any of the younger men?"

"That's up to the superintendent, not me."

"Is he a better gardener than you?"

"How would I know? He never comes here."

"Do you think the tree population is adequate in Egypt?"

"It's the only population that can never be too large."

"I agree."

"A tree is a gift," the gardener said emphatically. "During its lifetime, it offers us shade, flowers, and fruit; after its death comes wood. Thanks to trees, we eat, we build, we feel blessed when the soft north wind fans us through the branches. I dream of a country of trees where the only other inhabitants are birds and the souls of the dead."

"I intend to have trees planted in every province," revealed Ramses. "Every village square will have a patch of shade where the generations can meet and the young can listen to the wisdom of their elders."

"May the gods smile upon your work, Majesty. No government program could be more useful."

"Will you help me implement it?"

"How could I . . . ?"

"The Agriculture Department is full of hardworking scribes. To steer them in the right direction, I need a man who loves nature and knows its secrets."

"I'm only a gardener, Majesty, a—"

"You have the makings of an excellent secretary. Come to my office tomorrow and ask to see Ahmeni. He'll know what I want you to do and help you get started."

Ramses went on his way, leaving Nedjem amazed and stunned. At the edge of the huge garden, between two fig trees, the king thought he saw a slim, white figure. Had a goddess just appeared in this magical spot?

He hurried toward the apparition.

In the soft glow of sunset he made out dark hair and a long white gown. How could a woman be so beautiful, at once aloof and enticing?

"Nefertari . . ."

She ran into his arms. "I managed to slip away," she confessed. "Your mother agreed to stand in for me at the lute concert tonight. Have you forgotten me yet?"

"Your mouth is a lotus bud, your lips cast magic spells, and I have a crazy desire to kiss you."

Their kiss renewed them. Clinging together, their promise was reborn.

"I'm a wild bird you've trapped in the net of your hair," said Ramses. "You're a garden with the fragrance of a thousand different flowers, you make me feel drunk . . ."

Nefertari let down her hair as Ramses slipped the straps of her linen dress off her shoulders. In the warmth of a peaceful, sweet-smelling summer night, they came together.

FIFTEEN

The first ray of sunlight woke Ramses. He stroked his sleeping wife's delicious back and kissed her on the neck. Without opening her eyes, she twined around him, fitting her body to his powerful frame.

"I'm so happy."

"Happiness is what you are, Nefertari."

"Let's never stay apart so long again."

"It's not something we can control."

"Won't our lives ever be our own?"

Ramses held her tight.

"You aren't answering," she said.

"Because you know the answer, Nefertari. You're the Great Royal Wife, and I'm Pharaoh. We can't escape that fact, even in our dreams."

Ramses rose and walked to the window, looking out over the Theban countryside, lush green in the summer sun.

"I love you, Nefertari, but I'm wed to my country as well. I have to keep this land fertile and prosperous. When Egypt calls, I must not ignore it."

"Is there so much left to do?"

"More than I thought. I forgot I would have to govern men, not merely a country. A few weeks is all it would take to overturn the law of Ma'at and undo the work of Seti and all our ancestors. Harmony is the most fragile of treasures. If I relax my vigilance, Egypt will soon be awash in evil and horror."

Nefertari crossed to meet him, pressing her naked body to his. The merest touch of her scented skin told him their understanding was complete.

Sharp raps sounded at the bedchamber door. Before they answered, it flew open, and a wild-eyed Ahmeni entered. As soon as he noticed the queen, he looked away.

"It's serious, Ramses, very serious."

"Isn't it a bit early to come bursting in like this?"

"Come with me. There isn't a moment to spare."

"No time to wash and have some breakfast?"

"Not this morning."

Ramses always took Ahmeni at his word, especially when his usually levelheaded friend was as flustered as this.

The king drove his own two-horse chariot. The one behind him carried Serramanna and a bowman. The ride made Ahmeni queasy, but he was glad Ramses drove so fast. They came to a halt in front of one of the gates to the temple of Karnak, hopped down, and studied the stela covered with hieroglyphs any literate passerby would be able to read.

"Look," said Ahmeni. "There, the third line down."

The drawing of three animal pelts, signifying birth and designating Ramses as the Son of Light, was incorrect. The error robbed the inscription of its protective magic and damaged the Pharaoh's identity.

"I checked," a shattered Ahmeni informed them, "and the same mistake is on statues and tablets like this one all over town. It's deliberate, Ramses!"

"Who could have done such a thing?"

"The high priest of Amon and his stone carvers. They handled all the inscriptions for your coronation. If you hadn't seen for yourself, you'd never have believed me."

While the general meaning of the proclamations was unchanged, the altered royal name was definitely a serious matter.

"Call in the stone carvers," ordered Ramses, "and have the inscriptions fixed."

"Aren't you going to prosecute the ones who did it wrong in the first place?"

"They were only following orders."

"The high priest of Amon is ill; that's why he hasn't come to pay his respects to you."

"Do you have any proof that he's behind this? I can't afford to offend an important religious leader without due cause."

"All the evidence points to him!"

"You know better than to trust circumstantial evidence, Ahmeni."

"We can't let him get away with it. No matter how rich and powerful he is, he's still beholden to you."

"Compile a list of his assets for me, will you?"

Romay had no complaints about his new duties. After revamping maintenance procedures and appointing a new staff, he had tackled the royal menagerie, consisting of three wild cats, two gazelles, a hyena, and two gray cranes.

One animal remained beyond his control, however. Watcher, the Pharaoh's yellow-gold dog, was in the annoying habit of snacking on fish from the royal pond. Since the king's pet lion was his partner in crime, there was no way to stop their daily expeditions.

Early in the morning, Romay had helped Ahmeni haul in a heavy crate of papyrus. He wondered where the puny young scribe, who barely ate and slept only three or four hours a night, found so much energy. He spent the greater part of his days at his desk poring over papers, never showing the slightest sign of fatigue.

Ahmeni conferred with Ramses while Romay went on his daily tour of the kitchen, contending that Pharaoh's health, and therefore the health of the entire nation, depended on the quality of his food.

Ahmeni unrolled several papyrus scrolls on low tables.

"Here's the information on Karnak," he said with a hint of pride.

"Was it hard to gather?"

"Yes and no. The temple administrators weren't particularly happy to see me or answer my questions, but they didn't stand in my way when I checked their figures."

"And is Karnak as rich as we thought?"

"Richer. Eighty thousand employees, forty-six building sites on its outlying properties, four hundred fifty gardens, orchards, and vineyards, four hundred twenty thousand head of livestock, ninety boats, and sixty-five settlements of various sizes directly dependent on the largest religious establishment in Egypt. The high priest commands a veritable army of scribes and farmworkers. Factor in the property belonging to the god Amon, which the clergy controls, and the total is six million head of cattle and as many goats, twelve million donkeys, eight million mules, and fowl also numbering in the millions."

"Amon is the god of victory and the protector of the empire."

"There's no denying that, but his clergy are only men. Managing such enormous wealth exposes them to overwhelming temptations. I didn't have time to investigate any further, but the situation worries me."

"Anything specific?"

"The powers that be are anxious for Your Majesty to head north again. Otherwise, you're upsetting the status quo. All they want is to fatten their coffers and keep Karnak growing like a state within a state, until the day the high priest of Amon proclaims himself king of the south and secedes from the union.

"That would mean the death of Egypt, Ahmeni."

"And misery for the people."

"I'd need hard evidence, proof that there's been skimming. I can't face the high priest of Amon unless I have my facts straight."

"Leave it to me, Ramses."

Serramanna did not rest easy. Ever since Menelaus's bungled coup, he was aware that Ramses' life was in danger. The Greeks may have left the country, but the threat remained.

He kept a close eye on what he considered the trouble spots in Thebes: the military base, palace police headquarters, the barracks for the guard detachment. If a revolt was in the making, it would come from one of those places. The colossal Sard trusted his pirate's instincts, remaining wary of enlisted men and officers alike. In a number of instances, he had owed his survival to striking the first blow.

Despite his size, Serramanna moved like a cat. He liked to eavesdrop and observe from the shadows. No matter how hot it was, he wore a metal breastplate. In his belt he carried a dagger and a short, sharp-tipped sword. A frizzy mustache and sideburns made his massive face even more frightening; he used this to his advantage.

Career army officers, most of whom came from a wealthy background, hated Serramanna and wondered why Ramses had put such a lout in charge of the guardsmen. The Sard blithely ignored them. He didn't care about popularity. It wouldn't help him be the best fighter serving a good leader.

And Ramses was a good leader, captain of an enormous ship on a treacherous and adventure-filled course.

In short, his job was everything a Sardinian pirate could have wished for, and he was determined to keep it. He enjoyed a mammoth villa, fine food, and Egyptian beauties with breasts round as love apples, but these were not enough to satisfy him. Nothing could replace the thrill of proving himself in combat.

The palace guard was rotated the first, eleventh, and twenty-first of each month. They received their food and wine rations and were paid in grain. Each time the troops were relieved, Serramanna looked the new men over carefully before he assigned them. Any lapse in discipline, any slackening, resulted in a flogging and immediate dismissal.

The Sard walked slowly down the single row of soldiers. He stopped in front of a fair-haired boy who seemed slightly nervous.

"Where do you come from?"

"A village in the Delta, sir."

"Your favorite weapon?"

"The sword."

"Have a drink, soldier. You look thirsty."

Serramanna handed the fair-haired boy a flask of anise-flavored wine. He took two quick swallows.

"I'll post you in the hallway to the royal office. Your job is keeping everyone out of there during the last watch of the night."

"Yes, sir."

Serramanna had the men present arms, checked their uniforms, exchanged a few words with other soldiers, then sent them on their way.

The architects who designed the palace had set windows high in the walls so that cool air could circulate through the corridors on hot summer nights.

Everything was quiet. Outside, the frogs sang their courting songs.

Serramanna crept down the tiled hallway leading to Ramses' office. As he had suspected, the boy from the Delta was not at his post.

Instead, he was fiddling with the latch on the office door.

The Sard reached out one broad hand and lifted him by the scruff of the neck.

"A Greek, eh? Only a Greek could drink anise wine without flinching. Which faction do you belong to, my lad? One of Menelaus's leftovers, or part of some new plot? Answer me!"

The fair-haired boy twitched briefly, but made no sound.

Feeling the Greek go limp, the bodyguard put him down. He flopped on the floor like a rag doll. Without meaning to, Serramanna had broken the boy's neck.

SIXTEEN

Written reports were not Serramanna's province. He simply stated the facts to Ahmeni, who put them down on papyrus and alerted Ramses. No one knew anything about the young Greek, who had been recruited on the strength of his sword handling. His brutal death made it impossible to trace the real instigator, but the king, more grateful than ever for Serramanna's vigilance, refrained from reprimanding his bodyguard.

This time, the object of the break-in was not the

Pharaoh but his office, meaning affairs of state. Someone wanted confidential documents and information about the new king's future policies.

Menelaus's attack had been motivated by revenge; this incident was far murkier. Who had hired the young Greek to slink through the shadows and compromise Ramses at the beginning of his reign? Of course, there was Shaanar, who had been strangely quiet since the coronation. Could he be working behind the scenes, much more effectively than in the past?

Romay bowed to the king. "Majesty, your visitor has arrived."

"Show him to the garden pavilion."

Ramses wore only a simple white kilt and a single piece of jewelry, the gold bracelet on his right wrist. He collected his thoughts for a few moments, aware that the fate of Egypt would hinge on the interview he was about to conduct.

The elegant wooden pavilion stood in the shade of a willow tree. A low table was spread with silvery green grapes and fresh figs. Cups of light, refreshing beer would be ideal in the summer heat.

The high priest of Amon sat in an armchair with plump cushions and a matching footstool, resplendent in his wig, linen robe, bib necklace of pearls and lapis lazuli, silver bangles.

As soon as he saw his sovereign, the high priest rose and bowed to him.

"I trust you're quite comfortable," Ramses said.

"Your Majesty, I thank you for considering an old man's health."

"You're not feeling well?"

"At my age . . . well, you wouldn't understand."

"I was beginning to think we'd never meet."

"Heavens, no, Your Majesty. For one thing, I was confined to my bed for a time. For another, I hoped to bring the viziers of the north and the south along with me, and the Viceroy of Nubia."

"What a delegation! Did they reject your proposal?"

"At first, no; later they did."

"What made them change their minds?"

"They're high-ranking officials . . . they do not wish to displease Your Majesty. Still, their presence would have given my words added weight."

"If your cause is just, you have nothing to fear."

"Do you think it is?"

"Let me decide that, with Ma'at to guide me."

"I'm worried, Majesty."

"What can I do to ease your mind?"

"You asked for an accounting of Karnak's riches."

"And I got it."

"What do you conclude?"

"That you're a remarkable administrator."

"Should I take that as criticism?"

"Certainly not. Our ancestors taught, did they not, that spiritual and material welfare go hand in hand? Pharaoh endows Karnak, and you make it prosper."

"I still sense criticism in your tone, Your Majesty."

"Confusion, nothing more. Why don't we discuss your concerns instead?"

"It's rumored that Karnak's wealth and glory offend Your Majesty, and you wish to redistribute some of its privileges."

"Where have you heard this?"

"Here and there."

"And you believe these rumors?"

"When rumors are persistent, they may contain the germ of truth."

"If so, what do you think of the idea?"

"That Your Majesty would be well advised to preserve the status quo. That the wisest course would be following in your esteemed father's footsteps."

"Unfortunately, his reign was cut short before he had time to enact a great many necessary reforms."

"Karnak needs no reforms."

"That's your opinion."

"Then my worries were justified."

"Perhaps mine are, too."

"Yours? Your Majesty, I . . ."

"Is the high priest of Amon still Pharaoh's faithful servant?"

The prelate averted his eyes. To regain his composure, he ate a fig and drank some beer. The king was as direct in his questioning as he was unpretentious in dress, and the clergyman had been unprepared for either. However, the young pharaoh was careful not to push him, allowing him time to gather his wits.

"How can you doubt my loyalty, Majesty?" he said at length.

"Because of Ahmeni's investigation."

"That sniveling little scribe, that sneak, that rat, that—"

"Ahmeni is my friend, and his only ambition is serving Egypt. I take any insult to him as a personal affront."

"Forgive me, Majesty," stammered the priest. "But his methods . . ."

"Did he use undue force?"

"No, but he wouldn't let go. Worse than a jackal devouring its kill!"

"He's conscientious and thorough."

"But surely he found nothing wrong?"

Ramses looked the high priest square in the face. "Surely?"

Again, the prelate looked away.

"Egypt and everything in it belongs to the pharaoh, does it not?" asked Ramses.

"According to the legacy of the gods," intoned the priest.

"But the pharaoh may grant land to men who have proved themselves worthy."

"According to custom."

"Is the high priest of Amon authorized to act in Pharaoh's stead?"

"The high priest acts as his delegate at Karnak."

"With certain limitations; if I may refresh your memory."

"I don't see—"

"You've deeded land to secular individuals, putting them in your debt. Military officers, for instance, whose loyalty to me might then be compromised. Perhaps you need an army to defend your private domain?"

"Mere circumstance, Majesty! You can't be thinking—"

"There are three major cult centers in Egypt. Heliopolis is the holy city of Ra, the god of light. Memphis worships Ptah, the patron of arts and sciences. Thebes is the home of Amon, the hidden god. My father strove to maintain them in harmony. Your policies, however, have thrown them out of balance, giving Thebes a disproportionate importance."

"Majesty! Would you see Amon slighted?"

"Never. Amon's worldly representative is the one I question. As of today, I suspend you from your administrative responsibilities so that you may concentrate on religious devotions."

The prelate struggled to his feet.

"You know very well I can't do that."

"Why not?"

"Because my duties are secular as well as religious, exactly like yours."

"Karnak belongs to Pharaoh."

"That much is clear, but the temple can't run itself."

"I'll appoint an administrator."

"And bypass the ones I have in place? Majesty, I beg you to reconsider. Turning the priesthood of Amon against you would be most unwise."

"Is that a threat?"

"Just advice from an experienced leader to a young monarch."

"Do you think I'll follow it?"

"Support from the right quarters is critical to any king's survival. Of course, as your faithful servant I plan to follow your orders, whatever they may be."

Though visibly weary, the high priest seemed on surer footing.

"Don't fight a losing battle, Your Majesty. You're new at this; you think you can change things overnight, but it can't be done. The gods are slow to forgive. Remember what happened when Akhenaton turned his back on Thebes."

"Your net is tightly woven," Ramses told him, "but a falcon's beak can tear holes in it."

"Such a waste of energy! You belong in Memphis, not here. Egypt needs your strength to push back the enemies from our borders. Let me take care of Thebes, and I'll be behind you."

"I'll think it over."

The high priest smiled. "I knew you'd listen to reason. If you have the intelligence to match your spirit, you'll be a great pharaoh, Ramses."

SEVENTEEN

Each and every Theban notable had only one thing in mind: pleading his cause face-to-face with the new king. Ramses was an unknown quantity, aligned with no particular faction; who knew what unpleasant surprises he might have in store for even the best-connected courtiers? But to meet with the Pharaoh, one had to get past Ahmeni, who refused to let anyone waste his own time, much less Ramses'. Then there was the little matter of Serramanna's insistence on frisking each visitor!

Ramses canceled the rest of the morning's appointments, including the dikes inspector Ahmeni had recommended. Well, let Ahmeni take care of him. The king needed to consult with the Great Royal Wife.

After a refreshing dip, they sat on the edge of the pool, their naked bodies basking in the sun that filtered through the sycamores. The palace gardens were more beautiful than ever since Nedjem had been named to the Department of Agriculture.

"I finally met with the high priest of Amon this morning," Ramses confessed.

"Any headway?"

"None at all. He's forcing me to choose between caving in to him or declaring open warfare."

"What does he want you to do?"

"Leave Karnak as the most powerful temple in Egypt. He'll rule the south and let me keep the north."

"Out of the question."

Ramses looked at Nefertari in amazement. "I was certain you'd preach moderation!"

"If moderation leads to the country's ruin, it's no longer a virtue. The high priest wants to protect his own interests with no concern for the general welfare. He even presumes to dictate to the pharaoh. If you give in, everything Seti left you will be destroyed."

Nefertari spoke calmly, in her soft, soothing voice, yet her views were clear and firm.

"Meeting him head-on will be dangerous," Ramses told her.

"You have to take a stand, or you'll be seen as a weak ruler. The high priest of Amon will lead the opposition; we can be sure of that."

"I'm ready to take him on, but . . ."

"You're afraid it's for selfish reasons. That you have to prove your strength from the beginning."

"Are you a mind reader?"

"I'm your wife."

"Tell me what you think, Nefertari. Is it only my vanity leading me?"

"A pharaoh is larger than life. You are all that is generous, eager, and strong. You're acting on those qualities—acting as a ruler."

"But am I choosing the right battle?"

"The high priest wants to divide and conquer. There is

no evil greater than civil war. As Pharaoh, it's your duty to face him down."

Ramses laid his head on Nefertari's breast. She gently stroked his hair as all around them swallows flew, rustling the silken air.

The sound of a scuffle at the gates to the garden broke the spell. A woman was arguing with the guards, her voice growing louder.

Ramses threw on his kilt and headed for the gates.

"What's going on here?"

The guards stepped aside and there stood Iset the Fair, blooming and vivacious as ever.

"Majesty!" she exclaimed. "A word with you is all I ask!"

"Have I ever denied you?"

"No, but your security detail has, and of course your secretary, and—"

"Come this way, Iset."

A small boy stepped out from behind her. "Here's our son, Ramses."

"Kha!" Ramses picked him up and lifted him over his head. The frightened child burst into tears.

"He's very shy," said Iset.

The king sat the boy astride his shoulders. Soon Kha forgot his fear and began to laugh.

"Four years old . . . he's getting to be a big boy! What does his tutor say?"

"That he's too serious. Kha doesn't play much; he'd rather be reading. He already knows a lot of hieroglyphs; he can even write a few."

"He'll catch up with me before long! Come sit by the pool. I'm going to teach Kha to swim."

"Is she . . . is Nefertari with you?"

"Of course."

"Why have I had so much trouble getting in to see you? You shouldn't treat me like a stranger. You'd be dead if it weren't for me."

"What do you mean?"

"I sent that letter to warn you about the coup."

"What are you talking about?"

Iset hung her head. "All right, I admit there was a time when I resented being left in Thebes. I was so alone. But I never stopped loving you, and I refused to join forces with the members of your own family working against you."

"I never got your letter."

Iset turned white. "Then you thought I was against you, too?"

"Was I wrong?"

"Yes, you were wrong! By the name of Pharaoh, I swear I never betrayed you!"

"Why should I believe you?"

Iset took Ramses' arm. "How could I lie to you?"

Now they approached Nefertari, and her beauty took Iset's breath away. It was not so much her outward perfection as her integral radiance that disarmed and conquered everyone around her. Nefertari was truly a Great Royal Wife. No one could touch her.

Iset was untroubled by jealousy. Nefertari shone like the summer sky; her nobility inspired only respect.

"Iset! I'm so happy to see you."

As lesser wife, Iset bowed to her.

"Please don't. Come, Iset, have a swim. It's so hot today."

Iset had never expected such a welcome. Without a word,

she acquiesced, removing her clothes. Naked as Nefertari, she dove into the blue water.

As they swam, Ramses watched the two women he loved. How could his feelings for them be so different, yet so intense and sincere? Nefertari was the love of his life, unique and gifted, a queen. Iset the Fair was his carefree youth—desire, sensuality, passion. Still, she had lied and plotted against him; he had no choice but to punish her.

"Is it true I'm your son?" piped Kha.

"Yes, you are."

"The hieroglyph for son has a duck in it." The little boy carefully drew a duck in the sand with his finger.

"Do you know the one for Pharaoh?"

Kha drew a house, then a column.

"The house means protection, the column means greatness. *Per-ah*, great house—that's the real meaning of the word. Do you know why they call me Pharaoh?"

"Because you're taller than everybody and you live in a great big house."

"That's right, son, but the house is all of Egypt, and each person must find a home in it."

"Will you show me more hieroglyphs?"

"Wouldn't you like to play another game?"

Kha pouted.

"All right then," Ramses told him, and the boy brightened.

The king traced a circle with a dot in its center on the sandy garden path.

"The sun," he explained. "The sun is called Ra. His name is made of a mouth and an arm, because he's both word and deed. Now you try it."

The child drew a series of suns, each one closer to a perfect circle. Fresh from their swim, Iset and Nefertari inspected Kha's hieroglyphs.

"He's very advanced for his age," said the queen.

"It almost frightens me sometimes," said Iset. "His tutor doesn't know what to do with him."

"Then he needs another tutor," said Ramses. "My son should develop his talents, no matter what other children his age do. His ability is a gift from the gods. We mustn't hold him back. Wait here."

The king walked through the garden toward the palace.

Kha began to cry; his finger was sore. "May I pick him up?" Nefertari asked Iset.

"Yes. Yes, of course."

The boy quieted almost at once. Nefertari's eyes were full of tenderness. Iset felt bold enough to ask the question tormenting her.

"Despite the loss of your daughter, are you planning to have more children?"

"In fact, I've just begun to suspect I'm pregnant again."

"Ah . . . may the gods of childbirth smile upon you."

"Thank you, Iset. Your kind words will help me when my time comes."

Iset hid her dismay. She did not dispute Nefertari as Ramses' queen and hardly envied her the crushing responsibilities that came with the position of Great Royal Wife. What she did want was more children with Ramses, many more, and the honor attached to being their mother. For the time being, she remained the mother of his firstborn son, but if Nefertari gave birth to a boy, he would probably be given precedence over Kha.

Ramses returned with a miniature scribe's palette, complete with two tiny cakes of ink, one red, the other black, and three child-sized brushes. When he handed it to his son, the boy's face lit up. Kha clutched the precious kit to his heart.

"I love you, Papa!"

Once Iset and Kha had gone, Ramses again spoke his mind to Nefertari.

"I'm convinced she had something to do with the coup."

"Did you question her?"

"She admits she was upset with me, but she claims she tried to warn me. If she did, I never got her message."

"Why don't you believe her?"

"I don't think she forgives me for making you my consort."

"You're wrong."

"Her offense should be punished."

"What offense? A pharaoh can't hand out punishments based on fleeting impressions. Iset has given you a fine son. She wishes you no harm. Forgive the offense, if she ever committed one, and forget the punishment."

EIGHTEEN

Setau's outfit instantly set him apart from the palace regulars. His thick antelope-skin garment, cut like a winter tunic, had been treated with antivenom preparations. In an emergency, Setau could whip off his tunic, soak it in water, and produce a satisfactory snakebite remedy.

"This isn't the desert," Ramses told him. "You hardly need that portable pharmacy in Memphis."

"It's more dangerous here than in deepest Nubia. Snakes and scorpions everywhere, though you might not recognize them at first glance. Are you ready?"

"I fasted, just as you told me to."

"The treatments have gone well so far. You've built up an immunity to most kinds of snakebite, even certain cobras. Do you really want this added protection?"

"I gave you my consent."

"It's not without risk."

"Let's get on with it."

"Did you ask Nefertari about it?"

"Did you ask Lotus?"

"She says I'm slightly mad, but we see eye to eye."

Unshaven, square-jawed, refusing to wear a wig, Setau would have sent an ordinary patient running.

"If I've got the dose wrong," he warned his friend, "you could end up a vegetable."

"No use trying to scare me off."

"Drink this, then."

Ramses took the potion.

"What do you think?"

"Tastes good."

"That's because of the carob juice. The other ingredients are less appetizing: extracts of several different stinging plants and diluted cobra blood. Now you're protected against any bite there is. You'll only need a booster every six months."

"Setau, when will you come to work for me?"

"Never. And when will you stop being so naive? I could have poisoned you, just now."

"You're not a murderer."

"As if you'd know!"

"I learned a few things from Menelaus. What's more, you've been screened by Serramanna, my lion, and my dog."

"Quite the threesome. But are you forgetting that Thebes can't wait to see you leave and most of the notables hope to see you fail?"

"Should I let that stop me?"

"I don't have a secret remedy to protect you from men. They're far more dangerous than snakes."

"Yes, but men are what a pharaoh has to work with, if his goal is to build a just and harmonious society."

"Humph! You must be living in a dreamworld. Wake up, my friend. You're surrounded by schemers and villains. Still, you have one advantage: you feel the same mysterious force I do when I work with cobras. It brought you Nefertari, the most wonderful partner any king could have. I think you'll make it."

"It will be harder without your help."

"Flattery didn't use to be one of your faults. I'm heading north now, with a load of venom. Take care, Ramses."

Despite his brother's early show of strength, Shaanar was not discouraged. Who could tell what would happen when the young pharaoh locked horns with the high priest of Amon? It would probably end in a stalemate, undermining Ramses' authority. His word was far from carrying the weight of Seti's.

Shaanar was beginning to figure out his brother.

A frontal attack? Certain to fail, since Ramses would defend himself so forcefully that he would turn the situation to his advantage. It would be better to lay a series of traps, using trickery, lies, and betrayal. As long as Ramses remained unable to identify his enemies, he would expend his energy flailing at shadows. Once he was exhausted, Shaanar could move in for the kill.

While the new king was busy forming his government and bringing Thebes to heel, his brother had been quiet, seemingly detached. Soon he would have to make himself heard, or else be suspected of plotting in the background.

After much thought, Shaanar had concluded that his best course was to play Ramses for a fool, in a manner so blatant that the new pharaoh would have to lash out at him, never realizing that it was exactly the reaction his brother wanted. If his little experiment worked, Shaanar would know that Ramses could be manipulated.

And Shaanar would manipulate him for all he was worth.

For the tenth time, Ramses was lecturing Watcher about his fishing expeditions. It wasn't nice to steal from the palace ponds. It *was* nice to share his catch with Fighter, but didn't they both get enough to eat as it was? The yellow dog listened attentively, yet his expression told the king he was wasting his breath. With the lion as his accomplice, Watcher knew he could get away with murder.

The towering figure of Serramanna appeared in the doorway of Ramses' office.

"Your brother wants to see you, but he refuses to be searched."

"Let him in."

Serramanna stepped aside. Shaanar shot him an icy look in passing.

"Would Your Majesty be so good as to grant me a private interview?"

The yellow dog tagged after Serramanna, who always had a treat for him.

"It's been a long time since we talked, Shaanar."

"You have so much to do. I didn't want to be a nuisance."

Ramses circled his brother, inspecting.

"What are you looking at?" Shaanar said anxiously.

"You're thinner, brother dear."

"I've been trying to cut back these last few weeks."

Despite his dieting, Shaanar was still plump. His small

dark eyes shone in a moon face with the pudgy cheeks and the full lips of a true food lover.

"Why the beard?"

"I'll never stop mourning Seti," he said. "To lose our father so young . . ."

"I sympathize," Ramses said feelingly.

"I'm sure you do, but your duties leave you little time to dwell on it. It's not the same for me."

"What brings you here today?"

"You've been expecting me, haven't you?"

The king made no comment.

"I'm your older brother and my reputation is excellent. I've put our differences behind me; I can live with the fact I was passed over for the throne. But I can't resign myself to being a royal showpiece, of no real use to my country."

"I understand how you feel."

"My work as chief of protocol is no longer enough for me, especially since Romay, the new chief steward, has been handling most of it."

"What do you want, Shaanar?"

"I've thought long and hard before approaching you. I had to swallow my pride."

"There should be no question of such a thing between brothers."

"Will you meet my demands?"

"Not when I have no idea what they are."

"Will you hear me out?"

"Please go ahead."

Shaanar began to pace. "Could I ask to become vizier? Impossible. You'd be accused of favoritism. Head the police? The bureaucracy is too complicated. Chief royal scribe? Too much responsibility, not enough time for my royal duties. What about overseeing your construction proj-

ects? No, I have no experience. Agriculture? You've already
filled the position. Finance? You kept the incumbent. You
plan to reform the temples, but I have no inclination toward
the religious life."

"Where does that leave you?"

"With the one job I'm suited for: secretary of state.
You're aware of my interest in trade relations. Instead of
concentrating on negotiations for my personal gain, I want
to work toward strengthening diplomatic ties with our
neighbors, as well as within our dependent territories."

Shaanar finally came to a halt, asking, "Does my proposal shock you?"

"It's a tall assignment."

"My major goal would be avoiding war with the Hittites.
No one wants bloodshed. I've always promoted peace; will
you give me a chance to do something concrete about it?"

Ramses pondered. "I'll grant your request," he finally
told his brother. "But you'll need help, Shaanar."

"Admittedly. Do you have someone in mind?"

"My friend Ahsha. A professional diplomat."

"A minder?"

"A partner, I hope."

"As Your Majesty sees fit."

"Meet with him as soon as possible, then outline your
program for me."

On his way out of the palace, Shaanar could barely contain a whoop of joy.

He had twisted Ramses around his little finger.

NINETEEN

Ramses' sister threw herself at his feet.
"Forgive me, I beg of you," she sobbed. "Forgive my husband and me!"

"Get up, Dolora. Don't make a spectacle of yourself."

Dolora let him help her to her feet, but was still afraid to look at him. Tall and listless, she seemed about to swoon.

"Forgive us, Ramses. We didn't know what we were doing!"

"You wanted me dead. Twice your husband tried to have me killed. Sary, who practically raised me!"

"It was wrong of him, very wrong. I should never have played along. We were too easily influenced."

"By whom, sister dear?"

"The high priest at Karnak. He brainwashed us into thinking you'd be a bad king, that you'd lead the country into a civil war."

"You had no faith in me at all, then."

"My husband knew you as an impetuous boy, always itching for a fight. Now he sees the error of his ways . . . if you only knew how truly sorry he is!"

"And could our dear brother have been in on the plot?"

"No," lied Dolora. "He's the one we should have listened to. Once he was reconciled to our poor father's decision to name you as his successor, Shaanar became one of your staunchest supporters. His only thought now is serving Egypt in a position that will make full use of his talents."

"Why didn't Sary come with you?"

Dolora hung her head. "He fears the wrath of Pharaoh."

"As well he should. But luckily for both of you, our mother and Nefertari have been pleading in your favor. They want to keep peace in the family, out of respect for Seti's memory."

"Are you pardoning me?" asked his sister, astonished.

"I'm appointing you honorary superior of the harem at Thebes. A grand title, but not too tiring for you. Just make sure you behave yourself, Dolora."

"And . . . my husband?"

"He's going to head the brickyard at Karnak. Seti's additions to the temple are still being finished, so he'll have plenty to do. It's time he accomplished something constructive."

"But Sary has always been a scribe, an academic. He can't do manual labor!"

"Remember the teachings of the sages, Dolora. The hand and the mind must work together, or men turn evil. Now hurry and report to your new assignments, both of you. There's work to be done."

Leaving the palace, Dolora breathed a sigh of relief. Just as Shaanar had predicted, she and Sary had escaped the worst. Having just come to power, still in the sway of his mother and his wife, Ramses was inclined to be merciful.

Being forced to work was a real punishment to her, but less harsh than house arrest in some desert outpost or exile in the wilds of Nubia. As for Sary, his pride would suffer, but considering he could have been sentenced to death for treason, becoming a brickmaker was better than the alternative.

Their disgrace would be short-lived. Dolora's lies had enhanced Shaanar's credibility as a supportive and respectful brother to the king. Ramses, preoccupied with his new responsibilities, would believe that his old enemies, including his brother and sister, had finally fallen in line.

Moses was overjoyed to be back at Karnak. Once the period of mourning for Seti was over, Ramses decided to continue work on his father's great hypostyle hall, where Moses' work gangs were raising more than a hundred columns. The young Hebrew had a powerful build, broad shoulders, flowing hair, a full beard on his craggy face. He also had the respect and affection of his crew of stonecutters and hieroglyph carvers.

Moses had refused the post as master builder that Ramses offered him, not feeling equal to such responsibility. He could coordinate a project and motivate workers, yes, but draw architectural plans like the expert company at Deir el-Medina, no. He wouldn't be ready for that without more on-the-job training, more firsthand knowledge of construction materials.

The rough working conditions and physical labor helped

tame his soul. Every night, tossing in bed as sleep refused to come, Moses tried to understand why his mind was so troubled. He was living in prosperous times in a prosperous country, had a promising career, and was one of the Pharaoh's closest friends. He could have any woman he wanted, earned a good living . . . No matter how many blessings he counted, it was no use. Why did he always feel incomplete, why was he so restless and unhappy?

In the morning, he found relief in the bustle of the work site, the clang of mallet and chisel, the sight of huge blocks of stone sliding along a moistened track on wooden sledges, the constant alertness to danger, the slow satisfaction of raising a column.

Work was usually halted in the hot summer months, but Seti's death and Ramses' coronation had changed that. Moses had come up with a plan after consulting with the leaders of the various work gangs from Deir el-Medina, as well as the master builder, who explained his drawings in detail. Each day two sessions would be scheduled, the first from dawn to mid-morning, the second from late afternoon to nightfall, to keep the men out of the heat of day and allow them to rest. Furthermore, awnings would be rigged to provide some shade.

Moses had just passed the guard post at the entry to the hall of columns when the head stonecutter approached him.

"No one can work under these conditions," the man said flatly.

"Come on, the heat isn't that bad yet."

"It's not the heat. I'm talking about the brickmakers building the scaffolding for us. It's their new head man."

"New? Do I know him?"

"His name is Sary. Married to the Pharaoh's sister, Dolora. That's why he thinks he can do as he pleases!"

"What seems to be the problem?"

"It's too rough for him out here, so he only wants his gang to report every other day, but without the afternoon break or any extra water. Does he think he can treat his men like slaves? This is Egypt, not somewhere in Greece or Hittite territory. I stand by the brickmakers!"

"I don't blame you. Where can I find this Sary?"

"Sitting in the shade," the man said, gesturing toward the foremen's tent.

Sary seemed a different man. The affable, portly professor he had known was now almost gaunt, sharp-featured, jumpy. He alternately fiddled with a copper band on his left wrist, almost falling off now, and rubbed ointment into the big toe of his right foot, which was gnarled with arthritis. The only sign of his former station in life was an elegant white linen robe, the customary dress of successful scribes.

Reclining against a pile of cushions, Sary was sipping cool beer. He glanced up absently when Moses entered the tent.

"Why, hello, Sary! What brings you here?"

"Hello, Moses. I didn't realize you were still stuck in Karnak! This place is fine for the Pharaoh's *relatives*, but I thought he'd do better by a friend like you."

"I have no complaints."

"Ramses ought to promote you."

"Seeing a monument like this go up is already my dream job."

"Ha! It's more like a nightmare: the heat, the dust, the sweat and toil, the awful noise, and even worse, rubbing elbows with illiterate laborers . . . You're wasting your talents, Moses."

"Seti entrusted me with a mission. I plan to accomplish it."

"A noble attitude. But when you get fed up, you'll change your tune."

"And what are you contributing to Karnak?"

A scowl darkened Sary's face.

"Running the brickyard . . . now there's a plum assignment."

"The brickmakers are solid, respectable men. I'd take them over a bunch of self-indulgent scribes any day!"

"You were educated as a scribe, Moses."

"I wasn't taught to look down on others."

"Are you lecturing me, by any chance?"

"Look, Sary, I set the schedule here. It's the same in the brickyard as anywhere else, and I want you to follow it."

"I run my own department."

"All foremen answer to me."

"You'll have to make an exception."

"All right. If you won't follow the rules, I'll notify the master builder, who'll take the issue to the vizier, and he'll go to Ramses."

"Is that a threat?"

"It's the usual procedure in a case of insubordination at a royal construction site."

"You enjoy having the upper hand, don't you?"

"My only goal is to keep this project running as smoothly as possible."

"Don't make me laugh," sneered Sary.

"We're in this together," Moses told him. "Without cooperation, we'll never finish."

"Ramses will drop you, just like he's humiliated me."

"Listen, Sary. Get your brickmakers to work on the scaffolding, give them the midday break they're entitled to, and make sure they have plenty of water."

TWENTY

The wine was exceptional, the beef tasty, and the bean puree pleasantly spicy. "Say what you will about Shaanar," thought Meba, "he certainly knows how to entertain."

"Is everything to your liking?" asked Ramses' older brother.

"Simply wonderful! My dear fellow, you have the finest kitchen in Egypt."

Despite his long years as secretary of state, Meba was not merely being diplomatic. Shaanar treated his guests to the very best.

"Don't the king's politics strike you as inconsistent?" asked the veteran cabinet member.

"He's not an easy man to understand."

This veiled criticism satisfied Meba. His broad, kindly face had begun to show signs of strain. How could he be sure that Shaanar had not gone over to Ramses' side? Doing so would help keep the peace and safeguard the prince's rank. Still, the words he had just spoken seemed to prove the opposite.

"I can hardly approve of this new rash of appointments, turning excellent civil servants out of their offices and relegating them to lesser positions."

"I quite agree, Meba."

"Naming a gardener to Agriculture, what a farce! It makes me wonder what on earth Ramses plans to do with my department."

"That's exactly what I wanted to discuss with you today."

Meba squared his shoulders and adjusted the costly wig he wore year-round, even in the hottest weather.

"Are you trying to tell me something?"

"Let me give you all the details so that you can appreciate my situation. Yesterday, Ramses sent for me, out of the blue. I had to drop everything and head to the palace, where I was made to wait for over an hour."

"Weren't you . . . concerned?"

"I admit I was. His Sardinian even frisked me, over my protestations."

"You, the king's brother! Has it come to that?"

"I'm afraid so, Meba."

"Did you complain to the king?"

"They wouldn't let me. Apparently his security takes precedence over family feeling."

"Seti would never have stood for it!"

"Unfortunately, Seti is no longer with us."

"Men come and go, institutions remain. A prince of your stature must one day rise to the highest office."

"It's in the hands of the gods, Meba."

"Weren't you going to tell me about my department?"

"I'm coming to that. Now there I was, trembling with shame and indignation after the bodyguard searched me, when in walked Ramses, telling me he was naming me secretary of state!"

Meba blanched. "You, in my job? It's beyond comprehension!"

"You'll understand better when you hear he plans to monitor my every move. He wouldn't be able to control you, Meba, but I'll make a perfect figurehead. Our allies will be honored that Ramses cares enough about foreign policy to appoint his own brother to the State Department. They won't realize I'm only his puppet."

Meba was crestfallen. "So much for me . . ."

"And for me, despite appearances."

"This king is a monster."

"As other men of rank will soon discover. That's why we mustn't allow ourselves to be too discouraged."

"What are you suggesting?"

"What would you rather do, retire or help me keep fighting?"

"I can make trouble for Ramses."

"Pretend to step aside gracefully and wait for my instructions."

"Ramses had better watch out. Heading the State Department will give you plenty of opportunities, even with his operatives in place."

"You're still sharp, old friend. Now why don't you explain how you've kept the department running so smoothly all these years?

Meba was more than willing. Shaanar had neglected to mention Ramses' other major miscalculation: appointing Ahsha as his right-hand man. His pact with Ramses' friend must remain his most closely guarded secret.

Holding Lita by the hand, Ofir the Sorcerer walked slowly down the main street of the city of the Horizon of Aton, the abandoned capital where the heretic pharaoh Akhenaton had reigned with his wife, Nefertiti. The buildings were intact, but through the open doors and windows, sand blew in from the desert.

The Horizon of Aton had been a ghost town for more than fifty years. After Akhenaton's death, the court had abandoned his grandiose Middle Egyptian capital and returned to Thebes, Amon's cult center some three hundred miles to the south. Akhenaton's worship of the One God Aton, the golden orb, was repudiated in favor of more traditional beliefs

In Ofir's opinion, Akhenaton had not gone far enough. Sun worship was a travesty: God was beyond any representation, any symbol. God dwelt in the heavens, man on earth. Egyptians believed that their gods walked the earth; they rejected the notion of a single god. Therefore Egypt must be destroyed.

Ofir was descended from one of Akhenaton's advisers, a Libyan who had spent countless hours with the king, transcribing his mystic poems. He had later circulated them throughout the Near East, even among the inhabitants of the Sinai peninsula, particularly the Hebrews.

General Horemheb had ordered the execution of Ofir's great-grandfather, branding him a dangerous agitator and practitioner of black magic who had led Akhenaton astray and distracted him from kingly duties. When Akhenaton's son-in-law and successor, Tutankhamon, died young, General Horemheb took over, later appointing an old army crony to succeed him: Ramses I.

It was true that Ofir's great-grandfather had been working to avenge the humiliation his people had suffered, to undermine Egypt, to take advantage of Akhenaton's failing health, convincing him to abandon any semblance of a defense policy. And he had very nearly succeeded.

Today, Ofir was the torch bearer. He had inherited his great-grandfather's magical lore and talent for sorcery, as well as the hatred for Egypt that fueled his destructive fury. Bringing Egypt to its knees meant defeating the Pharaoh— defeating Ramses.

Lita stared blankly, yet Ofir continued to describe each public building, each private residence, the shops and craft establishments, the menagerie where Akhenaton had housed his collection of rare animals. They had already spent hours wandering through the empty palace where the king and Nefertiti had played with their six daughters, one of whom was Lita's grandmother.

On this new visit, Ofir noted Lita to be more attentive, as if her interest in the outside world was finally awakening. She lingered in Akhenaton and Nefertiti's bedchamber, slumped over an empty cradle, and wept.

When her tears were spent, Ofir took her by the hand and led her to a sculptor's workshop. In crates lay plaster heads of women, models for more permanent works in stone.

The sorcerer began pulling them out, one after the other.

Suddenly, Lita reached out for a statue, stroking its sublimely beautiful face. "Nefertiti," she murmured.

Then her hand darted toward another, smaller head, with remarkably delicate features.

"Merit-Aton, 'Beloved of Aton,' my grandmother. And her sister . . . and her other sisters . . . my lost family! I've finally found my family."

Lita clutched the plaster heads to her chest. One tumbled out of her grip and shattered on the floor.

Ofir braced himself for an outburst, but Lita stood mute and rigid. Then she dashed the rest of the heads against a wall and ground the pieces beneath her feet.

"The past is dying. Let me finish it off," she said with her vacant stare.

"No," objected the sorcerer. "The past never dies. Your grandmother and mother were persecuted because they believed in Aton. But I found you, Lita. I rescued you from exile and certain death."

"It's true, I remember now . . . My grandmother and mother are buried out there in the hills, and I should have joined them long ago. But you've been like a father to me."

"The time for revenge is at hand, Lita. What you suffered as a child was caused by Seti. Seti is dead, but he left his son to oppress us. Ramses must be humbled. You must punish him."

"I want to walk through my city," said Lita.

This time she was eager to touch the gates of temples, the doors of houses, as if taking possession of the empty town. At sunset, she climbed onto the terrace of Nefertiti's palace and contemplated her ghostly domain.

"My soul is empty, Ofir. Your thoughts will fill it."

"I want you to be queen, Lita, so that you can restore the One God to his rightful place."

"Words, Ofir. Only words. Hatred is what drives you. I can feel it. You're evil inside."

"Are you refusing to help me?"

"My soul is empty. You've filled it with your desire to do harm. You've patiently molded me into an avenger. Now I'm ready to fight for your revenge and mine, to cut like a sword."

Ofir knelt and thanked God for answering his prayers.

TWENTY-ONE

There was entertainment in the Theban tavern: a troupe of dancers, enticing Egyptian girls from the Delta, and lissome ebony-skinned Nubians. Moses looked on in fascination from his table at the back of the room, sipping a cup of palm wine. After a hard day's work, marked by two near-accidents, he felt the need to be alone in a noisy crowd, to be surrounded by people yet remain aloof.

Not far away sat an unusual couple.

The young woman was blond, voluptuous, attractive. The man, much older, had a disturbing countenance: gaunt, with jutting cheekbones, a prominent nose, very thin lips, a strong chin, he looked like a bird of prey. In the din, Moses could not overhear their conversation. He heard only meaningless snatches of the man's droning bass.

The Nubians were pulling patrons in to join in the fun. A tipsy middle-aged man laid a hand on the blonde's right shoulder, asking her to dance. Startled, she batted him away. When the man persisted, her hawk-faced companion extended his right arm and the drunk was instantly blasted back a good five paces, as if he'd been punched. Muttering an apology, he slunk away.

The gesture had been swift and unobtrusive, but Moses knew he'd seen correctly. This remarkable-looking character seemed to be gifted with extraordinary powers.

When the pair left the tavern, Moses tailed them. They walked toward the southern edge of Thebes, disappearing among the workmen's hovels, cramped lanes of single-story dwellings. For a moment he thought he'd lost them. Then he heard the man's firm footsteps.

This late at night, the streets were deserted. A dog barked. Bats swooped. The farther Moses went, the more curious he grew. He glimpsed the couple threading their way through humble dwellings that would soon be razed to make way for new construction. The neighborhood was uninhabited.

The woman opened a door with a loud creak rending the still of the night. The man was nowhere in sight.

Moses hesitated.

Should he go in and question her, ask who they were, what they were doing here? He realized how ludicrous he would seem, with no connection to the police and no business mixing in other people's private lives. What evil genius had inspired him to shadow them? Furious with himself, he wheeled—to find the hawk-faced man directly in his path.

"Following us, Moses?"

"How do you know my name?"

"I only had to inquire at the tavern. You're a well-known figure, friend of the Pharaoh's and all."

"And who might you be?"

"First tell me why you were following us."

"An impulse, nothing more . . ."

"That's a feeble explanation."

"Perhaps, but it's the truth."

"I don't believe you."

"Let me pass."

The man held out his hand.

In front of Moses, the dusty street quaked. A horned viper slithered out, its tongue darting furiously.

"A magic trick!" protested Moses.

"Don't let it near you. It's real enough; I merely roused it."

The Hebrew turned around. Another snake was behind him.

"If you value your life, come in with me."

The creaking door opened.

In the narrow back street, there was no escaping the reptiles. Where was Setau when he needed him? Moses entered a room with a low ceiling and a packed dirt floor. The man followed and shut the door behind him.

"Don't try to run. The vipers will get you. When I decide it's time, I'll put them back to sleep."

"What do you want?"

"To talk."

"I could flatten you with one punch."

The man smiled. "I wouldn't try it if I were you. Remember what happened in the tavern?"

The young blond woman was huddled in a corner of the room, a cloth covering her face.

"Is she sick?"

"She can't stand the darkness. Once the sun comes up, she'll feel better."

"Are you ever going to tell me what you expect of me?"

"My name is Ofir, I was born in Libya, and I practice magic."

"In affiliation with which temple?"

"None."

"You're a renegade, then."

"My young companion and I live like outlaws, always on the run."

"What other offense have you committed?"

"Not sharing the faith of the pharaohs."

Moses was dumbfounded. "I don't understand . . ."

"This fragile young woman is named Lita. She's the granddaughter of Merit-Aton, one of the great Akhenaton's six daughters. He's been gone these fifty years, his royal city abandoned, his name expunged from the annals—all because he tried to make Egypt worship Aton as the One True God."

"None of his followers were persecuted!"

"No, only forgotten, which is far worse. Ankhesenamon, his daughter and Tutankhamon's widow, was unjustly sentenced to death. Then Horemheb and his impious successors gained control of the Two Lands. If there were any justice, Lita would be Queen of Egypt."

"You want to overthrow Ramses?"

Ofir smiled once again. "I'm only an aging sorcerer, Lita is weak and despairing; the powerful Pharaoh of Egypt has nothing to fear from us. But there is one force that can topple him."

"What force is that?"

"The True God, Moses, the One True God whose wrath will soon be felt by all those who fail to acknowledge Him!"

Ofir's deep, rumbling voice shook the walls of the hovel. Moses was filled with an uneasy mixture of dread and fascination.

"You're a Hebrew, Moses."

"I'm an Egyptian citizen."

"You and I are alike, both exiles. We're looking for a purer land, untainted by crowds of gods. You're a Hebrew,

Moses, your people suffer, they wish to revive the faith of their fathers, affirm Akhenaton's grand design."

"The Hebrews are happy in Egypt—they are well paid and well fed."

"Their material needs are being met, perhaps, but that's no longer enough for them."

"If you're so sure, why don't you become their prophet?"

"I'm only a Libyan, with neither your credibility nor your influence."

"You're only a madman, Ofir! Turning the Hebrew community against Ramses would end in their utter ruin. They have no desire to rebel and leave the country. As for me, I'm the personal friend of a pharaoh with tremendous potential."

"A fire burns within you, Moses, the same as in the heart of Akhenaton. He still has followers. We're beginning to find one another."

"So you and Lita aren't alone?"

"We have to be very careful, but our movement is growing day by day. Akhenaton's way is the religion of the future."

"I doubt that Ramses would agree."

"You're his friend, Moses. You can make him see the light."

"Have I seen it?"

"The Hebrews will spread their belief in a single God throughout the known world, with you as their leader."

"Preposterous!" snorted Moses.

"Just wait and see."

"I have no intention whatsoever of opposing the king."

"Let him stay out of our way, and no harm will come to him."

"Stop your raving and go back to Libya, Ofir."

"The new land I spoke of doesn't exist yet. You'll be its founder."

"Sorry. I have other plans."

"You believe in the One True God, do you not?"

Moses was confused. "I don't have to answer that."

"Don't run away from your destiny."

Moses headed for the door. Ofir made no move to stop him. "The snakes have gone back underground," the sorcerer declared.

"Goodbye, Ofir."

"I'll be seeing you, Moses."

TWENTY-TWO

Shortly before dawn, Bakhen left his priest's cell, washed his shaved head and body, and put on a white kilt. Carrying a water jug, he walked to the sacred lake, where swallows circling overhead announced the new day. The broad lake, with stone steps at its four corners, contained the water of Nun, the watery chaos from which all life emerged. Bakhen drew off a bit of the precious liquid, which would be used in a variety of purification rites performed within the sanctuary.

"Bakhen? We meet again."

The priest turned to the man who had greeted him, dressed as a simple "pure priest."

"Ramses . . ."

"When I joined the army and you were my combat instructor, we fought. More or less to a draw, as I recall."

Bakhen bowed. "My past is no longer a part of me, Majesty. Today I belong to Karnak."

The former chief inspector of the royal stables and renowned cavalryman still had his rugged, square-jawed face, harsh voice, and forbidding manner; otherwise, he was very much the priest.

"Does Karnak belong to the crown?" asked Ramses.

"What kind of question is that?"

"I'm sorry to disturb you, Bakhen, but I need to know whether you're a friend or foe."

"Why would I oppose Pharaoh?"

"The high priest of Amon is battling me, or didn't you know?"

"Power politics . . ."

"Don't skirt the issue, Bakhen. There isn't room for two masters in this country."

The cavalry veteran was taken aback.

"I've just finished my novitiate and I . . ."

"If you're my friend, Bakhen, you must join me in this fight."

"What can I do?"

"Like every other temple in the land, Karnak should be an example of rectitude. If that were not the case, what would your reaction be?"

"I'd haul in the wrongdoers and tan their hides, just like I did with my horses!"

"That's how you can help me, Bakhen. Bring me proof that no one here is disregarding the law of Ma'at."

Ramses left him, taking the path around the sacred lake as calmly as the other pure priests who had come to fill their vessels with holy water.

Bakhen was unable to reach an immediate decision. Karnak had become his home, his world. Still, he thought, doing Pharaoh's bidding was the highest calling of all.

In Thebes, the Syrian merchant Raia had acquired three fine market stalls in the center of town. Cooks from noble families bought his specialty meats, while their mistresses fought over his latest Asian vases.

Since the end of the official mourning period, business had picked up again. Courteous, enjoying an excellent reputation, Raia had a faithful and growing clientele. He paid his employees well and praised them lavishly, so they always spoke highly of him.

After seeing his barber out, the merchant stroked his newly trimmed goatee and set to work on his ledgers. His staff was instructed not to disturb him for any reason.

Raia mopped his brow. The summer heat was hard on him. Even worse was the setback he had just suffered. The young Greek he hired had failed to break into Ramses' office and report on which matters were receiving the new king's attention. A predictable enough outcome; however, the Syrian's main objective had been to test Ramses' security. Unfortunately, his and Serramanna's measures appeared highly effective. Obtaining accurate information would not be easy, although bribery was always a viable alternative.

The merchant pressed an ear to his office door. He heard nothing in the antechamber; no one was spying on him. Just to be sure, he hopped on a stool and peered through a tiny hole in the partition.

Reassured, he entered the storeroom full of small alabaster vases from southern Syria, an ally of Egypt's. His ladies were especially fond of these, so Raia displayed only one at a time to whet their appetite. He searched for the one with a tiny red dot beneath the lip. Inside was an oblong fragment of wood with the vase's dimensions and price marked on it.

The code was easy to decipher, and the message from his Hittite employers was clear: oppose Ramses and back Shaanar.

"Beautiful piece," cooed Shaanar, stroking the vase that Raia was showing him, in full view of the upper-crust clientele that would never dare outbid the king's older brother.

"The work of an old craftsman who'll take his secrets to the grave with him," said Raia.

"I can offer you six high-yielding dairy cows, an ebony bed, eight chairs, twenty pairs of sandals, and a bronze mirror."

The merchant bowed. "A most generous offer, Your Highness. Would you do me the honor of affixing your seal to my ledger?"

Raia steered the prince toward his office, where they could conclude matters in private.

"I have excellent news," he said once the door was shut. "Our foreign friends are most receptive to your plan and would like to back you."

"Under what conditions?"

"No conditions, no restrictions."

"It sounds too good to be true."

"We'll discuss the details later. For the moment, we have an agreement in principle. Consider this an important victory. Congratulations, sir: I feel as if I'm talking with Egypt's next pharaoh, no matter how long the road we may have to travel."

For Shaanar, it was a heady sensation. This secret alliance with the Hittites was as effective and dangerous as a deadly poison. He must determine how it could be used to destroy Ramses without harming himself or compromising Egypt's strength. It was like walking a tightrope across a precipice. He knew he could do it.

"What will you reply?" asked Raia.

"Send my thanks and tell them I'm hard at work . . . as the newly appointed secretary of state."

"A cabinet post!" said Raia, clearly astonished.

"Under close supervision."

"My friends and I will count on you to make the most of the situation."

"What your friends should do is make incursions into the weaker Egyptian protectorates, buy up princes and tribes Egypt thinks it controls, and spread as many false rumors as possible."

"For instance?"

"Oh, imminent territorial conquests, total annexation of Syria, invasion of Lebanese ports, low morale among the Egyptian troops in the territories . . . We'll heat up Ramses' cool head."

"Allow me to express my admiration."

"I'm full of ideas, Raia. Your friends won't regret their decision to work with me."

"Perhaps it's forward of me to hope that my own recommendations may have played some part?"

"On top of the official payment for the vase, there will be a sack of Nubian gold."

Shaanar returned to the front of the shop. A man of his rank would never linger in a merchant's office, no matter how well known his penchant for exotic vases.

Should he tell Ahsha about this secret alliance with Egypt's major enemy? No, he quickly intuited. It was better if the right hand never knew what the left hand was doing.

In the sultry shade of a sycamore, Queen Mother Tuya was chronicling her late husband's reign, commemorating the essential dates in a blessed era of peace and prosperity for Egypt. Seti's every thought, every deed was fresh in her mind. She had been attuned to his hopes and fears. She treasured the memory of the intimate moments when their souls had communed.

In this slight, frail woman, Seti lived on.

Watching Ramses come near her, Tuya saw the stamp of his father's authority. The new pharaoh was all of a piece, without the inconsistencies that plague most men. Like an obelisk, he seemed able to withstand the strongest tempest. His youth and strength added to the impression of invulnerability.

Ramses kissed his mother's hands and sat down on her right.

"You write all day long."

"Even all night. Would you forgive me if I left anything out? You look worried, son."

Tuya could always read his mood in a minute.

"The high priest of Amon is challenging my authority."

"Seti saw it coming. Sooner or later, the clash was inevitable."

"What would my father have done?"

"You know perfectly well. There's only one possible course of action."

"Nefertari said as much."

"She's the Queen of Egypt, and like every queen, guardian of the law of Ma'at."

"You don't preach moderation?"

"When the possibility of secession exists, there's no room for compromise."

"Dismissing a high priest of Amon will have serious repercussions."

"Only one of you can rule the country. Which will it be?"

TWENTY-THREE

The donkeys followed their leader through the gates of the temple enclosure. The old one's hooves knew every step from the weaving workshops to the temple storerooms. He held the others to a steady, dignified pace.

It was a full shipment. Bakhen had been sent to help another priest with the receiving. Each length of linen, to be used for vestments, was supposed to be tagged with a number and entered in a ledger with a note on its origin and quality.

"Good stuff," said Bakhen's co-worker, a foxy-faced little man. "Been here at Karnak long?"

"A few months."

"You like the life here?"

"It's what I expected."

"What do you do on the outside?"

"Nothing. I'm a full-fledged priest now."

"I serve two months at a time, then go back to town. Work as a ferry inspector, but not as hard as here! The pace is killing."

"Then why do you do it?"

"That's for me to know. Listen, I'll pick out the first-quality material. You log the rest."

When each donkey was unloaded, warehouse workers carefully laid the linen on a cloth-covered sledge. Bakhen inspected it and made entries on a wooden writing board, including the date of delivery. It seemed to him that his fellow receiver was not as busy as he claimed. The greater part of his time was spent glancing furtively in all directions.

"I'm thirsty," he said. "Care for a drink?"

"Gladly."

The foxy little lay priest left the storeroom. He'd set his log on the back of the lead donkey, where Bakhen could see it. There were only scribbled approximations of hieroglyphs, nothing to do with shipments of first-quality linen.

When the lay priest returned, his water skin full of cool liquid, Bakhen was already back at work.

"Here, take some . . . making us work in this heat is inhuman, anyhow."

"I don't hear the donkeys complaining."

"Very funny."

"Almost quitting time for you, isn't it?"

"I wish! The cloth still has to be routed for shelving."

"What do we do with our receiving logs?"

"Give me yours, and I'll turn it in with mine at the main office."

"Is that far from here?"

"It's a hike, but not too bad."

"You're senior to me. Why not let me do the walking?"

"Oh, no. They wouldn't know you at the office."

"Then I ought to introduce myself."

"You don't know the routine, and they don't like wasting time."

"I'll have to learn eventually."

"Thanks for the offer, but all the same, you'd better leave it to me."

The man seemed disconcerted. He moved away so that Bakhen couldn't see what he was recording in his log.

"Writer's cramp?" Bakhen inquired.

"No, I'm fine."

"Just one thing: do you even know how to write?"

The lay priest turned indignantly toward Bakhen. "Why do you ask?"

"I saw your log book there, on the donkey's back."

"Nosy, aren't you?"

"Who wouldn't be, with how little work you've been doing? If you want, I'll fill out the log for you. Otherwise, you're going to have trouble at the office."

"Don't play dumb with me, Bakhen."

"Is there something I'm missing?"

"Oh, all right. You want me to cut you in. I can understand that, but still, your first day on the job?"

"What's the deal?"

The foxy little man came closer and spoke in a confidential tone. "The temple is rich, the richest in Egypt. Priests are paid nothing. We have to manage. Karnak will never miss a length of linen here and there. Go for the quality, find regular customers, and you make out very well. See?"

"Is the office staff in on it, too?"

"Just one scribe and two warehouse foremen. Since the linen we take is never logged, there's no way to trace it. A pretty good setup, eh?"

"Aren't you afraid of getting caught?"

"It's foolproof."

"But if someone talked . . ."

"Even if they did, no one would get excited, believe me. Now tell me how much of a cut you want."

"The same as the scribe, or whoever gets the best deal."

"You've got nerve! I think we can work together. In a few years we'll both have a nice little nest egg and we won't have to work our tails off. How about finishing up this shipment?"

Bakhen nodded and went back to work.

Nefertari laid her head on Ramses' shoulder as the sunrise flooded their bedroom with light. Both of them venerated this daily miracle, this renewed victory over darkness. Celebrating the morning rites, they associated themselves with the solar bark's journey through the realms of darkness, the gods' nightly battle with the monster intent on destroying all of creation.

"I need your magic, Nefertari. This won't be an easy day."

"So your mother agrees with me about Karnak?"

"Sometimes I have the feeling you're in league with her."

"We do see things the same way," she admitted with a smile.

"The two of you have convinced me. Today I plan to dismiss the high priest of Amon."

"Why did you wait this long?"

"I needed proof of mismanagement."

"And you got it?"

"I put Bakhen on the case. My old combat instructor turned priest. He uncovered a ring of warehouse workers skimming linen and reselling it. That means the high priest is either corrupt himself or no longer knows what goes on at Karnak. In either case, he needs to be replaced."

"Is Bakhen trustworthy?"

"He's young, but devoted to Karnak. What he uncovered disturbed him deeply. He knew he was honor-bound to report the wrongdoing he witnessed, yet I practically had to drag it out of him. Bakhen would never inform on others for the sake of his own advancement."

"When will you be seeing the high priest?"

"First thing this morning. I'm sure he'll deny any involvement and claim I'm accusing him falsely."

"Why are you so hesitant?"

"I'm afraid he'll retaliate by interfering with food redistribution. That's the price I'll have to pay for avoiding civil war."

Her husband's grave tone impressed Nefertari. This was no tyrant locked in a power struggle with a rival, but a pharaoh willing to take huge risks to preserve the unity of the Two Lands.

"I have a confession to make," she said dreamily.

"You knew more than you were telling me about Karnak?"

"Nothing of the sort."

"Then my mother is using you as her messenger."

"Wrong again."

"Does it have anything to do with the high priest's dismissal?"

"No, though it may affect the future of the kingdom."

"How long do you plan to keep me in suspense?"

"A few more months. Ramses, I'm pregnant."

He sheltered Nefertari gently in his strong arms. "The best doctors in the country will be at your side every moment."

"Don't fret so."

"How can I keep from worrying? I want our child, but your life and health mean even more to me."

"I'll have the best possible care."

"Suppose I order you to cut back on your public appearances?"

"No. I'm your partner, remember?"

Ramses was growing restless. By now the high priest was so late that his conduct bordered on an insult. What possible excuse could he offer? If he'd gotten wind of Bakhen's revelations, he was probably trying to stall the investigation, destroying evidence and discharging ringleaders and witnesses—tactics that would ultimately backfire.

As the sun reached its zenith, the Fourth Prophet of Amon requested an audience. The king admitted him at once.

"Where is the First Prophet and High Priest of Amon?" he demanded.

"He died just before noon, Your Majesty."

TWENTY-FOUR

A conclave was held by order of the Pharaoh. In atten-
dance were the Second, Third, and Fourth Prophets of
Amon at Karnak, as well as the high priests and priestesses
of the nation's other major cult centers. The only ones
failing to heed the call were the prelates of Dendera and
Athribis, the former being too old and infirm to travel, the
latter too ill to leave his residence in the Delta. They were
represented by two delegates with full voting powers.

This distinguished company met in a hall of Tuthmosis
III's complex at Karnak, the pharaoh of whom it was said
"His Monument Shines like the Sun." Here the high priests
of Amon were ordained, here they received instruction in
their duties.

"I need to consult with you," declared Ramses, "to
choose the new head of this great institution."

There was a murmur of approval. Perhaps this young
pharaoh was not as impulsive as some claimed!

"I thought by rights the Second Prophet assumed his
functions," offered the high priest of Memphis.

"I don't consider seniority a sufficient criterion."

"May I encourage Your Majesty not to rule seniority out entirely?" chimed in the Third Prophet of Amon. "In the secular domain, it is no doubt possible to fill high positions from the outside, but that would be a mistake where Karnak is concerned. A man of experience, a man of honor—"

"Honor! Since you bring it up, were you aware that employees have been stealing temple property within these very walls?"

An astonished rumble greeted the king's revelation.

"The culprits have been arrested and sentenced to work as weavers, since their crime was reselling linen. They will never again set foot inside a temple."

"Our late prelate . . . was he implicated in the affair?"

"Apparently not, but you can understand why I'm hesitant to appoint one of his assistants."

A stunned silence greeted the Pharaoh's remarks.

"Does Your Majesty have a name to put forward?" asked the high priest of Heliopolis.

"I expect this conclave to propose a serious candidate."

"How much time do we have?"

"According to custom, it is now my duty to visit a certain number of towns and temples, accompanied by the queen and select members of the court. Upon my return, you will inform me of the outcome of your deliberations."

Before leaving on the tour of Egypt that was a traditional part of the first year of a pharaoh's reign, Ramses visited the temple of Gurnah, on the West Bank of Thebes. Here Seti's *ka* was maintained in perpetuity. Each day, specially trained mortuary priests placed offerings of meat, bread, fruits, and vegetables on the altars and recited litanies to safeguard the immortal presence of the late king's soul.

The king contemplated one of the reliefs that depicted his father, forever young, addressing the gods. Ramses implored Seti's spirit to come out of the stone, burst forth from the walls, and surround him with all the force of an astral being.

With each passing day, Ramses had grown more acutely aware of Seti's absence, until it became both a trial and a summons. A trial, because he could no longer seek the advice of a knowing, generous mentor; a summons, since his dead father's voice unceasingly urged him to forge ahead, no matter what obstacles lay in his path.

In plush Theban villas, under shopkeepers' awnings, on doorsteps where mothers sat nursing babies, the topic of conversation was the same: which members of the court would Ramses and Nefertari take with them on their tour of the Two Lands, as the new pharaoh staked his claim in the pantheon of gods?

Everyone knew someone who had firsthand knowledge from a source close to the king or from a palace employee. It was widely held that the royal fleet would first head south, to Aswan, then turn around and sail down the Nile to the Delta. The crews had been told that the pace would be intense, with frequent short stops. There was general rejoicing that this rite of passage would be accomplished in good time, that the new king and queen would maintain the harmonious law of Ma'at.

As soon as the fleet was under way, Ahmeni buried

Ramses in a pile of briefs he was supposed to study before meeting with the nine provincial leaders, the temple administrators, and the mayors of the major population centers. The king's private secretary provided him with a biography of each important personage he would meet, outlining career, family situation, stated avowed ambitions, relations with other political leaders. When the information was less than solid or had not been verified, Ahmeni made note of the fact.

"This is a gold mine!" Ramses exclaimed. "How many days and nights have you spent putting it together?"

"I don't keep track. My only concern is accurate information. Without that, what basis is there for government?"

"Just skimming your masterpiece, I see that Shaanar has a network of rich, influential supporters."

"Does that come as any surprise?"

"I didn't realize how broad his base is."

"More hearts and minds for you to win over."

"You're an optimist."

"You're the king and you're meant to reign. Everything else is besides the point."

"Don't you ever rest?"

"I can rest when I'm dead. As long as I'm your sandal-bearer, it's my job to smooth the way for you. I'm your advance man, aren't I? Now try this camp stool out for me."

The Pharaoh's folding stool consisted of a leather seat on a sturdy frame. The legs broadened into duck's heads, encrusted with ivory.

"I've drilled your entourage," Ahmeni assured him. "Everything will be taken care of along the way. Your meals will be up to palace standards."

"You're even serious about food," teased Ramses.

"First of all, good food guarantees long life. Second,

moderation in food and drink preserves energy and con-centration. I've sent couriers ahead instructing the mayors and high priests in the cities where we'll be stopping to find lodging for all the members of our group. You and the queen, of course, will stay in the palaces."

"Have you made arrangements for Nefertari?"

"What do you think?" Ahmeni huffed. "Your wife's condition is of national concern. Her cabin is well ventilated and as quiet as we can make it. Five physicians will be on call and you'll receive daily updates. Just one small problem . . ."

"Concerning Nefertari?"

"No, concerning the landing stages. I've had alarming reports about the state of certain river ports, but I'm skep-tical. I think the provincial governors are simply looking for another handout. Fair enough, in view of your tour, but you mustn't cave in to pressure. You'll have to decide each case as you see it."

"How are our relations with the two viziers?"

"Terrible, from their point of view, but from ours, excel-lent. The viziers of the north and south are solid public ser-vants, but overcautious. They live in fear of being fired. Keep them on. They'd never dare betray you."

"I was thinking . . ."

"Of appointing me vizier? I hope not. I'm of far more use to you in my present capacity. I can work behind the scenes, without a huge bureaucracy to drag me down."

"Tell me how the courtiers feel about being invited."

"Thrilled to be included, but not too happy about Serramanna's security checks. He views every one of them as a potential criminal. I register their complaints. Then I file them away. Your Sard is doing an excellent job, and he can't be too careful."

"My dog and my lion are helping, too."

"They'll be well looked after."

"How is Romay working out?"

"I've had glowing reports. You'd think he'd been your chief steward for ages. Your household has never run more smoothly. Your instinct didn't fail you."

"Is Nedjem having as much success?"

"He takes his role as secretary of agriculture very seriously. Spends a couple of hours every day quizzing me on administrative matters, then confers with his technical advisers. He won't see much of the scenery on this trip!"

"And my beloved brother?"

"Shaanar's ship is a floating palace. He's been hosting receptions right and left, proclaiming the future glories of Ramses' Egypt."

"And he thinks I'll fall for that?"

"It's not as insincere as you might think. He really seems excited about the appointment."

"Are you saying that Shaanar may actually begin to support me?"

"In his heart of hearts, of course not. But the man is clever and knows how far he can go. You had the foresight to indulge his taste for power and keep him in the limelight. Let's hope he enjoys it too much to make any trouble."

"Let's *pray* he does."

"Time for bed now. Tomorrow will be a long day: at least ten audiences and three receptions. Will your bunk be comfortable?"

"Bunk?" thought Ramses. He had a headrest, a mattress of plaited skeins of hemp attached to a mortise-and-tenon frame, with lion's feet on the four legs, a footrest decorated with cornflowers, poppies, and lotus blossoms to sweeten his sleep.

"You'll need more pillows," noted the secretary.

"One is enough."

"Heavens, no!" Ahmeni protested. "Look at this paltry excuse for a pillow," he said, plucking it from the head of the bed.

Then he recoiled, stiff with horror, as the black scorpion he had uncovered stirred and prepared to attack.

TWENTY-FIVE

Serramanna was nearly inconsolable. He simply couldn't fathom how a scorpion had been sneaked into the Pharaoh's cabin. Close questioning of the servants yielded no results.

"They're not involved," the Sard informed Ramses. "I need to talk to your chief steward."

Romay had little use for Serramanna, yet did not protest when the king requested him to cooperate in the investigation.

"How many of your staff have access to the royal bedchamber?" probed the bodyguard.

"Five. Well, five from the permanent staff."

"What does that mean?"

"Occasionally I need to use temporary workers."

"Any at our last stop?"

"I did hire one man to take the bed linens in to the local laundry."

"What was his name?"

"It's in the payroll ledger."

"Don't bother checking," said the king. "He would have used an assumed name, and besides, we won't have time to turn back and track him down."

"No one told me about this outside hiring! You've made a mockery of my security measures!"

"Has something happened?" asked Romay, staring.

"That's for me to know! In the future, I want to search every single person boarding His Majesty's ship. I don't care whether it's a general, a priest, or a street sweeper."

Romay turned toward Ramses, who nodded his agreement.

"What about meals?"

"One of your cooks will taste every dish under my supervision."

"As you like."

Once Romay was out of the cabin, Serramanna slammed his fist into a beam, so hard that the wood cracked. "That scorpion wouldn't have killed you, Majesty," the giant offered, "but it would have made you good and sick."

"And I'd have had to give up the rest of the tour . . . a sign of the gods' disapproval. That's how someone wanted to make it look."

"It won't happen again," promised the bodyguard.

"I'm afraid it may, as long as we don't know who's behind it."

Serramanna frowned.

"Do you suspect anyone?" asked the king.

"Men aren't always as grateful as they should be."

"Out with it, man."

"Romay is in the perfect position . . . He could have been lying about the outside help."

"Go ahead and investigate."

"It's my job," said Serramanna.

Stop after stop, the new king and queen's grand tour was a triumph. Ramses' presence and Nefertari's charm won over every provincial governor, high priest, mayor, and other notables. Ramses made sure not to downplay his older brother, considering Shaanar's extensive contacts and the general relief at his appointment to the State Department. In the first place, it showed that there was no serious division within the royal family; furthermore, the prince's love of country and vision for Egypt would guarantee a strong defense policy, essential for preserving civilization from barbarian attack.

In each new town, the royal pair paid homage to Tuya, who inspired reverence whenever she appeared. Frail, silent, low-key, Tuya's mere presence represented continuity and legitimacy.

As the fleet neared Abydos, the cult center of Osiris, Ramses summoned his friend Ahsha to the prow of the flagship. No matter what the hour or day, the young diplomat was unruffled and impeccable.

"Glad you came along, Ahsha?"

"Your Majesty is winning the hearts of his subjects, which is well and good."

"Everyone loves a pharaoh," said Ramses ironically.

"Even if you're dealing with hypocrites, at least they acknowledge your authority."

"What do you think of Shaanar's new position?"

"A bit unconventional."

"In other words, it shocked you."

"I have no right to question Pharaoh's decisions."

"Do you consider my brother incompetent?"

"In the current international climate, diplomacy is a highly skilled profession."

"Who would dare to challenge Egypt's might?"

"Your personal triumph here at home mustn't blind you to the Hittite threat. The enemy realizes you're going to take a hard line against them, so they'll dig in. They may even be considering direct aggression."

"Any precise indications?"

"Not yet. Just speculation on my part."

"You see, Ahsha, my brother is a good representative, the perfect host at receptions and banquets. Foreign ambassadors will be charmed by his speeches. Who knows, he may even begin to believe his own rhetoric! But he can't be effective if the temptation to work against me is too strong. I'm not convinced by his sudden change in attitude, and that's where you come in."

"What do you need me to do?"

"I'm appointing you chief of the Secret Service. As you know, that means you'll be in charge of a courier network connecting the entire kingdom, including every document that leaves Shaanar's hands."

"Are you ordering me to spy on him?"

"That will be one of your duties."

"Won't Shaanar suspect me?"

"I've warned him that his every move will be watched. That may help keep him honest."

"What if he finds a way around me?"

"You're too good to let that happen, my friend."

Approaching the sacred site of Abydos, Ramses felt heartsick. Everything here spoke to him of his father, the namesake of Set, the Destroyer, who slew his brother, Osiris. As an act of conciliation, Seti had built a magnificent sanctuary where the mysteries of Osiris's death and resurrection were celebrated. Ramses and Nefertari had been initiated into these mysteries, imprinting on their souls the certainty of eternal life, the promise of which they must in turn communicate to their people.

The banks of the canal leading to the temple landing were completely empty. Yes, this was holy ground; yes, Osiris's resurrection was a solemn celebration; all the same, the absence of a welcoming party took the royal entourage by surprise.

Serramanna was the first one off the ship, sword in hand and flanked by his fellow guardsmen. "I smell trouble," muttered the Sard.

Ramses was close behind. In the distance, behind a row of tall acacias, stood the temple of Osiris.

"Careful, now," warned Serramanna. "Let me have a look around first."

Sedition at Abydos? The king could hardly credit such a sacrilege.

"The chariots," he ordered. "I'll take the lead."

"But Majesty . . ."

He realized it would be futile to protest. Providing security for such an unreasonable monarch was a virtually impossible task.

The royal chariot drove briskly toward the temple enclosure. To Ramses' amazement, the outer gateway was open. Alighting, he entered the open-air forecourt.

The temple facade was covered with scaffolding. On the ground lay a statue of his father depicted as Osiris. Here and there, tools lay scattered. Not a workman was in sight.

In shock, the Pharaoh entered the sanctuary. No offerings on the altars, no priest reciting the daily rites.

The temple had evidently been abandoned.

Ramses emerged and hailed Serramanna, standing at attention by the gate.

"Go find the men in charge of the construction."

Relieved, the giant Sard sprang into action.

The young Pharaoh's anger blazed hot as the bright blue sky over Abydos. Serramanna and his men had rounded up the priests, administrators, temple personnel, and construction workers who were supposed to keep the temple running and in good order. Each of them bowed, bent his knee, and touched his nose to the ground, terror-stricken by the monarch's ringing voice as he lectured them on their laziness and negligence.

Ramses accepted no excuse. It was no use claiming that Seti's death had interrupted the temple's normal operation. If so, every crisis would cause them to panic and effectively shut down an important religious establishment.

Yet the harsh punishment they feared as he spoke was not forthcoming. The new ruler merely required them to double their offerings to his late father's *ka*. He ordered them to lay out an orchard, plant additional trees, gild the temple doors, return to their construction work and finish the statues, resume the daily rites. He announced that a bark would be built for use in the celebration of the mysteries of Osiris. The farmers working on temple lands would no longer pay shares to the government and the temple itself would receive generous grants, providing that it was never again allowed to fall into such a sorry state.

The men of Abydos filed silently out of the forecourt, thankful for the king's leniency and vowing not to provoke his anger a second time.

His fury spent, Ramses entered the central chapel, representing the heavens, where a secret light shone in the darkness. He communed with his father's soul, now one with the stars, as the bark of the sun continued its eternal voyage.

TWENTY-SIX

Shaanar was jubilant.

Not because of the near miss with the scorpion; he had never really expected Sary's latest scheme to work. The king's old tutor was too blind with hatred to think straight. Cutting Ramses down to size would be no easy task, Shaanar realized. Yet experience had taught him that even the strictest security measures could be breached.

No, Shaanar was jubilant because Ahsha, at the end of a

very successful dinner party, had just told him a fabulous bit of news. In the stern of Shaanar's ship, they could have a private conversation. The few guests still on deck had been drinking heavily, and the ship's physician was attending a high government official whose vomiting had captured the attention of the rest of the partygoers.

"Head of the Secret Service . . . I must be dreaming!"

"Effective immediately."

"And spying on me is part of your job, I suppose?"

"Exactly."

"To all appearances, then, I'll have no real freedom of movement and only be nominally in charge."

"That's how Ramses sees it."

"Then he'll be completely in the dark, Ahsha! I'll play my role to the hilt. And you, it seems, will become the king's chief adviser on Hittite policy?"

"Most likely."

"Does our agreement still suit you?"

"More than ever. I'm convinced that Ramses will be a tyrant. He's completely self-absorbed. His vanity will lead the country to ruin."

"My sentiments exactly. But will you back me all the way?"

"My position is firm."

"Why do you dislike Ramses so much, Ahsha?"

"Because he's Ramses."

Set in the lush green countryside, the temple of Dendera was a blend of divine and earthly beauty, a hymn of praise to Hathor, the goddess of love and joy. Tall sycamores planted around the enclosure shaded the main temple and its outbuildings, including the famous school of music and dance. As patroness of Hathor's priestesses, Nefertari had looked forward to this stop on the tour, hoping for a few hours of meditation within the closed sanctuary. After the incident at Abydos, the royal fleet had been forced to sail southward, but the queen refused to skip Dendera.

Ramses seemed lost in thought. "Is something on your mind?" Nefertari asked her husband.

"I'm thinking about the new high priest of Amon. Ahmeni prepared briefs on the likely candidates, but none of them has exactly what I'm looking for."

"Have you consulted with your mother?"

"She agrees with me. Seti passed them over in the first place; they're hoping I'll forget that."

As Nefertari studied the images of Hathor's face, stunningly beautiful in stone, a strange glow suddenly illuminated her gaze.

"Nefertari . . ."

Lost in her vision, she did not respond. Ramses took her hand, fearing she would leave him forever, transported to heaven by the sweet-faced goddess of love, until she sighed and nestled against him.

"I was far, far away . . . In a sea of light with a voice that sang to me."

"What did it say?"

"To forget the official candidates. We'll need to find the new high priest all by ourselves."

"I scarcely have time for that."

"Listen for the voices from on high, like every pharaoh since the dawn of time."

Attending the concert held in their honor, Nefertari listened blissfully as the women sang and danced in the temple garden. Ramses, however, seethed with impatience. Would he have to wait for a miracle to find a high priest of Amon untainted by personal ambition?

He wished he could return to the ship to talk it over with Ahmeni, but was obliged to tour the temple complex, the workshops and warehouses. Everything was as beautiful as it was orderly.

Ramses finally found solace by the shores of the sacred lake. The serene water, the lovely beds of irises and corn-flowers, the soft tread of priestesses coming to carry water for the evening rites, would have soothed the most troubled spirit.

Nearby, an old man was pulling weeds and tucking them into a sack. His gestures were slow but precise. On one bent knee, he kept his back turned to the king and queen. His irreverence could have earned him a reprimand, but he was so absorbed in his task that the king let the old man go about his work.

"Your flowers are wonderful," Nefertari told the gardener after a while.

"I say nice things to them," he replied gruffly. "If I don't, they grow crooked."

"I've noticed that, too."

"Oh? A pretty girl like you, digging around in the dirt?"

"I enjoy working in the garden, when my schedule permits."

"How busy can you be?"

"My work is rather time-consuming."

"Are you a priestess?"

"For one thing."

"Forgive me, madam. I don't mean to pry. You share my love of flowers; that's all I need to know."

The old man grimaced in pain. "My bad knee . . . sometimes it's hard for me to get back up."

Ramses reached out an arm to help him.

"Thank you, Prince. You *are* a prince, aren't you?"

"Does the high priest of Dendera force a man of your years to do manual labor?"

"He does."

"They say he's old and cranky, in poor health, unable to travel."

"So he is. Do you love flowers, like the pretty lady?"

"Planting trees is my favorite pastime. Could you tell me where I can find the high priest, old man? I'd like a word with him."

"What about?"

"I wonder why he isn't attending the conclave at Karnak that's helping to choose a replacement for the high priest of Amon."

"And if you were to leave an old servant of the gods alone with his flowers?"

By now Ramses was certain that the high priest of Dendera was none other than this old gardener. "I hardly think a bad knee would be enough to stop the head of Dendera from boarding a ship for Thebes."

"There's also the frozen shoulder, the aching back, the—"

"Is the high priest of Dendera unhappy with his lot, perchance?"

"On the contrary, Majesty. His only wish is to live out his days in peace within these temple walls."

"What if Pharaoh asked him personally to attend the conclave, to give his fellow prelates the benefit of his experience and insight?"

"If our young Pharaoh is already wise in the ways of men, he would spare a tired old servant. Now would Your Majesty kindly hand me that cane on the garden wall?"

The king did as he was asked.

"See for yourself, my lord, how lame poor Nebu is. Why force him out of his beautiful garden?"

"As high priest of Dendera, will you at least consent to give your king some advice?"

"At my age, the less said, the better."

"Not according to the sage Ptah-hotep, whose maxims have guided us since the age of the pyramids. I value your wisdom. Could you please tell me who you consider most qualified to become the new high priest of Amon?"

"I've spent my whole life in Dendera and never set foot in Thebes. I'm really in no position to answer. Excuse me, Your Majesty, but it's almost my bedtime."

Ramses and Nefertari spent part of the night on the flat roof of the temple. Thousands of souls glimmered in the night sky; the undying celestial bodies revolved around the Pole Star, at the axis of the Visible and the Invisible.

Then the royal couple withdrew into a palace with windows overlooking the countryside. Although their rooms were small and the furnishings rustic, for the short time before the first birdsong their chamber was a paradise. Nefertari had fallen asleep in Ramses' arms. They shared their dream of happiness.

After performing the morning rites, eating a copious breakfast, and bathing in the pool adjoining the palace, Ramses and Nefertari prepared to depart. The assembled clergy saluted them. All of a sudden, Ramses veered off from the procession and slipped into the garden, skirting the sacred lake.

Nebu was on his knees, casting a critical eye on the grouping of marigolds and larkspur he had just planted.

"How did you like the queen, Nebu?"

"What do you expect me to say, Majesty? She's the soul of beauty and intelligence."

"So her opinion would count with you."

"Her opinion on what?"

"I hate to take you away from your garden, but you need to come to Thebes with us, at the special request of the queen."

"But what on earth would I do there, Majesty?"

"Become the high priest at Karnak."

TWENTY-SEVEN

When the royal fleet docked at Karnak, lighting up the waters of the Nile, all of Thebes was bubbling with excitement. What was the meaning of the Pharaoh's unannounced return? Contradictory rumors spread like wildfire. Some were certain the king planned to cut the temple staff and reduce Thebes to the rank of a sleepy provincial capital. Others claimed Ramses had fallen sick and was returning to die with his face toward the Peak of the West. The young

Pharaoh's star had risen much too fast. Now the gods were taking their revenge.

Raia, the Hittite agent, fretted and fumed. He no longer seemed to have the inside track. Thanks to his network of trade contacts, including shopkeepers in the major population centers as well as traveling merchants, he had been able to track Ramses' progress along the Nile without ever leaving Thebes. Yet he had no explanation for the king's precipitous return. Ramses had stopped at Abydos according to schedule, but then instead of continuing north he had backtracked, stopping briefly in Dendera.

Ramses was hard to figure. He acted on the spur of the moment, without confiding in advisers whose loose lips would have provided grist for the Syrian's mill. Raia foresaw a whole new set of challenges. Ramses would make a formidable adversary, and Shaanar would be hard pressed to outmaneuver him. If open conflict ensued, the king might prove much more dangerous than Raia had calculated. It would never do now to wait and see. His first step must be a quick and decisive move to eliminate any weak links in his chain of informants.

In a blue crown and long, pleated linen robe, scepter in hand, Ramses was truly majestic. A hush fell when he entered the hall where the conclave was in progress.

"Have you come up with a name for me?" he asked.

"Majesty," declared the high priest of Heliopolis, "our deliberations continue."

"As of this moment, they're finished. Allow me to present the new high priest of Amon at Karnak."

An old man shuffled into the hall, leaning on his cane.

"Nebu!" exclaimed the high priest of Sais. "I thought you were too ill to travel!"

"I am, but Ramses performed a miracle."

"At your age," protested the Second Prophet of Amon, "you should be thinking about retirement. The administration of Karnak and Luxor is a daunting responsibility!"

"I quite agree, but the Pharaoh's will must be done."

"My decree is already written in stone," revealed Ramses. "Tablets will soon go up proclaiming Nebu's appointment. Do any of you consider him unfit to fill this position?"

There were no objections.

Ramses gave Nebu a golden ring and a staff of electrum, an alloy of gold and silver, as symbols of his office.

"I hereby name you high priest of Amon. The treasury and granaries of this great domain are now beneath your seal. As guardian of Amon's temples and estates, be scrupulous, honest, and vigilant. Work not for your own advancement but to increase the divine *ka*. Amon can fathom the human soul, read each person's mind and heart. If Amon is well satisfied, he will keep you at the head of his clergy, granting you long life and a happy old age. Do you swear to respect the law of Ma'at and fulfill your duties?"

"I swear on the Pharaoh's life," declared Nebu, bowing to Ramses.

The Second and Third Prophets of Amon were furious and humiliated. Not only had Ramses saddled them with a prelate who would be at his beck and call, he had also named a complete unknown, Bakhen, as Fourth Prophet.

This young zealot would back up the doddering high priest and become the real master of Karnak. The temple's independence would be compromised for years to come.

The two dignitaries no longer saw any way to maintain control over the richest domain in Egypt. Squeezed between Nebu and Bakhen, they would sooner or later be forced to resign, prematurely ending their careers. In their confusion, they groped for an ally. Shaanar immediately came to mind, but now that the king's older brother was a cabinet member, he might be singing a different tune.

Since he had nothing to lose, however, the Second Prophet arranged to meet Shaanar as the representative of all Karnak's clergy members unhappy with Ramses' decision. They met in an open summer house by a fish pond. A servant offered the Prophet a cup of carob juice and discreetly withdrew. Shaanar rolled up the papyrus he was studying.

"You look familiar."

"My name is Doki. I'm the Second Prophet of Amon."

The little man appealed to Shaanar. With his shaved head, narrow forehead, bulging eyes, long nose, and pointed chin, he resembled a crocodile.

"What can I do for you?"

"You'll probably think me too forward, but I'm not used to polite society."

"Get on with it, then."

"An old man named Nebu has just been named high priest and First Prophet of Amon."

"A position you hoped would be yours, unless I'm mistaken."

"Our late prelate made no secret of the fact that I was his chosen successor, but the king passed me over."

"It's dangerous to question his decisions."

"Nebu will never be able to manage Karnak."

"Bakhen, my brother's friend, will be the one really in charge."

"Forgive me for being blunt, Your Highness, but do you find this arrangement satisfactory?"

"I accept it as the Pharaoh's will."

Doki was disappointed. As he feared, Shaanar was in Ramses' camp now. He composed his crocodile face and rose to leave.

"I won't take any more of your time."

"Just a moment. If I understand you correctly, you refuse to accept the situation."

"The king is trying to undermine Amon's clergy."

"Do you have the means to oppose him?"

"I'm not alone."

"Whom do you represent?"

"The majority of the administration, as well as the priests."

"And are you prepared to act?"

"Sir, I beg your pardon! Outright sedition is not for the clergy."

"Make up your mind, Doki. You don't seem to know what you want."

"I need help."

"First prove to me that you're serious."

"But how?"

"That's for you to determine."

"I'm only a priest, a—"

"You're a man of action or you're a nobody. If all you're going to do is bemoan your fate, I'm not interested."

"What if I managed to discredit the Pharaoh's yes-men?"

"Do it first, then come and see me. You understand, though, that this conversation never took place."

Doki's spirits lifted. He left Shaanar's residence with a headful of impossible schemes. Sooner or later, he'd hit on one that would work.

Shaanar was skeptical. This Second Prophet had possibilities, but he seemed a bit indecisive. Once Doki realized what a serious step he'd taken, he'd probably back off. But no potential ally could be discounted, and this way he would find out what the little priest was made of.

Ramses, Moses, and Bakhen inspected the construction under way at Karnak, a project Seti had envisioned but left his son to complete: a vast hall of columns. Delivery of the huge stone blocks was on schedule. The various work gangs were coordinating their efforts to raise the towering pillars, which represented papyrus stalks rising from the primordial ooze.

"How are things going with your workmen?"

"Sary gave me some trouble, but I think I brought him back in line."

"What seems to be the problem?"

"He's too hard on his workers. I suspect that he's also skimping on their rations and pocketing the difference."

"Let's take him to court."

"I don't think that will be necessary," said Moses with a hint of amusement. "I'd rather be able to keep an eye on him. The moment he goes too far, I'll be on his case."

"If you press him, he may file countercharges."

"Never fear, Your Majesty. Sary's too much of a coward for that."

"Wasn't he your professor once?" interrupted Bakhen.

"Yes," answered Ramses. "And a good teacher, too. But something came over him. After what he did to me, most other men would have banished him to the desert. I'm hoping that honest work will straighten him out."

"It hasn't yet," said Moses, shaking his head.

"I know you'll get results, though it won't be here. In a few days we're heading north, and you're going to come along, Moses."

His friend looked less than pleased "The colonnade . . . it's not finished!"

"I'm putting Bakhen in charge as Fourth Prophet of Amon. You'll brief him before we go. He'll see to the hall's completion and also oversee my additions to Luxor. Rows of colossal statues in the forecourt, a pylon gateway, obelisks—it will be wonderful! Keep things moving, Bakhen. I may only be granted a short time to live, and I want to dedicate this masterpiece."

"I'm honored by the trust you place in me, Majesty."

"I don't name straw men, Bakhen. Old Nebu will do his job well, and so will you. He'll run the temple and the estates, you'll do the building. Both of you will alert me to any difficulties. Now get to work and forget about everything else."

Pharaoh and Moses left the construction site and walked down a lane of tamarisks toward the chapel of Ma'at, the goddess of truth and justice.

"This is where I come to meditate," the king confided. "It calms my spirit and helps me see more clearly. I envy the priests. The soul of the gods is in every stone here. Every chapel reveals their truths."

"Why are you taking me away from Karnak?"

"You and I have work to do. Remember when we were

schoolboys discussing the future with Ahsha, Ahmeni, and Setau? I was convinced that only Pharaoh had true power. I was drawn to it like a moth to a flame, and it would have consumed me if my father hadn't taken me in hand. Even when I'm at rest, that power moves in me, telling me to build."

"You have a new project?"

"On such a scale that I can't even tell you yet. I'll need to think more during the journey. If I decide to proceed, there's a major role for you."

"I have to admit you surprise me."

"Why?"

"I was sure you'd forget your old friends and concentrate on the court, the corridors of power."

"You misjudge me, Moses."

"But won't power change you?"

"A man changes according to the goals he sets himself. My sole concern is the glory of Egypt, and that will never change."

TWENTY-EIGHT

Sary fumed. The king's brother-in-law and former tutor, reduced to being foreman of a sorry bunch of brick-layers, when he had once headed the royal academy! With another of his old students, Moses, always on his back, the overgrown thug! Day after day, Sary found the physical hardship, the taunts, more difficult to bear. He had tried to turn the workers against the Hebrew superintendent, but Moses was so popular that the attempt failed miserably.

Yet Moses was only following orders. Sary knew he must start at the top. He wanted revenge, revenge on the source of all his unhappiness.

"I hate him, too," admitted his wife, Dolora, nestling deeper into her pillows. "But what you're proposing scares me half to death."

"What have we got to lose?"

"I'm afraid, darling. Schemes like this have been known to backfire."

"So? Right now you're a social outcast; I'm literally cov-ered with mud. How can we go on like this?"

"I understand, Sary, really I do. But would we have to go that far?"

"Are you with me, or will I have to do it alone?"

"I'm your wife." He helped her to her feet.

"Have you thought it over carefully?"

"I've thought of nothing else for the last month."

"What if word gets out that we—"

"Not a chance."

"How can you be so sure?"

"I've covered everything."

"Is that really possible?"

"You have my word."

"Isn't there any way around—"

"No, Dolora. Now, are you with me?"

"Let's go."

Inconspicuously dressed, the pair walked down a lane leading to a section of Thebes where many immigrant workers lived. Dolora clutched her husband's arm nervously, hesitating at every turn.

"Are we lost, Sary?"

"Of course not."

"Are we almost there?"

"Not much farther now."

Inquisitive stares greeted them. But Sary marched stubbornly on as his wife grew increasingly apprehensive.

"Here we are."

He knocked at a low red door with a dead scorpion nailed to it. An old woman answered. The couple went down a wooden stairway leading to a sort of small, damp grotto ablaze with oil lamps.

"He's here," announced the old woman. "Sit on these stools and wait."

Dolora preferred to remain standing. The place gave her the shivers. Black magic was against the law in Egypt, yet certain sorcerers still dared to sell their services at exorbitant prices.

The plump and obsequious Lebanese magician padded toward his clients.

"Everything is ready," he announced. "And the consideration?"

Sary emptied a leather pouch into the man's right hand: ten chunks of perfect turquoise.

"The object you are purchasing has been placed within the grotto. Next to it you will find a fish bone. Use that to write the name of the person upon whom your spell is cast. Once you smash the charm, that person will fall ill."

As the magician spoke, Dolora retreated behind her shawl. When he left, she grabbed her husband by the wrists.

"Let's leave. I can't bear it!"

"Steady. It's almost over."

"Ramses is my brother!"

"He *was* your brother. Now he's our worst enemy. No one will help us, Dolora. We have to help ourselves. It's safe; he'll never be able to trace us."

"There's no other way?"

"It's too late to back out, Dolora."

Deep in the grotto, on a sort of altar painted with crude designs of grotesque animals and leering faces, sat a thin limestone tablet and a long fish bone whittled to a point. The stone was speckled with brown. The magician had probably soaked it in snake's blood to make the spell even deadlier.

Sary began to scratch the hieroglyphic symbols for Ramses' name into the limestone. His wife shut her eyes in horror.

"Now you," he ordered.

"No, I can't."

"The spell won't work unless it's performed by a married couple."

"I don't want to kill my brother!"

"He won't die. The magician swears it. He'll become an invalid, Shaanar will become his regent, and we can go back to Memphis."

"I can't."

Sary placed the fish bone in his wife's right hand and closed her fingers around it.

"Write 'Ramses.' "

He guided her trembling hand as she completed the crude inscription. Now for the last step: breaking the tablet. Sary picked it up, while Dolora again hid her face. She refused to witness such depravity.

Hard as he tried, Sary could not smash the tablet. The thin limestone seemed hard as granite. He groped for a rock on the floor of the grotto and angrily pounded the magic tablet, but could not even make a dent in it.

"I don't understand. It's only limestone, it's thin . . ."

"Ramses is protected," screamed his wife. "Nothing can harm him, not even black magic! Let's leave here as fast as we can."

Sary and Dolora wandered through the unfamiliar streets. With a panicky feeling in the pit of his stomach, Sary was having trouble retracing his steps. Doors slammed in their faces, eyes peered from slits in shutters. Despite the heat, Dolora still huddled behind her shawl.

A thin man with a hawklike profile approached them, an eerie gleam in his dark green eyes.

"Might you be lost?"

"No," replied Sary. "Out of our way!"

"Just trying to help."

"We're all right."

"These streets can be dangerous."

"We can take care of ourselves."

"You wouldn't stand a chance against armed bandits. A man carrying precious stones is asking for trouble in these parts."

"I'm carrying nothing of the sort."

"You paid the Lebanese magician in turquoise, didn't you?"

Dolora clung more tightly to her husband.

"Do you believe everything you hear?" countered Sary.

"Both of you were careless. I believe you forgot something?" The thin dark man produced the slab of limestone bearing Ramses' name.

Dolora turned away and buried her head on her husband's shoulder.

"Are you aware that an act of black magic perpetrated against Pharaoh is punishable by death? Rest assured, however, I have no intention of turning you in."

"What do you want?"

"To help, as I already told you. See the house to your left? Go inside, your wife needs something to drink."

The dirt-floored dwelling was humble but clean. A plump young blonde helped Sary ease his wife onto a wooden bench with a reed mat on top of it, then fetched Dolora some water.

"My name is Ofir," said the thin dark man. "And this is Lita, great-granddaughter of Akhenaton and rightful heir to the throne of Egypt."

Sary was too amazed to speak. Dolora was slowly coming around.

"Is this some kind of joke?"

"It's the truth."

Sary turned toward the fair young woman. "Is this man lying?"

Lita shook her head, retreating into a corner of the room, as if removed from her surroundings.

"Don't mind her," Ofir advised. "She's been through so much that the road back to normal life will be long and difficult."

"What happened to her?"

"As a child, she was threatened with death, beaten, imprisoned, forced to renounce her faith in Aton, the One God, and ordered to forget her name and her parents. In other words, they tried to destroy her soul. If I hadn't come along, she'd be no more than a raving maniac."

"Why are you helping her?"

"Because my own family was persecuted, like hers. We live only to seek our revenge, which will place Lita on the throne of Egypt and banish false gods from this holy land."

"Ramses isn't the cause of your suffering!"

"Of course he is. He belongs to an evil dynasty that has deluded and tyrannized the people."

"How do you manage to live?"

"Aton still has his followers, who give us food and shelter in the hope that our prayers will be answered."

"There can't be many left."

"More than you'd imagine, but completely underground. Even if Lita and I were the only two, we'd keep on fighting."

"A tired old heresy," protested Ramses' sister. "No one cares a thing about it anymore."

"*You* should," Ofir said firmly.

"Let's get out of here," begged Dolora. "These people are out of their minds."

"I know who you are," revealed Ofir.

"You don't!"

"Dolora, the Pharaoh's sister, and your husband, Sary, who used to be Ramses' tutor. He's mistreated you both and you want revenge."

"That's no concern of yours."

"I retrieved the fragment of limestone you used to cast a spell on him. If I bring it to the vizier and testify against you . . ."

"This is blackmail!"

"Join our cause and the evidence disappears."

"What's in it for us?" asked Sary.

"Using magic against Ramses is an interesting concept, but not just any magic will work. The spell you tried would have been adequate for a mere mortal, but not a king. At his coronation, Pharaoh's body was surrounded with special protective forces. They need to be removed, layer by layer. Lita and I can see to that."

"What do you ask in exchange?"

"Bed and board, a place where our followers can meet in secret."

"Don't listen," Dolora whispered to her husband. "The man is dangerous. No good will come of this."

Sary turned to face the sorcerer.

"It's a deal," he said.

TWENTY-NINE

Ramses lit the oil lamps to reveal the *naos*, Karnak's innermost sanctuary, which he alone was allowed to enter, or the high priest as his designate. The shadows parted to reveal the holy of holies, a pink granite chapel containing the earthly image of Amon, "The Hidden One," whose true form no human being would ever know. Slowly burning incense cones perfumed this most sacred of places, where divine energy became incarnate in both the Visible and the Invisible.

The king broke the clay seal affixed to the door, pulled the latch to the *naos*, and opened the doors of the reliquary.

"Wake in peace, creator of all life. Look upon your son whose heart is full of love for you, who comes to seek your counsel so that his every deed fulfills your purpose. Wake in peace and shine upon this earth that lives only through your love. Let your divine energy flow through every living thing."

The king shone the light on the holy statue, unwrapped the colored bands of linen around it, purified it with water from the sacred lake, anointed it with unguents, and rewrapped it with fresh, clean cloth. Then, bringing them to

life with his voice, the Pharaoh presented the offerings—
the same ones the priests would be placing on every altar at
Karnak—a ritual followed each morning in every temple
throughout the land.

At last came the supreme offering, in the name of Ma'at,
the immortal law.

"Through her you live," the king told Amon. "Her fragrance invigorates you, her dew nourishes you. Your eyes are
the law, your whole being is the law."

Leaving the Divine Power with a fraternal embrace,
Pharaoh closed the doors of the *naos*, latched it shut, and
resealed it with clay. As high priest, Nebu would next perform this rite in Ramses' name.

When Ramses left the *naos*, the entire temple was astir.
Priests were clearing the altars of the portion of consecrated food that was designated for human consumption;
breads and cakes were coming out of the temple ovens;
butchers were cutting meat for the noon meal, craftsmen
beginning their day's work, and gardeners cutting flowers
for the chapels. The day would be peaceful and happy.

Close behind Serramanna, Ramses' chariot headed for
the Valley of the Kings. Despite the early hour, the day was
already torrid. Nefertari rode serene, though mindful of the
heat. A damp cloth around her neck, as well as a parasol,
helped keep her cool in the blazing valley.

Before returning to Memphis, Ramses wished to see his
father's tomb once more and pray before the sarcophagus,
known as "master of life" because deep inside this golden
chamber Seti's soul lived on.

The two chariots came to a halt in front of the narrow entrance to the Valley. Ramses helped Nefertari down, while Serramanna, despite the security measures already in place, had a look around. Even here, he did not rest easy. The Sard inspected the guard detachment controlling access to the Valley and noted nothing amiss in their behavior.

To Nefertari's surprise, Ramses did not head straight for the tombs of Seti and his father, Ramses I, which sat side by side. Instead, he veered to the right, toward a site where workmen hacked at the rock, swept up the chips, and carted them away.

A master builder from the company of Deir el-Medina had his scrolls spread over several blocks of polished stone. He bowed to the royal pair.

"This is where I'm building my tomb," Ramses informed his wife.

"So soon?"

"In the very first year of his reign, a pharaoh must see work begun on his house of eternity."

The veil of sadness that had fallen over Nefertari's face now lifted. "Death is our constant companion," she agreed. "Being prepared can only ease the passage."

"Does this seem like a good spot to you?"

The queen turned slowly around, as if taking possession of the place, sounding out the rock and the depths of the earth. Then she stood very still, eyes shut tight.

"It will be your resting place," she affirmed.

Ramses held her close.

"Even though Ma'at requires that your body must lie in the Valley of the Queens, the two of us will never be separated," he told her. "Your tomb will be the most beautiful ever created in this hallowed land. The story of our love will be told through the centuries."

The Valley's powerful spell and the grave import of the moment forged a new link between the king and queen. The stone carvers, quarrymen, and master builder sensed its luminous intensity. They were a man and a woman in love; above and beyond that, they were a pharaoh and his consort, whose life and death bore the stamp of the eternal.

The day's work had been interrupted, the tools fell silent. Each workman felt mysteriously connected to the royal pair, without whom the Nile would stop flowing, no fish would leap in its currents, no birds would fly, the breath of life would desert humanity.

Ramses and Nefertari broke from their embrace, still holding each other's gaze. They had just crossed the threshold into a marriage of true minds.

As the men began to swing their picks once more, Ramses approached the master builder.

"Show me your plans," the king ordered, then studied the drawings.

"The first corridor needs to be longer. Add a forechamber with four pillars. Go deeper into the rock here and open out the Hall of Ma'at."

Taking the brush the master builder held out to him, the king sketched his modifications in red, specifying the required dimensions.

"Starting from the Hall of Ma'at, we'll angle right into a short, narrow passageway leading to the golden chamber, with eight pillars. The sarcophagus will lie in the center. Put in several radiating chapels for the funerary furnishings. What do you think?"

"Technically, it's quite feasible, Majesty."

"Let me know immediately if you run into problems during construction."

"My job is to make sure there aren't any."

The royal couple and their escorts left the Valley of the Kings and turned back toward the Nile. Since the king had not informed Serramanna of their destination, the bodyguard scanned the surrounding hilltops carefully. Ramses was by nature so audacious that keeping him safe was virtually impossible. One day his luck was bound to run out.

At the edge of the cultivation, the royal chariot took a sharp right, passing in front of the nobility's necropolis and the funerary temple of Tuthmosis III, the illustrious pharaoh who had pacified Asia and assured Egyptian domination throughout the Near East and beyond.

Ramses stopped at an empty spot at the edge of the desert, not far from the workmen's settlement. Serramanna immediately ordered his men to fan out; a potential attacker could be lurking in the wheat fields to their rear.

"What do you think of this place, Nefertari?"

The lithe and elegant young queen had taken off her sandals, the better to gauge the energy coming from the earth. Her bare feet trod lightly on the burning sand as she paced, circled, and came to rest on a flat stone in the shade of a palm tree.

"Power dwells here, exactly like the power within your heart."

Ramses knelt and gently massaged his queen's delicate feet.

"Yesterday," she confessed, "I had a strange, almost frightening sensation."

"Can you describe it?"

"You were lying safe inside a sort of stone shell.

Someone was tying to break the stone, to remove the protection and destroy you."

"Did it work?"

"My spirit clashed with the dark force and overcame it. The stone remained intact."

"A bad dream?"

"No, I was awake. I *saw* it, far away, but real, so real . . ."

"Are you better now?"

"Not completely. I still feel uneasy, as if someone is hiding in the shadows, out of reach, intent on hurting you."

"I have countless enemies, Nefertari, is it any wonder? They'd stoop to anything. Either I never do anything that would put me in danger—meaning nothing at all—or I simply go about my business. I choose to go forward."

"Then it's my duty to protect you."

"Serramanna takes care of that."

"He'll counter any physical attacks on you, but what about the invisible ones? That will be my role, Ramses. My love will surround you with a wall no evil can penetrate. But it's not enough. We need more . . ."

"What do you have in mind?"

"Something to preserve your name and your life for good."

"It will be born here, on the soil your bare feet have trodden. I know you've seen it, a massive guardian with a body of stone, a soul made of everything that endures. On this spot I'll build my Eternal Temple, the Ramesseum. I want us to conceive it together, like our child."

THIRTY

Serramanna groomed his whiskers, put on perfumed oils, dressed in a purple tunic with a flared collar, and checked his haircut in a mirror. Considering what he planned to say to Ramses, he needed to look respectable, like someone whose opinion counted. He had hesitated long enough. His suspicions had grown so strong that he had to get them off his chest.

He approached the king in his dressing room. Ramses would be receptive when it was bright and early.

"You're looking smart," said Ramses. "Don't tell me you're quitting as captain of my bodyguard to become a haberdasher!"

"I thought . . ."

"You thought that considering the delicate nature of your business, you'd better put a good face on it?"

"Who told you?"

"Just a guess."

"I'm right, Majesty!" blurted the Sard.

"You do have a way with words, Serramanna. Now explain yourself."

"The scorpion that was supposed to put you out of commission . . . someone planted it in your room."

"Obviously. Go on."

"It bothered me to have that happen, so I investigated."

"And you don't like what you found."

"No, Your Majesty, I don't."

"Are you afraid, Serramanna?"

The color drained from the Sard's broad face. Anyone but the Pharaoh of Egypt would have earned a punch in the mouth for such an insult.

"I'm responsible for your security, Majesty. You don't always make it easy."

"Are you saying I'm unpredictable?"

"If you could slow down a bit . . ."

"You'd be bored."

"Even when I was a pirate, I liked to do a good job."

"What's stopping you?"

"Passive protection is no problem, but am I allowed to go any further?"

"Out with it, man."

"I suspect someone close to you. Whoever sneaked in the scorpion had to know the location of your cabin."

"That could be any number of people."

"Possibly, but my instincts tell me I'm close to fingering a suspect."

"Fingering?"

"Well, I have my methods."

"Justice is the basis of Egyptian society, my friend. As the first servant of the law of Ma'at, Pharaoh is not above the law."

"In other words, I'll receive no official order to proceed."

"Wouldn't it only get in the way?"

"I understand," said Serramanna with a gleam in his eyes.

"I'm not sure you do, Serramanna. Follow your instincts, but take care. I won't have you roughing people up. Official order or no, I consider myself responsible for your actions."

"No one will get hurt."

"Give me your word."

"Do you trust a pirate?"

"A man of courage knows how to keep his word."

"When I say 'hurt,' I mean . . ."

"Give it, Serramanna."

"All right, Your Majesty. You have my word."

A spotless palace was one of Romay's obsessions. As Ramses' new chief steward, he was responsible for the king's personal comfort. The sweepers, floor scrubbers, and other cleaning personnel were busy as bees under the direction of a finicky scribe who hoped to bolster his position by pleasing Romay. He checked every job and was quick to threaten salary cuts for substandard performance.

Night was falling when the scribe left the sparkling-clean palace. Tired and thirsty, he made haste toward a tavern where they served his favorite beer. As he passed through a narrow street packed with laden donkeys, he was grabbed by the collar of his tunic and dragged backward into a darkened shop. The door slammed shut behind him. Frightened out of his wits, the palace official did not even cry out.

Two enormous hands gripped his neck.

"You're going to talk, scum!"

"Let go! You're choking me."

Serramanna loosened his grip.

"You follow the boss man's orders, eh?"

"Boss man?"

"Romay, the chief steward?"

"You can't fault my work."

"Romay hates Ramses, doesn't he?"

"I don't know. No, no, I don't think so. And I'm the king's faithful servant!"

"Romay is a scorpion fancier, I hear."

"Scorpions? He's scared to death of them."

"You're lying."

"No, it's the truth, I swear!"

"You've seen him handle scorpions."

"Never!"

The Sard began to have doubts. Usually, this method yielded excellent results. The man did appear to be telling the truth.

"Are you looking for someone who handles scorpions?" the scribe ventured.

"You know of someone?"

"A friend of the king's called Setau . . . he lives for his snakes and scorpions. They say he even speaks their language and they obey him."

"Where can I find this Setau?"

"He has a laboratory in the desert outside Memphis. His wife is a Nubian sorceress, as strange as he is."

Serramanna released his captive, who rubbed his neck and breathed deeply.

"Can I go now?"

The Sard shooed him away. "Wait," he said suddenly. "I didn't hurt you, did I?"

"No, not at all."

"Go, but never tell anyone we spoke, unless you'd like to test my grip again."

The scribe bolted into the darkness. Serramanna walked

calmly out of the shop and headed in the opposite direction.

His instincts had pointed toward Romay. After his sudden promotion, the steward was in the ideal position to harm the king. He was also the type of man Serramanna mistrusted; a jovial facade often cloaked ruthless ambition. Still, he might as well admit he'd been wrong about Romay, since the mistake had provided him with an interesting prospect.

Interesting, but tricky. Ramses held friendship sacred. Going after Setau would be risky, especially considering his defense capabilities. Nevertheless, Serramanna was honor-bound to follow every lead. As soon as they returned to Memphis, he would pay very special attention to this unconventional couple who lived on such easy terms with reptiles.

"I've received no complaints about you," noted Ramses a few days later.

"I've kept my promise, Majesty," Serramanna asserted.

"Are you quite sure?"

"Sure as can be."

"Any results?"

"Not yet."

"No new developments?"

"Only one false lead."

"But you haven't given up, I take it."

"My job is to protect you . . . within the limits of the law, of course."

"Is there anything you're neglecting to mention, Serramanna?"

"Do you think I'd be able to, Majesty?"

"Who knows what a pirate might do?"

"A *former* pirate. I like my new life too much to take needless risks."

Ramses' eyes narrowed. "Your prime suspect wasn't the right one, but you want to keep trying."

Serramanna nodded evasively.

"For the time being, you'll have to call off the investigation."

The giant Sard was crestfallen. "I was careful, just as I promised . . ."

"Not because of anything you've done—but because tomorrow we're leaving for Memphis."

THIRTY-ONE

Romay was swamped with preparations for moving the court from Thebes to Memphis. Not a single society lady must miss her pot of rouge, not a single gentleman must want for a comfortable chair. Meals on board ship must be the same high quality as in any royal palace. Ramses' dog and lion must enjoy a plentiful and varied

diet. Then there was the cook who had fallen ill, the wash-
erman who was late, the weaver who had mixed up the
towel order . . .

But Ramses had spoken, and Romay would obey. He had
expected to spend his life refining his prize recipes. Now he
was struck with admiration for this demanding and ambitious young pharaoh. Yes, Ramses was hard on his
entourage. He could appear intolerant, and burned with a
fire that might singe those who ventured too near. But he
was as fascinating as the falcon with wings outspread, protecting the sky. Romay wanted to prove himself to his king,
even at the expense of his own peace of mind.

The steward, personally carrying a basket of fresh figs,
arrived at the gangway to the royal flagship. Serramanna
blocked his path.

"Mandatory search."

"I'm His Majesty's steward!"

"Mandatory search," repeated the bodyguard.

"Are you trying to provoke an incident?"

"Are you trying to hide something?"

Romay looked shaken. "What do you mean?"

"Are you or aren't you?" growled Serramanna.

"I think you've finally gone off the deep end, Sard. All
right, if you're so security-conscious, take this basket to the
king yourself. I have a thousand other things to do."

Serramanna lifted the white cloth covering the basket.
The figs were gorgeous, but what evil might they conceal?
One by one, he gingerly lifted out each piece of fruit and
set it aside, fully expecting to see a scorpion's deadly tail
darting out at him.

When the basket was empty, there was nothing to do but
refill it, taking care not to bruise the perfectly ripened fruit.

Iset the Fair was lovelier than ever.

She bowed to Ramses, weak-kneed as any young noble-woman newly presented at court.

Firmly and tenderly, he helped her up.

"You weren't always such a fragile flower."

"No, Majesty," she acquiesced, her face grave, almost anxious, but her eyes smiling.

"Is something worrying you?"

"May I speak confidentially?"

They sat side by side on low chairs. "I can spare a few minutes," said the king.

"That's all?"

"My time is no longer my own, Iset. I have more work than there are hours in the day, which is as it should be."

"You're moving the court to Memphis."

"Correct."

"I've received no directive . . . am I to go with you or stay here in Thebes?"

"Do you understand the reason for my silence?"

"I've been trying to."

"The decision is up to you, Iset."

"Why?"

"I love Nefertari."

"You love me, too, don't you?"

"You ought to hate me."

"You rule an empire, but can you see into a woman's heart? Nefertari is special, unique, and I know it. But no one can stop me from loving you—not you, not your wife, not even the gods—no matter what place you give me in your life. Why shouldn't a lesser wife glean every scrap of happiness she can? Seeing you, talking to you, sharing a few stolen moments of your day, is all that keeps me going. Why should I have to give it up?"

"Then you've already made up your mind."

"Yes. I'm coming to Memphis with the court."

Forty or more boats sailed from Thebes to the cheers of the ever-growing crowd that Ramses and Nefertari attracted. The new high priest had assumed control without incident, the mayor and vizier retained their positions. The court had thrown elaborate banquets. The people rejoiced because the Nile had risen sufficiently to guarantee their continued prosperity.

Romay allowed himself a rare break in his activities. Everything on board the flagship was perfectly under control, unless you counted Serramanna. The Sard seemed to have some grudge against him. An unannounced search of every cabin and each crew member was his latest move. Someday the lummox would be cut down to size, and no one would mind. His lack of respect for social position had already earned him an impressive number of enemies. Only the king's support kept him in his job. But would he last?

The steward smoothed the already perfect bed linens, steadied the armchairs, rechecked the table settings, and bustled up to the bridge with a skin of cool water for the king's pets to share as they lay on their shaded platform.

From one of the windows of Nefertari's spacious cabin, Ramses observed the steward, amused and pleased.

"I've finally found a steward who thinks it's more than an

honorary position," he commented. "Quite an accomplish-
ment, in my book."

A hint of fatigue dulled his wife's habitual glow. Ramses
sat down on the bed and held her to him.

"Serramanna would hardly agree with you. He and
Romay have taken a dislike to each other."

The king was astounded. "Why on earth . . ."

"Serramanna seems to suspect him of something."

"It doesn't make sense."

"Let's hope not."

"Don't you trust him, either?"

"He hasn't been with us long."

"But I've given him his chance to shine."

"After a while, he'll forget that."

"You're pessimistic today."

"I hope Romay proves me wrong."

"Have you any reason to doubt his loyalty?"

"No, it's only that Serramanna makes me wonder."

"You know how I count on your opinion . . ."

She laid her head on his shoulder. "No one can be indif-
ferent to you, Ramses. They're either for you or against you.
Your power is too much for some people."

The king stretched out on his back. Nefertari snuggled
against him.

"My father's power was certainly greater than mine."

"You're the same, but different. Seti imposed his
authority without having to say a single word. His force was
hidden. You're like a fire, a raging river. You blaze a trail
without a thought for the difficulties ahead."

"I have a plan, Nefertari, an important new plan."

"Only one?" she teased.

"This one is really big. Ever since the coronation, I've

had a vision. It can't be denied, and if my plan succeeds, it will change the face of Egypt."

Nefertari soothed her husband's forehead. "Can you call it a plan, or is it still a dream?"

"I can make my dream a reality, but I'm waiting for a sign."

"I thought you were sure."

"I am, but I can't move ahead without the gods' approval."

"Do you want to keep it a secret?"

"Just putting it into words seems daring at this stage, but as Great Royal Wife, you should be the first to know."

Ramses explained and Nefertari listened. Yes, the plan was important, almost too important for words.

"You're wise to wait for a sign," she concluded. "I'll help you look for it."

"If it doesn't come . . ."

"A sign will come, if we know how to read it properly."

Ramses sat up and looked at his queen, who was hailed Beauty Among Beauties throughout the land. She was the womanly ideal of ancient love songs, with limbs of porcelain and turquoise, her slender body as restful as heavenly waters.

The king gently laid his ear on his wife's firm stomach.

"Do you feel our child growing?"

"This one will be strong, I promise you."

One of the straps of Nefertari's dress had slipped off her shoulder to reveal the swell of her bosom. Ramses bit the gauzy linen, baring his wife's sublime breasts. In her eyes he saw the flow of the celestial Nile, the well of desire, the magic of two bodies joined in a love without limits.

THIRTY-TWO

For the first time since his coronation, Ramses set foot in his father's office in Memphis. Bare white walls, three high barred windows, one large table, a straight-backed armchair for the king and chairs with woven seats for visitors, a chest for papyrus.

Intense emotion choked him.

Seti's spirit still moved in this austere study where he had spent so many days and nights at work, governing Egypt, keeping his country secure and happy. The room spoke to Ramses not of death, but of an invincible spirit.

Tradition dictated that each new pharaoh should build his own home, create his own surroundings. Ramses was expected to order this building pulled down. And such had been his intention, until he stepped inside the space once more.

From one of the windows, Ramses could see the inner courtyard where the royal chariot was housed. Then he touched the desk, opened the chest containing blank papyrus, and sat on the straight-backed chair.

Seti's soul did not turn him away.

The son had succeeded the father, the father accepted the son as Lord of the Two Lands. Ramses would keep the office intact and work here whenever he was residing in Memphis. It would stay plain as he found it, a precious reminder of the essential.

On the table sat two springy twigs from an acacia tree, lashed together at the bottom. This was the diviner's rod Seti had used to find water when their expedition was lost in the desert. It had marked a turning point in Ramses' education in the art of kingship. Seti had shown him that Pharaoh must master the elements, the very mystery of creation. Pharaoh must go to the heart of all matter and draw on its hidden powers.

For Pharaoh was more than a head of state. He was also a conduit to the Invisible.

With his age-stiffened fingers, Homer packed his mixture of sage leaves into the bowl of his pipe, an oversized snail shell that was finally seasoned to his satisfaction. Between two puffs, he treated himself to a sip of full-bodied wine, flavored with anise and coriander. Thus was the old Greek poet enjoying the cool of evening, in a comfortable armchair beneath his beloved lemon tree, when the maid announced a visit from the king.

As Ramses came into his limited view, Homer was astonished at how regal he had become. The poet struggled to his feet.

"Please don't get up."

"Majesty, how you've changed!"

"Majesty? Aren't we becoming high-toned!"

"You've been crowned king of Egypt. A monarch of your bearing commands respect. I can tell that you're not the hotheaded young man I used to lecture . . . though I hope Pharaoh still listens to me."

"I'm happy to see you continue in good health. Do your living conditions still suit you?"

"The maid is finally used to me, the gardener is quiet, the cook is a treasure, and the scribe who takes down my verses seems to approve of them. What more could I ask?"

Hector, the black and white cat, jumped into the poet's lap and began to purr.

As was his habit, Homer had rubbed his whole body with olive oil. Nothing could be more healthful or smell better, according to him.

"Making progress with your poem?"

"Listen to how I have Zeus address the immortals: '*Attach a golden cord to the sky, and when I have a mind to pull, I can drag up all the earth and sea, tie it around the horn of Olympus, and leave this world dangling in the air.*' Not too bad, eh?"

"In other words, I'm new on the throne and Egypt is up in the air."

"How would I know, sitting here in my garden?"

"Your muse and the servants' gossip should keep you well enough informed."

Homer scratched his white beard. "Could be . . . the reclusive life is not without its convenient aspects. It was time you returned to Memphis, Ramses."

"I had a tricky situation to resolve first."

"Finding a high priest of Amon who won't work against your interests . . . tough, but you pulled it off. Choosing an old and unworldly man showed unusual political savvy for one so young."

"I chose him on merit."

"Why not? The point is for him to obey you."

"If conflict between the north and south broke out, Egypt would be ruined."

"A strange country, but so endearing. I'm getting so used to your customs I've even started to drink my wine plain on occasion."

"Are you taking care of yourself?"

"There must be two doctors for every Egyptian, I swear! A dentist, an ophthalmologist, and a general practitioner have all made house calls. They've given me so many potions I can't begin to remember them. Though I admit the eyedrops have helped a bit with my vision. If I'd had them in Greece, I might not have lost so much of my sight. I won't go home now . . . too much fighting, too many factions, too many warlords and princelings mired in their rivalries. To write, I need peace and quiet. Concentrate on building one great nation, Majesty."

"My father undertook to do so."

"Here's a phrase of mine: *'What good are heartrending sobs, since the gods have condemned all men to a life of sorrow?'* You can't escape the common lot, and yet your role is to be placed beyond the suffering mass of humanity. The fact that there is a pharaoh, that there have been for centuries, allows your people to believe in happiness, experience it, and even to share it."

Ramses smiled. "You're beginning to undertand the mysteries of Egypt."

"Don't waste time pining for your father, and don't try to imitate him. Only become what he was: irreplaceable."

Ramses and Nefertari had celebrated rites in every temple in Memphis and recognized the high priest for his excellent administration of the city's famous art schools, where the finest sculptors in Egypt trained and worked.

The dreaded moment had now arrived when the king and queen must pose for these same sculptors. Enthroned, with their heavy crowns and scepters, they were required to sit motionless for hours on end while the sculptors, "those who give life," captured the royal couple in stone, forever young. Nefertari bore the ordeal with dignity, while Ramses grew increasingly restless. On the second day, unable to spend a moment more away from work, he called for Ahmeni.

"The inundation?"

"Fair," answered his private secretary. "The farmers were hoping for more, but the reservoir foremen are hopeful. The water supply will be adequate."

"How is my Agriculture appointee making out?"

"He leaves the administrative details to me and never sets foot in his office. He travels from field to field, farm to farm, solving all kinds of practical problems day in and day out. It's not what you'd expect from a department head, but . . ."

"He's on the right track. Are the farmworkers complaining?"

"The harvest was good, the granaries are full."

"Livestock?"

"Numbers on the rise, according to the latest tallies. No reports from the field on new diseases."

"And my darling brother's department?"

"Shaanar is a model cabinet member. He met with his staff, praised you to the high heavens, and asked that they all give their best for Egypt. He's taking his position very seriously, starts early in the morning, consults with his advisers, does his homework, and defers to Ahsha. Your brother is becoming a credit to your government!"

"Are you serious, Ahmeni?"

"The State Department is no laughing matter."

"Have you been to see Shaanar?"

"Of course."

"How did he treat you?"

"Courteously. He didn't object in the least when I asked him to furnish me with a weekly report of his activities."

"Surprising. He should have shown you the door."

"He's playing the part so well that he's even convinced himself. As long as you can keep tabs on him, I wouldn't worry."

"Keep him in line for me, will you?"

"I've already seen to that, Majesty."

Ramses got up, set the scepters and crown on his throne, and dismissed the sculptor in mid-sketch. Relieved, Nefertari followed his lead.

"Posing is torture," the king confessed. "If anyone had told me how awful it was, I never would have consented. Fortunately, this likeness will be the only one we sit for."

"Every station in life has its share of hardships. Your Majesty must never shirk his duties."

"Watch out, Ahmeni. They may raise a statue to you if you become a sage."

"No chance of that, with the pace you have me keep."

Ramses drew closer to his friend. "What do you think of Romay, my new chief steward?"

"A good man, but tormented."

"How so?

"Obsessed with the smallest detail in his quest for perfection."

"He's like you, then."

Ahmeni folded his arms. "Anything wrong with that?" he asked crossly.

"I want to know if Romay's behavior appears at all unusual to you."

"Quite the opposite. If you had a hundred Romays, then I could rest easy. Is there some problem with him?"

"Not yet."

"You have nothing to fear from Romay. If Your Majesty is finished with me, I need to get back to the office."

Nefertari tenderly took her husband's arm.

"Ahmeni is a rock."

"He's a one-man government."

"You spoke of a sign. Have you seen it?"

"No, darling."

"I feel it coming."

"What form will it take?" asked Ramses.

"I'm not sure, but it's heading for us like a horse at full gallop."

THIRTY-THREE

In early September, the floodwaters spread until Egypt resembled an immense lake from which the occasional hilltop village emerged. Those who did not seek work at one of Pharaoh's construction sites devoted their time to relaxation and boat travel. Well sheltered on hillocks, livestock fattened on forage. On estates the laborers fished in the fields they had only lately tilled.

At the southern tip of the Delta, just above Memphis, the Nile stretched for nearly fifteen miles. On the northern fringe, it was ten times wider, pushing out into the sea.

Papyrus and lotus plants grew dense, as if the country were reverting to the days before man walked the earth. The water's benediction purified the earth, drowned vermin, and spread the fertile silt that gave the land its abundance.

Every morning since mid-May a technician had descended the stairs to the Memphis Nilometer. The cubit ruler carved into its walls provided accurate records of the yearly inundation and a means of calculating the rate of the river's rise. At this time of year, the waters begin to recede almost imperceptibly until the level drops markedly toward the end of September.

The Memphis Nilometer was a kind of square well built of stone blocks. The technician climbed carefully, afraid of slipping. In his left hand, he carried a wooden tablet and the fish bone he used as a writing instrument. With his right, he braced himself against the wall.

His foot touched water.

Amazed, he stopped dead and studied the marks on the wall. His eyes must be playing tricks on him! He checked, checked again, then turned and ran up the stairs.

The canal district supervisor for the Memphis region raised unbelieving eyes to the Nilometer technician.

"These figures can't be correct."

"That's what I thought at first, but I double-checked again today. There's no doubt about it."

"Are you sure what month it is?"

"The first part of September, I know!"

"You've been a reliable worker, set to move up a grade at your next evaluation. Because of your record, I'll agree to forget this incident, provided that you resubmit the report after rectifying your error."

"There's been no error."

"Are you going to force me to take disciplinary measures?"

"Check for yourself, sir, please."

The technician's steady confidence unnerved his superior.

"You know as well as I do that these measurements are impossible!"

"I can't say I understand, but there you have it . . . The exact same measurement, recorded two days in a row."

The two men went together to check the Nilometer.

Afterward, the district supervisor could no longer deny that something out of the ordinary was taking place: instead of receding, the Nile was rising for the second time that year.

Sixteen cubits, the ideal water level. Sixteen cubits, or "perfect joy."

The news swept the country fast as a speeding jackal, causing an uproar. Ramses, in the first year of his reign, had performed a miracle! The reservoirs would be filled to the brim, the next season's crops irrigated throughout the dry months. The Two Lands would know the best of times, thanks to this royal magic.

Thus Ramses took Seti's place in his subjects' hearts. The new pharaoh was beneficent, endowed with supernatural powers, able to control the inundation and banish the specter of famine.

Shaanar was in a rage. How could people be so backward! They insisted on attributing a natural phenomenon to magic. The September flooding *was* highly unusual, of course, even incredible, as no Nilometer station in Egypt had records of any such occurrence. But Ramses had nothing to do with it! Even so, in every town and village the new pharaoh was being feted and his name praised to the heavens. After all, he was destined to equal the gods . . .

The king's older brother canceled his appointments and gave his entire department a day off in celebration, following the lead of his fellow cabinet members. Doing otherwise would be a tactical error.

Why did Ramses have all the luck? In the space of a few hours, his popularity had surpassed Seti's. A number of his adversaries caved in, deciding it would be hopeless to oppose him. Instead of forging ahead, Shaanar must proceed more cautiously than ever, slowly weaving his web.

His persistence would pay off in the long run. Fortune was notoriously fickle, and when Ramses' luck ran out, Shaanar would make his move. Until then, he would choose his weapons. He would have to strike accurately and hard.

Cries rose from the street. Shaanar thought there must be a scuffle, but the noise grew louder until it was almost deafening. The whole city was cheering! The secretary of state climbed the few steps to his building's roof terrace.

The spectacle that greeted him, along with thousands of his countrymen, turned him to stone.

A huge blue bird, something like a heron, was circling the skies of Memphis.

"The phoenix," thought Shaanar. "It can't be . . . the phoenix is back?" He struggled in vain to rid himself of the foolish notion, eyes fixed on the soaring bird. Legend had it that the phoenix returned from the netherworld to announce an exceptional ruler and herald the beginning of a new era.

A bedtime story, a priestly fantasy, a tall tale for the simple folk! Yet there it was, a splendid blue creature circling wide over Memphis, as if touring the city before choosing a new direction.

If he were an archer, Shaanar would have shot the bird down to prove that it was only a migrating waterfowl, confused and disoriented. Order a soldier to do it? None of them would obey him and people would think he was mad.

The entire city breathed as one, watching the phoenix. Suddenly, a hush fell.

Shaanar took heart. They knew, of course! If the blue bird really was the phoenix, it would do more than fly over Memphis. According to legend, it would have a precise destination. When the heron departed, it would take the crowd's delusion along with it. The people would stop believing in his brother's second miracle and perhaps even reassess the first one.

Ramses' luck was already deserting him! The odd baby cried. Then there was silence.

The huge blue bird soared on. In the clear air, the graceful movement of its wings could be heard, like the rustling of cloth. The people's joy gave way to disappointment. They'd missed the chance of a lifetime. This must not be the phoenix, appearing only once every fifteen centuries, but some poor dazed heron separated from its flock and hopelessly lost.

Relieved, Shaanar went back to his office. This showed how right he was never to heed old wives' tales. No bird, no man could live through the ages. No phoenix flew in to mark a pharaoh with greatness. Still, there was a lesson to be learned from the incident: knowing how to manipulate public opinion was crucial. People craved dreams in the same way they needed food. Not every ruler was born to be popular, but he could create a consensus by carefully fostering illusions.

The shouts rang out once more.

An angry, frustrated crowd, Shaanar surmised. He heard Ramses' name. Perhaps not in all honor and glory . . .

Back on the terrace, he was astonished to see the crowd exploding as the phoenix landed atop the city's greatest monument, the sacred obelisk.

Insane with rage, Shaanar conceded that the gods were indeed proclaiming a new era. The age of Ramses.

"Not one sign, but two," Nefertari concluded. "The second inundation, and now the phoenix. Could there be a better beginning?"

Ramses was reading the stack of reports that had just reached him. The Nile's unprecedented return to the ideal water level was a blessing for Egypt. And the entire population of Memphis had beheld the huge blue bird perched on the tip of the great obelisk at the temple of Heliopolis, a ray of sun preserved in sacred stone. There the phoenix remained, contemplating the chosen land of the gods after such a long absence in the great beyond.

"You look puzzled," observed the queen.

"Such powerful omens, it's enough to make anyone wonder."

"You think they're a warning?"

"No, Nefertari. I think they mean I should go ahead and not concern myself with doubters or stumbling blocks."

"Then it's time to set your plan in motion."

He took her in his arms. "According to the Nile and the phoenix."

A breathless Ahmeni burst into the audience chamber.

"The superior . . . of the House of Life . . . He wants to talk to you."

"Show him in."

"Serramanna is trying to frisk him . . . He'll cause a scandal!"

Ramses hurried toward the antechamber, where a robust

man of sixty, with a priest's shaved head and white robe, faced off with the colossal Sard decked out in helmet and breastplate, sword in hand.

The superior bowed to Pharaoh. Serramanna noted that Ramses seemed less than pleased.

"No exceptions," grumbled the giant. "Otherwise I can't vouch for your security."

"What brings you here?" the king inquired of the priest.

"An urgent request from the House of Life, Majesty. You're needed there."

THIRTY-FOUR

When Seti first brought Ramses to Heliopolis, it was to undergo an ordeal on which his future hinged. Today he entered as a pharaoh, passing through the gateway to the great temple of Ra, vast as Amon's cult center at Karnak.

On this holy ground, with its own canal, stood a complex of buildings: the shrine of the sacred stone, the sanctuary of Atum, the creator, in the shade of a sycamore; the chapel of the willow with the dynastic list carved into its trunk; the memorial chapel of Djoser, builder of the step pyramid at Saqqara.

Heliopolis was a place of enchantment. Garden paths, lined with stone niches holding statues of the gods, led through stands of acacia, willows, and tamarisks. Orchards and olive groves thrived. Beekeepers harvested rich loads of honey, dairymen husbanded high-yielding milk cows, craftsmen trained in the temple workshops. And all included a hundred villages contributing to the upkeep of Heliopolis, which were in turn protected by the temple.

Here the lore of the ancients had been handed down and codified in rituals. A long oral tradition of mythology continued. Scholars, ritualists, magicians transmitted their knowledge in silence and secret.

The superior of the House of Life at Heliopolis, which served as the model for all other institutions of religious learning in Egypt, had grown unaccustomed to the world outside.

"Your father often spent time among us," he now revealed to Ramses. "His fondest wish was to enter a religious order, although he knew it could never come true. You, Majesty, are young, bursting with energy and ambition. But will you live up to the name you bear?"

Ramses controlled his anger with some difficulty.

"Have you any cause to doubt it?"

"Heaven will answer in my place. Follow me."

"Is that an order?"

"You're lord of all you survey, and I am your servant."

The superior of the House of Life did not lower his eyes. Ramses had faced tough adversaries since becoming Pharaoh, but none as formidable as this.

"Follow me, please."

"Show me the way."

The superior walked in a measured pace toward the sanctuary of the primordial stone, from which an obelisk covered with hieroglyphs rose. Atop it sat the phoenix, perfectly still.

"Could I ask you to take a good look at this bird, Majesty?"

The midday sun was so dazzling that the phoenix was lost in a blur.

"Is your intention to blind me?"

"I leave that up to you, Majesty."

"Do you expect a king to act on a dare?"

"If it's in his nature."

"Explain the reason for your attitude."

"The name you bear, Majesty, is the basis of your legitimacy. Until now, it's been only a name. Will it remain so, or will you lay claim to it, no matter what risk that entails?"

Ramses looked straight at the sun.

The golden disk did not burn his eyes. He saw the phoenix rise, flap its wings, and move heavenward. Still the young monarch's gaze remained fastened on the shining orb that ruled the day.

"You are truly Ramses, Ra-Begot-Him, Son of Light. May your reign proclaim the victory over darkness."

The young king understood that he would never have anything to fear from the sun. He was its earthly incarnation; it was his source of energy.

Without another word, the superior made his way toward an oblong building with high, thick walls. This was the House of Life proper. In its center was the mound where the divine stone lay hidden, covered with a ram's fleece. Alchemists used it to perform transmutations, and pieces of it were buried with the initiates to aid in their passage from death to resurrection.

The superior showed the king into a huge library where

works on astronomy and astrology, prophecies and royal annals were preserved.

"According to our annals," declared the superior, "the phoenix was last seen in Heliopolis fourteen hundred and sixty-one years ago. Its appearance in Year One of your reign coincides with the intersection of two astronomical calendars: the fixed-year calendar, which loses a day every four years, and the real-year calendar, which loses a half-day a year. At the exact moment you ascended to the throne, these two cosmic cycles came together. A stela will be erected to mark the event, if you so desire."

"What lesson am I to draw from your revelations?"

"That chance does not exist, Majesty, and that your destiny belongs to the gods."

A miraculous September flood, the return of the phoenix, a new era . . . it was all too much for Shaanar. Dazed and forlorn, he put up a brave front at the ceremonies organized in Ramses' honor. Every sign pointed to the dawn of a new age under this young ruler. The gods had clearly chosen him to govern the Two Lands, preserve their union, enhance their prestige.

Only Serramanna was out of sorts. Maintaining security for the king was harder every day. Dignitaries traveled in packs to shake his hand, it seemed. Even worse, Pharaoh rode his open chariot through the main streets of Memphis, to the cheers of his people. Drunk on his own popularity, he refused the safety measures his guard captain recommended.

As if exposing himself to urban dangers were not

enough, the king also ventured into the countryside, most of which lay under the floodwaters. Peasants repaired their tools and plows, stocked granaries, while children learned to swim with floats. Overhead flew cranes with red and black beaks. Herds of belligerent hippos lazed in the muddy river. Allowing himself only two or three hours of sleep a night, Ramses visited a staggering number of villages. He earned the loyalty of provincial administrators and mayors, and gained the trust of the common folk.

When he returned to Memphis, the inundation was beginning to recede and farmers prepared for sowing.

"You don't even look tired," remarked Nefertari.

"What could be tiring about mingling with my people? But you, my darling, are you all right?"

"There's nothing I can put my finger on . . ."

"What do the doctors say?"

"They put me on bed rest."

"Then why aren't you in your bed?"

"With you away, I had to—"

"I won't leave Memphis again until you deliver."

"And your secret project?"

Ramses frowned. "Perhaps just one short trip, with your permission."

The queen smiled. "Your wish is my command."

"Egypt is so beautiful, Nefertari. My travels have made me realize how dazzling it is, the miracle child of water and sunlight, the epitome of Horus's strength and Hathor's beauty. We must devote our every waking moment to this country. You and I are meant not to govern, but to serve her."

"I believed that once."

"What do you mean?"

"Service is the noblest of human achievements. Only by

serving a higher goal can we find fulfillment. *Hem*, 'the servant,' is such a lovely word. It encompasses everyone from the seasonal construction worker or day laborer all the way up to Pharoah, the most powerful man in the land, the servant of the gods and of his people. Since the coronation, though, I see things differently. Neither one of us can simply serve. We must also direct, guide, steer the helm that keeps the ship of state on a steady course. No one else can do that for us."

The king grew somber.

"I felt the weight of that responsibility when my father died. I was so used to having someone who could guide, give advice, take charge. With him around, no problem was insurmountable, no misfortune without recourse."

"And that's what your people expect from you."

"I looked straight into the sun and it didn't burn my eyes."

"The sun is within you, Ramses. It gives life, it makes all things grow, but it can also be deadly if it's too strong."

"The desert sun is strong, but there's life in the desert."

"The desert is the netherworld on earth. It's not for human habitation, except for eternal dwellings that will outlast the ages. A pharaoh's greatest temptation is to immerse his thought in the desert, leaving behind the world of men."

"My father was a man of the desert."

"As every pharaoh should be, but he must also look toward the Valley and see it flourish."

Ramses and Nefertari fell silent in the still of the evening, as sunset gilded the single obelisk towering over Heliopolis.

THIRTY-FIVE

Once the windows in Ramses' bedchamber went dark, Serramanna left the palace, first making sure that his handpicked guards were at their posts. Jumping on the back of a superb black horse, he galloped through Memphis in the direction of the desert.

Egyptians did not like to go abroad at night. In the absence of the sun, demons were liable to creep out of their lairs and attack unwary travelers. The hulking Sardinian scoffed at these superstitions. He could hold his own against a horde of monsters. When his mind was made up, he was unstoppable.

Serramanna had hoped Setau would show up at court for the celebrations in Ramses' honor, but true to his eccentric reputation, the snake handler stayed home. In the course of his continuing investigation of the scorpion incident, the Sard learned that no one liked Setau. They feared his evil spells and loathed his reptilian companions, while forced to acknowledge he was doing a booming business. Selling venom for pharmaceutical purposes was beginning to make him a fortune.

Though not giving up on Romay, Serramanna had to admit that Setau made an excellent suspect. Suppose that he was staying out of sight because he didn't dare face Ramses since planting the scorpion? His reclusiveness was practically an admission of guilt.

Serramanna needed to see Setau in person. The ex-pirate was used to sizing up his opponents. He owed his survival to his ability to read them, so before he could make his move, he needed a good look at Setau. And since the man was hiding, he would have to flush him out.

As cropland gave way to desert, Serramanna dismounted and tethered his horse to the trunk of a fig tree, whispering a few words of reassurance in the animal's ear. Then he walked noiselessly toward Setau's complex. There was barely a crescent of moon, but the night was clear. A laughing hyena troubled him not in the least. It reminded him of boarding a ship by surprise.

The laboratory was lighted. What if Setau took some extra persuading? He'd promised Ramses to go easy, but if there were extenuating circumstances . . . He cautiously hunched down, skirted a rise, and approached the building from the rear.

His back to the wall, the Sard listened.

Low moans issued from the laboratory. Was the snake charmer torturing some poor wretch? Serramanna scrambled to a slit in the wall and peeked inside. Pots, jars, filters, caged snakes and scorpions, knives of various sizes, baskets . . . all kinds of equipment littered the shelves and workbenches.

On the floor lay a couple in a naked embrace. A beautiful black woman groaned in pleasure, her slender body arching. Her swarthy, square-jawed partner was stocky and virile.

The Sard looked away. While he freely indulged his own

taste for women, he was no voyeur. Yet this woman's beauty had stirred him. Interrupting such passionate lovemaking would be criminal, so he resigned himself to waiting. Spent, Setau would be easier to interrogate.

He smiled to himself thinking of the Memphis belle he'd be meeting for dinner the following evening. According to her best friend, she liked big, strong men.

A strange sound to his left caught his attention.

The Sard looked around to see a huge cobra ready to strike—one opponent he'd rather not face. He backed away, bumped into the wall, and froze. A second cobra stood in his way.

"Get away, you monsters!"

The giant's dagger had no effect on the snakes. If he did kill one of them, he realized, the other one would attack him.

"What's going on here?"

Naked, carrying a torch, Setau inspected the intruder. "You came to rob my laboratory. Good thing my watchdogs are always on the alert. Unfortunately for you, their bite is definitely worse than my bark."

"You can't get away with murder, Setau!"

"So you know my name. No matter, you're a burglar caught redhanded, waving a dagger. The judge will rule that it was self-defense."

"I'm Serramanna, the captain of Ramses' bodyguard."

"I thought I recognized you. Why do you need to steal from me?"

"I wanted to see you, have a look at your place, that's all."

"At this time of night? Not only are you interrupting me and my wife, you're lying through your teeth."

"It's the truth."

"Why this sudden wish to see me?"

"Security reasons."

"What does that mean?"

"My job is to protect the king."

"You think I'm a threat to Ramses?"

"I didn't say that."

"But you think it—why else spy on me?"

"I have to check every lead."

The two cobras inched closer to the Sard. Setau's eyes blazed with fury.

"Call them off."

"Are pirates afraid to die?"

"That way, yes."

"Get away from me, Serramanna, and never show your face here again. Next time I'll let them at you."

At a signal from Setau, the cobras backed away. The Sard, drenched in sweat, walked straight between them, heading back to his horse.

One thing was clear in his mind: Setau had the soul of a criminal.

"What are they doing?" asked little Kha, watching farmworkers herd a flock of sheep through a sodden field.

"After the sowing, the sheep help work the seeds into the soil," explained Nedjem, the new agriculture secretary. "The inundation leaves a huge amount of silt on the banks and fields. That helps us grow good wheat."

"And the sheep are helpers?"

"Just like cows and every other animal in creation."

The inundation had begun to recede, and the sowers were out in the fields, blessing the river's abundance. They began early in the morning, having a limited number of days with the right conditions for planting while the soil was moist and easily worked. After hoeing to break up the waterlogged clumps of soil, the seeds were scattered and the furrows covered. Livestock followed to help pack down the soil.

"The country is nice," said Kha, "but I still like my scrolls and hieroglyphs better."

"Would you like to visit a farm?"

"All right."

Nedjem took the little boy by the hand. Even his walk was serious, out of keeping with his age, like his academic gifts. Kindhearted Nedjem was so concerned for the child, with his lack of interest in toys and playmates, that he'd begged Iset the Fair to let him act as Kha's tutor, if only to take the little prince outside his gilded cage and introduce him to the wonders of nature.

Kha took in everything around him—not as a surprised and delighted child, however, but as a full-fledged scribe mentally compiling a report.

The farm had silos, barns, a barnyard, bread ovens, a kitchen garden. At the gate, Nedjem and Kha were invited to wash their hands and feet. Then the owner welcomed them, delighted to have such important visitors. He showed off his pampered and productive dairy herd.

"My secret," he confessed, "is finding the right pasture, where they don't get too hot and have plenty of grass."

"The cow is the animal of the goddess Hathor. That's why cows are good to us."

The farmer's eyes widened. "How do you know that, Prince?"

"I read it in a story."

"You already know how to read?"

"Will you do something for me?"

"Anything."

"Bring me a piece of limestone and a reed tip."

"Yes, right away."

The farmer glanced at Nedjem, who winked his approval. Writing implements in hand, the boy began to walk around the barnyard, then the barns themselves, to the farmhands' astonishment.

An hour later, the slab of limestone was covered with writing when he returned it to his host.

"I checked my figures," Kha told him. "You own a hundred and twelve cows."

The child rubbed his eyes and clung to Nedjem.

"Now I'm sleepy," he confessed.

By the time the old man settled Kha in his arms, the boy was asleep. "Another one of Ramses' miracles," Nedjem said to himself.

THIRTY-SIX

Athletic as Ramses, broad-shouldered, with a high forehead, flowing dark hair, and a bearded, weather-beaten face, Moses walked casually into the King of Egypt's office.

Ramses rose and the two men embraced.

"This was where Seti worked, isn't it?"

"Yes. I haven't changed a thing. His thoughts live on in these walls. I want them to be my inspiration."

Light filtered through the three high windows designed to keep air circulating through the room. The late summer heat was agreeable.

Ramses shunned his straight-backed royal armchair and sat on a plain seat of woven straw, facing his friend.

"How are you, Moses?"

"Fine, but I don't have enough to do."

"We never see each other these days. I'm afraid that's my fault."

"You know I can't stand to be idle. Why did you bring me to Memphis? I was better off working at Karnak."

"You're not enjoying high society?"

"The courtiers bore me. It's Ramses, Ramses, Ramses. Soon they'll be making a god of you. It's stupid and pointless."

"Have I done something wrong?"

"The September flooding, the phoenix, the new era . . . The facts are undeniable, and they explain your popularity. But do you have supernatural powers, are you predestined? The people think so."

"And you don't agree?"

"It may be true. But you're no god."

"Did I ever claim to be?"

"Be careful, Ramses, or too much flattery will go to your head."

"You don't seem to understand the role and the function of a pharaoh. You don't give me much credit, either!"

"I'm only trying to help you."

"I'm going to give you the chance to do that."

Moses' eyes shone with curiosity. "You're sending me back to Karnak?"

"I have a much more important assignment for you, if you accept."

"More important than Karnak?"

The king rose and leaned his back against the window frame.

"I have an important plan. So far I've only shared it with Nefertari. We agreed it would be best to look for a sign before I went ahead. The second inundation and the phoenix . . . in the end the gods gave me two signs. The House of Life confirmed that a new era really has begun, according to the laws of astronomy. Of course I'll continue the work my father began, in Karnak, in Abydos, and elsewhere. Still, I think a new era should be marked with new creations. Is that vanity, Moses?"

"Every pharaoh must build, according to tradition."

Ramses looked concerned.

"The world is changing. The Hittites constitute a permanent threat, and Egypt is a prime target. Those are the truths that led me to conceive of my project."

"Increasing your military strength?"

"No, Moses. Moving the strategic center of the country."

"Do you mean . . ."

"Yes, building a new capital."

The Hebrew was dumbstruck. "What? How will . . ."

"The northern border is where Egypt's fate will be decided. Therefore, my government should have its seat in the Delta to keep up with the latest developments in Lebanon, Syria, and our protectorates under threat from the Hittites. Thebes will remain the city of Amon, the home of Karnak and Luxor. I'll make sure they're grander and more beautiful than ever. On the West Bank, the Peak reigns in silence over the Valley of the Kings, the Valley of the Queens, the mortuary temples on the plain."

"But what about Memphis?"

"Memphis is the fulcrum of the Two Lands, where the Delta joins the Nile Valley. It will remain our economic and administrative capital. But we must go farther to the north and east, Moses. We can't pretend we exist in splendid isolation, or forget that we've been invaded before. We must remember that Egypt is a tempting prize."

"Isn't the line of fortresses enough of a deterrent?"

"In case of danger, I'll have to move quickly. The closer I am to the northern border, the less time it will take information to reach me."

"Building a capital is a perilous undertaking. Look what happened to Akhenaton."

"Akhenaton made some fatal errors. The site he chose, in Middle Egypt, was doomed from the start. He forgot about the good of his people and pursued his mystical fantasies."

"He challenged the clergy of Amon, and so have you."

"If the high priest of Amon is faithful to the law and loyal to the king, I'll have no quarrel with him."

"Akhenaton believed in a single god. The new capital was supposed to be a shrine to His glory."

"His father, the great Amenhotep, left him a prosperous country. He left it in ruins. Akhenaton was weak and indecisive, lost in his prayers. Under his reign, hostile powers seized Egyptian territory. If you're trying to defend him, it won't be easy."

Moses hesitated. "Today his capital lies abandoned."

"Mine will be built to last several generations."

"You almost frighten me, Ramses."

"Take heart, Moses!"

"How many years does it take to raise a city starting from nothing?"

Ramses smiled. "It won't start from nothing."

"Explain yourself."

"While I was Seti's co-regent, he took me to see the main sites associated with our dynasty. Each trip was a learning experience, though I couldn't always see the point at the time. Today I'm beginning to make more sense of our travels. One of the places we visited was Avaris."

"The capital of the Hyksos invaders? You can't be serious."

"Seti was the namesake of Set, who murdered his brother, Osiris. My father had the strength to dominate the forces of destruction, feed on their energy, and use it to build."

"And now you want to make Avaris the city of Ramses?"

"Yes, and that's what I plan to call it. *Pi-Ramses*, the city of Ramses, the capital of Egypt."

"It's madness!"

"Pi-Ramses will be magnificent, inviting. Poets will sing its praises."

"How long will it take to build?"

"I haven't forgotten your question. In fact, it's why I called you here."

"Does this mean what I'm afraid it does?"

"I need someone I can trust to supervise the work and keep the project on schedule. I need Avaris turned into Pi-Ramses as quickly as possible."

"Do you have a time frame?"

"Less than a year."

"That's impossible!"

"No, it isn't, thanks to you."

"You think I can move stone with the speed of a falcon and put blocks together through sheer force of will?"

"Stone, no. But with bricks it could go that fast."

"I'm beginning to see . . ."

"Your fellow Hebrews make up most of the brickmaking companies around the country. If we bring them all together, you'll form a group of highly skilled workmen capable of taking on such a large-scale project."

"Aren't temples supposed to be made of stone?"

"I'll enlarge the temples already in place. That can be done over several years. We'll use brick to build the palaces, government offices, villas for the nobles, houses, apartments. In less than a year, Pi-Ramses will be habitable and become a working capital."

Moses appeared unconvinced.

"I still say it's impossible. The blueprints alone . . ."

"The blueprints are in my head! I'll sketch them myself on papyrus and you'll take it from there."

"The Hebrews are a fairly independent lot. Each clan has its own chief."

"I'm not asking you to become a political leader, only a project administrator."

"Winning their trust won't be easy."

"I have faith in you."

"As soon as the news is out, other Hebrews will try to take my place."

"Will they be able to?"

Now Moses smiled. "No one will be able to meet your deadline."

"We'll build Pi-Ramses to shine in the Delta and cast a glow over all of Egypt. Get to work, Moses."

THIRTY-SEVEN

Abner the brickmaker could stand it no longer. Just because Sary was Ramses' brother-in-law, he thought he could treat his Hebrew workers like dirt. He shorted their overtime pay, cut their rations, and denied them time off, claiming their work was substandard.

When Moses was in Thebes, he had kept Sary in line. Now that he was gone, the situation was worse than ever. Yesterday evening the foreman had caned a fifteen-year-old boy, accusing him of not getting the bricks to the boat fast enough.

It was the last straw.

When Sary arrived at the brickyard, the entire work gang was seated in a circle. Only Abner was standing in front of the empty baskets.

"Get up and go to work!" snarled Sary, who grew thinner by the day.

"We demand an apology," Abner said calmly.

"Am I hearing right?"

"The boy you beat last night is home in bed. He did

nothing wrong. You owe him an apology, and we deserve one, too."

"Have you lost your mind, Abner?"

"We won't go back to work until you agree."

"Don't make me laugh!" Sary snorted.

"All right. We'll file a complaint instead."

"You're pathetic, Abner. And stupid. I already called the police in to investigate. They ruled that the boy was injured in an accident entirely of his own fault."

"That's a lie!"

"A scribe took his sworn statement in my presence. If the boy tries to change his story, he'll be accused of perjury."

"How can you twist the truth so!"

"If you men don't get back to work at once, you'll face stiff penalties. You're supposed to deliver bricks for the mayor's new mansion, and the mayor of Thebes doesn't like delays."

"But the law——"

"Don't talk to me about the law, Hebrew. It's over your head. If you file a complaint, your family and friends will suffer the consequences."

Abner believed him. He was afraid of Sary. With the rest of the gang, he went back to work.

Dolora, Sary's wife, was more and more fascinated by the strange personality of Ofir, the Libyan sorcerer. His hawk-like face was unsettling, yet his voice mesmerized, and when the subject was Aton, the solar disk, his enthusiasm was catching. A discreet houseguest, he had agreed to meet with a number of the princess's friends and speak about the unjust persecution Akhenaton had suffered, the need to promote the concept of a single god.

Ofir cast a spell over people. No one walked away from these sessions unchanged. Some were upset by his views, others persuaded. He slowly entangled some worthwhile connections in his web, attracting more support for Aton— and Lita—with each passing week. Even though the throne of Egypt remained only a remote possibility, a movement was beginning to form.

Lita attended these talks without joining in. The young woman's dignity, bearing, and reserve were the deciding factor for quite a few notables. She clearly belonged to a royal lineage that ought to be given consideration. Sooner or later, there was bound to be a role at court for Lita.

Ofir never criticized, made no demands. In a low, per-suasive voice, he evoked Akhenaton's profound convictions, the beauty of his poetry in honor of Aton, his love of truth. Love and peace: was that not the message of the persecuted king and his direct descendant, Lita? And this message her-alded a magnificent future, a future worthy of Egypt and her civilization.

When Dolora introduced the sorcerer to the former sec-retary of state, Meba, she was proud of herself. Proud that she had snapped out of her habitual apathy, proud to be serving a noble cause. Ramses had abandoned her; the sor-cerer gave meaning to her existence.

The old diplomat, with his broad, reassuring face and stately manner, made no attempt to hide his reluctance.

"I'm only doing this as a favor to you," he told Dolora.

"I appreciate it, Meba. You won't regret it." She showed him to where the sorcerer sat beneath a persea tree, weaving two strands of linen into a thin cord that would hold an amulet.

He rose and bowed.

"It's a very great honor for me to receive a cabinet member."

"I'm nothing now," Meba said bitterly.

"Injustice can strike anyone at any time."

"That's small consolation."

Ramses' sister chimed in: "I explained everything to our friend Meba. Perhaps he'll agree to help us."

"Let's not fool ourselves, my dear. Ramses showed me the door."

"You want revenge," said the sorcerer evenly.

"That's going too far," protested Meba. "I still have some influential friends who—"

"They're out to protect their own interests, not help you. I have another goal in mind: proving Lita's legitimacy."

"You're dreaming. Ramses has an extraordinarily forceful personality. He's not about to step aside. What's more, the miraculous happenings of late have made him very popular. Believe me, it's a lost cause."

"It's a challenge. I agree we can't fight him on his home turf."

"What's your plan, then?"

"Interested?"

"Well . . ." Meba fiddled with the amulet around his neck.

"That gesture provides a clue to one solution: magic. I know how to break through the spells protecting Ramses. It will be long and difficult, but I can do it."

The elder statesman recoiled.

"I can't offer you my assistance."

"I'm not asking for it, Meba. But there's another area that needs to be addressed: the spread of ideas."

"I don't follow."

"Aton's believers need a respected and respectable leader. And when Aton regains his supremacy, that leader will be in the forefront, overthrowing a pharaoh who's lost all credibility and is unsure how to react."

"Oh, my. It would be risky!"

"Akhenaton was disgraced, but never Aton. There's no law against worshiping him. It's a growing religion, and his followers are determined. Where Akhenaton failed, we'll succeed."

Meba's hands trembled. "I'll have to think about it."

"Isn't it exciting?" asked Dolora. "A new world is opening up to us, a world where we'll find our rightful place!"

"Yes, of course. Let me think it over."

A most satisfactory meeting, Ofir thought afterward. A cautious, fainthearted diplomat, Meba did not really have the makings of a leader. But he hated Ramses and dreamed of regaining his former glory. Unable to make up his mind, he would turn to his confidant, Shaanar, the man Ofir really hoped to attract. Dolora had told him a great deal about the new secretary of state and his old rivalry with Ramses. Unless he'd changed completely, Shaanar was proceeding in stealth, his desire to destroy his brother intact. The sorcerer felt sure that Meba would put him in touch with this powerful figure, destined to become their most valuable ally.

After a long and exhausting day of work, Sary's right big toe was red and swollen, twisted with arthritis. Standing on it was so painful that he could barely drive his official chariot. His only satisfaction had been taking disciplinary measures against the Hebrews, who had finally comprehended that it was useless to challenge his authority. Thanks to his connections in the police department and his relationship with the mayor of Thebes, he was free to vent his frustrations on the brickyard riffraff.

Having Ofir and his silent muse as houseguests was beginning to wear on his nerves. They tried to stay out of his way, of course, but their influence over Dolora was getting out of hand. Her newfound devotion to Aton was exasperating. With all the time she spent in prayer or listening at the Libyan's feet as he sermonized, she was bound to neglect her conjugal duties.

Tall, dark, and languid, she waited for him on the doorstep to their villa.

"Go get the liniment and rub my feet," he barked at her.

"A hard day at the brickyard?"

"Don't make fun of me! You can't imagine what it's like. Those Hebrews are hopeless."

Dolora took his arm and led him gently to their bedchamber. Sary reclined against a heap of pillows as his wife washed and oiled his feet, massaging liniment into his sore toe.

"Is your sorcerer still hanging around?"

"Meba called on him today."

"Your father's secretary of state?"

"He was interested in what Ofir had to say."

"You think Meba will join your movement? He's too much of a chicken."

"He's still an important and well-respected figure. Attracting him would really help our cause."

"Ofir and Lita have certainly managed to brainwash you."

"Sary! How dare you talk that way!"

"All right, forget it."

"This is our only chance to reclaim our position. And then this faith is so pure, so appealing . . . don't you just melt when Ofir talks about Aton?"

"Who means more to you, your husband or that hook-nosed sorcerer?"

"What? There's absolutely no comparison."

"He's with you all day long, while I spend my time with a bunch of lazy Hebrews. A blonde and a brunette to choose from . . . Your Libyan is one lucky fellow."

Dolora stopped rubbing the inflamed digit.

"You're raving, Sary! Ofir is a sage and a holy man. It must be ages since he's had any thought of—"

"But I'll bet you do."

"You're disgusting!"

"Take off your dress, Dolora, and keep on massaging me. I'm no holy man."

"Wait, I forgot to tell you something."

"What?"

"A royal courier delivered a letter for you."

"Let me see it."

Dolora went to fetch the letter. Sary's toe felt better already. What could this official business be? Perhaps an appointment to an office job, where he wouldn't have any Hebrews to supervise?

His wife returned with the scroll. Sary broke the seal on the papyrus, unrolled it, and read.

He winced, the color draining from his face.

"Bad news?"

"I'm to report to Memphis with my work gang."

"That sounds like a promotion!"

"Yes, but the letter is signed by Moses, chief of royal construction."

THIRTY-EIGHT

Every Hebrew brickmaker in the country answered the summons. When letters from Moses reached their various work sites, the response was overwhelmingly positive. Moses' reputation had spread throughout the land during his tenure at Karnak. He was known for championing the rights of his fellow Hebrews. Being Ramses' friend gave him a remarkable advantage, and now he had been named to oversee all royal construction projects! A new hope stirred: surely Moses would improve their salaries and working conditions.

Moses was frankly surprised by the positive reaction. A few local leaders were upset, but there was no questioning Pharaoh's orders. They yielded to Moses' authority, welcoming him when he toured the tent city north of Memphis, checking on the workers' comfort and sanitary conditions.

Suddenly Sary blocked his path.

"What's the meaning of this summons?"

"I'll be making an announcement."

"What am I doing here with all these Hebrews?"

"There are several other Egyptian foremen."

"Are you forgetting that my wife is the king's sister?"

"Are you forgetting that I'm your boss now?"

Sary chewed his lips.

"My lot of Hebrews is unruly. I cane them when I need to, and I don't plan to stop."

"Judicious use of physical discipline can make men listen with their third ear, the one on the back. But anyone who uses the cane without reason should be punished in kind. In fact, I'll see to it personally."

"Don't try to bully me."

"Watch yourself, Sary. I can have you demoted. By now you should be an excellent brickmaker yourself."

"You wouldn't dare."

"Ramses has given me full authority. Keep that in mind."

Moses brushed past Sary, who spat in the young Hebrew's footsteps.

Dolora was excited to be back in Memphis, but it could prove to be a nightmare. Ramses had been officially informed of his sister's return, along with her husband, but nothing had come of it. They had taken a modest villa, passing Ofir and Lita off as servants. The trio, over Sary's halfhearted objections, had every intention of continuing to proselytize as they had in Thebes. Given the number of foreigners living in Memphis, the country's economic capital, their work would be easier here. The south was more traditional and resistant to new religious concepts. Dolora considered the summons to Memphis a favorable sign.

Sary remained skeptical and preoccupied with his own fate, pondering what announcement Moses was about to make to thousands of agitated Hebrews.

Guarding the entrance to the State Department was a statue of the god Thoth in the form of an enormous pink granite baboon. Thoth, the scribe god, had created all the world's languages, and members of the Foreign Service sought his patronage. Learning several foreign tongues was a requirement for diplomats, since the knowledge of hieroglyphs was not for export. In the field, ambassadors and couriers used the local language.

Like other high-ranking officials in the department, Ahsha often meditated in the chapel to the left of the entrance and laid narcissi at the shrine to Thoth. Before addressing delicate issues of national security, it was wise to seek indulgence from the god of learning.

His offering made, the rising star of Egyptian diplomacy passed through several busy departments on his way to Shaanar's spacious office.

"There you are, Ahsha. What kept you?"

"Afraid I overslept; I was making rather merry last night. I do hope I haven't inconvenienced you."

Shaanar's face was red and puffy; he was obviously worked up about something.

"Tell me," Ahsha said soothingly.

"Have you heard about the Hebrew brickmakers camped north of town?"

"Yes, but I didn't take much notice."

"Neither did I, but apparently we should have!"

"What could brickworkers possibly have to do with us?" Well bred and elegant, Ahsha had nothing but disdain for manual laborers, although he hardly knew any.

"You'll never guess who's behind it. The new chief of royal construction—Moses!"

"Is that so surprising? He supervised Seti's additions to Karnak; it's a logical promotion."

"If only that were all. Yesterday Moses called an assembly and announced he was leading them to the Delta, where an all-Hebrew work crew will build a new capital for Ramses!"

A long silence followed this revelation as Ahsha, ordinarily unflappable, registered the shock.

"Are you quite certain . . ."

"Absolutely certain. Moses is carrying out my brother's orders."

"A new capital . . . simply impossible!"

"Not for Ramses!"

"How ambitious a project is it?"

"Pharaoh himself drew the plans and chose the site. And what a site—Avaris, the abandoned city of the Hyksos invaders we had so much trouble getting rid of!" Shaanar's moon face suddenly brightened. "What if Ramses really has gone mad? A project on this scale can only lead to ruin. Men of sound mind will have to take over eventually . . ."

"I wouldn't be overly optimistic. It's true that Ramses has a great deal at stake, but his instinct is solid. It's actually the smartest thing he can do. Moving the capital so far northeast and so close to the border, he's sending the Hittites a clear warning signal. They'll see that Egypt is taking nothing for granted, is aware of the danger but won't give an inch. The king will have better access to information about enemy actions and be able to react more quickly."

Shaanar sat down, disheartened. "It's a catastrophe. Our strategy is full of holes now."

"I wouldn't be too pessimistic, either," Ahsha advised. "On one hand, Ramses' dream may never become reality, and on the other, why should we change our plans?"

"But my brother is obviously taking an aggressive stance on foreign policy . . ."

"That comes as no surprise, but his policy will still be based on the intelligence he receives. We may as well let him think he's in charge."

Shaanar's confidence returned. "You're right, Ahsha. We won't let a new capital get in our way."

Queen Mother Tuya had missed the gardens of her Memphis palace. The times she had strolled there with Seti seemed too few and far between, the years she had spent with him too brief. She remembered his every word, his every glance, and had often imagined a peaceful old age at his side, basking in shared memories. But now Seti roamed through paradise and she walked alone in this marvelous garden, shaded by pomegranates, tamarisks, and jojoba trees. On either side of the path bloomed cornflowers, anemones, lupine, and ranunculi. Tuya sat pensively by the lotus pond, beneath a wisteria arbor.

When she saw Ramses approaching, her sadness vanished.

In less than a year as Pharaoh, her son had grown so self-assured that it was hard to believe he had ever doubted his capabilities. He kept up the same vigorous pace his father had, with seemingly inexhaustible reserves of energy.

Tenderly, respectfully, Ramses kissed his mother and sat down beside her.

"I need to talk to you."

"That's what I'm here for, my son."

"Do you approve of the men I've chosen for my cabinet?"

"Do you recall Seti's advice to you?"

"I did my best to follow it: 'Look deep in the souls of men. Look for advisers who are upright and firm, able to give an impartial opinion yet ever mindful of their oath of obedience.' Have I succeeded? Only the next few years will tell."

"Do you fear opposition so soon?"

"It's inevitable, at the rate I've been going. I know I'll run up against proud hearts and vested interests. When the idea for this new capital came to me, it was like a lightning bolt. I saw it and knew it was true."

"The *Sia*," said his mother, nodding, "direct intuition, without reasoning or analysis. It was the source of many of Seti's decisions. He believed it was handed down from pharaoh to pharaoh."

"Do you give my new capital your blessing?"

"Since the *Sia* spoke to your heart, why would you need my approval?"

"Because my father's spirit is in this garden, and both of us hear his voice."

"The signs were clear, Ramses. Your reign opens a new era, and Pi-Ramses will be your capital."

The Pharaoh took his mother's hands in his own.

"You'll see my city, mother, and be glad."

"A word, son. I'm concerned about your protection."

"Serramanna is a professional."

"I'm talking about your magical protection. Have you thought about building your Eternal Temple?"

"I've picked the site, but for now Pi-Ramses is my priority."

"Don't forget your Eternal Temple. If the forces of darkness are unleashed upon you, it will be your strongest ally."

THIRTY-NINE

The setting was magnificent.

Fertile land, broad fields, thick grass, flower-lined footpaths, apple orchards full of honeyed fruit, a flourishing olive grove, teeming ponds, salt marshes, dense thickets: here sat Avaris, once so despised, now reduced to a handful of houses and a temple to the god Set.

This was where Seti had taught his son the meaning of power. This was where Ramses would build his capital.

The beauty and lushness of the countryside surprised Moses; the Hebrews and their Egyptian foremen were part of the expedition Ramses had led in person, with his pets in tow. Serramanna, on high alert, rode ahead with a scouting party of ten.

The little town of Avaris dozed in the sun. Its only inhabitants were government workers in dead-end jobs, slow-moving peasants, and papyrus gatherers. The place seemed suspended in time.

The expedition had made a stop in Heliopolis, where Ramses had made an offering to his patron, Ra, then headed toward Bubastis (home to Bastet, the pleasure-loving cat goddess) and along the Pelusiac branch of the Nile, dubbed the "Waters of Ra." Near Lake Menezaleh, Avaris was at the western end of the "Road of Horus," leading across the Sinai coastline toward Palestine and Syria.

"A strategic location," commented Moses, studying the map Ramses had shown him.

"Do you understand the reasons for my choice now? With the aid of a canal, the Waters of Ra will give us access to the lakes around the isthmus of el-Qantara. In an emergency, we can reach the fortress of Sileh by boat, and the smaller frontier outposts as well. I'll be reinforcing the eastern side of the Delta, standing in the way of invasions, and closer to the source of any potential trouble in our protectorates. The summers are milder here. Our garrisons won't suffer from the heat and they'll remain more alert."

"You're a man of vision," said Moses admiringly.

"How do things look with your workers?"

"They seem happy with the plan, but the increased wages you're offering probably have a lot to do with that."

"If I'm generous, they'll give me their best. I want a splendid city."

Moses bent to study the map again. Four major temples were planned: to the west, one to Amon, "The Hidden"; to the south, the temple of Set, the local deity; to the east, a shrine to Astarte, the Syrian goddess; and to the north, the temple of Wadjet, "The Verdant," patroness of the fertile Delta. Near the temple of Set would be the river landing. This was the meeting point of two broad canals, linking the Waters of Ra and the Waters of Avaris, which surrounded the city and supplied drinking water. Close to the port lay warehouses, granaries, and workshops. Farther north, in the center of town, were the palace, government buildings, noblemen's villas, and residential neighborhoods where grand and humble dwellings stood side by side. The main street led away from the palace toward the temple of Ptah, with two side roads leading to the sanctuaries of Amon and Ra. Set's temple was set apart, on the opposite side of the canal connecting the Ra and Avaris branches.

There were also four military barracks, one between the Pelusiac branch and the government buildings, the three others along the Waters of Avaris—the first behind the temple of Ptah, the second bordering the residential neighborhoods, the last near the temples of Ra and Astarte.

"Production of ceramic tile is ready to start tomorrow," revealed Ramses. "From the smallest house to the biggest hall in the palace, Pi-Ramses will sparkle with color. But first they have to be built, and that's where you come in, Moses."

With his right index finger, Moses showed where the various buildings in the monarch's plan would be situated.

"It's ambitious. I like the way you think on a grand scale. Still . . ."

"Yes, Moses?"

"No offense, Majesty, but one temple is missing. It could easily go there." He gestured between the temples of Amon and Ptah.

"What god would it honor?"

"The god who created the institution of Pharaoh. The temple where your rededication will be celebrated."

"For that to happen, I'll have to reign thirty years. To build it now would be tempting fate."

"You've left room for it, though."

"Leaving it out of my plans would also be tempting fate. If I do reach Year Thirty of my reign, I want you at my side, along with our other old friends."

"Thirty years . . . who knows what God has in store for us?"

"For the moment, he's telling us to build the capital of Egypt together."

"I've divided the Hebrews into two groups. The first will transport blocks of stone to the temple sites and work under Egyptian supervisors. The second will manufacture the thousands of bricks to be used in your palace and government buildings. Coordinating the two groups will be awkward; I'm afraid my newfound popularity won't last. Do you know what the men call me? *Masha*, 'Rescued from Drowning.'"

"Is this some miracle I haven't heard about?"

"No, an old Babylonian legend they're fond of repeating. It's a pun on my name, which means 'He Who Is Born.' In their eyes, the gods have blessed me. A Hebrew, educated at the royal academy and friend to Pharaoh! God saved me from drowning in poverty and misfortune. A man with my luck deserves to be followed. That's why the brickmakers trust me."

"Treat them well. You have my permission to use the royal granaries if you lack provisions."

"I'll build your capital, Ramses."

The Hebrew brickmakers tied white headbands around the black wigs that stopped above their ears, and wore mustaches or trim beards. They were possessive of their expertise. Syrian and Egyptian brickmakers tried to compete with them, but the Hebrews remained the best and most sought after in the trade. The work was hard and closely supervised by Egyptian foremen, but the pay was decent and the leave days liberal. Here in Egypt, the food was good, lodging fairly easy to find. The hardier souls among them even built themselves comfortable homes with salvaged materials.

Moses had made no secret of the fact that at Pi-Ramses the pace would be more intense than usual, but promised bonuses in compensation. Many a Hebrew would prosper here, providing they spared no effort. Under normal conditions, three workmen could produce eight to nine hundred small bricks a day. At Pi-Ramses, they would have to manufacture different sizes: larger bricks for foundations, then a multitude of smaller ones. Usually foremen and stonemasons were responsible for the foundations.

By the end of the first day, the Hebrews realized that Moses would be as harsh a taskmaster as he had promised. Any hope of spending their afternoons asleep in the shade of a tree quickly vanished. Like his co-workers, Abner threw himself into his work: mixing mud from the Nile with chopped straw. Finding the right consistency was the trick. Several huge flats had been set aside and trenches dug to a canal for water to moisten the river silt. Then, keeping time to songs, the men worked the mixture with picks and hoes, a technique that resulted in stronger bricks.

Abner performed his tasks quickly and well. As soon as the mixture felt right to him, he loaded it in a basket, which a laborer hauled to the workshop, where it was poured into a rectangular wooden mold. Unmolding was a delicate operation; occasionally Moses supervised it in person. The bricks were left to dry for some four hours, then stacked and transported to the various work sites, beginning with the best-cured and therefore lightest-colored ones.

Humble as it was, the well-made mud brick proved to be a remarkably solid building material. Correctly laid, it would last for ages.

A competitive spirit awakened among the Hebrews. The

higher salary and bonuses played a part, of course, but so did their pride in being part of such a colossal undertaking and their determination to rise to the occasion. If their enthusiasm waned, Moses got them fired up again. Thousands of perfect bricks were being produced each day.

Pi-Ramses was coming to life, springing out of the Pharaoh's dream to become reality. Foremen and stone cutters, following the king's plans, laid solid foundations; laborers tirelessly carted load after load of the Hebrews' bricks.

Beneath the Delta sun, a city was taking shape.

At the close of each day, Abner admired Moses more. The Hebrew chief moved from group to group, checking the quality of the food, sending those who were sick or overworked off to rest. Contrary to his expectations, his popularity continued to grow.

Abner had already earned enough bonus money to build his family a fine new house, right here in the new capital.

"Pleased with yourself, little friend?"

Sary's hollow face wore an evil grin.

"What do you want with me?"

"I'm your foreman. Have you forgotten that?"

"I do my job."

"Not for long."

"What?"

"Your bricks are below the standard."

"That can't be!"

"Two building foremen found bad bricks in the loads you sent them. They've written you up. If I turn it in to Moses, you'll be fired, maybe even put in jail."

"What's this all about? Why are you lying?"

"You have one alternative: buying my silence. Hand your pay over to me and the report will disappear."

"You're a jackal, Sary!"

"You have no choice, Abner."

"Why do you hate me so?"

"You're a Hebrew, one among many. Let's say you're paying for all the rest."

"You have no right!"

"I need an answer. Now."

Abner hung his head. Sary had beaten him again.

FORTY

In Memphis, Ofir felt more at ease than he had in Thebes. The northern capital was home to many foreigners, who seemed for the most part to fit in perfectly. Some adhered to Akhenaton's doctrine. The sorcerer revived their flagging faith, promising that it would bring them happiness and prosperity in the near future.

Those who were privileged to see Lita, silent as ever, were greatly impressed. None of them doubted that royal blood flowed in her veins, nor that she was the ill-fated pharaoh's rightful heir. The sorcerer's patient, well-reasoned arguments for the existence of a single god worked wonders, and Dolora's Memphis villa was the setting for productive meetings that netted a daily increase in the number of believers.

Ofir was not the first foreigner to propagate original ideas, but he was the only one to revive the heresy quashed by Akhenaton's successors. His capital and burial place had been abandoned, no person of rank had been entombed nearby in the necropolis. It was generally conceded that Ramses, after bringing Karnak under his control, would stand for no religious troubles. Therefore, Ofir took care to be sparing in his criticism of the king and his policies, which might invite disapproval.

The sorcerer was finally getting somewhere.

Dolora brought him a drink of cool carob juice.

"You seem tired, Ofir."

"Our work demands a constant effort. How is your husband doing on his project?"

"He's very unhappy. According to his last letter, he spends his days scolding lazy, dishonest Hebrews."

"I've heard the work is going very quickly, though."

"Everyone says it will be splendid."

"But dedicated to Set, the evil lord of the powers of darkness! Ramses wants to snuff out the light, hide the sun. We have to stop him."

"I'm convinced of it, Ofir."

"Your support is essential, as you know. Will you consent to let me use every means at my disposal to keep the Pharaoh from destroying Egypt?"

The tall, languid woman bit her lips. "Ramses is my brother!"

Ofir gently took Dolora's hands.

"He's already done us so much harm. Of course, I'll abide by your decision, but why wait any longer? Ramses isn't waiting for anything! And the further he goes, the stronger his magical defenses become. I'm not sure I'll be able to break through them if we stall."

"It's such a big step . . ."

So Dolora was still unwilling to attack her brother. Ofir let go of her hands.

"There may be another way."

"What are you thinking?"

"Queen Nefertari is rumored to be pregnant."

"It's no rumor. She's already showing."

"Have you any affection for her?"

"Not in the least."

"I'll ask one of my compatriots to bring what I need tonight."

"I'll stay in my room!" cried Dolora, retreating hastily.

The man arrived in the middle of the night. The house was quiet; Dolora and Lita slept. Ofir opened the door to the merchant, took the sack from him, and paid with two linen sheets Dolora had donated.

The transaction took only a few moments.

Ofir shut himself up in a small room to which he had blocked all the openings. A single oil lamp gave off a dim light.

On a low table, the sorcerer laid out the contents of the bundle: a statuette of an ape, an ivory hand, a crude figurine of a naked woman, a miniature pillar, and another figurine of a woman, this one holding snakes in her hands. The ape would supply him with the technique of the god Thoth. The hand was for action. The naked woman gave him power over the queen's reproductive organs. The pillar represented the lasting effect of his spell. The snake woman would poison Nefertari's body with black magic.

Ofir's task would not be easy. The queen possessed great personal strength, and, like her husband, had been endowed with protective forces at the time of her coronation. But pregnancy weakened those defenses. The new life inside her sapped Nefertari's own life force.

It would take at least three days and nights for the spell to take hold. Ofir was slightly disappointed not to be attacking Ramses directly, but without his sister's consent that would be impossible. When he had Dolora completely in his sway, he would try again. For now, he could begin to weaken the enemy.

Leaving the daily business of governing in the hands of Ahmeni and his cabinet members, Ramses made frequent visits to Pi-Ramses. Thanks to Moses' leadership and organization, as well as a strict schedule, the work was progressing by leaps and bounds.

The atmosphere was upbeat. The men were happy with the quality and quantity of their rations. On top of that, generous bonuses were paid as promised, on the merit system. The hardest workers would make a tidy bundle and be able to set themselves up either in the new capital or another town, perhaps even buy a plot of land. There was also a well-equipped infirmary to care for the sick and injured. Unlike other construction sites, Pi-Ramses was not plagued with workers feigning illness in order to go on leave.

The king was safety-conscious; several foremen were permanently assigned to site security. All but a few minor injuries had been avoided when the temple of Amon's granite blocks were set in place. Thanks to a scrupulously observed rotation of work gangs, the men never reached the point of exhaustion. Two days off every six days allowed them to rest and recuperate.

Moses alone drove himself relentlessly. He rechecked all work, resolved conflicts, made urgent decisions, reorganized substandard work crews, reordered materials and supplies, wrote reports, slept an hour after lunch and three hours each night. Their leader's energy impressed the Hebrew brickworkers so deeply that they toed the line for him. No supervisor in their experience had ever defended their interests as he did.

Abner could have spoken to Moses about Sary's extortion, but he was afraid of how his foreman might retaliate, given his strong police connections. Labeled as a troublemaker, Abner would be deported and never see his wife and children again. Once he'd started receiving payments, the foreman had stopped harassing him and been almost pleasant. It seemed the worst was over. The Hebrew walled himself in silence and molded his bricks with the usual care and speed.

That morning, Ramses was touring the work site. As soon as his visit had been announced, the Hebrews washed, trimmed their beards and mustaches, tied fresh white bands around their best wigs, and lined up their bricks in perfect order.

The first chariot that stopped in front of the brickyard discharged a glowering giant with sword and shield in hand. Was one of the workers about to be disciplined? The presence of twenty archers did little to lighten the mood.

Serramanna filed stonily down the tense and motionless

rows of Hebrew brickmakers. When they had passed inspection, the Sard signaled one of the soldiers to let the royal chariot advance.

The brickmakers bowed to Pharaoh, who called them by name, congratulating them on their work. Cheers greeted his announcement that new wigs and white Delta wine were to be distributed; but what touched the men most deeply was the attention the king paid to the freshly molded bricks. He picked up several at random, weighing them in his hands.

"Perfect," he declared. "Double rations for a week and an extra day off. Where is your foreman?"

Sary stepped forward.

Ramses' old teacher was the only one not especially eager to see the monarch. If Sary had never plotted against Ramses, he might still be head of the royal academy and a court insider.

"Satisfied with your new assignment, Sary?"

"I thank Your Majesty for granting me the privilege."

"If my mother and Nefertari hadn't interceded, your punishment would have been much stiffer, believe me."

"I'm aware of that, Majesty, and hope my new attitude will convince you to forgive my past transgressions."

"They're unforgivable, Sary."

"The remorse I suffer weighs on my heart."

"It can't weigh too heavily; it's been quite some time, and you're still around."

"Is it too much to hope for Your Majesty's pardon?"

"I don't hold with that notion, Sary. There's no way around the law of Ma'at. You've flouted it, and your soul is forever stained. Make sure you cause Moses no trouble. This is the last chance I'm giving you."

"I swear to Your Majesty that—"

"Enough said, Sary. Be glad of the chance to take part in creating Pi-Ramses."

When the king climbed back in his chariot, cheers rose again, even louder this time. Reluctantly, Sary chimed in.

FORTY-ONE

As planned, construction proceeded more slowly on the temples than on secular edifices. Nevertheless, immediate shipments of granite began, and expert stone haulers, including a number of Hebrews, made regular deliveries to the work site.

Thanks to the brickmakers' industriousness, the royal palace rose quickly from its stone foundation, already dominating the center of the capital. Shipping was under way, the warehouses were open, carpenters were turning out fine furniture, ceramic tile was being mass-produced. Villas seemed to pop up overnight, neighborhoods grew, the barracks would soon be ready to house their first troops.

"The palace lake will be splendid," announced Moses. "It ought to be dug by the middle of next month. Your capital is going to be beautiful, Ramses. It's built with love."

"You can take credit for that, Moses."

"All I've done is execute your plans."

The king detected a slight reproach in his friend's tone of voice. Just as he was about to ask why, a courier from Memphis galloped up. Serramanna made him stop at a respectable distance. The messenger jumped down and approached his sovereign, panting.

"Your Majesty's presence is urgently requested in Memphis. The queen has been taken ill."

Ramses collided with Dr. Pariamaku, chief of the palace medical staff, a learned and commanding man of fifty with long, expressive hands. An experienced surgeon, he had a reputation as an excellent doctor, though strict with his patients.

"I want to see the queen," demanded Ramses.

"The queen is sleeping, Majesty. The nurses applied a massage oil mixed with a sleeping draft."

"What's wrong with her?"

"There are signs of a premature delivery."

"Isn't that dangerous?"

"Very high-risk, I'm afraid."

"I order you to save Nefertari."

"I still predict a favorable outcome."

"What makes you say that?"

"My staff performed the usual tests, Your Majesty, placing barley and wheat in two cloth sacks that were sprinkled with the queen's urine for several days in a row. Both grains sprouted, indicating she will give birth successfully. Since the wheat sprouted first, she will have a girl."

"I've heard the opposite."

Dr. Pariamaku gave him an icy stare. "Your Majesty must be referring to another technique, in which the grains are covered with soil. In any case, we must hope that the seed of your heart, implanted in the queen's heart, is firmly fixed in the infant's skeletal system. High-quality sperm gives a straight spine and excellent bone marrow. Need I remind you that the bones and tendons come from the father, the flesh and blood from the mother?"

The doctor was rather pleased with his lecture. And such an illustrious student!

"Need I remind you that I studied anatomy and physiology at the royal academy, Doctor?"

"Of course not, Majesty."

"Nothing led you to expect complications?"

"My learning has certain limits, Majesty . . ."

"My power has none, Doctor. I demand a safe delivery."

"Majesty . . ."

"Yes, Doctor?"

"Your own health must be closely monitored. I have not yet had the honor of examining you, which is among my foremost responsibilities."

"No need. I've never been sick a day in my life. Call me the moment the queen wakes up."

The sun was low in the sky when Serramanna granted Dr. Pariamaku entry into the king's office.

The distinguished physician was ill at ease.

"The queen has awakened, Majesty."

Ramses rose.

"However . . ."

"Out with it, Doctor!"

Pariamaku, who had boasted that he would be able to handle Ramses, was beginning to miss Seti, taciturn and uncooperative as the late king had been. Ramses was like a raging storm—best to stay out of his way.

"The queen has just been taken to the delivery room."

"I demanded to see her immediately!"

"The midwives decided there wasn't a second to lose."

Ramses snapped the reed pen in his hand. If Nefertari died, would he have the strength to go on?

Six midwives from the House of Life, wearing long tunics and turquoise necklaces, helped Nefertari to the delivery room, an airy, flower-filled pavilion. Like all Egyptian women, the queen would give birth naked, straight-backed, squatting over stones with a bed of reeds on top of them. This symbolized each newborn's destiny, its life span determined by Thoth.

The first midwife would support the queen from behind, the second would ease her through each stage of labor, the third would catch the baby, the fourth would attend it, the fifth was the wet nurse, and the sixth would hold two *ankh* amulets—the "key of life"—for the queen until the infant's first cry was heard. Though aware of the dangers facing them, the six women moved serenely.

After thoroughly massaging Nefertari, the head midwife had applied poultices over her lower abdomen. Judging it necessary to hasten what promised to be a painful labor, she inserted a paste of turpentine resin, onion, milk, fennel, and salt into the vagina. To ease the labor pains, she prepared dried earth to be mixed with warm oil and rubbed on the genital area.

The six midwives knew that Nefertari's labor would be long and its outcome uncertain.

"May the goddess Hathor grant the queen a child," chanted one of the women. "May no sickness touch it. Begone, demon of darkness, with your insidious ways. You will never embrace this infant, put it to sleep, harm it, or carry it off. May the spirit move in the child, may no evil spell touch it, may the stars be favorable."

As night fell, the contractions came closer together. Bean paste was packed around the queen's teeth so that she could clench them without undue strain.

Professional, focused, reciting ancient incantations to banish pain, the six midwives helped the Queen of Egypt bring forth new life.

Ramses couldn't stand it a moment longer. When Dr. Pariamaku reappeared for the tenth time, he thought the king might fly at his throat.

"Is it finally over?"

"Yes, Majesty."

"Nefertari?"

"The queen is alive and well and you have a daughter."

"How is the baby?"

"Too soon to tell . . ."

The king pushed past the physician and charged into the delivery room, where one of the midwives was cleaning up.

"Where are they? The queen and my daughter?"

"In a palace bedchamber, Majesty."

"Tell me the truth!"

"The baby is very weak."

"I demand to see them."

Relieved, radiant, but exhausted, Nefertari slept. The head midwife had given her a sedative.

The baby was remarkably beautiful. Fresh, her eyes at once astonished and curious, the child of their love greeted life for the miracle it was.

The king held her. "She's perfect! Why do you think something's wrong?"

"The cord broke on the amulet we were putting around her neck. A bad omen, Majesty, a very bad omen."

"Have the signs been read?"

"We're waiting for the prophetess to complete her predictions."

The prophetess appeared a few minutes later. With the six midwives, she formed the circle of the Seven Hathors, foreseeing the newborn's destiny. Huddled around the infant, they went into a trance.

Their meditation seemed to last a very long time.

Grim-faced, the prophetess broke away from the circle and approached the king.

"The time isn't right, Your Majesty. We have been unable—"

"Don't lie to me."

"We may be wrong."

"Just tell me what you see."

"The next twenty-four hours are critical. If we don't find a way to dispel the demons eating away at her heart, your daughter won't live through the night."

FORTY-TWO

The royal infant's blooming wet nurse had been personally checked by Dr. Pariamaku. Her milk had the pleasant odor of carob flour. To augment her milk supply, the nurse had been drinking fig sap and eating roasted fish spines ground up in oil.

Much to the distress of the doctor and wet nurse, the baby would not take the breast. Another nurse was called in, with the same result. The final remedy, a special reserve of milk kept in a hippopotamus-shaped vessel, worked no better. The child would not take the thick milk flowing from the animal's teats.

The doctor moistened his tiny patient's lips and was preparing to wrap her in damp cloths when Ramses took her in his arms.

"She's becoming dehydrated, Majesty!"

"Your treatments can't help her. She'll take her strength from me."

Holding his tiny daughter tight to his chest, the king went to Nefertari's bedside. Despite her exhaustion, the queen was radiant as ever.

"I'm so happy, Ramses! Nothing can harm her now."

"How do you feel?"

"Don't worry about me. Have you thought of a name for our baby?"

"That's up to the mother."

"We'll call her Meritamon, 'Beloved of Amon.' She'll see your Eternal Temple finished. While I was in labor, I had the strangest sensation . . . you need to start work on it right away. It will be your best defense against the forces of evil and keep us united against adversity."

"You'll have your wish, I promise."

"Why are you holding her so tight?"

Nefertari's gaze was so clear, so trusting, that Ramses was unable to keep the truth from her.

"Meritamon isn't well."

"What's wrong with her?"

"She won't take the breast, but I'll make her better."

The queen sank back into the bed. "I've already lost one child, and now death is trying to take our daughter. It's dark, dark . . ."

Nefertari swooned.

"Your diagnosis, Doctor?" asked Ramses.

"The queen is very weak," Pariamaku replied.

"Can you save her?"

"I don't know, Majesty. If she survives, she mustn't have any more children. Another pregnancy would be fatal."

"And our daughter?"

"I've never seen anything like it. She seems so peaceful,

now that you're holding her. The midwives may be right, although I find their hypothesis absurd."

"What is it, then?"

"They think she's under some sort of magic spell."

"A spell, here, in my palace?"

"That's why I didn't take it seriously. Still, it might be a good idea to consult the court magicians . . ."

"But what if one of them is involved? No, there's only one thing left to do."

Meritamon slept in her father's powerful arms.

The court buzzed with rumors: Nefertari's child was stillborn; the queen was near death; Ramses was mad with despair. While not daring to believe them, Shaanar hoped there might be some truth to these excellent reports.

On the way to the palace with his sister, Dolora, Shaanar put on a grave and tearful face. His sister seemed genuinely grief-stricken.

"Been taking acting lessons, sister dear?"

"Can't you see that I'm upset?"

"You don't care about Ramses or Nefertari."

"No, but the baby . . . the baby isn't responsible."

"I had no idea you were so sentimental. If the rumors are true, things are looking up for us."

Dolora could never tell Shaanar what was really upsetting her: Ofir's successful spell. To break through the royal couple's defenses and shatter their lives, the Libyan must have extraordinary reserves of black magic.

Ahmeni, paler than ever, received Dolora and her brother.

"Given the circumstances," said Shaanar, "we thought the king might like his family nearby."

"Sorry, he'd rather be alone."

"How is Nefertari?"

"The queen is resting."

"The baby?" asked Dolora.

"Dr. Pariamaku is attending her."

"Can you tell us anything more definite?"

"That's all I know."

As Shaanar and Dolora left the palace, they saw Serramanna and his guard detail escorting a scruffy-looking, bareheaded man, dressed in a strange antelope-skin tunic studded with pockets. They were walking briskly toward the royal couple's private apartments.

"Setau! You're my last hope."

The snake charmer walked up to the king and gazed at the baby in his arms.

"I don't care for babies, but that one's a beauty. The mother's looks, of course."

"Meet our daughter, Meritamon. She's dying, Setau."

"Come again?"

"She's under a spell."

"Has it come from inside the palace?"

"I'm not sure."

"What has it done to her?"

"She won't take the breast."

"Nefertari?"

"Sinking fast."

"I suppose good old Pariamaku has resigned the case?"

"He's not at all sure what to do."

"Is he ever? Put your daughter down in the cradle. Gently, now."

Ramses did as he was told. The moment he let go of Meritamon, her breathing grew labored.

"Your strength is all that's keeping her alive. Just as I feared. What's this now? The baby isn't even wearing an amulet! Don't they know anything in this palace?"

Setau dug a scarab amulet out of a pocket, strung it on a fine cord with seven knots, and put it around Meritamon's neck. The scarab bore the inscription: "Ravenous death will not take me, divine light will preserve me."

"Pick her up again," ordered Setau, "and show me the palace laboratory."

"Do you think you'll be able to—"

"We'll discuss it later. Every minute counts now."

There were several sections to the palace laboratory. Setau shut himself up in the room where male hippopotamus tusks were stored. He selected one and carved it into an elongated crescent moon. He smoothed the surface without damaging the ivory, then carved several symbols with the power to repel the forces of darkness visiting themselves upon the vulnerable mother and child. A winged griffin with a lion's body and falcon's head, a female hippo brandishing a knife, a frog, a shining sun, a bearded dwarf with fists full of snakes—these, he considered, were best suited to the situation. Describing his magical helpers aloud as he carved, he empowered them to attack and destroy all demons, male and female, in their path. Next, he prepared a potion of viper venom to clear the opening to Meritamon's stomach, though even the minutest of doses might be too much for a newborn.

When Setau emerged, Dr. Pariamaku was running frantically toward him.

"Hurry! The baby is almost gone."

Looking out at the sunset, Ramses held his daughter, trustfully slumbering against him. Despite his magnetism, her breathing was growing ragged. Nefertari's baby, the only child of their union who might survive . . . If Meritamon died, Nefertari would follow. Anger welled up in the king's heart, an anger that would repel the creeping shadows and save his daughter from their evil grip.

Setau entered the chamber, holding the newly carved tusk.

"It ought to break the spell," he explained. "But it's not enough. We can't reverse the damage to her internal organs unless she swallows this potion."

When he told them what it was made of, Dr. Pariamaku shook his head.

"I can't recommend this, Majesty!"

"Are you sure it will work, Setau?"

"I admit it's dangerous. You have to decide."

"Let's go ahead," said Ramses.

FORTY-THREE

Setau laid the carved tusk on Meritamon's chest. Snug in the cradle, her huge eyes inquisitive, the infant breathed peacefully.

Ramses, Setau, and Dr. Pariamaku remained silent. The talisman seemed to be working, but would it last?

Ten minutes later, Meritamon began to fuss.

"Have them bring a statue of the goddess Opet," ordered Setau. "I'm going back to the laboratory. Doctor, moisten the baby's lips, and make sure that's all you do."

Opet, the female hippopotamus, was the patroness of midwives and wet nurses. In the heavens, she took the form of a constellation separating the Great Bear (linked to Set, and therefore potentially destructive) from the reborn Osiris. Magicians from the House of Life had charged the statue with positive energy. Filled with mother's milk, it was placed at the head of the cradle.

Meritamon stopped crying and dozed off again.

Setau reappeared, holding a crudely carved tusk in each hand. "Not pretty," he said, "but they ought to do the trick."

He laid one tusk on the baby's stomach and the other at her feet. Meritamon did not stir.

"A field of positive forces is protecting her now. The spell has been broken, the evil undone."

"Is she out of danger?" asked the king.

"Not unless she takes the breast. The passage to her stomach has to open, or she'll die."

"Give her your potion."

"No, you."

Ramses gently parted his sleeping daughter's lips and poured the amber liquid into her tiny mouth as Dr. Pariamaku looked the other way.

Moments later, Meritamon opened her eyes and cried.

"Quick!" said Setau. "The statue!"

Ramses picked up his daughter, Setau removed the thin metal stopper in the statue's nipple, the king brought the baby's mouth to meet it.

Meritamon gulped the life-giving liquid, barely stopping to catch her breath, and gurgled with contentment.

"What can I do to thank you, Setau?"

"Nothing, Ramses."

"I'll appoint you director of the palace magicians."

"They can get along without me. How's Nefertari doing?"

"Amazingly well. She can walk in the garden tomorrow."

"And the baby?"

"She can't get enough of life."

"What were the Seven Hathors' predictions?"

"The black cloud over Meritamon's future has lifted.

They saw vestments, a woman of great nobility, the stones of a temple."

"Sounds forbidding, for a princess."

"You deserve a richer life, too, Setau."

"My snakes, my desert creatures, and Lotus are enough for me."

"You'll have unlimited credit. As for your venom production, the palace will pay top price for it and redistribute it to the hospitals."

"I don't want any favors."

"It's no favor, since your pharmaceuticals are the best in Egypt. You deserve to make a profit and invest in more research."

"There *is* one thing . . ."

"Anything."

"Do you still have any of that red Faiyum wine from Year Three of your father's reign?"

"I'll have several jars of it sent your way tomorrow."

"Let me know how many vials of venom I'll owe you."

"For you, no charge."

"I don't like presents, especially coming from the Pharaoh."

"Think of it as a gift from a friend. It would make me feel better. Tell me, where did you learn the technique you used to save Meritamon?"

"My snakes teach me almost everything, and Lotus knows the rest. Nubian sorcerers are peerless, believe me. The amulet I put around your daughter's neck will do her a world of good, providing you have it recharged every year."

"I'm giving you and Lotus an official residence."

"In town? You can't be serious. How would we do our work? We need the desert, the dark, the danger. Speaking of danger, that was quite an unusual spell they cast on Meritamon."

"Explain."

"I had to use extreme measures because the spell was so strong. There was some foreign wizardry at work—Syrian, Libyan, Hebrew, maybe. Without three magic tusks, I'd never have been able to break through the negative force field. Not to mention the fact that it takes an exceptionally twisted mind to go after a newborn baby."

"A palace magician, do you think?"

"That would surprise me. No, someone comfortable with evil."

"He'll try again."

"Of that you can be sure."

"How can we find him and put him out of commission?"

"I haven't the least idea. Any fiend so powerful is certainly a master of deception. It could even be someone you've met, who would have seemed perfectly ordinary. Or he could be hiding in some well-concealed lair."

"How can I keep my wife and my daughter safe?"

"Stick to the proven methods: amulets and rituals."

"What if that's not enough?"

"You'll need to surround yourself with energy more powerful than black magic."

"A base that generates energy," mused Ramses.

The Eternal Temple . . . that would be his best hope.

Pi-Ramses was growing.

Not quite a city yet, but buildings and houses mushroomed in the imposing shadow of the palace. Its stone foundations rivaled those of its Thebes or Memphis counterparts. The work was proceeding at lightning pace. Moses seemed tireless and continued to run a model work site. Seeing results so quickly made everyone from master builders to rough laborers eager to see the project to completion. Some planned to live in the capital their own hands were helping to build.

Two Hebrew clan chiefs, resentful of Moses' growing authority, had tried to challenge him. Before he could even respond, the brickmakers had unanimously demanded that he remain their leader. From that moment on, Moses became the uncrowned king of his people without a homeland. He was so consumed with the task of building Pi-Ramses that his mental turmoil abated.

The news that Ramses would soon be touring the work site made him glad. Bad omens had followed his last visit. The sighting of certain birds made the men uneasy about the queen and her baby. For days, their spirits were low. Moses told them not to worry, betting that Ramses would be back before they knew it—and Ramses was proving him right.

Serramanna, try as he might, could not stop the workers from lining up on both sides of the royal chariot's route through town. Then men wanted to touch their pharaoh, to have his magic rub off on them. The Sard muttered curses. What if one of them had a dagger? Why wouldn't Ramses listen?

The king headed straight for Moses' temporary quarters. When he alighted, Moses bowed, but once they were inside, out of public view, the old friends embraced.

"If we can keep going at this rate, we may just meet your ridiculous deadline."

"Let me guess: you're ahead of schedule!"

"So it seems."

"This time I want to see everything."

"I think you'll be pleased. May I ask after Nefertari?"

"The queen is very well indeed. So is our daughter. Meritamon will be a beauty, like her mother."

"I hear you had a close call."

"Setau was the one who saved them."

"With his pharmaceuticals?"

"No, he's become quite adept at magic. He broke an evil spell someone cast on my pregnant wife."

Moses was aghast. "Who'd dare try such a thing?"

"We don't know yet."

"You'd have to be hard as stone to attack a mother and child. And insane, to make an attempt on the royal family."

"I wonder if there's a connection to my building a new capital. I've ruffled a lot of feathers."

"I don't think so. It's too big a jump from discontent to murder."

"If it turned out a Hebrew was guilty, how would you feel?"

"A criminal is a criminal, no matter what his background. But I think you're on the wrong track."

"If you learn anything at all, don't keep it from me."

"What? Don't you trust me?"

"Would I talk to you this way if I didn't?"

"No Hebrew would stoop so low."

"I have to be away for several weeks, Moses. Take good care of my capital."

"The next time you come, you'll hardly recognize it. Don't wait too long, though. We wouldn't want to postpone the opening ceremonies."

FORTY-FOUR

June brought stifling heat and a round of festivities marking the beginning of Ramses' second year on the throne. Already more than a year since Seti's departure for the dome of heaven!

The royal couple's boat moored at Gebel el-Silsila, where the great river narrowed. According to tradition, the spirit of the Nile resided here, a genie pharaoh must reawaken for the life-giving waters to rise again.

After the offering of milk and wine and the ritual prayers, the royal pair entered a chapel carved into the river bluffs. Inside, it was pleasantly cool.

"Did Dr. Pariamaku speak to you?" Ramses asked Nefertari.

"He prescribed something new to give me back my energy."

"Nothing else?"

"Is he hiding the truth about Meritamon?"

"No, you can rest easy on her account."

"Then what was he supposed to tell me?"

"Courage is not the good doctor's greatest virtue."

"Tell me."

"All right. He said it's a miracle you survived childbirth this time."

A shadow passed over Nefertari's face. "You're telling me I can't have any more children, aren't you? I'll never give you a son."

"Kha and Meritamon will be the legitimate heirs to the throne."

"Ramses should have more children. Many sons. If you want me to step aside, to join a religious order . . ."

The king clasped his wife to him. "I love you, Nefertari. You're the light of my life. You were meant to be Queen of Egypt. Our souls are joined for eternity. Nothing and no one can come between us."

"Iset will bear your children."

"Nefertari . . ."

"Ramses, listen. It's meant to be. You're no ordinary man, you're Pharaoh."

As soon as they arrived in Thebes, the royal couple proceeded to the site where Ramses was to raise his Eternal Temple. The location had grandeur and pulsed with the energy that flowed from the looming Peak—symbol of the West, the afterlife—and the fertile Theban plain.

"I should never have neglected this project and focused so much on Pi-Ramses," the king admitted. "My mother's warning and the threat of black magic opened my eyes. Only a temple of millions of years can shield us from the forces of darkness."

Noble and resplendent, Nefertari paced the vast stretch

of rock and sand, so sterile in appearance. Like Ramses, she was a child of the sun, never burning, only glowing from its touch. Time froze. She was the founding goddess. Each place her feet touched became holy ground.

The Great Royal Wife walked out of eternity to claim this sun-baked soil, adding her spiritual signature to her husband's seal.

The two men collided on the gangway to the Pharaoh's ship and stopped dead, face-to-face. Setau was shorter than Serramanna but just as broad of shoulder. Their eyes locked.

"I was hoping not to find you anywhere near the king, Setau."

"Sorry to disappoint you."

"There's talk of black magic nearly killing the queen and her baby."

"Still no idea who was behind it? Some security Ramses has here."

"You're asking for it," the Sard growled.

"Be my guest. But watch out for my snakes."

"Is that a threat?"

"Take it any way you want. To me, a pirate is a pirate, no matter how you dress him up."

"It would save me a lot of time if you'd just confess."

"For someone in your position, you're not very well informed. Haven't you heard that I saved the princess's life?"

"To cover your tracks. You don't fool me, Setau."

"As if you'd be hard to fool."

"Make the slightest move in the king's direction and I'll bash your skull in."

"You talk big, Serramanna."

"Try me."

"An unprovoked attack on a friend of the king's would land you in jail."

"That's where you'll end up."

"You'll beat me to it, Sard. Now get out of my way."

"Where are you going?"

"To meet Ramses, at his request, and drive the snakes away from his future temple."

"I'm watching you, sorcerer."

Setau shoved past Serramanna.

"Stop spouting foolishness and get back to guarding the king."

Ramses spent several hours at the temple of Gurnah, on the West Bank of Thebes, meditating in the chapel dedicated to his father's perpetual memory. He had brought an offering of grapes, figs, juniper berries, and pine cones. Here Seti's soul could rest in peace, nourished by the subtle essence of offerings.

And here Seti had first announced that Ramses would be his successor. At the time, the full weight of his father's words had not registered. While Seti lived, Ramses moved in a dream, safe in his father's giant shadow, lost in admiration of a mind that moved like the divine bark through the celestial reaches.

When the twin crowns of Egypt, one red, one white, had been placed on his head, the sheltered life of the prince regent was instantly replaced with the harsh reality of governing—much harsher than he had ever imagined. On the temple walls, grave and smiling gods brought the sacred to life. Within these walls, a pharaoh's eternal spirit honored the gods and communed with the Invisible. On the outside were men. Humanity—courageous and craven, upright and hypocritical, generous and greedy. And caught in the middle of these opposing forces was Ramses, entrusted with maintaining the link between gods and men, no matter what his own desires and failings might be.

Only one year on the throne, but how long since he had ceased to live for himself?

When Ramses climbed into the chariot with Serramanna at the reins, the sun was low in the sky.

"Where to, Your Majesty?"

"The Valley of the Kings."

"I had every boat in the fleet searched."

"Anything suspicious?"

"Nothing."

The Sard was edgy.

"Is that really all you have to report, Serramanna?"

"It is, Your Majesty."

"Are you sure?"

"It's only a feeling I have."

"Something to do with black magic?"

"Feelings don't count, only facts. Until I have evidence, it would be wrong to name names."

"Let's get moving, then."

The horses galloped toward the Valley, the entrance to which was guarded night and day. In the late summer afternoon, the rocky walls were radiating heat absorbed during the day. It was stifling, like riding into the suffocating blaze of an oven.

Dripping sweat and red with effort, the ranking officer of the guard detachment bowed to the Pharaoh and assured him that no robbers would find their way into Seti's tomb.

Ramses directed the chariot not toward his father's final resting place but to his own. Their workday finished, the stone carvers were cleaning their tools and arranging them in their baskets. At the unexpected sight of the sovereign, a hush fell. The workmen huddled in back of their foreman, who was finishing his daily log.

"We've finished the corridor into the Hall of Ma'at. May I show you, Your Majesty?"

"I'll go alone."

Ramses went through the entrance to his tomb and descended a short flight of stairs carved into the rock, symbolizing the sun's nightly disappearance. The walls of the corridor below were carved with vertical columns of hieroglyphs, prayers that a pharaoh, depicted as youthful for all eternity, addressed to the power of light, saying the litany of its secret names. Next came the secrets of the hours of darkness, the hidden room, the trials the old sun must overcome before it could be reborn with the morning.

Passing through this vale of darkness, Ramses next encountered his likeness worshiping the gods, alive in the next world as they were on earth. Skillfully drawn, brightly painted, these images preserved the king's spirit through all eternity.

On the right was the chariot room with its four pillars. The shaft, carriage, wheels, and other parts of Ramses' ritual chariot would be stored here, that it might be reassembled in the other world and serve him as he battled the forces of darkness.

From this point on, the passage narrowed. The walls were decorated with scenes and texts relating to the ritual opening of the mouth and the eyes, carried out on the statue of the risen, transfigured king.

Then all was rock, barely hewn by the stone carvers' chisels. It would take them several more months to finish the Hall of Ma'at and the golden chamber where the sarcophagus would be laid to rest.

Ramses' death rose up before him, calm and mysterious. No word would be missing from the ritual texts, no scene from the tableau of the afterlife. The young king felt himself move beyond his earthly body, into a world whose laws were beyond any human understanding.

When the Pharaoh emerged from his tomb, a peaceable night had fallen on the valley of his ancestors.

FORTY-FIVE

The Second Prophet of Amon, Doki, hurried from the temple of Amon to the royal palace. The king was here in Thebes and had summoned Karnak's top officials. The crocodile-faced priest rushed on, cursing his idiot of a secretary. Knee-deep in livestock tallies, the fool had neglected to pass on the Pharaoh's message. He could go live with the livestock!

Serramanna frisked Doki and showed him to the Pharaoh's audience chamber. Across from him, in a chair with arm rests, sat old Nebu, the high priest and First Prophet of Amon. Wizened and slouching, his bad leg propped on a pillow, Nebu took whiffs from a bottle of flower essences.

"Please forgive me, Your Majesty. I'm only late because—"

"Don't mention it. Where's the Third Prophet?"

"He's in charge of the rites of purification at the House of Life and wishes to remain in seclusion."

"Granted. What about Bakhen, the Fourth Prophet?"

"He's on site at Luxor."

"Surely he could take the afternoon off!"

"They're raising the obelisks, a delicate operation, I understand. If you want me to send to Luxor . . ."

"No matter. The high priest is in satisfactory health, I hope?"

"No," replied Nebu listlessly. "I can barely get around. Most of my time is spent in the archives. My predecessor didn't pay much attention to older forms of worship, and I hope to revive them."

"And you, Doki? More concerned with affairs of this world?"

"Someone has to be! Bakhen and I run the temple and its estates—under the guidance of our revered leader, of course."

"I may be lame, but there's nothing wrong with my vision. My young subordinates have come to understand that. The mission the king has given me will be carried out to the fullest. I've set high standards."

The firmness in his voice startled Ramses. Weary as he might seem, Nebu was clearly in charge.

"We rejoice in your visit, Majesty. It shows that the creation of your new capital doesn't mean you're abandoning Thebes."

"That was never my intention, Nebu. What pharaoh worthy of the name would turn his back on the city of Amon, god of victories?"

"Then why stay away so long?" he asked, almost accusingly.

"It's not the high priest of Amon's place to question government policy."

"I agree completely, Majesty, but it *is* his place, I believe, to concern himself with the future of his temple."

"Put your mind at ease, Nebu. The hall at Karnak has the biggest and most beautiful colonnade ever built, does it not?"

"By Your Majesty's grace, would you permit an old and unworldly man to inquire as to the true motive for your visit?"

Ramses smiled. "Which of us is more impatient, Nebu?"

"You feel the fire of youth, I hear the call of heaven. I can't waste what little time I have left in idle chatter."

The clash left Doki speechless. If Nebu continued to be so defiant, the king was bound to lose his temper.

"The royal family is in danger," revealed Ramses. "I've come in search of stronger magic to protect us."

"Why Thebes?" asked the high priest.

"Because this is where I'll build my temple of millions of years—my Eternal Temple."

Nebu gripped his cane. "Excellent. But first I suggest you augment your *ka*, the special power with which you are endowed."

"How is that?"

"By finishing work on the temple of Luxor, where your *ka* is paramount."

"Looking out for your own interests by any chance, Nebu?"

"Under different circumstances, I might have pleaded my case, but not after what you've just told us. Luxor is Karnak's direct connection to divine power and might—the power you need to maintain."

"I'll make note of your advice, high priest. For now, prepare to officiate at the ground-breaking of my Eternal Temple on the West Bank of Thebes."

To ease his feverish excitement, Doki downed several cups of strong beer. His hands shook. Cold sweat ran down his back. He'd suffered so much injustice, but his luck was finally changing!

He was only Second Prophet of Amon, yet he had just been entrusted with a state secret of the highest importance. Ramses had made a serious error in judgment, and if Doki played his cards right, he might become high priest after all.

The Eternal Temple . . . an unexpected opportunity, the solution he thought he'd never find. But he had to get control of himself, move slowly and cautiously, not waste one precious second, know what to say and when to say nothing.

His position at Karnak would allow him to skim commodities destined for the project, simply removing a line here and there from the inventories. Since he was in charge of the scribes who kept the ledgers, the risk was nonexistent.

Perhaps he was overly optimistic. Was he really capable of embezzlement on such a scale? The high priest and the Pharaoh were no fools. One false move and he'd be done for. Still, it was the chance of a lifetime. A pharaoh built only one Eternal Temple.

From Karnak to Luxor it was a half-hour's walk down an avenue of sphinxes. Consulting the archives of the House of Life, where all the secrets of heaven and earth were stored, and reading the books of Thoth, Bakhen had come up with a plan to enlarge Luxor according to Ramses' stated intentions. Thanks to Nebu's support, the work had proceeded at a rapid pace. A spacious courtyard adorned with statues of Ramses would be added onto the original temple of Amenhotep III. In front of the elegant pylon gateway, six colossal statues of the new pharaoh would guard the entry, while two towering obelisks would rise toward the heavens, warding off evil forces and protecting the royal *ka*.

The richly colored sandstone, the walls covered with electrum, the silver flooring, would combine to make Luxor the finest achievement of Ramses' reign. The poles with their banners affirming the holy presence would reach to the stars.

But the strange events of the last hour had plunged Bakhen into despair. An oversized barge hauling the first obelisk from the Aswan quarries whirled madly in the middle of the Nile, trapped in an uncharted whirlpool. The captain, busy taking soundings from the bow to check for sandbanks, had seen the danger too late. Panic-stricken, the helmsman had lost his grip. At the moment he hit the water, one of the rudders broke. The other jammed and was useless.

The barge's spinning had unbalanced the cargo. The shifting obelisk—two hundred tons of solid pink granite—had already snapped several of the ropes that secured it. The rest would soon give way. Soon, the monolith would be flung into the river.

Bakhen clenched his fists and cried.

The accident would be the end of his career. He would and should be held responsible for the wreck, the loss of the obelisk, the death of several men. In his haste to see Luxor finished, he, Bakhen, had ordered the barge to sail north before the yearly flood, ignoring the danger to the crew. What made him think he could defy the laws of nature?

The Fourth Prophet of Amon would gladly have given his life to undo this disaster. But the boat spun faster and faster, the hull creaked and shuddered. The obelisk was a work of art, complete except for the gilding on the pyramidion, to make it glitter in the sunlight. Now its splendor would be wasted on the bottom of the river.

On the far shore, a man was gesticulating—a whiskered giant with sword and helmet. His shouts were lost in the whipping wind.

He was yelling at a swimmer, Bakhen finally realized, begging him to turn back. Instead, the man's rapid strokes brought him closer and closer to the spinning barge. At the risk of drowning in the current or being hit by an oar, the swimmer managed to reach the prow and pull himself along the hull with a dangling rope.

Then he gripped the jammed rudder, struggling with both hands to free it. With superhuman effort, braced against his heels, the muscles of his arms and chest popping, he dislodged the huge block of wood.

The boat righted itself and stopped for a few seconds, parallel to shore. The wind was right for the helmsman to steer it out of the whirlpool. Soon the oarsmen were able to help.

The moment the barge reached the shore dozens of stone carvers and laborers ran up to unload the giant pillar.

The daring swimmer appeared at the top of the gangway, and Bakhen knew him at once. Ramses, the King of Egypt, had risked his life to save the obelisk.

FORTY-SIX

On six meals a day, Shaanar was ballooning. Whenever he lost all hope of winning the throne and finally taking revenge on Ramses, he ate. Food made him feel better, helped him forget about his brother's burgeoning new capital and flagrant popularity. Even Ahsha failed to raise his spirits, convincing as his arguments seemed. Power would take its toll on Ramses, he argued; the honeymoon would soon be over, his path would be strewn with obstacles . . . yet Ahsha had nothing concrete to back up his claims. The Hittites were strangely inactive, daunted by the young monarch's miraculous debut.

In short, things were going from bad to worse.

Shaanar was gnawing on a plump goose drumstick when his steward announced Meba, the former secretary of state whom the prince had replaced, laying all the blame for the switch on Ramses.

"I don't want to see him."

"He's insisting."

"Send him away."

"He claims he has important information concerning you."

The former department head was not one to exaggerate; his entire career had been built on proceeding with caution.

"All right, then."

Meba was the same as ever: a broad, reassuring face, a pontificating manner, a droning voice. A high government official who had felt he was set for life and could never imagine what had really caused his dismissal.

"Thank you for seeing me, Shaanar."

"Always a pleasure, old friend. May I offer you anything to eat or drink?"

"Water would do very nicely."

"You haven't given up wine and beer, now, have you?"

"Since I left the department, I've suffered from dreadful headaches."

"So terribly unfair of my brother to force you out. Perhaps in time I can find a place for you."

"Ramses isn't the type to go back on his decisions. And look how far he's come in one short year!"

Shaanar bit into a goose wing.

"I was quite resigned," the former diplomat admitted, "until your sister, Dolora, introduced me to someone quite unusual."

"Do I know him?"

"A Libyan named Ofir."

"Never heard of the fellow."

"He's in hiding."

"Why is that?"

"Because he's protecting a girl by the name of Lita."

"What kind of story is this?"

"According to Ofir, Lita is the direct descendant of Akhenaton."

"But all his descendants are dead!"

"And what if it's true?"

"Ramses would banish her on the spot."

"Your sister has fallen in with them and other believers in Aton, the One God replacing all others. In Thebes they had quite an extensive membership."

"I hope you're not joining! No good can come of this foolishness. Ramses represents the dynasty that put an end to Akhenaton's experiment, and condemns it still."

"I'm well aware of that. Simply meeting with this Ofir made me nervous. But in retrospect, I think he could be the key to defeating Ramses."

"A Libyan who lives on the run?"

"Ofir has a certain advantage: he's a sorcerer."

"There are hundreds in Egypt."

"How many of them would be able to cast a spell over Nefertari and her baby daughter?"

"Whatever do you mean?"

"Dolora is convinced that Ofir is a wise man and Lita is destined to be queen. Since she's asked me to head her movement, your sister tells me everything. Ofir is a master of black magic, determined to break through the royal couple's magical defenses."

"Are you quite certain?"

"Once you've seen him, you'll believe it. But that's not all, Shaanar. Have you given any thought to Moses?"

"No . . . Why Moses?"

"In many respects, Akhenaton's beliefs parallel those of the Hebrews. I've heard rumors that the Pharaoh's oldest friend is obsessed with the concept of a single god. That he's disenchanted with our civilization."

Shaanar studied Meba attentively. "What are you getting at?"

"I think you should encourage Ofir to practice his magic, and introduce him to Moses."

"You're leaving out the girl. Akhenaton's heir . . . that bothers me."

"Me, too, but will it matter?" Meba countered. "Let's convince Ofir that we believe in Aton and back his Lita. Once the sorcerer has undermined Ramses' health and recruited Moses, we'll get rid of the Libyan and his princess."

"An interesting plan, old friend."

"I'm counting on you to improve it."

"What's in this for you?"

"I want my job back. The Foreign Service was my life. I miss receiving ambassadors, hosting state dinners, holding secret talks with foreign dignitaries, nurturing relationships, setting traps, juggling protocol . . . It's hard to understand unless you've been part of it for as long as I was. When you become king, appoint me to my old position."

"I'll take it under consideration. You intrigue me, Meba."

The old diplomat beamed. "If it's not too much trouble, I might take some of that wine you offered me. My headache is gone."

Bakhen, the Fourth Prophet of Amon, prostrated himself before his pharaoh.

"I have no excuse to offer, Majesty. I take complete responsibility for my failure."

"What failure?"

"The obelisk could have sunk, we almost lost the crew . . ."

"Your nightmares mean nothing, Bakhen. Only reality counts."

"It doesn't undo my carelessness."

"It's not like you, I agree. What were you thinking?"

"I wanted Luxor to be your masterpiece."

"Did you think I'd settle for only one jewel in my crown? Rise, Bakhen."

The former soldier was burly as ever. He looked more like an athlete than a holy man.

"You were fortunate, Bakhen, and I like the men around me to be lucky. There's magic in knowing how to stay out of harm's way."

"If you hadn't been there . . ."

"You were even able to make me appear! Nice trick. In fact, it's one for the royal annals."

Bakhen was afraid some terrible punishment would be pronounced after these ironic remarks. Instead, Ramses turned his piercing gaze toward the barge. The gigantic pillar was being unloaded without further incident.

"It really is a splendid obelisk. When will the other one be ready?"

"By the end of September, I hope."

"The hieroglyph carvers had better get busy!"

"Aswan is hotter than here, and in the quarries—"

"Excuses, excuses! Go to Aswan yourself and see that the work's done on schedule. And what about the colossal statues?"

"The sculptors have found the perfect sandstone at Gebel el-Silsila."

"Get them moving, too. Send someone today to make sure they're not wasting a minute. Why isn't the courtyard finished?"

"We're going as fast as we can, Your Majesty!"

"Wrong, Bakhen. When you're building a home for the Pharaoh's *ka*, a refuge for the creative force that keeps the universe in motion, you can't behave like a simple foreman, quibbling over technique, unsure of your materials. Your mind has to meet the stone like a bolt of lightning for the temple to spring from the ground. You've been slow and lazy: that's your real mistake."

Dumbstruck, Bakhen was unable to protest.

"When Luxor is finished, my *ka* will prosper. It's energy I need. Find more workmen—the best available."

"Some of them were assigned to your site in the Valley of the Kings."

"Bring them back here. My tomb can wait. One more thing I want you to take care of: my Eternal Temple on the West Bank. I need to start on it as soon as possible—another safeguard."

"You're planning . . ."

"A colossal complex, a temple so powerful its magic will repel adversity."

"But Luxor, Your Majesty."

"There's also Pi-Ramses, an entire new city. Call forth the sculptors from every province and weed out all but the best."

"Majesty, there are only so many hours in a day!"

"Make time, Bakhen. That's what I do."

FORTY-SEVEN

Doki met the sculptor in a tavern in Thebes where neither of them was known. They sat in the darkest corner, near a noisy bunch of Libyan laborers.

"I got your message and here I am," said the sculptor. "Why all the mystery?"

Wearing a wig that sat low on his forehead and covered his ears, Doki was unrecognizable.

"Have you mentioned this meeting to anyone?"

"No."

"Not even your wife?"

"I'm single."

"Your girlfriend, then?"

"I don't see her until tomorrow night."

"Give me back my letter."

The sculptor handed the papyrus scroll to Doki, who tore it to shreds.

"In case we can't reach an agreement," he explained, "there should be no evidence that we were ever in contact."

The sculptor, a broad-backed and forthright fellow, took a dim view of this.

"I've hired out to Karnak before with no complaints, but no one ever made me sneak into a tavern and listen to mumbo jumbo."

"I'll get to the point, then. How would you like to be rich?"

"Is this a joke?"

"No. I can offer you a quick way to make a fortune, but it does involve risk."

"What kind of risk?"

"Before I tell you, we have to agree on something."

"Go on."

"If you turn me down, you get out of town for good."

"And if I don't?"

"Perhaps we should leave it at that," said Doki, rising.

"All right, I agree. Don't go."

"Do you swear on the Pharaoh's life and the wrath of the goddess of silence?"

"I do."

Giving one's word was considered magic, a commitment of one's entire being. Breaking it caused a person's *ka* to flee, weakening the spirit.

"All I'm asking is for you to carve hieroglyphs on a stela," Doki revealed.

"That's what I do for a living! Why all the mystery?"

"You'll see when the time comes."

"About the payment . . ."

"Thirty dairy cows, a hundred sheep, ten fattened steers, a light boat, twenty pairs of sandals, furniture, and a horse."

The sculptor was stunned. "All for a simple stela?"

"Yes."

"Only a fool would say no. You're on!"

The two men shook hands.

"When do I start?"

"Tomorrow at dawn, on the West Bank."

Meba had invited Shaanar to a country villa belonging to one of his former staffers. The former secretary of state and the king's older brother arrived by different routes, two hours apart. Shaanar had elected not to inform Ahsha of the meeting.

"Your sorcerer is late," complained Shaanar.

"He promised he'd be here."

"I'm not used to waiting. If he doesn't show up soon . . ."

Ofir made his entrance, accompanied by Lita.

Shaanar's irritation vanished. He stared in fascination at this disturbing stranger. Gaunt, with high cheekbones, a hooked nose, thin lips, the Libyan was like a vulture about to devour its prey. The girl had a blank, hangdog look about her.

"You do us a great honor," declared Ofir in a deep voice that sent a chill down Shaanar's spine. "We hardly dared to hope for such a favor."

"My friend Meba told me about you."

"Aton be praised."

"That's one name I wish you wouldn't mention."

"I've devoted my life to pursuing Lita's claim to the throne. The fact that you're willing to meet with me must mean that you acknowledge it."

"Quite right, Ofir, but aren't you ignoring one major obstacle—Ramses himself?"

"On the contrary. The current pharaoh is endowed with exceptional force of character and breadth of vision. A tremendous challenge. Breaking down his defenses is bound to be difficult. However, I do have a few secret weapons."

"If you're caught practicing black magic, you face the death penalty."

"Ramses and his dynasty have tried to wipe out the memory of Akhenaton. If I fight him, I fight to the finish."

"Then it's no use preaching moderation."

"No," Ofir said firmly.

"Let me tell you about my brother. He's a violent man, determined and uncompromising. If he finds a movement to resurrect Aton, he'll crush it in a minute."

"That's why we need to attack him from behind."

"Good plan, but hard to execute."

"My magic will eat away at him like acid."

"What if we had an undercover agent? I'm thinking of someone in his inner circle."

The sorcerer's eyes narrowed to an inscrutable slit, like a cat's.

"Yes," thought Shaanar. "I've hooked him."

"Who is it?"

"Moses. An old school friend of Ramses', the Hebrew he put in charge of building his capital. If you can convince him to help you, I'll sign on."

For the commanding general at the southern outpost of Elephantine, it was the good life. Since Seti's pacification campaign a few years earlier, led by the Pharaoh in person, the Nubian provinces under Egyptian control were quiet as well as profitable.

The southern frontier was well guarded. No Nubian tribe would have dreamed of attacking or even protesting against the line of fortifications. Nubia belonged to Egypt for good. Tribal chieftains sent their sons north to be edu-cated. They returned as loyal subjects of the pharaoh, under the guidance of the Viceroy of Nubia, who was appointed directly by the king. While the thought of living abroad was painful to native Egyptians, the post was highly sought after because of the considerable privileges attached to it.

Still, the general wouldn't want to trade places. Elephantine was so tranquil, the climate was wonderful, and besides, he'd been born here. The garrison trained at dawn, then reported to the quarry, overseeing the docks where granite was loaded on northbound barges. His fighting days were far behind him—the further the better.

Since his appointment to the garrison, the general had become a customs official. His men inspected shipments from the deep south and calculated tariffs. His headquar-ters was cluttered with government documents, but he'd rather face a mountain of papyrus any day than a fierce band of Nubian warriors.

In a short while he'd take a quick boat trip down the Nile to check the fortifications from the river. He always enjoyed it, with the soft breeze, the lush banks, the scenic cliffs. Smiling, he thought ahead to his dinner engagement with the young widow he was tenderly consoling.

A strange sound startled him: footsteps, running.

"Urgent message. From Nubia. Sir," panted his lieu-tenant.

"Which detachment?"

"Desert patrol."

"The gold mines?"

"Yes, sir."

"What did the courier tell you?"

"A serious matter."

In other words, the scroll couldn't be tossed on the piles

of papyrus and wait a few days. He lifted the seal, unrolled it, and skimmed it with growing alarm.

"It's a fake. A joke!"

"No, sir. You can talk to the messenger."

"*Attack,*" he read, incredulous. "*Nubian rebels . . . Convoy carrying gold to Egypt!*"

FORTY-EIGHT

The new moon had just risen.

Bare-chested, Ramses wore a wig and an Old Kingdom kilt. The queen was dressed in a long, form-fitting white dress. In place of a crown, she had the seven-pointed star of the goddess Sechat, whom she represented in the evening's ritual. The cornerstone of the Ramesseum, the Pharaoh's Eternal Temple, was being laid.

Ramses thought of the time he had spent in the quarries of Gebel el-Silsila, working mallet and chisel right alongside the stone cutters. He remembered how he had wanted to stay there, and how his father showed him he was dreaming.

Twenty ritualists from the temple of Karnak assisted the royal couple, with three of the Four Prophets presiding:

Nebu, Doki, and Bakhen. The next day two architects would descend on the site with their work gangs.

The complex would be vast—five hectares, Ramses had decreed. Room for the temple itself, as well as numerous annexes, including a library, storerooms, and a garden. This holy city, economically self-sufficient, would nurture and celebrate the supernatural power present within the Pharaoh.

Stunned by the scope of the project, Bakhen refused to dwell on what lay ahead, focusing his attention on the king and queen performing the ceremony. After marking the symbolic corners of the future temple, they pounded in stakes and stretched a cord around them, invoking the memory of Imhotep, father of architecture, builder of the first pyramid.

Then Pharaoh dug a section of the foundation with a hoe and laid within small bars of gold and silver, amulets, and miniature tools, which he covered with sand. With a sure hand, he laid the first cornerstone with a lever, then molded a brick. His example would give rise to the temple, its floors, walls, ceilings. Next came the ritual purification: Ramses walked around the temple site scattering incense, known as "That Which Makes Divine."

Bakhen held up a wooden model of the monumental entrance. Blessing it, the king was opening the mouth of his Eternal Temple, bringing it to life. Henceforth the Word was in it. Ramses struck the door twelve times with the white club called "She Who Illuminates," summoning the presence of the gods. He lit a lamp, showing the way to the inner sanctuary where the Invisible would reside.

He concluded with the ancient words affirming that this temple was built not for him but for his true master, the law, the beginning and end of every temple in Egypt.

Bakhen had the sensation he was witnessing a miracle. What had happened here, before the eyes of a privileged few, was beyond human understanding. This space, still empty, already belonged to the gods. The power of Ramses' *ka* was palpable.

"The stela commemorating today's events is ready," declared Doki.

The sculptor in Doki's hire appeared with a small stone tablet covered with hieroglyphs. The text forever consecrated the site of the Ramesseum. The magical symbols transformed the earth into heaven.

Setau came forward, holding a blank papyrus and a flask of fresh ink. Doki gave an involuntary jump. This rough-looking character had been given no role in the ceremony!

Setau wrote on the papyrus, in horizontal lines from right to left, then read his text aloud.

"May any living mouth be sealed which would speak ill of the Pharaoh or so intend, either night or day. May this temple of millions of years be the magical haven protecting the royal person and shielding him from evil."

Doki was sweating profusely. No one had mentioned this magical incantation. Fortunately, it had no effect on his plan.

Setau rolled up the papyrus and presented the scroll to Ramses. The king affixed his seal to it and placed it at the foot of the tablet, where it would be buried. Now the king's gaze would come to rest on the hieroglyphs and bring them into existence.

He whirled around.

"Who carved these hieroglyphs?"

The sculptor stepped forward. "I did, Majesty."

"Who gave you the text to inscribe on the tablet?"

"The high priest of Amon himself, Your Majesty."

The man prostrated himself, partly out of respect and

partly to avoid Ramses' rising fury. The traditional inscription for the groundbreaking of a temple of millions of years had been modified and distorted, destroying its protective value.

Nebu! The high priest must be in league with the forces of darkness. He'd sold out to Ramses' enemies. The Pharaoh felt like smashing the old man's head in with the ceremonial mallet. But then a strange force seemed to emanate from the newly consecrated ground, a wave of soothing warmth rising up his spinal column, the "tree of life." A door opened within his heart, changing his outlook. Violence was not the answer. Out of the corner of his eye, he saw Nebu make a gesture that confirmed his opinion.

"Rise, sculptor." He got to his feet. "Now go find the high priest and bring him to me."

Doki gloated. His plan was working perfectly. The old man's protests would be ineffectual, the punishment merciless, and the office of high priest vacant. This time, the king would call on a man who knew more about running Karnak. He, Doki, was that man.

The sculptor was well rehearsed. He stopped in front of an old man holding a gilded staff in his right hand, with a golden ring on the middle finger, the two attributes of the high priest of Amon.

"You're sure that's the man who gave you the text for the stela?"

"I am."

"Then you're a liar."

"No, Majesty! I swear it was the high priest in person who—"

"Sculptor, you've never laid eyes on him."

Nebu retrieved his ring and staff from the elderly ritualist to whom he had handed them.

Frantic, the sculptor began to cry out. "Doki! Where are you, Doki! You were the one who told me to go after the high priest of Amon. I knew it was wrong to fool with magic!"

Doki made a run for it.

The sculptor went after him, blind with rage, fists flying.

Doki succumbed to his injuries. The sculptor, accused of assault with intent to kill, falsification of hieroglyphs, bribe-taking, and perjury, would appear before the vizier and be sentenced either to death by suicide or else forced labor in a remote desert prison.

The day after the incident, at sunset, Ramses placed the correctly reworded commemorative stela with his own hands.

The groundbreaking was complete. The Eternal Temple was born.

"Did you suspect Doki?" Ramses asked Nebu.

"It's human nature," replied the high priest. "Satisfaction with one's lot in life is the exception, unfortunately, not the rule. As the sages so aptly put it, envy is a fatal disease that no physician can cure."

"We'll have to find another Second Prophet."

"Are you thinking of Bakhen, Majesty?"

"Of course."

"I won't oppose your decision, but I'm not sure it's time yet. You've put Bakhen in charge of both the renovations at Luxor and the construction of your Eternal Temple, and that was wise of you. He's a young man worthy of your trust in him. But don't overburden him, don't pull him in too many directions at once. When the time is right, he can move up through the hierarchy."

"What are you suggesting?"

"Replace Doki with an old man like me, preoccupied with priestly duties. That way the temple of Amon at Karnak will no longer be a source of worry for you."

"Good idea. You can choose him yourself. Have you taken a look at the plans for the Ramesseum?"

"My life has been a long and happy one, with only one regret: that I won't live long enough to see your Eternal Temple finished."

"Who knows, Nebu?"

"My bones ache, Majesty, my eyes are growing dim, I'm hard of hearing, and I have trouble staying awake these days. The end is near, I can feel it."

"I thought sages lived to be a hundred and ten."

"I've been blessed in my life. I don't mind if death wants to take me and share my good fortune with others."

"You see pretty clearly, I'd say. If you hadn't handed your staff and your ring to the ritualist, what would have happened?"

"Needless to speculate, Majesty. Ma'at was watching over us."

Ramses looked out over the expanse where his temple of millions of years would be built. His Eternal Temple.

"I see a grandiose building, Nebu, a temple of granite, sandstone, and basalt. The pylons touch the sky. The doors are gilded bronze. Trees shade the sparkling ponds. The granaries are full of wheat, the treasury full of gold and silver, precious stones, and rare vases. Living statues fill the courtyards and chapels. A rampart stands guard over all these wonders. At sunrise and sunset, the two of us go up to the roof terrace and survey this slice of eternity. Three spirits will live forever in this temple: my father's, my mother's, and my wife, Nefertari's."

"You're forgetting the fourth one, which should be the first: yourself, Ramses."

The Great Royal Wife approached the king. Her hands cupped an acacia seedling.

Ramses knelt and planted it as Nefertari sparingly watered.

"Take care of this tree for us, Nebu. It will grow with my temple. Let us pray that the gods let me come to rest one day in its peaceful shade, forgetting the world of men. That the Lady of the West will show herself in the leafy branches, then bend down and take me by the hand."

FORTY-NINE

Moses stretched out on his sycamore bed.

It had been an exhausting day. Fifty minor incidents, two injuries at the palace, rations delivered late to the third barracks site, a thousand reject bricks to haul away. Nothing out of the ordinary, just an accumulation of headaches that slowly wore him down.

The old questions began to plague him. Building this

new capital was a joy, but raising temples to several different divinities, including the evil Set, seemed an offense to the One God. His work on Pi-Ramses meant contributing to the greater glory of a pharaoh who would only perpetuate the old ways.

In a corner of the room, near the window, someone moved.

"Who goes there?"

"A friend."

A gaunt figure with a hawklike face stepped out of the shadows and moved through the flickering lamplight.

"Ofir!"

"I need to talk to you."

Moses sat up. "I'm tired and I want to sleep. Come see me on the site tomorrow. I'll try to find time for you."

"I'm in danger, my friend."

"Why is that?"

"You know why! Because I believe in One God, the savior of humanity. The God your people worship in secret, the God who will one day reign supreme, replacing false idols. And Egypt is where it must start."

"Are you forgetting that Ramses is Pharaoh?"

"Ramses is a tyrant, obsessed with his own power. He cares nothing for religion."

"You'd better not discount his power. Ramses is my friend, and I'm building his capital."

"I appreciate your loyalty, but you're being torn in two, Moses, and you know it. In your heart, you reject this pharaoh's supremacy. You long for the rule of the One True God."

"You're raving, Ofir."

The Libyan stared hard into his eyes. "Be honest with yourself, Moses."

"Do you think you know me better than I know myself?"

"Why not? We recognize the same fundamental error and share the same ideal. If we join forces, we can transform this country and the future of its inhabitants. Like it or not, Moses, you've become the leader of the Hebrews. With you in charge, the factional fighting has ceased. They've become a people."

"The Hebrews are subject to Pharaoh's authority, not mine."

"I refuse to accept his authority, and so do you."

"You're wrong. I know my place."

"Your place is at the head of your people, guiding them toward the truth. Mine is to bolster Lita, the legitimate heir of Akhenaton, and reinstate the supremacy of the One True God."

"Stop your ranting, Ofir. Inciting a revolt against Pharaoh can only lead to disaster."

"Do you know of any other means to our end? Or don't you think the truth is worth fighting for?"

"You and Lita, all alone? It's laughable."

"It's not just the two of us anymore."

Moses raised an eyebrow. "No?"

"Since the last time we met," Ofir informed him, "the situation has changed considerably. The movement is larger and far more ambitious than you can imagine. Ramses isn't as invincible as he seems, and unfortunately for him, not as all-powerful as he thinks. A good part of the country's elite will follow us once you blaze the trail, Moses."

"But why me?"

"Because you're a proven leader. Lita has to remain in the background until it's time for her to take the throne. I'm the keeper of the flame, not a man of influence. We need your voice to make our ideas heard."

"I wonder who you really are, Ofir."

"A simple believer, like Akhenaton, convinced that the One God will rule all nations, once proud Egypt bends to His will."

"Madness," thought Moses. "I shouldn't have let him get started." And yet the man's words held a strange fascination. Ofir gave voice to his own repressed and highly subversive thoughts.

"It can never happen," said Moses.

"Time is on our side," Ofir reassured him. "Take charge of the Hebrews, give them a country, let them acknowledge the Supreme Being. Lita will govern Egypt, we'll be your ally. Our alliance will foster the truth that will sweep the world."

"It's only a dream."

"I'm no dreamer, and neither are you."

"Ramses is my friend, I tell you, and he rules with an iron fist."

"No, Moses, he's not your friend, but your worst enemy—the enemy of what you know to be the truth."

"Get out of my room, Ofir."

"Think over what I've said and prepare for action. It won't be long before we join forces."

"Don't count on it."

"I'll be seeing you, Moses."

The Hebrew spent a sleepless night.

Ofir's words swept through his mind like a tidal wave, washing away all his fears and objections. Whether or not he was ready to admit it, this was exactly what he'd been waiting for.

Side by side, the Pharaoh's dog and pet lion were licking chicken carcasses clean as Ramses and Nefertari sat entwined beneath a palm tree, admiring the scenery. With some difficulty, the king had convinced Serramanna to let them leave Thebes for a day in the country, bringing Fighter and Watcher as bodyguards.

The news from Memphis was excellent. Little Meritamon was thriving on her nurse's milk. Her brother, Kha, flourished under the watchful eyes of Nedjem, the agriculture secretary. Iset the Fair had been delighted to learn of the princess's safe birth and sent warm congratulations to Nefertari.

The late evening sun shone gold on Nefertari's silken skin. The sound of a flute drifted through the soft air. Cowherds sang as they rounded up their cattle; heavily laden donkeys lumbered homeward. In the west, the sun glowed orange, while above Thebes the Peak turned red.

The hard day gave way to the tender night. How beautiful Egypt was, resplendent in her golds and greens, the silver Nile and the blazing sunset. How beautiful Nefertari was, in her sheer linen dress. An intoxicating scent wafted from her recumbent body. Her expression was grave and peaceful, a noble window on her luminous soul.

"Do I deserve you?" asked Ramses.

"What a strange question."

"Sometimes you seem so far above all the sound and the fury . . ."

"Haven't I done my job?"

"Oh, yes, you do everything perfectly, as if you'd been a

queen all your life. I love you and admire you, Nefertari."

Their lips met, warm and vibrant.

"I'd made up my mind not to marry," she confessed, "and to live in a cloister. It wasn't that I didn't like men, but they all seemed driven by ambition. Sooner or later it made them small and weak. But you were beyond ambition, for fate had chosen your path in life. I admire you and love you, Ramses."

They both knew that they thought as one and that nothing would ever come between them. Conceiving the plan for the Eternal Temple had been their first magical act as royal couple, the source of an adventure that only death would end, and then only outwardly.

"But I'll have to keep reminding you of your duty," she added.

"Which one?"

"To have sons."

"I already have one."

"You need more. If your life is long, you may outlive some of them."

"Why couldn't our daughter succeed me?"

"According to the astrologers, her nature has a contemplative bent, just like Kha's."

"That might be a good attribute in a ruler."

"Depending on circumstances. Tonight our country is perfectly serene, but what will tomorrow bring?"

The sound of a horse's hooves shattered the quiet. Serramanna leapt to the ground in a cloud of dust.

"Forgive the disturbance, Majesty. Emergency dispatch."

Ramses skimmed the papyrus the Sard handed him.

"A report from the commanding general at Elephantine," he explained to the queen. "Nubian rebels have attacked a convoy carrying gold for our principal temples."

"Any dead?"

"A couple of dozen. Even more injured."

"Was it just robbery or the start of an uprising?"

"No one knows yet."

Shaken, Ramses began to pace. The lion and dog, sensing their master's mood, sidled up to him.

The king said the words the Great Royal Wife was dreading.

"I'll leave at once. Pharaoh must set his own house in order. In my absence, Nefertari, you will govern Egypt."

FIFTY

Pharaoh's war fleet was made up of roughly twenty boats with bow and stern curving upward from the water. A broad sail was lashed to the single sturdy mast. In the center was a huge cabin for crew and troops. The smaller forward cabin housed the captain.

Aboard the flagship, Ramses had personally checked the port and starboard rudders. A covered pen had been built for his pets. The dog snuggled up between the lion's front paws, replete from their frequent feedings.

Sailing up the Nile to Nubia, Ramses felt a renewed fascination with the barren, green-flecked hills, the bright blue sky, and the thin band of lush growth the river carved through the desert. It was a land of fire, unforgiving and yet beyond all conflict, like his soul.

Swallows, crested cranes, and pink flamingos flew over the fleet, while high in the palm trees baboons whooped at their passage. The soldiers spent their time gambling, drinking wine, and dozing in shady corners, as if they were on a pleasure cruise.

Their arrival in the land of Kush, beyond the Second Cataract, was a rude awakening. The men disembarked in silence, pitching their tents on the desolate shore and building a palisade. Then they awaited Pharaoh's orders.

A few hours later, the Viceroy of Nubia and his military escort reported to the monarch, seated on his traveling throne of gilded cedar.

"What do you have to say for yourself?" asked Ramses.

"We have the situation well in hand, Majesty."

"I asked for an explanation."

The Viceroy of Nubia had grown quite stout. He dabbed at his forehead with a white cloth.

"A deplorable incident, to be sure, but we mustn't blow things out of proportion."

"An entire shipment of gold lost, soldiers and miners slaughtered—doesn't that justify my intervention?"

"The message that was sent to you may have been somewhat alarmist, but of course we're honored by your presence."

"My father pacified Nubia and entrusted you with preserving the peace. Now your laxness and dawdling have compromised it once again."

"It was fate, Majesty, fate!"

"You're the Viceroy of Nubia, royal standard-bearer, superintendent of the southern desert region, head of a royal cavalry division, and you dare speak to me of fate!"

"My performance has been flawless, I can assure you, Majesty. But it's too big a job for one man: meeting with village mayors, making sure the granaries are stocked, checking the—"

"What about gold production?"

"Mining and shipping are under my close supervision, Majesty."

"Is that why you let the convoy go unescorted?"

"How could I know that a handful of madmen was on the loose?"

"I thought that was part of your job."

"I can't be everywhere at once."

"Take me to the scene of the attack."

"It's on the gold route, a barren and lonely spot. It won't tell you anything."

"Who were these rebels?"

"Some miserable tribe. They probably primed themselves with drink."

"Have you searched for the perpetrators?"

"Nubia is a very large province, Majesty, and my troop levels have been cut."

"In other words, no serious investigation has been attempted."

"Only Your Majesty could order a military sweep."

"That's all, Viceroy."

"Shall I help Your Majesty hunt down the rebels?"

"Just tell me the truth: is Nubia prepared to rise up in support of them?"

"Well, it's unlikely, but—"

"Is the rebellion already under way, then?"

"No, Majesty, but there does seem to be some unrest. That's why we really were hoping you'd come to help us."

"Drink up," Setau told Ramses.

"Can't I get along without it?"

"Yes, but I'd rather err on the side of caution. Serramanna can't do a thing to guard you from snakes."

The king drank the dangerous brew made from nettle extracts and diluted cobra blood. Setau gave him regular doses to build up his immunity to snakebite. At least he could eliminate one risk along the gold road.

"Thanks for bringing us along. I love it here, and Lotus is glad to be home. Just imagine the specimens we'll find!"

"It's no vacation, Setau. Nubian warriors have earned their fierce reputation."

"Why not let the poor devils have their gold, and quiet things down?"

"They committed robbery and murder. No one can flout the law of Ma'at with impunity."

"Nothing can change your mind, I suppose."

"No, nothing."

"Have you considered your personal safety?"

"This mission isn't one I can delegate."

"Tell your men to take special care. Snake venom is strongest at this time of year. They need to use asafetida. The odor of the gum resin will repel some reptiles. If anyone is bitten, send for me at once. Lotus and I will be sleeping in our wagon."

The expeditionary force marched along the rocky trail, led by a scout, then Serramanna and Ramses on surefooted horses. Next came oxen pulling wagons, donkeys laden with weapons and water gourds, and finally the foot soldiers.

The Nubian scout was convinced that the rebels were still close by the site of the attack. Nearby was an oasis, the perfect place to stash their loot until they attempted to trade it.

According to the map supplied by the viceroy, the gold route was studded with wells, and reports from the Nubian mines had indicated no recent problem with the water supply. They could advance without fear through the heart of the desert.

The scout was surprised to encounter a decomposing donkey. Usually the convoy leaders selected only the healthiest animals for their long marches.

As they neared the first water stop, the men's spirits rose. To quench their thirst, refill their gourds, sleep in the shade of their cloth shelters . . . from the top officers down, every soldier was looking forward to the same prospect. Since night would fall in three hours or less, the king would certainly make camp here.

When the scout reached the well, a chill ran through him despite the torrid heat. He ran back to Ramses.

"Majesty! The well is dry."

The Pharaoh's troops did not have enough water to survive a march back to their point of departure. The only choice was marching forward, in hope of making it to the next well. But since the provincial government's information had proved unreliable, it might mean the next well would be just as dry.

"We could leave the main road," suggested the scout, "and branch out to the right toward the rebels' oasis.

Between here and there is a well they might use on their raids."

"Rest until dusk," ordered Ramses. "Then we'll head off again."

"A night march is dangerous, Majesty! Snakes, the potential for ambush . . ."

"It's our only option."

Ramses was reminded of an earlier expedition, with his father. Their soldiers had faced an identical situation—local insurgents poisoning the wells on the gold route. In his heart of hearts, he admitted that this time he'd underestimated the danger. He knew from experience that a simple peacekeeping mission could end in disaster.

The king addressed his men, telling them the truth. They were worried, but the more experienced soldiers kept up the morale. Pharaoh was their leader, and Pharaoh was a miracle worker, they told their comrades.

Despite the risks, the foot soldiers enjoyed the night march. The rear guard, more alert than ever, would counter surprise attacks. The scout would keep them from stumbling into danger. With the full moon, he could see far into the distance.

Ramses thought of Nefertari. If he failed to return, the burden of ruling Egypt would fall on her. Kha and Meritamon were too young to take the throne. Factional fighting would resume, more desperate than ever for having been temporarily quelled.

Then, without warning, Serramanna's horse reared, throwing him to the rocky ground. Stunned, he rolled down a sandy slope and came to rest in a gulch not visible from the trail.

A curious sound, like heavy breathing, caught his attention.

Just in front of him, a viper rasped, threatened and ready to strike.

Serramanna had lost his sword in the fall. Unarmed, all he could do was back away, avoiding any sudden movements. But the hissing viper, slithering sidewise, blocked his path.

He tried to stand, but the pain in his right ankle stopped him. Unable to run, he'd be easy prey.

"Away from me, snake! I promised I'd die by the sword!"

The hissing viper inched closer. Serramanna threw sand in its face, making it even more furious. The moment it was about to dart out at him, a forked stick pinned the snake to the ground.

"Nice shot!" Setau said in self-congratulation. "One chance in ten I'd make it." He grabbed the snake by the neck, its tail thrashing wildly.

"What a beauty. Light blue, dark blue, and green . . . a lovely specimen, don't you agree? Luckily for you, the hissing carries and it's pretty easy to recognize."

"I suppose I should thank you."

"The bite of this viper causes local swelling. Then the whole limb is affected and begins to hemorrhage. That's all. Only a small amount of venom, but very toxic. With a strong heart, you might survive it. Honestly, this snake isn't half as dangerous as it looks."

FIFTY-ONE

Setau plastered Serramanna's sprained ankle with herbs, then applied linen dressings soaked in salve to reduce the swelling. In a few hours, it would be fine. Suspicious, the Sard wondered if the snake charmer might not have masterminded the whole incident to make himself look like a hero, innocent of any wrongdoing and a true friend to Ramses. However, Setau had made no attempt to capitalize on the rescue, which spoke well of him.

At dawn, they stopped to rest until mid-afternoon. Then the march resumed. There was still enough water for man and beast, but soon it would have to be rationed. Despite the men's fatigue and anxiety, Ramses stepped up the pace and exhorted the rear guard to continuing vigilance. The insurgents would never attack head-on; they would try for the advantage of surprise.

In the ranks, there was no more joking or talk of home. In time, the men fell silent.

"There it is," announced the scout, pointing.

Puny weeds, a circle of parched stones, a wooden frame

to hold the weight of a large water skin hanging from a frayed rope: the well. Their only salvation.

The scout and Serramanna ran forward. For a long moment they peered down, then slowly straightened. The Sard shook his head.

"The place has been dry for ages. We're all going to die of thirst. No one's been able to find a permanent water source. We'll have to fill our skins in the great beyond."

Ramses called the men together and told them the situation was serious. By the next day, their water would be gone. They could neither advance nor retreat.

Several soldiers threw down their weapons.

"Pick those up," ordered Ramses.

"What's the use?" asked an officer, "if the desert is going to get us?"

"We've come here to reestablish order, and we won't leave until we've done so."

"How can our dead bodies fight the Nubians?"

"My father once found himself in a similar situation," said Ramses, "and he saved his men."

"Then why don't you save us, too?"

"Take shelter from the sun and water the animals."

The king turned his back on his army and faced the desert. Setau came to join him.

"Do you have a plan?"

"I'll walk until I find water."

"That's crazy."

"I have to do as my father taught me."

"Stay here with us."

"A pharaoh doesn't surrender so easily. I won't wait for death to come to me."

Serramanna approached them. "Majesty . . ."

"Don't let the men panic and keep up the watch, day and

night. They need to remember they're under threat of attack."

"I can't let you go off alone into this desert. As your chief of security . . ."

"Keep my army safe for me."

"Hurry back. Your troops need a general."

As the foot soldiers looked on in horror, the king walked away from the dried-up well and into the red desert. Reaching a rocky butte, he scaled it easily, surveying the desolate scene from the top.

Like his father, he needed to probe the earth's hidden secrets, find the veins of water that sprang from the ocean of energy, flowed through the rock, and filled the heart of the mountains. Ramses' solar plexus ached, his vision blurred, his body burned as if consumed with fever.

He took the divining rod tied to the sash of his kilt, the same wand his father had used to see into the earth. Its magic, he knew, would still work, but where should he even start looking in all this sand?

A voice spoke within the king's body, a voice from beyond this earth, a voice deep as Seti's. The pain in his solar plexus grew so intense that he was forced to walk slowly down the cliff. He no longer felt the burning heat of day. His heartbeat slowed like a desert animal's.

The sand and rocks changed shape and color. Ramses' gaze gradually penetrated the layers of sand; his fingers gripped the two pliable acacia branches bound together with linen thread.

The rod quivered, paused, went dead. He walked and the voice grew more distant. He retraced his steps, going left, the direction of death. The voice came, louder. The rod twitched. Ramses bumped into a huge pink granite boulder, lost in the sea of stone.

The force from the earth tore the rod straight out of his hands.

He had found water.

Parched, sunburned, sore, the soldiers rolled away the boulder and dug where the king told them. Fifteen feet down, they hit water. Their cheers reached the sky.

Ramses had them sink a series of wells, linked by an underground gallery, a technique he had picked up on his last desert expedition. In this way, he could not only save his army, but provide for future irrigation over a fairly wide area.

"Can you see the gardens already?" asked Setau.

"That will be our greatest gift to Nubia," answered the king.

"I thought we were here to put down an insurrection," protested Serramanna.

"We are."

"Then why do you have your soldiers digging ditches?"

"It's often part of their mission, according to our custom."

"Pirates don't try to be fishermen." He sniffed. "If we're attacked, will we be prepared to defend ourselves?"

"I thought I put you in charge of our security."

While the soldiers completed their project, Setau and Lotus were busy trapping snakes, outstanding in both variety and size. They milked a quantity of priceless venom.

Serramanna uneasily stepped up the scheduled watches and also instituted barracks-style training. The men seemed to have forgotten the stolen gold and the rebel threat. Their pharaoh worked wonders, and soon he'd be leading them home.

"Amateurs," scoffed the ex-pirate.

Many Egyptian soldiers were temporary recruits who soon reverted to the laborers or farmers they really were. They had never experienced the heat, blood, and death of combat. There was no better training for war than being a pirate, always on the alert and ready to dispatch any enemy with a ready weapon. Discouraged, Serramanna made no attempt to teach the men some of the more vicious attacks and surprise defenses he knew. These greenhorns would never learn to fight.

Yet he had the feeling that the Nubian rebels were not far off and for the past two days or more had been sneaking up on the Egyptian camp, spying. Ramses' pet lion and dog also sensed a hostile presence. They grew agitated, slept less, prowled around sniffing the air.

If the Nubians were anything like some of the pirates he had known, the Egyptian forces were doomed.

The new capital of Egypt was going up at an astonishing rate, but Moses no longer saw it. To him, Pi-Ramses was now a foreign place, full of false gods and men deluded into meaningless beliefs.

Faithful to his promise, he kept the work moving along. Yet everyone noticed how short his temper was becoming, especially when he dealt with the Egyptian foremen. His complaints about their strictness were usually unfounded. Moses spent more and more time with his Hebrew brethren, discussing their people's future with small groups of men each evening. Many were satisfied with their life in Egypt and felt no urge to go in search of an independent homeland. The risk seemed too great.

Moses kept after them, stressing their faith in a single god, their unique culture, the need to throw off the Egyptian yoke and reject false idols. He changed a few minds, but many more remained closed to him. Still, Moses was recognized as a leader who had done them a world of good. No one took his opinion lightly.

Ramses' old friend was living on less and less sleep. His waking dream was of a fertile land where the god he cherished would reign supreme, a land the Hebrews would govern on their own, defending its borders as their most prized possession.

At last he understood the nature of the fire consuming his soul for so many years now. He could name this unquenchable desire; he could see the truth and lead his people toward it. He knew, and was filled with dread. Would Ramses accept such heresy, such a challenge to his power? Moses would have to convince him, make him see the light.

Memories flooded his mind. Ramses was far more than an old playmate. He was a true friend, who burned with a different version of the fire that consumed Moses. He would never take part in a coup against Ramses. He would meet him face-to-face and win him over. No matter how impossible that might seem, Moses was confident.

For God was with him.

FIFTY-TWO

The Nubian rebels had half-shaved heads, hoop earrings, broad noses, ritual scars on their cheeks, beaded necklaces, and panther-skin loincloths. They encircled the Egyptian encampment while most of Ramses' soldiers dozed in the afternoon heat. Their huge acacia bows launched a number of successful hits before the Egyptians could muster a response.

What kept the rebel chief from giving the order to attack was the sight of a small band of men, also armed with sturdy bows, behind a palisade of shields and palm fronds. In the lead was Serramanna, who had been expecting them. His handpicked archers would have a clear shot into the Nubian ranks, as the Nubian chief could see. The advantage was his, but even so . . .

Time stood still. No one moved a muscle.

The rebel chief's lieutenant advised him to start shooting and take down as many of the enemy as possible, while a few fleet warriors stormed the palisade. But the chief had been in a battle or two, and didn't like the look of Serramanna. The hairy giant might well have a trick or two up his sleeve. He didn't look like the other Egyptians they'd encountered. His hunter's instincts warned him to be careful.

When Ramses emerged from his tent, all eyes were upon him. In a close-fitting, flaring blue crown, a short-sleeved, tucked linen tunic, and gold-trimmed kilt with a bull's tail dangling from the sash, the Pharaoh held a shepherd's crook in his right hand, a sign of his magical powers. He clutched the end of it to his chest.

Behind him marched Setau, carrying the king's white sandals. He thought of Ahmeni, the king's official sandal-bearer, and almost smiled despite the tenseness of the situation. How amazed their friend would be to see him decked out in wig and white loincloth, clean-shaven, exactly like a seasoned courtier except for the odd-looking sack suspended from his waist.

As the Egyptian soldiers looked on nervously, Pharaoh and Setau walked to the edge of the camp, stopping less than a hundred paces from the Nubians.

"I am Ramses, Pharaoh of Egypt. Who is your head man?"

"I am," said the chief, stepping forward.

Two feathers stuck in his red headband, muscles bulging, the rebel chief held a light spear trimmed with ostrich plumes.

"If you're no coward, come here."

The lieutenant made a sign of disapproval. But neither Ramses nor his sandal-bearer was armed, while he had his spear and his adviser a double-edged dagger. The chief glanced over at Serramanna.

"Stay on my left," he ordered his lieutenant. If the hairy giant gave the order to shoot, the chief would be protected by a human shield.

"Are you afraid?" asked Ramses.

The two Nubians broke away from the war party and walked toward the king and his sandal-bearer, coming to a halt only ten paces in front of them.

"So you're the Pharaoh who oppresses my people."

"Nubians and Egyptians live in harmony. You broke that peace when you killed the members of the convoy and stole the gold being shipped to our temples."

"The gold is ours, not yours. You're the one who's a thief."

"Nubia is an Egyptian province, subject to the law of Ma'at. Murder and robbery must be severely punished."

"Your laws mean nothing to me, Pharaoh. I make my own. Other tribes are prepared to join us. Killing you will make me a hero! Every warrior in Nubia will be at my command, and we'll rid our country of Egyptians once and for all!"

"Kneel down," ordered the king.

The chief and his lieutenant looked at each other, bewildered.

"Lay down your arms, kneel, and submit to the law."

The chief leered at him. "If I bow to you, will you grant me your pardon?"

"You've placed yourself outside the law. To pardon you would also go against it."

"You show me no mercy."

"I know none."

"Why should I bow to you?"

"Because it's the only freedom permitted you as an outlaw."

The lieutenant jumped in front of his chief, waving the dagger.

"Let Pharaoh's death set us free, then!"

Setau, who hadn't taken his eyes off the two men, opened the sack at his waist, releasing a sand viper. Slithering with deadly speed, it bit the Nubian's foot before he could spear it.

Crying out, he bent over to slash the bite with his dagger and let out the poison.

"He's already colder than water and hotter than flame," intoned Setau, looking the chief straight in the eyes. "He's sweating, his eyes are glazing over, he's starting to drool. Now his eyes and eyelids are stiffening, his face is swelling, his throat is burning. He's about to die. He can't get up, his skin is turning purple, his whole body is shaking."

Setau held up his sack full of vipers. The Nubian war party backed away.

"Kneel," Pharaoh ordered once more. "Or prepare to die an awful death."

"You're the one who's going to die!"

The chief held his spear over his head, then froze as a terrible roaring filled his ears. Turning, he barely caught a glimpse of the lion's mane and gaping jaws before it clawed his chest open and snapped his neck with its jaws.

At a signal from Serramanna, the Egyptian bowmen fired at the scattering Nubians. The foot soldiers advanced and disarmed the war party.

"Tie their hands behind their backs!" shouted the Sard.

As news of Ramses' victory spread, hundreds of Nubians left their hideouts and villages to pay him homage. The king gave a white-haired tribal chief the use of the newly created fertile zone around the water hole. He was also put in charge of the prisoners of war, who were to do farmwork under police supervision. Escapees and repeat offenders would get the death penalty.

Then the Egyptian forces marched to the oasis, which had served as the rebel stronghold. Meeting only feeble resistance, they took possession of the gold that would one day grace statues and temple doors in the motherland.

At nightfall, Setau found two lengths of palm rib for kindling, held them between his knees, set a piece of dead wood between them, and twirled until sparks flew. The soldiers on watch would have a fire to keep away cobras, hyenas, and other pests.

"Have you collected more snakes?" asked Ramses.

He nodded. "Lotus is glad we came here. We've found enough now; tonight we'll rest."

"It's a wonderful country."

"You seem to like it as much as we do."

"It tests me and takes me beyond myself. Its power is mine."

"Without my viper, the rebels would have killed you."

"But they didn't, did they?"

"It was still a risky plan."

"It spared a great deal of bloodshed."

"Do you ever consider being more cautious?"

"What for?"

"I'm only Setau the snake charmer. It's all right if I fool around with reptiles. But you, Ramses, are Lord of the Two Lands. Your death would plunge Egypt into disarray."

"Nefertari could run the country."

"You're only twenty-five, Ramses, but you can't act so young anymore. You'll have to send others into battle."

"Pharaoh can't be seen as a coward."

"No; just don't overdo it. I'm only telling you to be a bit more careful."

"But I have the best protection: Nefertari's magic, you and your snakes, Serramanna and his royal bodyguard, Watcher and Fighter . . . I'm the luckiest man on earth."

"Save your luck for when you need it."

"I'll never run out."

"Pig-headed as ever, I see. I might as well go to bed."

Setau turned his back on the king and stretched out beside Lotus. Her contented sigh convinced Ramses to slip away. His friend might not get to rest for long.

How could he make Setau realize his real place was high in the government? Ramses' failure to recruit him was his first major setback. Should Setau be free to go his own way or be forced into an official position?

Ramses spent the night gazing at the starry sky, his father's new home, where he dwelt with the souls of all the departed pharaohs. He thought about his accomplishments: finding water in the desert, putting down the rebellion, just as his father had done. It made him feel proud, but he was far from content with his victory. The earlier campaign had not had lasting results. This time would be the same. He would have to get to the root of the problem, but how could he determine what it was?

In the first light of dawn, Ramses sensed a presence at his back and slowly, very slowly, turned around.

There stood an enormous elephant. It had crept into the oasis, stepping nimbly around the dried palm ribs strewn all around. The lion and watchdog had opened their eyes but sounded no warning, as if they did not sense a threat to their master.

The big bull elephant with flapping ears and long tusks

was his friend. Years earlier, Ramses had saved him, removing a spearhead from the tender trunk.

The King of Egypt stroked that trunk now, and the lord of the savannahs trumpeted in joy, waking the whole encampment.

The elephant sauntered away, covering a hundred paces in a few long strides, then turned to look back at the king.

"He's telling us to follow," said Ramses.

FIFTY-THREE

Ramses, Serramanna, Setau, and a handful of veteran soldiers followed the elephant across a strip of arid plain, then up a thorny slope to a plateau topped with a venerable acacia tree.

The elephant waited for Ramses to catch up.

Following the huge beast's gaze, he discovered a splendid view. The oversized spur of rock where they stood, a landmark for navigation, looked down on a vast bend in the Nile. Ramses, mystical spouse of Egypt, contemplated the life-giving waters, the divine river in all its majesty. On the nearby rocks, hieroglyphic inscriptions dedicated the spot to the goddess Hathor, queen of the stars and patroness of sailors, who often stopped here.

With its right front foot, the elephant sent a boulder tumbling down the cliff. It landed in a sandy coulee between two promontories. To the north, the cliffs were vertical, almost straight down to the water. To the south, they sloped gradually into a vast open stretch, broadening westward.

On the shore below, a boat hollowed out of a palm trunk was moored, with a boy sleeping inside.

"Go get him," the king ordered two of his soldiers.

The boy saw them coming and took to his heels. He would have gotten away if he hadn't tripped on a rock and sprawled on the riverbank. The Egyptian soldiers twisted the young Nubian's arms and brought him before the king.

The runaway's eyes darted in fear. Were they going to cut off his nose? "I'm not a thief," he cried. "The boat belongs to me, I swear it, and—"

"Answer my question," Ramses told him, "and you'll go free. What do they call this place?"

"Abu Simbel."

"You may go."

The boy ran back to his dugout and paddled away with all his might.

"We can't stay here long," advised Serramanna. "I don't think this spot is secure."

"No sign of any snakes," complained Setau. "Bizarre. Could Hathor have driven them off?"

"Don't follow me," the king commanded.

Serramanna stepped forward. "Majesty!"

"Don't make me say it twice."

Ramses began the descent toward the river. Setau restrained the Sard.

"You'd better do as he says."

Serramanna reluctantly gave in. The king on his own, in the middle of nowhere, in hostile territory! No matter what Ramses said, he would remain on guard.

Reaching the riverbank, Ramses turned to face the sandstone cliff.

Here was the unknown heart of Nubia. And he, the Son of Light, would need to reveal it, make of Abu Simbel a wonder outlasting the centuries and sealing the pact between Egypt and Nubia.

The Pharaoh spent several hours in meditation, immersing himself in the spirit of Abu Simbel: clear sky, sparkling water, hard rock. The province's main temple would be built here, concentrating divine energy and radiating a protective force field so strong that the clash of arms would be forever stilled.

Ramses observed the sun. Its rays did not merely glance off the cliff, but penetrated to the heart of the rock, lighting it from inside. He would tell his architects to capture this miracle.

By the time the king climbed back to the top of the cliff, Serramanna's nerves were stretched to the limit. He was tempted to quit for good, but the elephant's placid attitude changed his mind. He refused to appear less patient than an animal, even the most majestic of animals.

"We're going back to Egypt," decreed the king.

After cleansing his mouth with natron, Shaanar surrendered his face to the barber, who was also skilled in the painless removal of body hair. Ramses' older brother was extremely fond of massages. He particularly liked having his scalp rubbed with perfumed oils before the hairdresser came to do his wig. These small pleasures lightened his days and helped him present his best face to the world. He might not be as handsome or athletic as Ramses, but he could be just as well groomed, if not more so.

His clepsydra, a costly water clock, told him the hour was drawing near for his appointment.

His litter, comfortable and roomy, was the finest in Memphis except for the Pharaoh's, which he one day planned to occupy. Shaanar had the bearers drop him off at the canal that gave heavy barges passage into the main river landing.

Ofir the sorcerer sat in the shade of a willow tree. Shaanar leaned against the trunk and watched a fishing boat go by.

"Any progress, Ofir?"

"Moses is an exceptional man, with a mind of his own."

"In other words, you can't convince him."

"I didn't say that."

"I need facts, Ofir. Vague impressions won't do."

"The road to success is a long and winding one."

"Spare me the philosophy. Have you signed him on, or haven't you?"

"He listened. It's a beginning."

"Interesting, I admit. Did he indicate any approval?"

"Moses is familiar with Akhenaton's ideas. He knows they've contributed to the Hebrew faith and that a collaboration could be fruitful."

"And the Hebrews will follow him?"

"He's more popular than ever. Moses is a born leader. Once Pi-Ramses is finished, he'll rally his people."

"How long will that be?"

"A few more months. He has the brickmakers working at lightning speed."

"Ramses and his capital! His fame will spread beyond the northern border, I'm afraid."

"Where is the Pharaoh now?"

"In Nubia."

"A dangerous place."

"Don't fool yourself, Ofir. The royal couriers have relayed excellent reports. More miracles for Ramses: he found a spring in the desert, opened up new farmland. He's bringing back the gold for the temples. A successful expedition, an exemplary victory."

"Moses knows that he'll have to confront the Pharaoh."

"His closest friend . . ."

"His belief in the One God will lead him to it. And our support will be crucial."

"That's your role, Ofir. You understand why I have to remain in the background."

"I'll need your help."

"In what form?"

"A place in Memphis, servants, a communication network."

"Granted, on the condition that you submit regular reports on your activities."

"Confidential reports."

"When are you going back to Pi-Ramses, Ofir?"

"Tomorrow. I plan to tell Moses how our numbers are growing."

"I'll take care of your material concerns; you focus all your attention on convincing Moses to fight for his faith, against Ramses' tyranny."

Abner the brickmaker hummed to himself. In less than a month, the first Pi-Ramses barracks would be finished and the initial detachment of foot soldiers transferred from Memphis. The premises were spacious and well ventilated, the fittings remarkable.

Thanks to Moses, Abner now headed a small crew of his fellow craftsmen, experienced and industrious as himself. Sary's extortion was only a bad memory. Abner would move his family to the new capital and work in public building maintenance. The future was looking bright.

Tonight he would enjoy a meal of Nile perch with his comrades. Then they would play a game of snake, advancing their pieces along the serpent's back while avoiding various pitfalls. Abner had a feeling it was his lucky night.

Pi-Ramses was changing. The construction site was gradually turning into a real city. It didn't seem long now until the dedication, the moment when Pharaoh would bring his capital to life. It had been his special privilege, Abner reflected, to serve a great king's vision and work with Moses.

"How are you, Abner?"

Sary wore a Libyan tunic with wide vertical stripes of black and yellow, cinched at the waist with a green leather belt. His face had grown even more emaciated.

"What do you want with me?"

"Asking after your health, that's all."

"Move along."

"Is that any way to talk to me?"

"I think you've forgotten I was promoted. I don't report to you anymore."

"Proud as a peacock, aren't we, Abner? Easy, now."

"I'm busy this evening."

"What could be more urgent than old friends?"

The Hebrew was growing uneasy, to Sary's amusement.

"You're a reasonable fellow, Abner. You want a nice little life for yourself, but you know that everything has a price. And I'm the one who sets it."

"Buzz off!"

"That's right, Hebrew. You're an insect. Bugs don't complain when you squash them. I expect half of your wages and bonuses. When the work is done here, you'll volunteer to stay on as my servant. Mmm, I'll enjoy having a Hebrew houseboy. I'll keep you busy, don't worry. You're lucky, Abner. If I hadn't noticed you, you'd end up as vermin."

"You can't make me, I tell you, I—"

"Stop babbling and do as I say," the foreman snarled in parting.

Abner crouched in a corner, hanging his head. This time Sary had gone too far. This time he'd speak to Moses.

FIFTY-FOUR

Peerless Nefertari, her beauty like the morning star at the dawn of a good year, her touch like a lotus flower. Luminous Nefertari, catching him in the dark loops of her fragrant hair.

To love her was to be reborn.

Ramses gently massaged her feet, then kissed her legs, letting his hands wander over her lithe, tanned body. She was the garden where the rarest flowers grew, the pool of clear water, the distant country of frankincense trees. When they came together, their desire was strong as the surge of a cresting river, tender as a woodwind tune in the twilight.

As soon as the expedition returned from Nubia, the king had gone straight to his wife, ignoring well-wishers and advisers. Nefertari and Ramses had celebrated their reunion beneath the verdant foliage of a sycamore. The refreshing shade of the great tree, its turquoise leaves and notched fruit red as jasper, were one of the treasures of the palace at Thebes where they had managed to slip away.

"You were gone forever . . ."

"The baby?"

"Kha and Meritamon are both doing wonderfully. Your son thinks his little sister is very pretty but a little noisy. He's already trying to teach her to read. His tutor made him stop."

Ramses held his wife closer. "That's a mistake. Why hold him back?"

Before Nefertari could answer, her husband's lips sought hers as the sycamore branches bent discreetly over them in the cool north wind.

Bakhen, carrying a long staff, marched in front of the royal pair. It was the tenth day of the fourth month of the inundation season, Year Three of Ramses' reign, and he was leading them to inspect the newly completed additions to the temple of Luxor. A long procession followed them down the avenue of sphinxes leading from the temple of Karnak.

The new facade of Karnak imposed silence. The two obelisks, the colossal royal statues, and the massive yet elegant pylon gateway formed a composition worthy of the greatest builders of old.

The obelisks repelled negative energy and attracted divine power to the temple, where it would nourish the *ka* produced here. At the bottom were dog-faced baboons, symbols of the god Thoth's intelligence, uttering the sounds that helped bring forth each new dawn. Each element, from hieroglyph to colossal statue, contributed to the daily rebirth of the sun, which now sat in glory above the twin towers of the pylon and central doorway.

Ramses and Nefertari passed through it, entering a great

open-air forecourt with huge columns lining the walls, a powerful expression of the *ka*. Between them stood colossal statues of the king, a testimony to his indomitable strength. Tenderly clinging to the giant's legs was Nefertari, both frail and steadfast.

Nebu, the high priest of Amon, slowly made his way toward the royal pair, his golden staff tapping in time.

The old man bowed.

"Majesty, here is the home of your *ka*, the endless source of energy for your reign."

The feast of the dedication of Luxor involved the entire population of Thebes and its environs, the humble as well as the grand. For ten days, there was singing and dancing in the streets; taverns and open-air drinking establishments were crammed. By the grace of Pharaoh, free beer filled every belly.

The king and queen presided at a banquet recorded in the royal annals. Ramses proclaimed the temple to his *ka* completed, decreeing that no architectural feature would be added in the future. Still to be addressed was the decoration of the facade and forecourt walls. It was generally agreed that the young Pharaoh was wise to wait and decide on appropriate symbolic themes. The House of Life would provide him with expert advice.

Ramses appreciated Bakhen's attitude. The Fourth Prophet of Amon made no mention of his own contributions, but praised the architects who had designed Luxor with careful attention to the principles of harmony. When the feasting was over, the king presented the high priest of

Amon with the Nubian gold, which would henceforth be shipped with stringent security measures.

Before departing northward, the royal pair visited the site of the Eternal Temple. Bakhen's competence was in evidence there as well. Graders, unskilled laborers, and stonecutters were hard at work. The Ramesseum was beginning to rise from the desert floor.

"Hurry, Bakhen. I want the foundations laid as quickly as possible."

"The Luxor work gangs will start working here tomorrow. Then we'll have full crews and enough skilled workers."

Ramses noted that his plan for the complex had been followed to the letter. He could already picture the chapels, the great hall with pillars, the offering tables, the laboratory, the library . . . millions of years would flow through the veins of stone.

The king toured the holy site with Nefertari, describing his vision, as if he were already touching the carved walls and columns covered with hieroglyphs.

"The Ramesseum will be your greatest monument."

"Perhaps."

"Why do you doubt it?"

"Because I hope to build temples all over the country, make hundreds of homes for the gods. I want my country drenched with their energy. I want the land of Egypt to be heaven on earth."

"What could surpass your Eternal Temple?"

"In Nubia, I met an old friend. An elephant. He led me to an extraordinary place."

"Does it have a name?"

"Abu Simbel. A stopping place for sailors, protected by Hathor, where the Nile is at its most beautiful, the river blends with the rock, the sandstone cliffs seem ripe to give birth to a temple."

"But so far south . . . Won't the technical difficulties be overwhelming?"

"We won't let them overwhelm us."

"No pharaoh before you has attempted such a thing."

"True, but I'll succeed. From the moment I first saw Abu Simbel, I haven't been able to get it out of my mind. The elephant was a messenger from the gods, I'm sure of it. Abu stands for elephant, and as you know, the hieroglyph can also be read as 'start' or 'beginning.' A new start for Egypt, the beginning of her territory, must be there in the heart of Nubia, at Abu Simbel. It's the only way to assure a lasting peace."

"It's a wild idea."

"Of course it is! But also an expression of my *ka*—the fire within me captured forever in stone. Luxor, Pi-Ramses, Abu Simbel are each my desire and my brainchild. If I spent my time on day-to-day matters, I wouldn't be acting like a pharaoh."

"My head rests on your shoulder and I feel secure in your love. But you can also rest on me, like a colossal statue on its pedestal."

"Do you approve of my new project?"

"Think more about Abu Simbel. Let it grow inside you until your vision is dazzling and imperious. Then act upon it."

Within the enclosure of the Eternal Temple, Ramses and Nefertari felt a strange force move within them, making them invulnerable.

Workshops, warehouses, barracks were ready to be occupied. The main thoroughfares led through residential neighborhoods and ended at the major temples, still under construction, but with each inner sanctum in usable condition.

The brickmakers' work was finished, and an army of landscapers and painters took their place, not to mention the decorative artists who would give Pi-Ramses its outward face. But would Ramses smile on it?

Moses climbed to the roof of the palace and contemplated the city. Like Pharaoh, he had worked miracles. The men's physical labor and his own careful organization had not been enough. The spark had come from enthusiasm, not human but divine in origin, the sign of God's love for his creation. And Moses longed to offer this city to his God, not leave it to Amon, Set, and the like. Such an outpouring of talent wasted on those mute idols . . .

His next city would be built to the glory of the One God, in his own country, on holy ground. If Ramses was truly his soul mate, he would understand.

Moses pounded on the edge of the balcony.

The King of Egypt would never tolerate a minority revolt, never let a descendant of Akhenaton take over the throne. To believe otherwise was, at best, an impossible dream.

Below, near one of the side entries to the palace, stood Ofir.

"May I speak to you?" called the sorcerer.

"Come up."

Ofir had learned to blend in wherever he went. At Pi-Ramses he could pass for an architect coming to offer Moses valuable advice.

"I'm giving up," declared Moses. "No use trying to argue."

The sorcerer eyed him coolly. "Has something happened to change your mind?"

"I've thought it over, that's all. It's a losing battle."

"I came to tell you that our ranks have been growing steadily. There are influential people who believe Lita should take the throne with the blessing of the One God. In that case, the Hebrews will be free."

"You mean to overthrow Ramses? Are you mad?"

"Our convictions are firm."

"Do you think your sermons will sway the king?"

"Who said we'll stop at sermons?"

Moses stared at Ofir as if he were meeting a stranger.

"You can't mean . . ."

"Of course I can, Moses. You've reached the same conclusion I have, and that's what bothers you. Akhenaton was defeated and persecuted only because he refused to use force against his enemies. No fight can be won without bloodshed. Ramses will never accommodate us or anyone else. We'll have to fight him from within. And you will lead the Hebrews in their revolt."

"The dead will number in the hundreds, even thousands. Is carnage what you want?"

"If you prepare your people, they'll win, with God on their side."

"I won't listen to another word. Be gone, Ofir."

"I can see you in Memphis as well as here."

"Don't count on it."

"There's no other way, and you know it. Don't try to ignore the voice inside you. We'll fight the good fight together, and God will triumph."

FIFTY-FIVE

Raia, the Syrian merchant, fingered his goatee. Business was booming. The quality of his preserved meats and Asian vases attracted an ever-growing clientele among the upper classes of Memphis and Thebes. The creation of the new capital, Pi-Ramses, meant yet another market would open up. Raia had already secured a permit to set up shop in the heart of the commercial district and was training the sales force to deal with demanding customers.

Increasing his inventory, he had ordered a hundred precious vases, all new designs, from his Syrian sources. Each piece was unique and would be priced accordingly. Raia's personal opinion was that Egyptian craftsmen did better work, but the buying public's taste for the exotic (not to mention its rampant snobbery) was lining his pockets.

Although the Hittites had ordered their agent to back Shaanar and oppose Ramses, after a single unsuccessful attempt on the king, Raia had given up trying. Pharaoh was too well protected and any further activity on the Syrian's part might lead the investigators to him.

Over the last three years, Ramses had proved as strong a

ruler as his father, with the added energy of youth. He was like a raging torrent, sweeping all obstacles out of his way. No one had the authority to oppose him, even if the number of building projects he had undertaken was sheer madness. The court and the people were at once enthralled and subjugated.

Raia checked his shipment. Among the new pieces were two alabaster vases.

He shut the storeroom door, then listened at it. Satisfied that he was alone, he stuck his hand inside the vase with the small red check mark under the rim and pulled out a pine tag inscribed with the vase's dimensions and origin.

Raia knew the code by heart and easily worked out the message his contact in southern Syria had forwarded from the Hittites.

Stunned, the secret agent destroyed the message and went running out of the shop.

"Superb," said Shaanar, admiring the blue swan-necked vase Raia had just unpacked for him. "The price?"

"Rather high, I'm afraid, Your Highness. But it's one of a kind."

"Let's discuss it, shall we?"

Gripping the vase to his chest, Raia followed Ramses' older brother to one of his villa's roofed terraces, where they could speak without fear of being overheard.

"If I'm not mistaken, Raia, you're following emergency procedure."

"Correct."

"What's going on?"

"Our friends have decided to take action."

It was the news Shaanar had hoped for, but also dreaded. If he were Pharaoh, he would put Egyptian troops on high alert and shore up the border defenses. But Egypt's most dangerous enemy was offering him a way to get back at his brother. He would have to use this vital secret to his sole advantage.

"Could you be more specific, Raia?"

"You look disturbed."

"Who wouldn't be?"

"It's true, Your Highness. I'm still in shock myself. This decision will change the face of relations between Egypt and the Hittites."

"More than that will change, Raia. The fate of the whole world hangs on it. You and I will be major players in the drama that unfolds."

"But I'm only an agent."

"You'll be my contact with the Hittites. A good part of my strategy depends on the accuracy of the information you provide."

"You make it sound so important."

"Do you hope to stay in Egypt, once we win?"

"I'm at home here."

"You'll be rich, Raia, very rich. I never forget a favor."

The merchant bowed. "Your humble servant, Sir Prince."

"Do you have any details?"

"Not yet."

Shaanar took a few steps, leaned over the railing, and looked north.

"This is a great day, Raia. One day we'll tell ourselves it marked the beginning of the end of Ramses."

Ahsha's Egyptian mistress was a marvel. Playful, inventive, insatiable, she had elicited new and subtle responses. A definite improvement over her pretty but boring predecessors, two Libyan girls and three Syrians. Ahsha demanded imagination in his lovemaking. That alone could release the unexpected melodies straining within the body. He was just getting around to sucking his lady love's sweet little toes when he heard his steward hammering at the door, despite strict orders.

Outraged, Ahsha flung the door open without thinking to cover himself.

"Forgive me, sir. An urgent message from your office."

Ahsha consulted the wooden tablet. It was brief: "Report at once."

At two in the morning, the streets of Memphis were deserted. Ahsha's horse quickly covered the distance between his residence and the State Department. Not stopping to make the customary offering to Thoth, Ahsha took the stairs four at a time and sped to his office. He found his secretary waiting.

"I thought I should let you know immediately."

"About what?"

"A dispatch from one of our agents in northern Syria."

"If it's another false alarm, you'll be in trouble."

The bottom of the papyrus scroll looked blank, but when heated with the flame of an oil lamp, hieratic characters appeared. This shorthand method of writing hieroglyphs sometimes made them almost unreadable. The hand of the Egyptian spy on their payroll in Syria was unmistakable.

Ahsha read and reread the message.

"Glad I sent for you?" asked the secretary.

"Please leave."

Ahsha spread out a map and checked the information against it. If his calculations were correct, the worst was in store.

"The sun isn't even up," grunted Shaanar, yawning.

"Read this," advised Ahsha, handing his chief the secret message.

Shaanar's eyes opened wide. "What? The Hittites have taken control of several villages in central Syria, well outside the zone of influence acceptable to Egypt . . ."

"The message is definite."

"No casualties, it looks like. They could just be testing the limits."

"It wouldn't be the first time. But the Hittites have never gone so far south."

"What do you make of it?"

"They're preparing a full-fledged campaign in southern Syria."

"Is that a statement or a guess?"

"A guess."

"How could we find out for sure?"

"In light of the situation, I assume more messages will follow."

"Whatever the case, let's keep this quiet as long as possible."

"We're taking quite a risk."

"I know we are, Ahsha. But that's what we have to do. We were trying to coax Ramses into a waiting game, but it seems the Hittites are restless. We'll have to keep the Egyptian army off guard as long as we can."

"I'm not so sure," objected Ahsha.

"Why?"

"Number one," he ticked off. "That would only buy us a few more days, hardly enough time to stop a counter-offensive. Number two, my secretary knows I received an urgent message. Any delay in informing the king will look suspicious."

"Then having the inside track does us no good at all!"

"Wrong, Shaanar. Ramses appointed me head of the Secret Service. He trusts me. In other words, he'll believe what I tell him."

Shaanar smiled.

"A very dangerous tactic. They say Ramses is a mind reader."

"A diplomat thinks in code. What I want you to do is communicate your concerns, once I've alerted him. That will make you look credible."

Shaanar settled into an armchair. "Damnably intelligent, Ahsha."

"I know Ramses. Underestimating his insight would be a fatal error."

"I agree. We'll follow your scenario."

"Just one more problem: being sure of the Hittites' real intentions."

Shaanar knew what those intentions were. But he judged it wiser not to reveal his sources to Ahsha, whom he might be forced to sacrifice to his Hittite friends as the situation evolved.

FIFTY-SIX

Moses shuttled from building to building, checking the walls and windows. He drove his chariot all the way across town, pressing the painters to hurry and finish their work. It was only a matter of days until Ramses and Nefertari arrived for the official dedication of Pi-Ramses.

A thousand flaws jumped out at him, but how could they be fixed in so short a time? The brickmakers had agreed to lend a hand to the frantic workmen finishing the site. In the final rush, Moses' popularity remained intact. His enthusiasm was catching, even more so as the dream was becoming reality.

Despite his exhaustion, Moses spent long evenings with his Hebrew brethren, listening to their grievances and hopes. He had grown comfortable in his role as leader of an emerging people. His ideas frightened most of the men, yet they were drawn to his personality. When the grand adventure of Pi-Ramses was finished, would Moses be taking his fellow Hebrews in a new direction?

Overtired, the young supervisor slept only fitfully. In his dreams, Ofir's gaunt face loomed. Aton's messenger had spoken the truth: when push came to shove, sermons and speeches would never be enough. They would have to act, and action often meant violence.

Moses had fulfilled the mission Ramses had given him, acquitting himself of any obligation toward the King of Egypt. Yet he still owed loyalty to his oldest friend and vowed to warn him of the dangers facing him. Once his conscience was eased on that score, he would be free—completely free.

According to the royal courier, the Pharaoh and his wife would arrive around noon the following day. The population of the surrounding towns and villages had flocked to the outskirts of the new capital so as not to miss the event. Overwhelmed, the security forces could not stop the crowds from spilling in.

Moses was hoping to spend his last few hours as construction supervisor outside the city, strolling in the countryside. Just as he reached the edge of town, however, an architect ran up to him.

"The statue is breaking loose! The giant statue!"

"At the temple of Amon?"

"We can't seem to stop it."

"I told you not to touch it!"

"We thought—"

Moses' chariot sped back through town. The scene in front of the temple of Amon was chaotic. A two-hundred-ton statue of the king seated on his throne was slowly slipping toward the facade. It could either collide with the building, causing enormous damage, or fall from its sledge and shatter. What a sight to greet Ramses at the dedication!

Fifty or more men strained desperately, holding the ropes that secured the giant sculpture to a wooden sledge. Where rope touched stone, several leather pads had already split.

"What happened?" asked Moses.

"The foreman climbed up on the statue to help guide it into place. He fell, and the men pulled the wooden brakes to stop the sledge. It jumped the track and kept going. There was dew on the ground, the runners were already wet . . ."

"You should have a gang of at least a hundred and fifty!"

"There isn't a hand to spare."

"Bring me jugs of milk."

"How many?"

"Thousands! And get more men here as fast as you can."

Seeing Moses in action, the struggling workers quieted. When he climbed along the right side of the statue, perched on the granite apron, and poured milk in front of the sledge to lay a new track, they took hope. A brigade formed to pass jugs to Moses. Following his directives, the first spare hands to arrive on the scene tied long ropes to the sides and back of the sledge, slowing the statue's momentum.

Little by little, the colossus moved back on track.

"The braking beam!" shouted Moses.

Thirty men sprang into action, hauling the notched log into place. It would halt the sledge at the spot where Ramses' statue would sit, in front of the temple of Amon.

The colossus, righted and slowed, slid easily into place.

Dripping with sweat, Moses hopped down, glowering. The men feared the punishment that was sure to come.

"Bring me the man responsible for this fiasco, the man who fell off the statue."

"Here he is."

Two workmen pushed Abner forward. He fell to his knees in front of Moses.

"Forgive me," he groaned. "I had a spell, I . . ."

"Aren't you one of my brickmakers?"

"Yes. My name is Abner."

"Why were you working here?"

"I . . . I'm in hiding." He gulped.

"Have you lost your senses?"

"I can explain."

Abner was a Hebrew; at least he deserved a hearing. Moses could see that the man was distraught and would only talk to him one-on-one.

"Come with me, Abner."

An Egyptian architect stepped in front of them. "This man is responsible for a serious incident. Letting him off would be an insult to his co-workers."

"I'll question him and take it from there."

The architect bowed to the project supervisor. If Abner had been an Egyptian, Moses would surely have shown less consideration. Lately he had shown a favoritism toward his fellow Hebrews that was bound to backfire.

Moses helped Abner into his chariot and fastened a leather strap around him.

"Enough falls for one day, don't you think?"

"Please, Moses, forgive me!"

"Get a grip on yourself, man, and tell me what happened."

In front of Moses' residence was a breezeway. The two men hopped down from the chariot and went inside. Moses took off his wig and kilt, gesturing toward a large jug.

"Get up on the ledge," he ordered Abner, "and pour that water slowly over my shoulders."

As Moses briskly rubbed his skin with herbs, the brickmaker emptied the heavy jug.

"Cat got your tongue, Abner?"

"I'm afraid."

"Why?"

"Someone's after me."

"Who?"

"I can't say."

"If you won't tell me, I'll turn you in for disciplinary action."

"No! I'll never work again."

"Wouldn't that be fair?"

"No! I give you my word."

"Then talk."

"I've been the victim of extortion." Abner sighed.

"Who's doing this to you?"

"An Egyptian."

"Out with it, man!"

"I can't name names. He has connections."

"Then I can't help you."

"If I tell you, he'll try to get even!"

"Don't you trust me?"

"I was planning to tell you, but I'm too scared."

"Stop shaking and give me a name. I'll take care of him for you."

Abner trembled so violently that the jug slipped from his hands and shattered.

Groaning, he said, "Sary."

The royal fleet navigated the grand canal leading to Pi-Ramses. Every member of the court, it seemed, was accompanying the Pharaoh and the Great Royal Wife. No one could wait to see the new capital, which would be the place to live if you sought the king's favor. There was a great deal of negative speculation, bordering on criticism: how could a city built so quickly be any match for Memphis? It would be a major setback for Ramses, and sooner or later he'd be forced to abandon his new capital.

In the prow, the Pharaoh was watching the Nile fan into its Delta when the boat tacked toward the canal.

Shaanar sidled up to his brother.

"I know this is hardly the time, but I have a serious matter to discuss with you."

"Can't it wait?"

"I'm afraid not. If I'd been able to speak to you sooner, I wouldn't have to intrude on this happy occasion. But you were out of reach."

"I'm listening, Shaanar."

"You did me a favor appointing me secretary of state, and I wish I could repay you with nothing but the best of news."

"And that's not the case?"

"If reports reaching me are to be believed, the international situation leaves something to be desired."

"Get to the point."

"The Hittites seem to have gone beyond the limits our late father established and invaded central Syria."

"Is that fact or hearsay?"

"It's too early to tell, but I wanted to be the first to inform you. In the recent past, the Hittites have tended to engage in provocation, then back away. We can hope that this is simply another bluff. Still, it would be wise to take certain precautions."

"I'll consider it."

"Are you skeptical?"

"You said yourself that the reports haven't been verified. Once you have solid information, let me know."

"At your service, Majesty."

The current was strong, there was a good tailwind, and

the boat sailed briskly. Shaanar's announcement left Ramses thoughtful. Did his older brother really take his new position seriously? He was capable of inventing reports of a Hittite invasion, just to show how well he was running his department.

Central Syria . . . a neutral zone where neither nation maintained a military presence, relying instead on patchy intelligence networks. Since Seti had refrained from taking the Hittite stronghold of Kadesh, the fighting had been small-scale and intermittent.

Perhaps the creation of Pi-Ramses, a strategic threat, had roused the Hittites to action. They may have decided the young pharaoh was looking toward Asia and their empire. Only one man could sort out the truth for him: his friend Ahsha, head of the Secret Service. The official reports that reached Shaanar would be fragmentary, while Ahsha's sources would reveal the enemy's real intentions.

A mate who had shimmied to the top of the mast began to cheer.

"Ahoy! There it is, the port, the town . . . Pi-Ramses!"

FIFTY-SEVEN

Alone in a golden chariot, the Son of Light rode down the main thoroughfare of Pi-Ramses, toward the temple of Amon. At high noon, he appeared in full force, like the life-giving sun. Alongside the two plumed horses marched his lion, head high, mane in the wind.

Stunned by the power their monarch radiated, as well as the magic that permitted him to have the king of beasts as a bodyguard, the crowd at first was completely silent. A single cry rose: "Long live Ramses!" Then another, ten more, a hundred, a thousand . . . The jubilation was indescribable as the king made his slow and majestic way down the avenue.

Nobles, tradesmen, country folk were dressed for a feast day. Their hair shone with moringa oil, the women wore their best wigs, children and servants threw armfuls of flowers and greenery in the royal chariot's path.

An open-air banquet was being prepared. The steward of the new palace had ordered a thousand loaves of the whitest bread, two thousand rolls, ten thousand pastries, mounds of dried meat, milk, bowls of carob, grapes, figs, pomegranates. Roast goose, game, fish, cucumbers, and leeks would also be on the menu, not to mention thousands of jars of wine from the royal cellars and vats of beer brewed the previous evening.

The king had invited all his people to celebrate his capital's birthday.

No little girl was without a colorful new dress, no horse without bright bands of cloth and copper rosettes, no donkey without a garland of flowers around its neck. Pet dogs, cats, and monkeys would have an extra feeding. Elders, no matter what their station in life, would be served first, seated in comfort beneath sycamore and persea trees.

Official requests would be collected—for government positions, plots of land, livestock—and carefully examined by Ahmeni. Generosity and indulgence were the order of the day.

The Hebrews joined in the festivities. Their labors had earned them a well-paid leave as well as the satisfaction of building the new capital of the kingdom of Egypt with their own hands. Their accomplishments would go down in history.

A hush fell over the assembled crowd as the chariot drew to a halt before the colossal statue of the Pharaoh that had come so close to toppling the day before.

Ramses looked heavenward, meeting the giant's stony stare. It wore the twin crowns of upper and lower Egypt, one white, one red, entwined with the uraeus—the figure of a cobra spitting acid venom to blind the king's enemies. Seated on his throne, hands resting on his kilt, the granite Pharaoh looked on his works.

Ramses stepped down from his chariot. He, too, wore the double crown, and was dressed in a billowing robe of gauzy linen; beneath it shone a gilded linen kilt held in place with a belt of silver. A broad gold collar covered his chest. He addressed the statue.

"You are my *ka* incarnate, the spirit of my reign and my city. I open your mouth, your eyes, your ears. I pronounce you a living being. Anyone who dares attack you will die."

The sun was at its zenith, directly overhead the Pharaoh. He turned to his people.

"Pi-Ramses is born, Pi-Ramses is our capital!"

Thousands of enthusiastic voices took up the chorus.

All day long, Ramses and Nefertari had traveled broad avenues, streets and alleys, visiting each section of Pi-Ramses. Dazzled, the Great Royal Wife dubbed it "The Turquoise City," a phrase that was instantly on everyone's lips. That was Moses' final surprise for the king: the facades of villas, houses, and modest dwellings had been tiled in a luminous blue. The faience workshop had been Ramses' idea, but he had never imagined that so many tiles could be produced in so short a time, providing the city with a visual unity.

A dashing Moses served as master of ceremonies. There was no doubt now that Ramses would name his old friend as vizier and closest adviser. It was obvious how well they understood each other and how perfectly Moses had translated the Pharaoh's plans and wishes for his new capital.

Shaanar was furious. Ofir had either lied about his influence over the Hebrew, or grossly miscalculated. Moses was poised to become a rich man, a government insider. Confronting Ramses over religious differences would be suicide. Besides, his people were so well assimilated that

they had no desire to change the status quo. Shaanar's only
true allies remained the Hittites. Dangerous as vipers, but
allies.

A reception was held in the royal palace, its great
columned hall adorned with harmonious scenes from
nature. In this enchanted setting, Nefertari appeared lovelier
and more charming than ever. The king's consort, magical
protectress of the royal residence, found the right thing to
say to each courtier.

Everyone admired the painted tile flooring, in delightful
patterns evoking garden ponds, flowers in bloom, ducks
flitting in a papyrus thicket, lotus blossoms, darting fish.
Pale green, light blue, off-white, golden yellow, and deep
purple blended in a tone poem singing the praises of creation.

Scoffers and nay-sayers were reduced to silence. Pi-
Ramses' temples were still far from completion, but in
terms of luxury and refinement, the palace was in every way
the equal of Memphis and Thebes. The court could feel
quite at home. The aristocracy and government officials
were already planning their villas in Pi-Ramses.

Another miracle for Ramses—an incredible string of
miracles.

"Nothing you see would be here without this man,"
declared Pharaoh, laying a hand on Moses' shoulder.
Conversations broke off.

"Protocol dictates that I should sit upon my throne,
Moses should prostrate himself before me, and I should
reward him for his faithful service with collars of gold. But

he is my friend, my oldest friend, and we have worked side by side. I conceived the idea for this capital; he carried out my plans."

Ramses took Moses in a solemn embrace, the highest accolade a pharaoh could bestow.

"Moses will remain a few more months as chief of construction, until his replacement is trained. Then he will come to work at my side for the greater glory of Egypt."

Shaanar's worst fears were confirmed. The two of them combined would be harder to deal with than an entire army.

Ahmeni and Setau congratulated Moses and were surprised to note his nervousness. They put it down to the emotion of the moment.

"I don't like the way he's building me up," their friend objected.

"You'd make an excellent vizier," Ahmeni said firmly.

"Still, you'd have to answer to this wretched little scribe," teased Setau. "He's the one who really gives the orders."

"Watch it, snake man!"

"The food is wonderful. If Lotus and I can scout out some new species, we may find a place nearby. Has anyone seen Ahsha? Why isn't he here today?"

"No idea," said Ahmeni.

"You'd think he'd be more diplomatic."

The three friends saw Ramses walk up to his mother, Tuya, and kiss her on the forehead. Despite the hint of sadness that would never leave her grave and lovely face, Seti's widow shone with pride. When she announced she was moving her household to the palace for an extended stay at Pi-Ramses, her son's triumph was complete.

The palace aviary was finished but not yet stocked with the exotic birds that would delight both the ear and the eye. Leaning against a pillar, arms crossed, features drawn and tense, Moses could not look Ramses in the eyes. He had to forget the man and address an adversary, the Pharaoh of Egypt.

"Everyone is sleeping, except for you and me."

"You look exhausted, Moses. Can't this talk wait until tomorrow?"

"No. I have to stop pretending."

"Pretending what?"

"I'm a Hebrew. I believe in the One True God. You're an Egyptian and you worship idols."

"Not this again."

"It disturbs you because it's the truth."

"You've been instructed in the wisdom of the Egyptians, Moses. Your One God, shapeless and unknowable, is the hidden power within each speck of life."

"He doesn't appear as a sheep!"

"Amon is the secret of life, revealing himself in the gust of wind that fills the sails of the bark, the curving ram's horns that mirror the harmony of all creation, the stone that gives shape to our temples. He is all of that and none of that. You know these ancient teachings as well as I do."

"It's all an illusion. There's only One God."

"Does that prevent him from taking the form of his many creatures, while remaining one?"

"He doesn't need your temples and your statues."

"I'm telling you, again, Moses, you've been under too much strain."

"I know what I believe. Even you can't change that."

"If your god makes you intolerant, be careful. He'll turn you into a fanatic."

"You're the one who ought to be careful, Ramses! A movement is gathering strength in this country, still tentative, but a force for the truth nonetheless."

"What do you mean?"

"In your grandfather's time there was Akhenaton, who shared our beliefs. He blazed the trail. Listen for his voice, Ramses. Listen to me. Or else your empire may crumble."

FIFTY-EIGHT

For Moses, the situation was clear. He hadn't betrayed Ramses' trust and had even warned him of the peril that lay ahead. He could proceed with an easy conscience, following his destiny and unleashing the fire in his heart.

The One God, Yaweh, lived in a mountain. He would go in search of it, no matter how difficult the journey might prove. A few other Hebrews had decided to risk losing everything and leave Egypt with him. As he finished packing, Moses remembered the one pressing matter he should resolve before he said goodbye to his native land.

It was only a short distance to Sary's estate on the west side of town. The house was set in an old and thriving palm grove. He found his old teacher drinking cool beer by a fish pond.

"Moses! What a pleasure to see the real power behind Pi-Ramses! To what do I owe this honor?"

"The pleasure is all yours, and it certainly isn't an honor."

Sary rose, insulted. "You may be the man of the hour, but you have no right to be rude. Remember who you're talking to."

"A second-rate crook?"

Sary struck out at Moses, but the Hebrew caught his wrist. He crumpled and fell to his knees.

"You've been hounding a fellow by the name of Abner."

"Never heard of him."

"You're lying, Sary. You threatened him and extorted his wages."

"He's only a Hebrew brickmaker."

Moses tightened his grip. Sary groaned. "I'm only a Hebrew, too," said Moses, "but I could break your arm and cripple you."

"You wouldn't dare."

"My patience is wearing thin, I warn you. Stop bothering Abner or I'll drag you headfirst into court. Now swear it!"

"I . . . I swear not to bother him again."

"In the name of Pharaoh?"

". . . the name of Pharaoh."

"Break your oath and you're done for."

Moses released him. "You're getting off easy, old man."

If he weren't in such a hurry to leave the country, he'd surely initiate formal proceedings. He hoped a warning would be sufficient, but leaving the house, his mind was not at ease. He had read hatred, not submission, in Sary's dark expression.

Moses hid behind a palm tree. He didn't have long to wait.

Carrying a bludgeon, Sary slipped out of the house, walking south toward the brickmakers' quarters.

Moses kept a good distance between them until he saw his old teacher go through the open door of Abner's house. Almost at once, he heard cries of pain.

He ran into the house and in the semidarkness saw Sary clubbing Abner, who crouched on the dirt floor, shielding his face with his hands. Moses grabbed the bludgeon from Sary and whacked him on the back of the skull. The Egyptian collapsed, blood streaming down his neck.

"Get up, Sary, and off with you!"

But Sary lay still as Abner crept closer.

"Moses . . . it looks like . . . he's dead!"

"He can't be. I didn't hit him that hard!"

"He isn't breathing."

Moses bent over and touched the body—the corpse?

He had just killed a man.

In the street outside it was quiet. "Run for it," said Abner. "If they arrest you . . ."

"You'll defend me, Abner. You'll explain I was saving your life!"

"Who'd believe me? They'd say it was a cover-up. Go, Moses, run fast!"

"Do you have a big sack around?"

"Yes, for my tools."

"Let me have it."

Moses stuffed Sary's body inside and hoisted the sack over his shoulder. He'd find some sandy spot where he could dig a shallow grave, then hide in an unoccupied villa until he could gather his wits.

The police dog let out a high-pitched whine and strained on his leash, which was most unusual for him. When the patrolman released him, the greyhound bolted toward a sand-strewn vacant lot.

The dog was digging fast. By the time the patrol caught up, the policemen saw him unearth an arm, then a shoulder, then the face of a dead man.

"I know him," said one of the policemen. "It's Sary."

"The king's brother-in-law?"

"That's the one. Look, there's dried blood on his neck!"

They freed the body. There could be no doubt: Sary had been killed by a blow to the back of the head.

All night long, Moses paced like a Syrian bear in its cage. What he'd done was wrong, trying to hide the body of a villain like Sary, fleeing justice when it would have absolved him. But there had been Abner, his fear, his hesitation . . . and they were both Hebrews. Moses' enemies would be sure to twist the incident and bring about his downfall. Even Ramses would side with them and punish him harshly.

Someone had just entered the half-finished villa. The police, so soon? He would put up a fight. He would never surrender.

"Moses, Moses, it's me, Abner! Come out if you're hiding here!"

He stepped from the shadows. "Will you testify in my favor, Abner?"

"The police have discovered Sary's body. You're accused of murder."

"But who . . ."

"My neighbors. They saw you."

"But they're Hebrews, like us!"

Abner hung his head. "They don't want trouble with the law. I know how they feel. Run, Moses. You have no future here in Egypt."

Moses was appalled. The king's construction supervisor and potential vizier, reduced to being a fugitive from justice! In the space of a few hours, to fall from the pinnacle into the abyss . . . God must have sent him this suffering to try his faith. Instead of a comfortable but empty life in a heathen country, God was offering him freedom.

"I'll leave at dark. Farewell, Abner."

Moses departed through the brickmakers' quarters. He hoped to convince a handful of followers to leave with him and form a sect that would eventually attract other Hebrews, even if their first homeland was only an isolated desert region. He had to set the example, no matter what the cost.

A few lamps shone. Children slept, housewives chatted on doorsteps. Beneath the awnings, their husbands drank herb tea before heading off to bed.

In the street where his closest followers lived, two men were fighting. As he drew near, he could see that it was his two most vocal supporters, quarreling over a stepladder one had supposedly stolen from the other.

Moses broke up the fight.

"You!"

"Stop fighting over a trifle and come with me. We'll leave Egypt and go in search of our new homeland."

The older of the two men eyed Moses with disdain. "Who made you our guiding star? If we don't obey you, will you kill us, like you murdered the Egyptian?"

Stricken, Moses found no answer. A grandiose dream shattered inside him. He was no better than a criminal on the run, utterly abandoned.

FIFTY-NINE

Ramses insisted on viewing Sary's body. He was the new capital's first fatality.

"It was murder, Your Majesty," affirmed Serramanna. "A violent blow to the back of the head with some kind of club."

"Does my sister know yet?"

"Ahmeni saw to it."

"Is the suspect in custody?"

"Majesty . . ."

"What aren't you telling me? No matter who it is, he'll be tried and sentenced."

"Majesty . . . there's a warrant out for Moses."

"That's absurd."

"The police have witnesses."

"Reliable witnesses?"

"All Hebrews. The most damaging statement came from a brickmaker named Abner. He saw it happen."

"What does he say?"

"That they scuffled, it got out of hand. Moses and Sary were not on the best of terms. My sources tell me they'd already quarreled in Thebes."

"What if all the witnesses had the wrong man? Moses can't be a murderer."

"A police scribe recorded sworn statements from all the brickmakers."

"Moses will explain."

"No, Your Majesty. He's on the run."

The Pharaoh ordered a search of every house and building in Pi-Ramses, but nothing came of it. Mounted policemen combed the Delta questioning villagers, but found no trace of Moses. The northeastern border patrol received strict guidelines, but they may well have come too late.

Ramses was frustrated to find that his daily updates gave no clue as to which route Moses had taken. Was he hiding in a fishing village along the Mediterranean? Had he stowed away in a boat heading south, or taken refuge in some remote monastery?

"You should eat something," urged Nefertari. "Since Moses disappeared, you really haven't had a good meal."

Ramses gave his wife's hands a tender squeeze. "Moses was exhausted. Sary must have provoked him. If he were here in front of me, he could explain. The fact that he ran away tells me he was at wit's end."

"Will he be able to live with himself?"

"I'm afraid he won't."

"Your dog is sad. He thinks you're neglecting him."

Ramses let Watcher jump on his lap. Wriggling with joy, the dog licked his master's face, then rested his head on his shoulder.

"My three years on the throne have been wonderful . . . The additions to Luxor completed, the Eternal Temple under way, the new capital dedicated, Nubia under control—and now this calamity! Without Moses, the world I've begun to build won't hold together."

"You've been neglecting me, too," said Nefertari in a hushed voice. "Can't I help you rise above this suffering?"

"Yes. Only you, my darling."

Shaanar and Ofir met by the docks at Pi-Ramses, now bustling with activity. Foodstuffs, furnishings, household goods, and countless other supplies needed in the new capital were being unloaded every day. Boats brought in donkeys, horses, cattle. The grain silos filled, cellars were stocked with fine wines. Discussions as heated as any in Memphis or Thebes were heard among the wholesalers vying to establish trade in the new capital.

"Now Moses is only an outlaw, Ofir."

"It doesn't seem to upset you much."

"You were wrong about him. He never would have changed sides. His rash action has cost Ramses a valued associate."

"Moses is an honest man. His faith in the One God is no mere whim."

"Let's stick with the facts. Either he'll turn himself in or he'll be arrested and sentenced. We no longer have any hope of using the Hebrews to our advantage."

"Those who believe in Aton are no strangers to hardship. We've struggled on for years. This won't stop us. I hope we can count on your help."

"Don't press me. I need to know about your concrete plans."

"Every night I work to undermine the health of the royal couple."

"How can you touch them? You know that they have the Eternal Temple now, too . . ."

"Ramses has many projects under way, but none of them are finished. We'll have to capitalize on the slightest sign of weakness, be ready to rush in when the first breach opens."

The sorcerer's manner, calm yet firm, impressed Shaanar. If the Hittites succeeded with their plan, Ramses' *ka* would certainly be compromised. Ofir's magical attacks would further sap the king's strength. Resilient as he was, eventually Ramses would falter.

"Keep it up, Ofir. Perhaps you've heard that I never forget a favor."

Setau and Lotus had decided to found a new laboratory at Pi-Ramses. Ahmeni, in his spanking new offices, worked day and night. Tuya kept the court running smoothly. Nefertari performed her religious and queenly duties. Iset the Fair and Nedjem were busy bringing up Kha. Meritamon was blooming. Romay the steward puffed from palace kitchens to wine cellar, wine cellar to state dining room. Serramanna tinkered with his security procedures. Life in Pi-Ramses was orderly and peaceful, but for Ramses, nothing was the same without Moses.

Despite their differences, his old friend's strength had been a gift that helped Ramses achieve his vision. Moses had put his soul into the city he left behind, and it showed. Their final conversation proved that his friend had fallen victim to evil influences, was caught in invisible bonds.

A spell—someone had cast a spell on him.

Ahmeni, juggling an armload of scrolls, hurried toward the king as he paced his audience chamber.

"Ahsha just got here. He wants to see you."

"Show him in."

Although suave in his elegant pale green robe with red trim, the young diplomat looked less the trendsetter than usual.

"It distressed me that you missed the dedication," Ramses told him.

"The head of the State Department represented me, Majesty."

"But where were you?"

"In Memphis, collecting the dispatches from my information network."

"Shaanar mentioned Hittite troop movements in central Syria."

"It's more than troop movements, and it goes much farther than Syria," Ahsha said with uncharacteristic gruffness.

"I thought my dear brother might be exaggerating. He likes to make himself look important."

"If anything, he minimized the danger. Now that I've checked my own sources, I'm convinced that the Hittites have launched a full-scale campaign in Canaan and Syria—all of Syria. Even the ports of Lebanon are under threat."

"Have there been direct attacks on our garrisons?"

"Not yet, but they've moved into areas we considered neutral and taken villages. Before this it's only been political maneuvering in our territories, apparently nonviolent, but the Hittites have taken de facto control of Egyptian territory—provinces under our jurisdiction and supposedly sending us tribute."

Ramses bent over the map of the Near East spread out on a low table.

"The Hittites are working their way down a corridor to our northeast. They plan to invade," the king predicted.

"Too early to say that, Majesty."

"Why else would they be heading in this direction?"

"To extend their territory, cut us off, sow panic in our protectorates, hurt Egypt's reputation, demoralize our army . . . take your pick."

"What does it look like to you?"

"Like war."

Ramses drew a quick slash of red ink across the Anatolian peninsula, home of the Hittites.

"A bloodthirsty people. Unless we stop them, they represent a threat to civilization as we know it."

"Diplomacy . . ."

"Too late for that."

"Your father negotiated . . ."

"A buffer zone around Kadesh, I know. But the Hittites won't honor it. They honor nothing. I demand a daily report on their movements."

Ahsha bowed. Ramses no longer spoke as a friend, but as a commanding pharaoh.

"Have you heard that Moses is a fugitive from justice, wanted for murder?"

"Moses? It's unbelievable."

"I think someone set him up. Put out a bulletin through your network, Ahsha, and find him for me."

Nefertari was playing the lute in the palace garden. To her right lay the cradle where her plump and rosy-cheeked daughter napped; on her left sat Kha, cross-legged, reading a tale full of wizards and demons. Just in front of her was Watcher, trying to dig up the tamarisk sapling Ramses had planted the day before. Nose in the dirt, front paws flying, he worked so doggedly that the queen didn't have the heart to scold him.

Suddenly he stopped and ran to the garden gate. His barking and jumping could only mean a visit from his master.

The sound of her husband's footsteps told Nefertari that his heart was heavy. She rose to meet him.

"Is it Moses?"

"No, I'm sure he's all right."

"Not . . . not Tuya."

"My mother is fine."

"Tell me what's wrong."

"It's Egypt, Nefertari. The dream is over . . . the dream of a country where peace and prosperity rule, where each day is a blessing."

The queen shut her eyes.

"War?"

He nodded. "There's no way around it."

"You're leaving, then."

"Who else should command the army? If we don't stop the Hittites, it's death to Egypt."

Little Kha glanced up at the embracing couple, then went back to his story. Meritamon napped. Watcher kept digging.

In the tranquil garden, Nefertari clung to Ramses. In the distance, a white ibis took flight above the wheat fields.

"So long apart, Ramses. Where will we find the courage to go on?"

"In the love that unites us and always will, no matter what happens. While I'm gone, you'll act as my regent, queen of my Turquoise City."

Nefertari looked off at the horizon.

"You're right to go," she told him. "Never negotiate with evil."

The white ibis soared majestically above the royal pair, bathed in the glow of sunset.